Advance Praise for *Life Is Everywhere*

"Lucy Ives is a daring writer with a wicked sense of humor. Her books announce a plethora of ideas, her purview broad, with interests ranging from ancient history to contemporary art. She brilliantly observes society and culture, and invents stories only she could imagine. Ives's sense of language and unique mind make her one of our most original contemporary writers."
—Lynne Tillman, author of *Mothercare*

"Writing novels is the way Lucy Ives discovers her thoughts about the at once disheartening and marvelous fact of being alive right here, right now. This brilliant and playful novel brims with wisdom."
—Alejandro Zambra, author of *Chilean Poet*

"*Life Is Everywhere* is simply dazzling. Part campus novel, part bildungsroman, part scenes from an unsalvageable marriage, the book blows past genre to deliver an unvarnished portrait of a woman on the verge: of a nervous breakdown, maybe, but also the possibility of her own self-realization. Lucy Ives has an ear for how people talk when they've lost the desire to speak. Her sentences are angry and elegant, replete with the accidental comedy of swimming with sharks. Witty, seductive, furious, and bold, this is a pitch-perfect aria of broken hearts and dubious morals. It is, what's more, a delightful read."
—Anahid Nersessian, author of *Keats's Odes: A Lover's Discourse*

"The superb Lucy Ives slays enemy and friend alike in this multi-valent successor to Jarrell's *Pictures from an Institution*."
—Jesse Ball, author of *Autoportrait*

Praise for Lucy Ives

"Ives, an accomplished poet, infuses even mundane actions with startling imagery." —*The New York Times Book Review*

"Emotionally precise in the extreme." —Lily Meyer, NPR

"There is perhaps no author better able to confront the acute absurdities of our reality than Lucy Ives, who veritably tackles the derangements of our era with glee, clarity, and brilliance." —Kristin Iversen, *Refinery29*

"Sontag says a good writer must be a fool and an obsessive, that the critic and the stylist are bonuses (so, inessential). But Ives—not just for her own erudition and syntactical artistry, remarkable as they are—counters that it is the critic and the stylist who are indispensable, for they are the ones who interface thought with language." —Jameson Fitzpatrick, *The Believer*

"Lucy Ives is as deeply funny and ferocious a writer as they come. She's also humane and philosophical when it matters most." —Sam Lipsyte

"I first knew Lucy Ives's work as a poet, and to have her prose is a gift, too." —Hilton Als

"A deeply smart and painstakingly elegant writer." —Wayne Koestenbaum

"A rampaging, mirthful genius." —Elizabeth McKenzie

Life Is Everywhere

LIFE IS EVERYWHERE

A Novel

Lucy Ives

Graywolf Press

Excerpt from *Margery Kempe* by Robert Gluck. Reproduced with permission from the author.

Excerpt from *Schizophrene* by Bhanu Kapil. Reproduced with permission from the author.

This publication is made possible, in part, by the voters of Minnesota through a Minnesota State Arts Board Operating Support grant, thanks to a legislative appropriation from the arts and cultural heritage fund. Significant support has also been provided by the McKnight Foundation, the Lannan Foundation, the Amazon Literary Partnership, and other generous contributions from foundations, corporations, and individuals. To these organizations and individuals we offer our heartfelt thanks.

MINNESOTA STATE ARTS BOARD   CLEAN WATER LAND & LEGACY AMENDMENT

Published by Graywolf Press
212 Third Avenue North, Suite 485
Minneapolis, Minnesota 55401

www.graywolfpress.org

Published in the United States of America

ISBN 978-1-64445-204-2 (paperback)
ISBN 978-1-64445-187-8 (ebook)

2 4 6 8 9 7 5 3 1
First Graywolf Printing, 2022

Library of Congress Control Number: 2022930737

Cover design: Kapo Ng

for M. E.

Contents

Life Is Everywhere

1
Paralysis

There is stultification wherever one intelligence is subordinated to another.

—Jacques Rancière

The Byzantine emperor Leo the Sixth, b. 866, d. 912, was known as "the Wise," *Leōn ho Sophos*, for his love of books. He was only moderately successful as a military campaigner and married four times, an activity condemned by the Church and therefore requiring complex administrative maneuvering. Leo is remembered to history for his intricate, prolific, and no doubt tedious sermons and, more gloriously, for the codification of all existing Byzantine law into a six-volume, sixty-book corpus called the *Basilika*, or Royal Laws. During the latter half of his reign, he issued an edict banning the production of blood sausage. This edict is thought to be the earliest written evidence of an outbreak of botulism.

They did not reveal themselves to human science until some nine hundred years later: the tube-shaped bacterium *Clostridium botulinum* with its proteinaceous emanation, botulinum toxin—a substance produced when the bacteria grow in the air-free conditions they require for flourishing (among which: brine baths, salt packing, tin cans). The toxin is among the most potent natural poisons on the planet, a microgram being lethal to humans when inhaled. It is, in a molecular sense, infernally clever, working upon nerve synapses to prevent the broadcast of stimuli by impeding release of the compound acetylcholine, a neurotransmitter. The biochemical radio silence caused by botulinum toxin is what we call paralysis. Early symptoms include blurred vision, mild loss of facial muscle control including ptosis (drooping eyelids), nausea, vomiting, diarrhea, constipation, cramps, and difficulty breathing. In more extreme poisonings, death occurs within forty-eight hours from respiratory failure. During the sufferer's decline, the brain remains functional. Consciousness continues, unabated.

Scroll back a tiny bit: At the end of the eighteenth century, the southern German countryside, reeling from various military incursions, was impoverished and health standards allegedly *sehr* lax. In 1793, at the village of Wildbad in Württemberg, thirteen people became ill and six died from consumption of a local delicacy, *Saumagen*, cooked pig's stomach filled with blood sausage, yum. Such incidents must have continued, for in 1802 the royal government in Stuttgart issued a public warning about blood sausage, that archaic culprit. In 1811, the medical section of the Department of Internal Affairs of the Kingdom of Württemberg once again warned against "sausage poisoning," as the ailment was termed. Medical professors weighed in. One Herr Doktor Johann Heinrich Ferdinand von Autenrieth studied symptoms and concluded housewives were to blame—in that they, disliking messy burst casings, refused to boil their sausages thoroughly.

Clarity came in the form of an unlikely figure: Justinus Andreas Christian Kerner, b. 1786, d. 1862, a medical man and, as a medical man might be in those days, visionary poet. In 1811, Kerner published a strange travelogue, *Die Reiseschatten* (*Travel Shadows*), recording the wanderings of one Lux, an imagined itinerant showman who specializes in shadow puppetry. The book was a fictionalized version of Kerner's own journeys through Germany and Austria following his graduation from the University of Tübingen, where he had trained to become a physician and studied with Autenrieth, enemy to housewives and undercooked *Wurst*. Kerner's later life as an artist included membership in the coterie of Romantic poets of Swabia, as well as investigation of paranormal phenomena. During the 1820s, Kerner came under the influence of Franz Mesmer's doctrine of animal magnetism. Kerner's most famous publication was a long Mesmer-influenced case study of 1829, *Die Seherin von Prevorst* (*The Seeress of Prevorst*), in which Kerner documented his treatment of the wife of a local merchant, Frau Friederike Hauffe, who was given to communion with the invisible spirits of the dead as well as privy to the pursuits of aliens living on the left and right sides of the moon. Far from curing Frau Hauffe, Kerner became convinced that she was a true psychic, a creature with one foot in the realm beyond—and, as if in confirmation of his diagnosis, she wasted away and died after discontinuing treatment with him.

Kerner also liked to make drawings of fanciful insect-like beings from random inkblots. He then used his semiautomatic illustrations as inspiration for poems. He termed this work *Klecksographien*, or blot-drawing; it was almost certainly known to Rorschach.

In the 1810s, Kerner, a young man, was still intimately involved with the academic medical establishment, as well as empiricism, a tool that he was using to secure his career and that he never entirely abandoned, even in his studies of the uncanny. In 1815, he sent a detailed report regarding rural sausage poisonings to his former professor, Autenrieth, who obliged Kerner two years later by publishing it in the *Tübinger Blätter für Naturwissenschaften und Arzneykunde*, a professional journal on the natural sciences and pharmacology. Kerner continued to collect food-poisoning cases and in 1820 brought forth a monograph, *Neue Beobachtungen über die in Württemberg so haüfig vorfallenden tödlichen Vergiftungen durch den Genuss geraücherter Würste* (*New Observations on the Deadly Poisonings Occurring So Often in Württemberg on Account of Consumption of Smoked Sausages*), whose title seems to indicate a raging epidemic. Kerner describes the symptoms of sickened individuals: "The tear fluid disappears, the gullet becomes a dead and motionless tube; in all mucous cavities of the human machine the secretion of the normal mucus stands still, from the biggest, the stomach, toward the tear canal and the excretory ducts of the lingual glands. No saliva is secreted. No drop of wetness is felt in the mouth, no tear is secreted anymore. No earwax appears in the auditory canal, also signs of drying out of the Eustachian tube become apparent. No mucus is secreted in the nose; no more sperma is secreted, the testicles decrease. Urination can only be performed by standing and with difficulty. Extreme drying out of the palms, the soles, and the eyelids occurs."

Paralysis attacks flow. Sources retreat. All channels are desolate and arid.

Fascinated, Kerner attempted to isolate the mysterious toxin. He investigated and manipulated the fatty parts of affected meats, administering what he termed a "fat poison," or "fatty acid," to a menagerie of nonhuman subjects—birds, cats, rabbits, frogs, flies, locusts, snails—as well as experimenting on himself with nonlethal doses, which he noted had a sour taste. Autenrieth, to his credit, was alarmed by his student's use of his own body as a testing ground for his theory of *das Fettgift* and requested that Kerner desist. Whether Kerner did eventually stop selectively paralyzing himself or not, in a monograph that followed in 1828 he made a breakthrough, concluding that "the nerve conduction is brought by the toxin into a condition in which its influence on the chemical process of life is interrupted. The capacity of nerve conduction is interrupted by the toxin in the same way as in an electrical conductor by rust." He also suggested, perhaps inspired by his own experience of the poison's activities (one wonders what he felt), that it might be used for therapeutic purposes. He went on to receive the not entirely flattering nickname of Wurst-Kerner, and the better-known writer Heinrich Heine famously mocked Kerner as the poet "who sees ghosts and toxic blood sausages."

So much for Kerner and *das Gift*, even if he was mostly correct. He did not quite perceive his fugitive (and extremely small) object. Meanwhile, the Europeans kept at their semiraw meats for the rest of the century, and, in 1895, a group of musicians dining on a pickled ham in the Belgian village of Ellezelles began to experience visual disturbances and muscle paralysis, among other miseries. Fanfare Les Amis Réunis (Brass Band [of] The Reunited Friends) had gathered for the burial of a local man who had lived a long life. Following the funeral repast, three members of the band died and ten more very nearly died. A microbiologist, Émile Pierre-Marie van Ermengem of the University of Ghent, was called in. Van Ermengem had studied internationally at various laboratories, including that of Robert Koch, founder of modern bacteriology, in Berlin, and was able to successfully identify an anaerobic microorganism he called *Bacillus botulinus*, later *Clostridium botulinum*. In other words, in the spleen of one of the deceased musicians and in the murderous ham, van Ermengem discovered numerous traces of microorganisms that thrived in the absence of air. He published his observations in 1897. *Botulus* is the Latin word for sausage. Thus was "botulism" born, although, as we know from the edict of Leo the Wise, it had been a human problem for at least a millennium.

In 1904, a batch of canned white beans became home to productive *Clostridium botulinum* in Germany. In 1906, there was an outbreak of botulism in the United States, also due to the toxin occurring in canned foods. In 1918, there was an influenza pandemic, which is mostly unrelated, except that it made manifest the genocidal effects of very small biological entities, with the H1N1 influenza virus causing the deaths of some fifty to one hundred million people, roughly 3 to 5 percent of the world's population, in two years. This pandemic happened, of course, to coincide with the end of the First World War, a conflict that saw German development of anthrax and glanders, both bacterial infections associated with domesticated herbivores (cattle, horses) but that may also affect humans. Before this time, smallpox had been Western warcraft's most effective agent. A ban on biological weapons was forthcoming, in the form of the Geneva Protocol of 1925, and in the United States relevant worthies seemed to feel that the use of bacteria, viruses, etc., was too unpredictable to be a reliable killing method.

Yet, during the Second World War, matters changed. In 1941, a US military attaché in Switzerland reported that German and French collaborators at the Koch Foundation laboratories near Paris were in the midst of producing botulinum toxin, abbreviated BoTx, for dissemination by airburst bombs. This, along with a lecture by a Japanese doctor, Hojo Enryo, "On Bacteriological Warfare," delivered at the Berlin Military Academy of Medicine, spurred American efforts. In 1942, the War Research Service, directed by George W. Merck, corporate pharmacologist, began its explorations, and, in Maryland, at Camp, and later Fort, Detrick, from 1943 all the way to '69, year of the American moonwalk, researchers toiled to isolate, purify, and crystalize BoTx type A, an endeavor in which they were successful—in part as they believed, beginning in 1943, that the planned D-Day invasion might involve a biological component, with German V-1 rockets armed with BoTx.

After the war, and after the nonuse of biological weapons and use, instead, of atomic ones, the BoTx consolidated at Fort Detrick was shared in a controlled way. At Johns Hopkins, one Dr. Daniel Drachman began injecting highly diluted quantities of the toxin into animals, showing that the resulting muscle atrophy did not lead to botulism. This outcome was taken up by a San Francisco–based ophthalmologist, Dr. Alan Scott, who was interested in correcting squints and ocular twitches without surgery. Scott began treating the extraocular muscles of nonhuman primates with the agent and found it was an effective cure, if one that needed to be repeated, as the localized paralysis tended to wear off in a few months. It was now the 1970s. In 1978, Scott attempted a trial with humans. An ophthalmologist in Amsterdam, Dr. P. V. T. M. de Jong, was working with the experimental treatment, too. In December of 1989, the American Food and Drug Administration licensed BoTx as an orphan drug called Oculinum, for the management of chronic facial spasms. In 1990, the FDA published a list of guidelines for the use of "botulin," and the next year Scott sold a patent for Oculinum to the then-Canadian pharmaceutical company Allergan, for nine million dollars. Oculinum's revenue in 1991, year of the fall of the Soviet Union, was thirteen million dollars.

For the next decade, Allergan researched additional applications for its neuroparalytic poison. A 1992 study found that cosmetic injection of *Clostridium botulinum*-A exotoxin into glabellar frown lines was more effective than the use of collagen, to which some people are allergic and which can cause blindness. The study observed that treatment of this particular type of frown line, a wrinkle that occurs between the eyes, may be disproportionately significant and even necessary, since it can indicate socially ambiguous emotions, such as terror, grief, and rage. Some people, for example, suffering from particularly deep frown lines, are assumed to be displeased or angry all the time, even when they are not. The toxin works to inhibit calcium metabolism in the presynaptic neuron at the cholinergic neuromuscular junction and therefore prevents neuromuscular transmission, resulting in reversible paralysis. In other words, a person's face can't move. This treatment differs from collagen injection in that it acts on the underlying muscular cause rather than cutaneous effect. You will need to keep the toxin freeze-dried until you are ready to use it. Before you inject a patient, ask her to frown. Make the injection into the corrugator muscle. You will learn that many treated patients say they like not being able to frown. You may find that this incapacity produces a positive self-image.

Today, Botox, as Oculinum was renamed for off-label use, supplies an annual revenue estimated at more than two and a half billion dollars. Additional studies investigating the so-called Facial Feedback Hypothesis have shown that Botox can also be effective in treating depression. Because humans are imitative animals and because afferent feedback from muscles and skin may influence emotions, a woman whose face can no longer arrange itself into a frown is not subject to increasingly intense waves of self-stimuli. She cannot further sadden herself by manifesting sadness. Therefore, much as, for the sufferer of botulism, the working of the toxin is first manifest in the face, so, too, for the Botox patient, relief from symptoms associated with depression is manifest on the countenance—in more ways than one.

Further study of the bacterium in its natural environment (soil, silt, lakes, coastal waters, oceans; intestinal tracts of mammals, their excreta) has shown that there is in fact a virus, or phage, that infects the bacterium, enabling production of the toxin by affecting the bacterium's DNA, even as the toxin is only produced when the bacterium is under stress and therefore releasing spores. Very little is known about the phage.

Meanwhile, the beings on earth most affected by botulism are not humans but rather waterfowl, which die at a rate of some ten to one hundred thousand per year. Special conditions are needed for the bacteria to produce spores and, thus, the toxin: warmth, protein, an anaerobic environment, wetness. Plant matter and invertebrate animals decomposing along the surface of a lake in sun meet these criteria. They are feasted upon by ignorant birdlife.

But the lives and/or corpses of herons and/or loons were not of particular interest to Faith Ewer. Neither a birder nor a twitcher was she, nor did she particularly enjoy leaving the limits of New York City, except by way of the major airport named for a dead president, and, then, only really—or, *really only*—to travel the francophone world, but mostly and usually to France itself, where she felt herself alluringly anonymous as well as just foreign enough to keep things stimulating. She was what is termed an expert, and this had the effect of making her, at least in her own imagination, a spy. There was tension in her back, near the neck and shoulders, and stale air in the room.

She looked up from the stack of word-processed pages from which she was reading. The one point of calm was the numbness in her face.

"Could someone open that door, please?"

A student, thin and stooped and male, a little beard like a rash on him, scuttled out of his seat and made this happen.

Faith, Dr. Faith Ewer, returned to her sentences. She muttered the line she had just read once more. What would have been ideal would have been to be able to start doing this a different week, say next week or the week after next or any other. Isobel, although she had been late, was here, too, glowering in the corner under a stack of muted raw-silk scarves.

Faith recalled the mass email lately composed by the departmental chair, regarding Professors Ewer and Childe, their gracious acceptance, their willingness to share the course for the remainder of the semester, given recent developments. *On top of all of their many other commitments*, the chair had enthused, *they have heroically granted my request!*

The chair knew what he was doing. He was a reformed sadist on his second marriage who, given an early interest in risky forms of self-medication, hadn't expected to live this long. His survival and recent transcendence to relative emotional stability had emboldened him. He was writing a book of experimental criticism, a series of aphorisms and poems that appeared, revoltingly, to have all the features of a sentimental memoir. He had numerous peculiar, friendly gestures for the dean, including literal backslapping. He kept talking about potlucks and informal symposia plus interdisciplinary drinks nights, then disappearing from campus abruptly every Wednesday. He blamed a punishing schedule of speaking engagements.

Faith did not wish to make herself suffer by using a search engine to ascertain if this might in fact be the case—that Florian Cádiz really was as sought after as she was beginning to fear that he might be. She mistrusted him instinctively but had collaborated with him closely for the past three years, largely because he was fresh meat, not yet poisoned by Isobel's dogmas, Isobel's inane and unfathomable popularity with the "hard" left. Faith, in return for his loyalty, had provided Florian cover. She had cleared a path for his administrative ascent. She'd found him a new publisher and even very nearly liked it when he expressed a moist joy on the afternoon he'd signed the contract for his fairly well reviewed third book, a study of metaphor in the writings of Lithuanian semiotician Algirdas Julien Greimas.

Cádiz was boyish but, Faith reminded herself, Cádiz (b. 1961) was not a boy. He had lived a significant portion of his life in free fall and had to possess preternatural instincts when it came to self-preservation. Cádiz was a cat. He was seldom to be found where you had left him.

Roger was another story. Roger Herbsweet had already been becoming famous, locally, for his bizarre treatment of students, his reliance on hypnotic suggestion and other cheap forms of mind control, and therefore none of the new mess was a surprise. He had a habit of taking up with his advisees, joining himself intensely to them, wrapping himself cephalopod-style around their intellects, sucking. Given that he mostly published weakly received translations of oddball Renaissance poets these days, it was far from clear where his vampirism got him. He seemed to like to drop his victims in the early stages of the dissertation process, either while they were attempting to have a prospectus approved or shortly thereafter. As they would at this point have declared their fealty to him in a rather public manner, it was usually impossible for them to go on. In a way, you couldn't fault him. He was weeding out the frail ones, keeping the profession pure. On the other hand, Faith couldn't help feeling that along the trail of hollow, celery-white corpses, bite marks in their skulls, were young people she had at some moment vaguely appreciated, even summoning a twinge of jealousy in response to something or other one of them might have said.

If Florian Cádiz was a cat, Roger Herbsweet was a dog.

You therefore kept Roger Herbsweet fenced in. You gave a creature like him simple and repetitive tasks. You praised him when he got it right, broke his jaw when he was wrong. You gave him a stump to piss on and personally selected the excess lambs to draw and quarter, and you yourself tossed the bloody fragments into his pen. You yelled at him from time to time, from a safe distance. Later, you fed him nothing living. You began to starve him. You told him what he was. You mocked his suffering, his hunger for fresh risk. And that was how you dealt with it, his *needs*.

But nobody had taken charge of Herbsweet. Worse than this, they seemed to have encouraged his feral habits by allowing him to maintain positions in not one but two departments—he spoke the languages very well, after all—and it was this, perhaps, that had led to the excess of privacy, the independence, which was now to be somebody or other's, perhaps even Herbsweet's himself, if they could pin it on him, downfall.

Briefly, the numbness in Faith's face reasserted itself.

Yes, she greatly regretted this schedule, even if she was slightly amazed by what she herself could withstand. Taking on an additional class, on top of her current seminar, Literature Says "No," in which she was unpacking the sinister side of the aesthetics of resistance (very relevant!), along with her roster of thesis and dissertation writers, was basically untenable, but here she was, doing it, simply because Florian had asked her, and in some odd way she preferred very much not to examine, Faith wanted to give Florian Cádiz pleasure. She returned time and time again to the recent email in which he announced the co-teaching plan. She mocked his stupid formal language, staring at it on the screen of her phone, but also she very nearly nibbled his words, smelled them, rested her face against them, nuzzled the spaces between them with the bridge of her delicate nose—broken and filed and reset during the summer before she went to college, when she was seventeen, at her father's suggestion.

Even before her appointment this morning, she had been looking at the message. And there were others, from the past year and the year before, with which she occasionally tantalized herself. They were just notes about coffee; jokes regarding students' sartorial habits and weight gain or loss, their obvious pandering; a reference to a crush Faith and Florian shared on a certain Argentinean philosopher; a series of adorable questions about how to approach a potential donor.

When at last summoned into the clean room in which her cosmetologist would minister to her with gloved fingers and an infinitely thin metal prick, Faith had separated her gaze from the interface with difficulty. She had responded as curtly as she could without inviting resentment to questions regarding the effects of injections past—her facial anamnesis, as it were—then settled into silent reverie, as she was asked to frown and received the benediction of treatment.

She had the sense that this afternoon she appeared, if not slightly startled, then, perhaps, slowed down. Time had broken around her eyes and lips. Time split its husk, poured its riches over her; it no longer held sway there. It was possible that she had replied to the questions regarding the recent history of her face in a somewhat leading fashion. Perhaps there had been one additional injection on account of the tale she told. Had there not been an extra spark of pain? Had she not mentally dedicated this brief moment of suffering to Florian?

In another era and another week she would have stayed home. Her husband, Marcus, whose firm was currently crafting an agreement between a Shanghainese hotel group and a midtown real estate concern, left the house early and returned late. Faith might easily have worked undisturbed from her wing of the apartment until the excessive paralysis had settled into the light paralysis of her face she had come to enjoy and even require. But duty was what it was. If someone wanted to bother to observe something out of the ordinary about her countenance, then so be it, but chances were nothing of the sort could possibly transpire. Not only were the students blind to anything save their own fears, her colleagues preened themselves so maniacally they had no time for others' appearances. Only Florian might notice, but sadly he was out of town.

Anyway, a lack of movement often presents itself as a non-presence, a void.

Here Faith realized that she had, perhaps, not been speaking for quite some time.

She looked up from the page, from a paragraph on squatters' rights.

Around the seminar table, students mostly wrote with their heads down. A few presumptuous individuals gazed at her directly, writing implements raised, as if Faith's thought was a pond in which they floated, buoyed by critical awe.

Maybe Faith perceived something. She wasn't sure. There was information, a kind of pressure on the air, energy emerging from these faces. It did not flow into her. It rather paused, frustrated, just above her skin.

Faith felt herself to be a statue, an artwork designed not to reflect human reality but to absorb and store it.

Maybe this, Faith thought, was power.

"Excuse me."

It was Isobel.

Professor Isobel Childe was seated in a corner of the seminar room, back straight as a yardstick, and, like a fourth grader, had her hand raised, entire arm in the air. No mild flick of the pen, this was a cab hail.

"Oh," said Faith, aware that her face did not indicate astonishment and that therefore the sound she made was incomprehensible and raw.

"I have a question." Dr. Childe's arm was slowly retracted.

"Yes?" It was easy enough for Faith to cause her voice to go up at the end of this short word.

"Where, exactly, are we—on the syllabus?" Isobel rummaged in a nest of papers on her lap above a lurid, floor-length paisley skirt.

Faith wondered, as she so often did, if this was a performance on Isobel's part, a ploy to humiliate her, or if Isobel might indeed not be quite sure where she, or anyone else in the room for that matter, was.

"The syllabus," Faith repeated, stalling.

Faith had a copy of the syllabus inside an interoffice envelope in her bag, but she made no move to retrieve it.

A stirring began within the ranks of the seminar table to gallantly produce the document on Faith's behalf. Faith permitted this convulsion to develop and richen on its own and, then, to unfurl.

Isobel was frowning. Isobel Childe was five years younger than Faith Ewer and had never visited a cosmetologist. She did not dye her hair, did not exercise, liked midcentury jewelry and copious quantities of kind bud, which she purchased from a former advisee of her ex-husband's who had since become a very successful dealer and who lived in a cavernous duplex in Brooklyn Heights. Isobel met the former student for lunch from time to time, accepting a package, usually in a tissue-festooned Diptyque or Barneys bag, evidence of the ex-student/dealer's wife's shopping interests, Isobel supposed. (Isobel had never met the woman.) She paid with an envelope of cash. The former student, Mark, was blond, gym-bodied, clean-shaven. He dressed in pristine athleisure and had a ten-thousand-dollar watch strapped on. He looked like a precocious senior partner at a corporate law firm on a Sunday, fresh from the squash court, scrubbed and scented, grim with the numbers but making the best of it, tan.

Mark, like Isobel's former partner, had been a sinologist in school. He was that sort of piercing, high-strung Protestant who absorbs languages and complex political histories with terrible ease. He was a natural diplomat, economist, scholar, hard-news journalist, or agent of the CIA. He could explain the past as a magic-free material scaffold that upholds and comprehensively predicts the present. "Always historicize," Fredric Jameson had written. Yes, the dictate suited Mark well.

Isobel had slept with this quiet American a number of times while her marriage was ending. She had found Mark, in that cliché, a big cat: he kept his eyes closed and was given to occult bursts of energy that he pressed into Isobel's flesh with his hands, nose, tongue, fingers, knees, penis, usually in that order. Given the age difference (almost eighteen years) Isobel had no ambition to recommence assignations. She did sometimes wonder if the dalliance had played a role in Mark's decision to abandon a promising and, for the time, cutting-edge dissertation on clandestine markets of the Cultural Revolution. She sometimes thought of the night he'd shown up in a Columbia sweatshirt and leather jacket after Terrence had consumed his usual ill-advised dose of temazepam. Mark's pale hair was a flower, and they'd fucked standing up in the kitchen. He smelled of cigarettes and detergent. He was twenty-three and she was forty and he wanted her to leave Terrence to run away with him and make babies, if she still could. He'd cried silently and kissed her with his wet face, attempting to pull her wordlessly out of the apartment.

He'd subsequently followed Isobel to Berkeley after she'd accepted a temporary appointment there, but by that point she couldn't bring herself to speak to him. For a month or more he'd trailed her around campus, always at a polite distance, and finally she'd relented and taken him back to her apartment for a twelve-hour session, after which she had sat him down and explained things. She wasn't his and wasn't anyone's and if he loved her he had to take her at her word. She was leaving Terry, she was accepting a new position in New York, and she was embracing a life of celibacy.

It was (1) that Mark had been able, after several months, to accept this news, and (2) that Isobel had been in deadly earnest, that they had managed to remain friends. The agony he'd felt in relation to her need for liberty had been instructive in a way no treatise, archive, method, or data set had ever been. He'd become freer, too.

How Mark's current business played into these revelations was a subject of lesser concern to Isobel. At first he had not wanted to accept her money, but then she'd told him her current salary plus how much she'd taken Terry for in the divorce (Terry, who'd been—provably—railing his female and a few of his male students on the side on a regular basis since the mid-1970s, plus engaging in a lucrative and not-exactly-progressive consulting practice on the side of *that* side, and who had his own share of guilt). Mark sighed, pocketed her cream-laid envelope.

Isobel had walked home that day, stowed the first of what were to be many, many packages in her freezer until evening. She'd always liked the smell and taste and touch of ice-cold marijuana. She liked to stretch it out, too, infusing cooking oils and butter. She baked various things. She was precise about it. She was pretty high right now.

Thus, if Isobel Childe appeared at all agitated, this was no more than a twentieth, some ridiculously small proportion, of her true agitation, which she could no longer feel. She, not Roger Herbsweet, was the preeminent scholar of the nineteenth-century novel, at least at this institution. It made no sense for someone who was around mainly to be the one person on staff who knew something about poetry to be focusing on prose. Yes, it *was* a novelist, as Florian had attempted to placate her back in April when everyone's courses had shown up online, but it was *LeGouffre*. Hardly Balzac. It was a cult figure! Barely literature! The course was evidently some sort of cultural history and didn't Isobel think that Herbsweet was finally getting with the departmental program? Wasn't this an encouraging sign? Didn't Isobel remember the days when he was trying to put together what was only the world's wackiest seminar on neocon poetics, The Gold Standard: Metonymy as Money, that legendarily deranged offering? Florian hadn't been around then, but that didn't mean he hadn't heard of it, the head-scratching and muttering up and down the administrative chain and the lack of a syllabus or even assigned readings. Roger *turned in* a syllabus now. Roger *showed up* to departmental meetings. He taught things other people could *understand*. He didn't cut his classes short and tell everyone they should take the rest of the day off and get on the A to Aqueduct-North Conduit Avenue, hit the racetrack and then the beach, if they wanted to truly comprehend the lyric. Roger was no longer the most popular professor in the department. He was rough and unpleasant but diligent enough. He was certainly feared and maybe hated. He was obviously morbidly depressed, but he was the sort of person who bent with the wind to avoid breaking. Isobel *was* the wind, Florian pursued, his whitened teeth glinting, his own fluency in four Western European languages advertised by sagging bookshelves. Isobel was the defining force in the building, and if she didn't believe Florian when he told her so, then she had only to look at the description of Roger Herbsweet's upcoming class, a manuscript-based Marxian reading of the career of a *rarissimo* (*rarissima*?) who'd produced something like .75 books in "their," Florian selected the pronoun with care, lifetime.

"Did you read his 'baby' monograph?" Florian wanted to know. They were still talking about Roger.

"His first book?" This was an edited version of young Herbsweet's dissertation, his one serious piece of scholarship, actually reported to be fairly presentable. Isobel had not read it, although a few years back she had availed herself of some notes and the book's index for use in a conference paper.

"Don't you think you're being a bit petty?"

"Not particularly!"

"And if I were to ask Faith if *she* wants to do some poetry?"

This had been more than sufficient, and Florian knew it. Faith was even slightly renowned for her bizarre forcing of postmodern poems into the service of unwieldy theories of globalization. Poets she wrote about, often academics themselves, published letters decrying her interpretations, begging their small publics to believe that they hadn't meant this or that sonnet or erasure as a comment on the worldwide standardization of shipping containers, to name just one such gaffe. Indeed, it was a practice from which Faith had seemed of late to be in quiet retreat. She wasn't one to apologize, but she was obsessively strategic. A request of this kind from Florian could really flummox her, maybe set her back a semester.

Anyway, if Isobel were being totally forthcoming with Florian, which she definitely was not, she didn't give a shit what Roger taught. She had come to Florian's office merely to complain about something it was fairly reasonable for her to complain about. She had come to seek advantage, and advantage was what she had got.

Or, so she had at the time believed.

The present state of affairs was an indication that this advantage, if that is what it had been, was mostly on Florian's side. Who knew how much chess Florian had played, bopping around the estates of his much divorced and remarried extended family as a precocious adolescent; Isobel was willing to bet that it had been a lot. Isobel had once heard Florian joke at a party that in the eighteenth century his family had been notorious for poisoning. When a student in the circle asked whom they'd poisoned, Florian tittered. He could barely contain himself. "Themselves!" he'd finally barked. "Or, I mean, one another." Then, producing an enigmatic smile, he'd swirled away.

It was easy to wish to know less about Florian. The more one knew, the more one felt that he had already foreseen and arranged everything that came to pass in the department.

Isobel was, for one, not yet willing to rule out a scenario in which Florian had somehow entrapped Roger, although she was pretty uncertain as to how that would have worked, particularly from a mechanical point of view. And here Isobel returned to the girl. This was the really damaging part, the negative human-interest theme—by means of which an imaginary author hoped to stimulate book sales, if this were the plot of a novel, which it was not.

The girl—the anonymous student, the unnamed plaintiff—as everyone in the whole fucking city now seemed to know, had been discovered under Roger's desk by a member of the four-person cleaning staff who did the building on Saturdays. It was the middle of the day and the girl had obviously been there awhile.

The first time Isobel had heard her name over the phone, she hadn't recognized it. Florian had had to remind Isobel that this girl was one of theirs, a doctoral student, that in fact it was Isobel who, something like three years ago, had demanded that the department accept her. This would have been when Florian was still new.

"It seemed like you wanted to work with her," Florian's voice said delicately, or as delicately as possible given the horrific compression, through Isobel's iPhone.

"Well, where has she been?" It was the evening of the previous Saturday and Isobel was just settling down with a spliff and some neo-Kantian descriptions of the probable end of the world that she planned to eviscerate in a group review.

"I'm in the department now," Florian told Isobel, a non sequitur. He sounded distracted. "It's not really very good."

Florian went on to explain the account he had received from

security. The member of the cleaning staff in question, one Tayisiya Musa, had been vacuuming the hall and saw that Professor Herbsweet's door had been left ajar, the agreed-upon sign that a faculty member was requesting some basic dust removal. Musa had nudged the vacuum in. She said that she was wearing earbuds and with the noise of the machine couldn't hear. Going under the furniture, specifically the desk, she felt something. The something was soft and large. Squatting down, Musa had come face-to-face with the rigid form of the aforementioned unnamed female student, who was on her hands and knees in a dress shirt and pantyhose. After some initial alarm, Musa assumed this was an incomprehensible game the students were playing. Musa turned off the vacuum and requested that the student, who was at this point motionless, relocate so that Musa could finish the carpet. She said that she had told the student she could go back to whatever it was she was doing in just a moment. She said that she found it odd that the student was so strangely dressed and that she wasn't wearing shoes, but that in the moment she was mainly concerned with getting the floor done. The student made no response. Her eyes were open and she stared straight ahead.

At first Musa found this offensive and was about to leave, but then she noticed that there was something in the student's face that suggested this was not a prank. She let go of her machine and went out to the reception area, where Sylvère Opie, an administrative aide, was snacking on stale Halloween candy and catching up on some paperwork.

Musa told Opie what she had seen and together they returned to Herbsweet's office, where the unnamed student remained, still in her position.

Opie told Musa that he knew this person slightly, that she was possibly an advisee of Herbsweet's. He'd seen her come and go. He went over and tried talking to the kneeling form, waving his hand in front of her face. Although now beads of sweat were visible on the student's increasingly grayish forehead and nose, she remained taciturn, immobile.

It was, Musa had said, as if they were encountering a piece of human furniture.

Opie called security.

Security called the Wellness Exchange.

Security received the OK to remove the student for an interview and observation, what was called "emergency counseling."

Musa and Opie went back to work.

The unnamed student, for her part, apparently did not resist. A thermal blanket was tied around her waist and an SUV issued to campus security used to convey her three blocks to Mental Resources, where she was transferred to a counselor.

"I just got off the phone with them," Florian concluded.

"With whom?" It wasn't that Isobel did not grasp the enormity of the situation; she was just disoriented. She had been at first mildly pleased that Florian had phoned her at all and then in his hour of need, but now she saw that he expected her to take care of this. Isobel needed to exercise tact. She had to avoid opening herself to the narrative.

"Security and the health person."

"The counselor?"

"Yes. The emergency counselor, the therapist. The one who's there for things like this."

"They called you?" Isobel felt she was maneuvering fairly well.

"She supposedly spoke," Florian clarified. "After a few hours. She apparently has her ID number memorized. It came out before her name."

"It's so handy at the library," Isobel was saying, meaning one's identification number.

"Right," said Florian, indicating that he did not in fact agree with Isobel. "I'm going over there."

"Are you sure that's a good idea, Florian?"

"I've been in the department *all day*, Isobel. Of course Roger's upstairs, but they easily could have come and got me. I mean, if something was wrong, nothing was keeping, really *keeping*, her in Roger's office."

Florian was fishing, in his way, but Isobel refused the invitation. She kept to already established facts. "But they didn't know who she was!"

"Well, now they know. The counselor called the police."

"What?"

"I'm reaching out to Erwin next."

Erwin Hogarth was the dean of the humanities. Erwin Hogarth would not be pleased.

"Thank you for letting me know."

"Shall I meet you there?"

"I'm sorry?"

"Isobel, you advised her master's thesis. Frankly, you're our ambassador."

Isobel breathed slowly, paging through her mind. She wasn't coming up with anything.

"I know this must be extremely upsetting. It's so radically weird! You didn't ask for this to happen, but I think we owe it to everyone to show Erwin a united front."

Isobel rose from her couch. She was very unhappy.

"I'm going to text you the address," Florian continued. "I'll let Erwin know how devastated you were to hear this, Isobel, about *your* advisee, your protégée, with whom you'd been working *so closely*. It's dreadful. I think he'll be extremely moved by your dedication to our students."

"Yes," Isobel told him, but Florian had already hung up.

Anyway, as Florian knew, Isobel lived approximately four blocks from the university's health facility. Even with an extravagant amount of procrastination and toking it wasn't going to take her long to get there. She thought about Erwin, for whom she had exactly zero personal regard but who at least seemed competent, and selected a sweater she had purchased in Montparnasse in the late 1970s, along with a tweed blazer that must at one time have belonged to Terry. She looked, she thought, examining herself in a narrow mirror near the door, like an interesting childless relative. Which was, she supposed, exactly what she was.

She surprised herself by arriving at the Wellness Exchange in advance of Florian.

She was sent up to the floor and sector in question.

"Hi," she told a receptionist.

Luckily, they were not used to faculty visits here and immediately understood the reason for her presence. "I'll take you back," the receptionist told Isobel, so kindly that Isobel wondered if maybe she, Isobel, might not like to check herself in for observation someday. All things were either a dusty pink or sea-foam green, as if babies might spontaneously arrive, requiring binary decor.

"Was this area originally used for something else?" Isobel asked her guide. She liked to test her powers of observation whenever possible.

The nurse seemed to smile, although Isobel could only see the back of her head. "Hmm," she said. "I don't think so!"

Isobel decided that she liked the response. "I didn't think so, either."

"Here we are." The nurse popped open a door. "She's your student, right?"

Isobel still didn't think so, but this was not the time to split hairs.

Here Isobel was astonished to find herself in the midst of an extremely vivid hallucination. She saw the unnamed student. It wasn't the young woman in front of her, who wore a rumpled fitted oxford shirt, probably Brooks Brothers, and a pair of what were obviously institution-issue sweatpants. It was the student who had sat at a seminar table on orientation day two years, she thought, ago, who was meek and miscalculated her responses to prickly queries from Faith.

Isobel hadn't been present, just walking by in the hall. She'd stopped to listen to the most fumbling explanation of an interest in transatlantic modernism and exchanges around free verse that she'd never hoped to hear! And, of course: she'd read the master's thesis. Now she remembered. Except that it had been about a minor American poet of the 1960s, hardly what the student had been admitted to study. It was an easy topic. Something they'd do in English.

Here Isobel's memory-image transmogrified. She recalled a potent scene in Honoré de Balzac's 1834 novel *La Duchesse de Langeais*, in which the title character is borne away by a gang of experimental Freemasons loyal to a soldier with whom she is engaged in an intrigue. For her seductions and refusal of actual sex with said soldier, the duchess is threatened with branding by the Mason clique. She's told that all the world will know of her coquetry, once she has a star-shaped burn on her forehead. Yet, rather than react with fear, the duchess tells her controlling lover that her brow is even hotter than the metal with which he threatens to brand her, that she desires his mark. Deflated by this upping of the ante, the soldier lowers his scorching tool. It's hard to say if this is what the duchess wants.

For there is always a fine line, Isobel thought, between submission and enthusiasm. Isobel had heard that psychoanalysis was the best way out of this sort of emotional predicament, but she'd never been able to bring herself to put much stock in it. She was alone now because she was of the determined opinion that any person she opened herself to would eventually reject her, much as Terry had. He'd numbed himself to her, fallen away from their shared life. This was structural, historical, inevitable.

Isobel could lie still in a pit of unending submission and yet be accused of resistance.

This door has been intended only for you. And now I am going to close it.

But the unnamed student did not have these sorts of problems.

The student was, if Isobel was not mistaken, dedicating her weekends to a full-blown sadomasochistic affair with Roger Herbsweet. Which, given the student's lack of any talent for scholarship, could be considered strategic, as Isobel, for one, was definitely not about to let this one get to dissertation stage.

Clever girl, thought Isobel.

It had not occurred to Isobel, then and there, in a room reserved for the counseling of the seriously distressed, that whatever liaison there had been between Herbsweet and this student might present a problem and a quasi-legal one, at that. Granted, she had understood Florian's alarm; she knew what the words *dean* and *police* meant. It's just that you had to believe this was going to blow over. These things always did. Roger would deny everything, and it would be this person's word against his. If she even gave her word. Much of the time, they didn't.

"Hello," Isobel said, employing low registers, making the greeting count. She hovered and the nurse pulled up a chair. Isobel took some time arranging herself. The nurse, apparently mistrusting Isobel, was doing something with some charts.

"I meant to write you." This was the student. She seemed relatively stable, if, like many young people these days, prone to category errors.

"Oh?"

"Thank you for the comments on my thesis. I'm sorry I've been out of touch for so long."

"That's fine," Isobel purred.

The nurse, observing what she took to be healthful banter, withdrew.

"I'm fine, too, by the way," the student whispered. "Tell him I said so."

"I will!" Isobel was suddenly aware of her own extreme discomfort.

"I just didn't know," the student paused.

Isobel waited.

"I just didn't know if I should, well, *you know.*"

Isobel did not know. Isobel did not want to know. "It's OK," she said. She intended this as only the least affecting thing she could say and was already calculating the likely speed with which she might be able to exit the interview.

"It's not OK!" The student did not scream or shout, but her voice was piercingly unwell.

Isobel allowed herself, with dread, to settle in. This would be an episode.

"I'm so sorry," said the student. Then: "I know you know. He must have told you."

Again, Isobel did not know. And had been told nothing.

Fortunately, here Florian and Erwin appeared. They both looked like they might jump out of their skins and, also, therefore, their ludicrous matching Barbour jackets, so anomalous and unwanted was the situation, and this put Isobel at greater ease. She made introductions. Then, when nobody was looking, she simply got up and left.

She bought a cheesecake on her way home.

So, yes, she had had to account for her actions. Here she was, paying through the nose, all on account of an ill-timed complaint to Florian about Herbsweet's course description. Isobel had assumed that Florian wouldn't catch her in her game, wouldn't know Isobel was attempting to expand the borders of her smallish but still extremely impressive intellectual kingdom. However, Isobel had been wrong in this and Florian demonically perceptive. Florian had exacted his punishment, and now Isobel was condemned to listen as Faith attempted to regurgitate the past thirty years of continental philosophy via what sounded like a series of floundering book-jacket blurbs. It was a little bit like sitting in on a reasonably accomplished oral exam by a student one had expected to fail, a thought that gave Isobel pleasure, even as she suffered. And so Isobel made the decision to do what she always did in the midst of oral exams and dissertation defenses: she interrupted in order to ensure that events were following their previously foreseen order. Isobel disrupted Faith. Therefore, Isobel won.

"What week are we on?" Faith was repeating, regarding the syllabus, looking past Isobel's shoulder.

Isobel was about to say something disparaging about Roger, but stopped herself, recognizing that Faith was capable of anything when it came to secondhand reports.

Faith, for her part, was now staring down at the surface of a Xerox that had been transmitted to her from somewhere within the students' ranks. She had turned to its second page only to discover that it had been illuminated with a series of ballpoint drawings of Mickey Mouses with breasts as well as phalluses, who were being orally and manually ministered to by a pair of extremely busty and dexterous Bugs Bunnies. Fortunately, it was impossible for Faith to move her face very much. She returned to the first page and tossed the syllabus back into the center of the table, whence somebody or other instantly retrieved it.

Again someone was raising their hand.

"Someone?" Faith asked, meaning by this a reiteration of her initial request.

"We're on week nine," said a student Faith did not recognize. "But technically it's week eight because we missed a week because, *um*."

"So you're on week eight?" This was Isobel.

"Yes," the student confirmed.

Faith decided that she wanted to take charge. After all, let Isobel come sit at the head of the table and deal with this, rather than wave her wand from the shadows!

"Could," Faith slowly brought about, "somebody please *read* what is written for week eight?"

There came a silence, which lasted.

These sheltered, perfectionist fetuses were terrified to read, even in English, on the off chance they might get something wrong.

It was enraging.

"Hello?" Faith asked them.

"Oh, I'll do it," said a female voice.

Faith peered over. She attempted to squint, but this did not prove feasible, given the treatment.

The volunteer was pushing hair from her brow.

Oh god. It was that one.

This student, who was also in Faith's "No" course and who Faith wished very ardently were *not* in it, began reading.

"Week eight colon," the student said.

Faith was in pain. "Are you insane?"

The student froze.

"Don't read the punctuation."

"Oh, no, of course not!" The student laughed meagerly and recommenced. "Week eight. October thirtieth. For class meeting. Begin PP. Clyve's translation will be consulted. DO NOT," the reader's voice increased irritatingly in volume, "EMPLOY ELLIS."

Faith waited. When nothing further was forthcoming she asked, "Is that all?"

The student nodded.

In some sense, Faith and Isobel had only themselves to blame for not having prepared anything substantial, which was to say, anything at all, for today's meeting. Then again, they had not spoken to each other directly in more than five years, so it had seemed pointless to examine their differences, which were fairly extreme, now.

Isobel sat forward. "You are reading *Passe-partout*?"

There was assent around the table.

Faith was not about to let this discussion get away from her. "And you are thinking about translation?" Faith spoke these words, making them musical and pleasant, grooming them with her best invisible comb. If one read the description of Faith's research interests on the departmental home page, one would see that Faith specialized in something called "translation theory," had published 1.5 books on the subject. Faith could feel Isobel frowning in the background and was pleased.

Jeff Santal, someone who might actually get himself a job one day, raised his hand. Faith resented Jeff, but in this instance he was a known quantity, if someone who was likely to give her late-career publications lukewarm reviews once he had tenure.

Jeff, feeling his moment arrive, lowered his hand. "Roger told us, early on, that the novella is the centerpiece of the course. I think he was pretty clear about it. 'C'est notre point de repère' is how he put it, actually quite a few times!"

Jeff spoke very good French and there was a hush.

Jeff cleared his throat. "I think we all also recall that early on Roger said that he had come across something remarkable. He said that this class was going to be his sandbox. He was really inspired, it seemed like."

"Oh?" said Faith.

"Well, he was quite open about it in a certain way. But in another way, it wasn't very clear. We're all supposed to be translating it."

"The novella?" Faith glanced at Isobel, who was now bent over, taking furious notes.

"Yes. We had discussed the title last week. Or, I mean," Jeff said, flustered in spite of himself, "the week before."

No one here wanted to be the first to name whatever it was that had happened, Faith thought. No one wanted to say "the incident," or "the *alleged* incident." Nobody was going to drop any references to fantasies of enforced servitude or BDSM. None of this was out of loyalty to Roger. No one was that deluded about Roger's character. Their reluctance was tactical. They understood, perhaps instinctively, that the official line had not yet gelled. Those who normally took an adversarial stance would disagree with the procedure lighted on by the administration. Others would be more conciliatory. They would speak of understanding, as well as the uncertainty we so often feel with respect to the actions of others, the so-called battle of the sexes, erotics and pedagogy, how consent can be so murky. They would say that it was right to move forward with consideration, without haste.

Jeff would probably fall into the latter camp. He would, at any rate, be able to imagine himself in Roger's shoes. (The experience of the unnamed student, who was without shoes on that fateful Saturday, was, at any rate, likely unimaginable to Jeff.)

"Good," said Faith. She meant several things by this, but mostly she was commending Jeff for sharing information.

Faith felt better now. She foresaw her coming liberation into the empty evening. She might even walk back to Chelsea. She would turn off her phone and take a circuitous route through the West Village, where there were a few tantalizing store windows she had not passed in a while.

Believing the matter of the syllabus to have been settled, Faith was about to resume reading from the rough draft of what she was privately calling "A Theory of 'No'; or, How to Do Nothing with Literature" when she noticed, with a certain sinking, that Jeff Santal had again raised his hand.

"I think we've understood the syllabus," Faith told him.

"Of course!" Jeff tucked his arm back under the table and leaned forward, performing a penitent face. "I thought I should say one more thing."

Faith checked in with Isobel.

The manic writing continued.

Faith was alone. She was alone with the animals. "And what is that?"

"About the title. It was interesting?"

Faith was beginning to lose patience. "And how was that?"

"Roger said that he didn't think anyone had translated the title correctly. He said that he felt this was a major problem in LeGouffre's reception in the anglophone world."

Faith pondered this. Démocrite Charlus LeGouffre was not really much better or much worse (i.e., less) known in the United States than any other nineteenth-century European novelist, with the obvious exceptions (Dickens, Dostoyevsky, Hugo). Dickens and Hugo were kept alive by Disney. Teenagers and lawyers got into Dostoyevsky, that perfect writer.

Faith sharpened her knife. "*How* is that a problem?"

Jeff blushed. "Ummm," he stammered, "if someone doesn't understand the title of a book then I guess that's—" Jeff trailed off, biting the inside of his own mouth.

Faith frowned. Or, she would have frowned, had she been able. However, Faith could not frown. She could have thoughts, but they were not manifest, save in her words, which—and here she realized abruptly that Jeff had not been blushing but rather attempting to keep himself from laughing in her face.

A miscalculation. Jeff's reviews of her future titles were not going to be *lukewarm*. They were going to be bald displacements, as when a baby bats an object off a table. He was going to tell everyone to forget her.

Faith considered the waste likely to be laid to her legacy in a decade. She became rigid, or, rather, even more rigid. She enjoyed once more and with even greater satisfaction the lack of sensation in her face. The inability to respond was power. The inability to imitate one's human sphere was true liberty. It was impossible for Faith to seem to care.

Jeff was now staring at Faith, aware that he had transgressed but baffled by the lack of rejoinder.

This was why they were trying to admit fewer men, Faith reminded herself. "Thank you, Jeff Santal," she said. "I think you've been speaking long enough. Does someone else want to pick up and explain Roger's theory of titles, if you don't mind?"

Nothing.

Faith waited.

Nothing, still.

Faith decided that she would take a different tack.

"Isobel!" Faith trilled. "You will be far more knowledgeable about this. Maybe you could start us out with an explanation of the title of the novella and how it has been translated!" Faith could recall that there were at least two different titles that had appeared with English translations of the work in question—a death knell for its reputation, you did have to hand it to Roger. But Faith couldn't, for the life of her, remember what either of these titles was. She wished that she had spent some time with Google this morning, as she had told herself she would, rather than once again sifting desperately through Florian's old emails for a sign.

"Sorry?" said Isobel, looking up.

Faith was vibrating curiously at the head of the seminar table.

Isobel had not been listening. She had been outlining the introduction to a new article about the fictional duchesse de Langeais. De Langeais was a stand-in for Balzac's real-life conquest, the duchesse de Castries, whose name Isobel enjoyed for its evocation, surely arbitrary, of the English verb *to castrate*. The Duchess of Castrates, ha. Isobel thought, too, of *La Duchesse de Langeais*'s original title, when it first appeared in serial format: *Ne touchez pas la hache. Don't Touch the Axe.* Itself a tool of castration—and, in the book, a punch line. "Don't touch the axe," an executioner advises the frustrated lover of the duchesse de Langeais, long before he meets his duchess. This is in England and the axe in question used to cut off the head of King Charles I. The lover later repeats the line, his first witticism, in Paris. But *la duchesse* cannot bear to see him succeed socially, even so slightly, and says something like, "Oh, we've all heard that one before, you turd." A third party stares at her in horror. But, in a way, de Langeais is right: it's a common enough warning.

Maybe the duchess fears that she herself is the axe. She is, after all, designed to be married. That is the contract. Be female, be a commodity, but marry and be capable of giving birth to dukes. This is what, Isobel surmised, the duchesse de Langeais hears from the mouth of a man who believes himself to be in love with her: It is dangerous to interact with an object designed for a specific task. In so doing, one risks one's own destiny.

Isobel bit her pen.

Isobel pondered the unnamed student, arranged in whatever position. *The position.* The position of ultimate submission. One is a table, a furnishing, a design object, an item adjusted to stimulate a sensitive organ, maintained in perpetual readiness. *Les outils qui parlent.*

That was Molière, a character's epithet for servants, "tools that have the power of speech."

But do not touch the axe. *Be* the axe, by all means, go right ahead. Buy it. Stare at a picture of it. But touch it and what you got was your own damn fault.

Isobel remembered that she was meant to be saying something and so she said, "Yes?"

"I'm asking about the titles." This was Faith.

"Which titles?"

"For the novella."

"I think it has one title."

"In English!"

Isobel was so engrossed in the challenge of retrieving these phrases that she did not linger on what was either Faith's rudeness or her despair. Isobel, for her part, was either about to be very pleased with herself or the contrary. "Ha!" Isobel said. *"Skeleton Key* and *The Passport.* Those are the English versions. Clyve and Ellis, respectively. Are we rating them?" Isobel sparkled, vaguely, beneath her scarves.

There was a little collective movement in the room, a listing to one side. It seemed that the students would be very pleased indeed if they were in fact rating them right now, these titles, a consensus that was lost on neither Faith nor Isobel.

The students wanted to vote.

Isobel looked at Faith, who was not looking at Isobel.

Faith said, "I think we can agree that your first assignment for the course—" She paused. "That your first assignment for the course that Professor Childe and I are now directing is to find your *own* English title for the novella."

Jeff was already raising his hand.

"Yes?"

"Do you mean that we should begin translating the novella into English?"

Faith did not need to think about this. "Just the title. You will want to read it, of course. And take notes. We will discuss next week."

"Will there be a new syllabus?" It was Jeff again.

"Do your best," Faith said. She was pushing her chair back from the table and taking out her smartphone.

If Jeff were female it would have been difficult to resist screaming at him, but Jeff was not female and so the situation was just barely manageable. It was clear to Faith that Roger had been using this class as a workshop for his own translation of *Passe-partout*, which she imagined he planned to publish with some insider-y literary press, a fun oddity at last correctly Englished for your pleasure, with a new introduction by the distinguished translator and scholar.

Isobel, meanwhile, rustled in her corner. She always seemed to travel with at least one plastic bag stuffed with irregular papers, as if she were constructing a very large hamster bed somewhere. Faith decided that they could encounter each other on email for organizational purposes, as necessary, but that there was no point engaging in actual conversation. She buried herself in her text messages, several of which had been sent by her son, who required something or other before dinner.

"Professor Ewer?"

This was someone talking to her.

Faith was typing the words *call you*. She said, "Yes?" but did not look up.

"I, uh, sorry. I'm just wondering how final papers for the class are going to work?"

Faith was forced to look up. The reason she was forced to look up was that she was speaking to someone who did not understand how things functioned, and this was, as ever, an extremely unwelcome surprise. It meant that she was speaking to someone who required an explanation as to how things functioned, which meant that this person wanted to be told (1) that things were dysfunctional, and (2) that everyone had long ago decided not to make any attempt to rectify things. This was not a child of divorce, for starters.

Faith sighed pointedly at this faulty state of affairs, which was to say, the young woman who had been reading aloud earlier.

"Hi," said this wretch. "Erin."

"*Erin,*" Faith repeated. On the screen of Faith's phone a dialogue box the size of a trio of aspirin in a row contained words she could not really see, which in fact read, *call youJesus.* Faith made the decision to hit the dot that launched them, irretrievably, into the ether.

"Sorry," Erin repeated.

Faith's pages were already in her bag and all she needed to do now was stand up, phone in hand, and she would be able to exit. She held herself in stillness, awaiting whatever ludicrous bid for parental attention was to come.

Erin waited, too.

The back of Faith's head hurt, although the numb feeling in the front of her face continued to be great, just great. Pressing hard against her numbness, the one point of grace in this moment, Faith, acting as proxy for Erin's avoidant mom or whoever it was, asked, "What do you want?"

"I don't know what to do."

"Then," said Faith, standing, "email someone who was paying attention." She trembled briefly from the effort of evading this moron's advances, left the room.

Erin Adamo was now the last remaining soul. This often happened, after her classes. The room did not smell very good. It smelled like loathing and the bodily emanations loathing produces, the psychic slime that gathers in crevices nearby asymmetrical relations. Erin Adamo had read plenty of books, but this was of little interest to her professors, possibly because Erin was not about to reveal to them what she considered her own valuable opinions on said books. No one remembered Erin's name as a consequence of Erin's inability to say enough at the right moments or too little, when awkwardness or evil threatened.

Just a moment ago she had made an effort. And she had approached Faith, in whose "No" course Erin was also enrolled. And Faith, true to her current research interests, had refused.

But it was also possible that this refusal was not a mere matter of politics. It could well have been personal, and this was a reality that Erin would need to confront, sooner or later, as it had some bearing on the future Erin was going to have to live in. Erin was going to need a job in years to come, and if Erin wanted to have a job that involved teaching at the university level, she was going to have to deal with the fact that the instructors she had met so far during her graduate career were all but entirely unwilling or unable to attach a name to her face from day to day. The outlook was, as they say, poor.

The other difficulty was that Erin was not too sure where else she could go.

By which Erin meant, in the city and in the American economy. She had been taught how to read words and create sentences and had long excelled at this, and, in the face of her own talent, reflected back to her by teachers since she had attained the age of ten, had prematurely forsworn the attractions of all other structures of human knowledge, including algebra, another once-sympathetic system.

This had been unwise, but being young, Erin had not managed to grasp exactly how fatally unwise it was. And now Erin was here, allegedly comparing poems written in American English to poems written in Japanese and French, although, as there were no tenured faculty members who concerned themselves with modern Japanese verse, Erin's options were currently limited to transatlantic relations. The only Axis power she seemed to be invited to incline her mind toward was Germany. So Erin read German, too. She attempted to believe that her specialty was poetry; however, no classes about poetry were offered this semester, Erin's third. There had been none the previous two semesters, either.

Erin's bag was still under the seminar table and she stooped to pick it up, in the process catching sight of a loose leaf of paper that had fallen to the carpet. Erin squatted and tugged the page out from under the chair leg where it was currently impaled. It was a section of Faith's manuscript, and for a moment Erin had a vision of arriving at Faith's office, slightly torn paper in hand:

Faith [*wears expression of amazement*]: I've been looking for that everywhere!

Erin [*striding toward Faith's desk, confident, offering cherished page*]: It's nothing!

Faith [*fervent*]: It is far from nothing! Without you I could not have completed my _____ (here insert crucial academic task).

Faith and Erin [*now friends for life*]: . . .

But of course nothing like this was going to take place, not least of all because Faith, like all those who benefited from birth in a postindustrial society, made use of word-processing software and did not need anyone to come to her to replace her "lost" pages. And even if some act of terror or technological crisis led to catastrophic memory loss, Faith would still say no. It did not matter what Erin did.

Thus, in discovering this fallen page, Erin did not discover a thing. She folded it in half, placed it in her bag. Maybe she would read it later and decide that Faith was an intellectual fraud, a rumor that had legs among the students these days. Or maybe it would be useful as a bookmark, a kind of talisman that might confer social power or mystical literacy upon the user. At home, Erin might even add it to her bulletin board. With it there, she would be able to study Faith's style at leisure.

Erin did not particularly want to think about going home, in part because of how many trains the transit would require. And there were other reasons not to think of it. Other reasons that stung Erin. Erin looked dully after something somewhere and found the classroom door.

Anyway, Erin could go uptown. Actually, it was not a mere option because she had said yes, as opposed to no. She had said that she was coming.

She stopped briefly in to the women's restroom near the stairs to examine her appearance. She wore black and gray because this was what she always wore, along with a red vintage coat with a torn lining, a recent thrift store buy. Today she had eaten a slice of American cheese, a cup of yogurt, a cellophane sack of trail mix. She had also consumed two glasses of water and the equivalent of five cups of coffee. She attempted to make an alluring face at the image of her face and washed her hands.

If only she hadn't so royally alienated Faith, because Isobel Childe certainly wasn't available to her at this point, either. It was something she could barely bring herself to think about, flicking water off her fingertips into the sink.

As she was exiting the building, the security guard at the desk, possibly the only person who worked here who recognized her from day to day, told her to have a nice evening. She had come out of the stairs with her back to him, but he said it anyway. That was the sort of person he was. He did things that were not, strictly speaking, necessary.

She turned awkwardly.

"Thank you," she said. "You as well."

"See you tomorrow," said the guard, whose name Erin did not know.

Erin went out onto the sidewalk. She would walk the six blocks to Union Square, avail herself of the 4 or 5 train. She wondered, briefly, if she should buy a snack on her way, considering that she was beginning to feel fairly pressing pangs, but reminded herself that she had little money and one of the few things in this world she was able to control with any certainty was her weight. She was, after all, not bad looking. She had gotten the sense from Roger Herbsweet that he might even approve her prospectus this semester if she lost another five pounds.

But Roger wasn't around anymore, Erin reminded herself. Roger had made an error, some people said. Roger had his foibles, others told her. Erin felt slightly foolish for having taken his class in hopes of solidifying a connection that might rescue her from the impasse in which she currently found herself. Perhaps Roger was actually a great guy and, due to his esoteric interests plus gruff attitude, grossly misunderstood by the graduate population. And the institution at large. And the world. And maybe Roger could return and would still become what Erin privately termed her "poetry teacher," meaning that together they could discuss whatever it was each of them happened to be writing in his or her nonprofessional capacity, for surely somebody as unconventional as Roger had to write poetry.

Erin strove to feel sorry for Roger Herbsweet but found that she could not. This inability expressed itself as a mental tightness, like trying to push a beanbag under a reasonably well made door (a shut door). She next attempted to imagine that the unnamed student had driven Herbsweet to a point of madness that was only answerable through the student's "punishment" via transformation into a redundant piece of office furniture. Given that (like all full-time professors) Herbsweet was already in possession of a relatively OK university-issue tabletop, fitted with cord-minding apertures in black plastic, a reddish mahogany-like laminate surface, he did not really require another. Erin tried to think of a scenario in which all this was the student's fault. The student had needs! Inappropriate needs! That idiot. That fool. That student needed . . .

Erin had to wait for the light to change. When the light changed, she had to wait for the coast to be clear. People were hit all the time by cars making sudden turns, particularly after sundown. She herself had only recently, at the end of the previous week, even, narrowly avoided a bus that was gliding into its stop in midtown, a very big swan of ungodly weight. She had been on her way to the Japan Society. The vehicle had missed her face, it seemed, by a mere five inches, ruffling the air with its mass. It hadn't touched her and she hadn't died. Yet, in that moment, she had begun to see the ease with which one is taken from this earth. Poof. A sizzle and then the collapse of the staircase that used to be one's elaborate personal narrative. Time stopped for the dying person, which meant that while consciousness still inhered, it touched on, it was, all times at once.

She'd begun the predictable movie:

The first thing on the screen was Ben's face. His fucked-up face. Apparently the movie ran in reverse. But, then again, Erin wasn't actually dying, so it made sense that whatever vision this semi-near-death experience inspired, it was basically an exploration of subjects of current concern, not the great existential themes. Thus: Ben's face. There it was, and the long bus flowed by, bopping to a standstill.

She was not going to call him. Nope. She was not going to bring him food at the friend's apartment where he might still be holed up like a genuine fugitive. She was not going to look at messages he had sent her two months ago, when things were still all right, when they were still whatever they had been. She would not look at his endearments, the begging, the threats. She would not read anything he had written.

Ben was her husband.

Erin worried the band of her wedding ring with her left thumb, a compulsive gesture. The metal was there and the callus beneath it.

Erin crossed the street. She walked a short block and made a right turn onto 14th. She descended the stairs in front of Whole Foods (a corny voice in her head blared "WHOLE PAYCHECK"), stuck a Metrocard through the reader in the turnstile, walked the corridor, the short stairs, the awkward interchange past the N/Q/R/W where a woman in a suit covered in white sequins was singing Alicia Keys into a microphone while behind her someone who appeared to be a sibling made the will of an electronic keyboard his own. She went down to the 4/5/6, surprised as she always was that she had not encountered anyone she knew among the two hundred or so souls streaming by underground. She wondered, briefly, if perhaps someone she knew was standing at her shoulder, a few feet away, on a neighboring platform, watching. She imagined that the watching happened calmly, that the watcher understood that there was no time to admit their acquaintance.

A 5 rumbled up. The platform filled. The moment came and Erin boarded.

They were still air-conditioning the cars, even in the second week of November. Today it might have hit eighty degrees for a couple of hours, Erin was not sure, not having spent a great deal of time out of doors. She did know that the university library was aggressively climate controlled, it did not really matter the season. She also knew that the library often smelled worse than the subway, a mixture of disinfectants and the vague but unshakable ghosts of feces and over-flowed toilets past. In the bathrooms in the stacks it was not unusual to open a stall to discover a toilet so brimming with shit it appeared that the disjecta had been not defecated by human bowels but rather shoveled in. Sometimes someone would have draped a clear plastic recycling bag over the horrifying bowl as if to signal "You probably already have pretty strong feelings about what you have discovered in this bathroom stall, but in case you're still deliberating, word to the wise, it's better not to pee or poo here. You could try to change a tampon or stand here and cry if you need to, but we wouldn't recommend it."

The sight was so common that Erin wondered if there might not be a secret society of students and faculty members who hung out at the wobbly, pen-scarred desks among the books, chugging laxatives. But, in truth, these toilets seemed to have a single author. The shitstorm was monographic and all the more disturbing for that, given the prolific nature of its creator. It indicated deep anxiety, as well as cultural issues where the gut in question was concerned.

Erin, on the subway, settled into the shoulder of her neighbor, which was bare and male and several inches from her eyes. She did not inhale but rather attempted to ease her mind into the human warmth generated in the packed car, the simultaneous hardness and slow, jiggling ease of human bones and human flesh pressed into various standing, stooping, leaning, lounging, cowering poses. Someone must long ago have determined that the only way to keep a city moving was to have seating at a minimum and, then, only at the edges. Bodies arranged vertically consumed space, ceiling to floor. No capacity went to waste. Equally amazing to Erin was the fact that no other city in the country had a public transit system of any comparable scale. This one, meanwhile, was decaying. She had read somewhere that, even without unanticipated flooding, tens of millions of gallons of water were pumped out of the tunnels every day, and every night grouters went out on leak patrol. She often rode the trains late and was used to seeing the strange carless utility and garbage trains, was accustomed to long, slow rides past work crews, their lamps with crisp, parchment-colored light that was so reassuring as the vehicle trundled by. They were all beneath the earth. All awaited some future destination, a translation or transformation, a result; the transit workers and the commuters were alike. The great, shared wish was to keep a passage open. Everyone wanted this, whatever *this* was, to continue, that there be a way, an aperture. They were like some of the rest of the world in this, in what could be called their cosmopolitanism, in what Erin considered the minimalism of their shared desire, which was neither nationalism nor a cult. Some people on the subway presumably anticipated Christian apocalypse: she had read their pamphlets, the cartoons depicting rapture and then a heaven full of men and women ranged like cattle over the clouds. But most people seemed only to be thinking an hour into the future, to merely want the subway to be a temporary state. They wished to enter, move, then exit once more. They did not really want to be here.

Erin's neighbor's shoulder stirred and withdrew. They were at 59th Street and here he removed himself from the car. A little more air hit her, the crowd thinning.

She and Ben rode the trains late at night together, at one and two and three in the morning. This was supposed to be a mark of change. The system wasn't as unpredictable as it allegedly had been in the 1980s and '90s when Erin, who had grown up in the city, was a child. She still remembered an afternoon when she was twelve or thirteen, when an empty car's doors had opened to reveal a thick black-red pool of blood more than three feet in diameter on the floor. The blood had glittered in the fluorescent lighting, so liquid and black and red, its perfect meniscus seemingly unbreakable even with the subway's motion.

Erin remembered thinking, in that moment, when she was an adolescent, that the blood she saw on the floor of the empty train car was beautiful, like plastic or glass, perfect in its strange smooth existence. The horror hadn't begun to descend until later, and then the horror remained for years. All of that blood, without a body. The empty train car in which blood rolled, from front to back.

But perhaps these days the pools of blood had merely gone some-where else.

Her best friend in high school had twice been attacked by a young man she did not know, who, when he saw her in a crowded train, had pushed her out the door at some deserted local stop in northern Manhattan and forced her against the tiled wall where he repeatedly inserted two of his fingers into her vagina with what she described as regular, mechanical thrusts. It happened once and then again. Each time she got away and he did not pursue her. And then she never saw him again for what Erin supposed was the rest of her best friend's life. He had been handsome, this rapist, in a red anorak, her best friend said. Her best friend's hair had begun falling out in the shower.

Erin did not know where her high school best friend was now. She had been her second best friend, after a bad experience in middle school. They had stayed in touch for a few years, not long. The friend was probably somewhere in the city. Erin had looked for her on Facebook and using various search engines, but hadn't been able to find so much as a photograph of her or mention. It worried Erin. But, then again, a lot of things worried Erin.

The last conversation she could recall between herself and the friend had concerned the friend's first college roommate, a woman who had a pair of angel's wings tattooed on her back.

Erin could recall wondering, she did not quite know why, if her high school best friend was going to be OK. The friend was attending a glamorous and mostly reputable university in the city, in fact the same university where Erin was now pursuing her PhD, and the friend seemed entranced by the roommate's tattoo, as if it were a sign confirming the existence of a hoped-for-but-never-before-verified alternate world. Erin remembered now that this message about the roommate and the roommate's wings had come in a letter. She could picture this, unfolding the pink ruled pages, because there had been an illustration of the roommate's back. The illustration had been annotated to the effect that the wings were slightly smaller than scale (than whatever scale one might imagine as appropriate for an angel). All the same, there was plenty of admiration. The best friend was beginning to have an idea about the future. She wrote about dropping out of school. She said that she did not know what she wanted to major in.

Maybe it was around this time that Erin had begun having her own difficulties. That would make sense. It would explain why it was so hard to remember what had occurred, as if there were a sash tied over Erin's eyes. Perhaps, given the problematic nature of Erin's present, it made sense that she could not remember much of the past decade-plus with ease. But Erin wasn't sure about this. She did have it in her to perceive that her amnesia might be meaningful. She felt she had been present—only, she could not see, could not move. She knew that she had, factually speaking, lived those years, that this was the plot, but when she attempted to go back to them and look, so much information was missing.

Why had she and her best friend stopped communicating? Erin recalled that she was afraid for her friend, yes. She was afraid because she had the sense that her friend was letting go, that she felt it was too difficult to go forward, that she might let go of life. Erin could see that things had become more complicated for the friend, rather than less. Her friend's family had no money and there was nothing there to catch her if she fell.

Erin had thought this, and she had also reflected that she herself was in danger of doing the very same thing, although she had no idea why. Sometimes Erin found that she could not understand simple sentences in American English. The mouths moved, but an inchoate whine came out. She had sat motionless in some spot on her college's campus and could not do what she was supposed to be doing. She could not walk, could not speak.

Maybe this was why she had not replied to that letter, serious as it was in spite of the pink stationery. Erin had not sent a letter or a postcard or an email. She had her friend's phone number in her dorm room but didn't make a call.

Erin was afraid, then, in the year of the collapse of office buildings. Erin was also, if it was possible to come to some point of reckoning with herself, afraid now.

Even now Erin rode the train with half a mind to bombings and mass shootings, stabbings, chemical attacks. Even now that she had survived her twenties, what had once seemed an unimaginable feat. A bomb had not been detonated beneath the United States. A bomb had not been detonated above the United States. Bombs were elsewhere. Everything was still here, yet something irreplaceable and ineffable was gone. They had everything now, all the possessions and all the food and ideas and moral authority, but the country was a hollow shell. It was filled with air you feared to smell because in the olfactory sense was the deepest, the most detailed memory. It carried you into the past in a way your eyes could never hope to do. Smell did not stop time, but it had an uncanny deal with time, for it could exist in more than one time at once. Perhaps this was why it was the most maligned of the senses, dealing as it did with invisible things and being, as it was, largely unresponsive to the machinations of power.

When Erin—mad, young Erin in her early twenties—felt that she was just about to be killed in some historical event beyond her control, she smelled the air. She tried to focus on smell. Smell told her that things were inevitably far worse and far better and different: no one was coming to kill her, but that did not mean she was safe. She was a human being. She was mortal. She was a flick, a lint, a grain.

The train hammered to a stop at 86th. Erin believed for a moment that she could feel the driver's fatigue. It was getting to be late in the week, after all.

She stepped over legs and wound among bodies. She walked the platform, went up stairs and more stairs.

It was amazing to her that everyone knew just what to do. Everyone ran down the stairs, their jackets flying. Everyone hiked up the stairs. They grumbled at those who were slow. There were scenes of rage and contrition lasting no more than twenty seconds as everyone went wherever they understood themselves to be meant to go. They brushed against one another and, in their confusion at these interactions, grew angry. They did not know who one another were. They were under the earth near the Atlantic Ocean moving in haste in stone-lined tunnels. They judged one another's appearances. They assessed facial symmetry; they cared about one another's bodily mass, but mostly insofar as it was an image. They cared about volumes.

This was the obsession of their culture. They made photographic images discussing volume and shared these with one another instead of speaking, although they spoke to those they knew. They touched one another and were strange to one another below the earth in this city, as in many other cities. They wondered who would look good in an image.

Erin came up onto the street, passing on the final stair a swollen middle-aged man in socks, no shoes, with a cardboard sign that read *PLEASE I AM ALONE.* Erin walked by.

Something had happened to Erin. She was not exactly sure what this thing was, but she knew that she moved and lived under its influence. It was sluggish and thick, like the plot of a pre-millennium video game. It was vague, yet absolute. As far as this thing was concerned, it did not matter that Erin had perceptions and thoughts, that time continued to unfold and Erin was conscious in it. This thing was a net, a gate, a spell. It had always been with Erin, but the quality of its presence was changing. She had been afraid before. She was more afraid now. The thing tightened.

At the same time, Erin knew that the thing was promised to her. It would occur. This gave her a certain amount of comfort. Sometimes she felt that she was upside down in the ocean, attempting to swim up but hitting sandy bottom, pawing at an obstacle that was supposed to be pliant air. At least the obstacle was real—or, if not real, then, "there." It didn't make sense that it was there and yet it was. It was there for her, sedimentary and cruel. It belonged to her, in its way.

A month and change earlier, in September, Erin had learned that the person she had lived with and slept with for the past decade, to whom she was married, although that was hardly the most salient fact of their relationship, which had begun when they were both in their early twenties, was, as in the well-known American myth, "living a double life." She had picked up his phone. There it was. Simple as that.

There had been no delay. She had confronted him immediately. It was like diving and drowning. A force did this, a mass. A spirit lived. It was not "her."

Her husband's name was Ben and he had gone away. She was beginning to learn all that she had not permitted herself to see. This was psychedelic, this period. It was an inversion, vivid, full of spontaneous visions.

Erin learned that underneath what we name, in the sentences we live alongside and within, there is something else. We can feel it when we speak, when we attempt to describe what happens and the people we know, but we will not talk about it. What is underneath is another version of what happens and another version of the people. We know these events and these people, too, but they are not a part of what we believe or say. We don't believe it, and we don't believe we live it. We don't say it. All the same, we live it anyhow.

Erin had gone into the underneath. This was who she was now. It felt muddy in her lungs, weird air.

Ben had been living a second, possibly realer life with a woman he worked with. They had sex at work and in the woman's apartment. It had been almost a three-year affair.

As much as Erin was now basking in dreck, she tried to remain agnostic. She was in agony, but she attempted not to characterize these events, not to understand them in relation to herself.

Ben had left the apartment weeks ago, maybe it was a month now, and on the few occasions when they had talked on the phone he told her that she had driven him into this way of living, that it had not been within his power to choose, that the insufficient affection she gave him forced him to seek alternate comfort. She was a bad woman, but he loved her. It was difficult being married to and loving a bad woman (whom one loved so much!). Erin had no idea how awful it was. It was so awful.

Often, Ben was drunk and drinking during these conversations. This was not unusual for him, but with some distance between them, it did strike Erin that Ben was very, very drunk. He worked himself into a lather and cursed her.

Erin wept, hearing her husband's curses. She held herself apart from what he said, and thus what she wept at was her own mis-understanding. She had only believed that he was unhappy, not that he considered her the exclusive author of his misery. Now she knew what he believed. This was what it was like, underneath all the social reality Erin had ever known. You scratched the surface of literature, money, drugstore makeup, film and television, all of the popular music of the 1990s on compact disc, all of the ideas of all of the world's fashion designers, abstract expressionism, the beauty of domesticated felines, the array of gummy candies origi-nating in Western Europe, quantum computing, take your pick, and there it was. You had not seen it. Willfully, you had not seen what was right there.

Erin had been dreaming about Ben's death for years. She dreamed that he slipped into a swamp or fell off a cliff. In these dreams she was inconsolable. She did not want him to die. Sometimes she woke up with a scream. Always, when she woke, he was there, snoring beside her, usually sleeping something off.

Erin had watched television and read books. She had seen many movies. She had studied the films of John Cassavetes. She knew what an alcoholic was. She knew that an alcoholic is a person who drinks to excess. She understood that an alcoholic does not experi-ence drinking as a pleasant accompaniment to other modes of liv-ing. Alcohol, for the alcoholic, is like a shovel. The alcoholic does not muse, does not unwind with a cocktail. The alcoholic digs in the wet.

Ben had an easy job, as jobs went. He was a low-level adminis-trator. And Ben had a very difficult job. He averaged two six-packs a night. This was just when he was home, mind you, an increasingly, as the years had worn on, infrequent occurrence.

She could see that Ben was trying to live a good life. Perhaps this was why she had not thought of him as an alcoholic like the others. He drank too much, in a way that seemed to her magisterial, towering. He drank so much that he should be dead. But she would not have called him an alcoholic.

All he had was a little paunch from the beer and an occasional bruise to an arm or cheek from a bike accident. He was young, and he was always either hung over or drunk, hung over or drunk. It was a pendulum, a schedule. It seemed normal. Yet Erin assumed that someday this would change.

They were several years into the marriage when Erin decided she would go back to school for a PhD. There were no real jobs in publishing; she didn't imagine she would be missing much.

Ben seemed at first nonplussed as far as this plan was concerned, but upon learning that Erin would not have to pay for the degree and would receive a small living stipend, he agreed that this was "not bad." People he drank with informed him of the salaries of full professors and he even manifested himself slightly enthusiastic. "You'll take care of me," he told her. This was when they were in their late twenties. Already Ben comported himself as if he were middle aged. He was increasingly stern, manipulative, different.

They were both grateful for what they had found together, or so Erin had believed.

Yet, when she had departed a year ago for a two-week trip to Paris for an academic conference and to see a friend from college, Ben had told her, in the airport, that she was free to leave but should "consider" how her actions made him feel. Then he had excused himself to go into the men's restroom and Erin had had to run to make her flight.

It was the sort of thing she might have thought about, but instead of thinking about it, she had done the opposite. On the plane, she drank wine and slept. In Paris, the conference was stilted and her friend was largely unavailable. Through another friend who made a living writing cultural items for a neoliberal weekly, Erin was introduced to a tall midwesterner who had been residing in the city for almost a decade and whose greatest ambition was to be mistaken for a French person. He met her at a café, high up on a winding street in the 16th, and after this they climbed higher, to a small place he knew with about seven tables, where they were to dine. He was a financial reporter, grinding away at the *New York Times*'s regional bureau, an enterprise he claimed was slowly being brought to its knees by the death of print and aftershocks of the financial crisis. He needed to find new work, he said, his mouth full of kibbeh. He was writing a novel, he told her. It was not easy going, he said. He talked and talked in the light of a very small lamp. Erin had been informed that he was extremely handsome, but she was having difficulty understanding him as anything other than pretty unhinged. He was a big man in a blazer, his square jaw going. His French was bass and quivering with correctly deployed rhotics. He trembled with some frisson and involuntarily—or so it seemed—threw a water glass to the floor, where it shattered. The waiter was apologetic, likely intimidated, and the Midwesterner was unable to stop laughing, tittering, really. The Midwesterner accepted a new glass and new water. The Midwesterner was telling Erin the story of his life, how he had been adopted as a young boy, but not so young that he could not remember. The strictness of his adoptive father, to whom he referred by the father's first name; this relationship that seemed to be an ongoing trial, one that the Midwesterner encountered everywhere he went, veiled in spectral guises. He spoke of his own precocity, how he was accepted to a rarefied college in the wilderness that only educated men, their horseback rides into the void of the American West, how they spoke to one another, men or boys, the students of the college, of their clarity of purpose. The Midwesterner seemed to have been adopted a second time by a successful alumnus of the elite wilderness school. He took care to let Erin know that he, the Midwesterner, was a valued commodity. He pertained to a network that was not about to let him go, but, by the same token, he could not afford to let them down, this network—for in this case, the case of letting the network down, he would almost certainly be unfairly benefiting from privilege, should he continue to meet with professional success, which was already foreseen and guaranteed.

Erin did not pertain to a network. The friend (also male) who had introduced her to the Midwesterner and the Midwesterner himself were part of networks. Their networks were, even, slightly distinct. Erin understood, vaguely, that she was meant to attach herself to these networks, as well, but given the gender difference, it often seemed like, in so doing, she would have to contend with the bodies of men, which were, if not exactly obstacles, still in her way. It was not for nothing that she had gotten married in her early twenties, that she had a husband at home.

The Midwesterner was telling Erin that he had an amazing dictionary at his apartment. He said that it might really interest her. He seemed inordinately happy.

The Midwesterner's apartment was in the right direction. Erin would be passing by it on her way to transportation. She said something about how interesting, yes, etymologies. She was wearing her hair long in those days, what felt like years ago now, and had combed it out straight. Anyone might have pitied her innocence.

Erin followed the Midwesterner down the steep hill of the 16th to the building where he rented a single room in a literal turret overlooking the Seine. The Eiffel Tower was visible, glittering creamily in blackness.

The Midwesterner did not turn on a light.

Erin assumed that he wanted her to admire the structure. "Amazing," she said. Then, "Can we look at the dictionary?"

The Midwesterner chuckled, covering her with his body.

"Oh," said Erin.

"Mmm," said the Midwesterner, beginning to lick her and paw her hips.

Erin had the sense that this moment was a business opportunity of a kind. It seemed, also, fairly indecent of her to consider refusal. It was a lot she was being offered. The Midwesterner had told her the story of his life. Here he was, having narrated the tale of his intellectual formation, pressing his body against hers. She allowed him to shuffle her over to an unmade bed at the center of the room.

Erin was agnostic, if aroused. It had been years since she had kissed a man who was not Ben. She hovered above the scene, thinking, This is how it happens. This was how a person becomes other than the person she has meant to be. She was wearing a long skirt, a dowdy tweed garment that hit below the middle of her calves, and now the Midwesterner, grunting, hitched this up. His fingers went to her crotch. Erin had on tights, underwear.

Erin said, "I need to tell you something." In the midst of her sleepy conviction that she did not have a choice where the Midwesterner's desires were concerned, it had occurred to her that she was also party to a very public contract and mentioning this contract now would at the very least be relevant, if not useful.

"What's that?" The Midwesterner was chewing on her ear. He was an urbane man, surprisingly without muscle, in spite of his trimness and size.

"I'm married."

The Midwesterner stopped chewing. "So?"

"I'm not sure what we're doing." Erin put it like that. She had not said, "I'm not sure I like what we're doing." She was attempting to be polite.

She had been raped multiple times when she was in college, in what she now thought of as a bizarrely elaborate scenario. It had been more like a feeling of drowning than of being raped, which she associated with violence and struggle, as per media depictions. Thus she did not have a name for that week of disjointed life. She had been traveling alone in Australia and in Melbourne, at a youth hostel, had encountered a Dutch boy about her age. He was canny, in expensive glasses, his English very good. He was renting a private room at the top of the hostel. It had a pair of bunk beds but he occupied it alone. He had invited her upstairs and then, over the course of several days, repeatedly drugged her with what she later concluded was Rohypnol, administered via soda. She could not remember much of this, just his weight on top of her and strange things that he had said, how he wanted to take her home with him to the Netherlands and introduce her to his parents, that he believed they should get married. Erin was fairly sure he had used condoms. He was an advanced student of agriculture, with side interests in engineering of the biochemical kind. He seemed to know exactly how to incapacitate her in such a way that she was conscious but barely, pliable. She was unsure how this period of captivity had ended, but she recalled someone knocking on the door. For several days after she had wandered the city. The Dutchman had gone away somewhere. *Dutchboy*, she thought. She was twenty-one, then. It was the mild Australian winter. She had tried to visit a museum. She had tried to think in words.

Someone will want me someday, Erin had tried to convince herself. She told herself that these "adventures," as she styled them, were proofs of her allure, which was not the same as beauty but which had its own reality and force. She attempted to feel a sort of satisfaction.

Unable to focus or know where she was in her own mind, she could not begin in time, in those few Australian days. She went outside and lay down on a chilly lawn in a public garden, the sun a white lattice that felt full of the hideous depth of human lives. The sun is showing me something, Erin had thought. The sun knows how far away I am.

Erin had felt the hard, curved earth beneath her. She closed her eyes and gazed upon black and orange ribbons. She believed that she could feel the planet spinning, wobbling in space. She lay against an object. Here was a point in time, irreplaceable. She did not know what she was, but she knew time and the existence of the ground. She listened to the ground, which was at once hollow and not. She could hear voices. It was so difficult to stay awake.

She knew that she had slept for an hour or more in the grass, in the park, in Melbourne, that day. Sleep had seemed irresistible, and in that sleep she had seemed to feel the feeling of staring not into the sky but into the earth's atmosphere, beyond which lay endless space. She was facing out. She faced away from human life, the burning of carbon.

No one had disturbed her supine form, and when she awoke she was able to order coffee from a stall. She could feel something in her subjectivity solidifying once more. There was damage, but she would be able to speak, at least. She could begin, as in a series, with counting. She had not resolved to forget these events; that had merely happened. She had forgotten, except when she did not forget, and at these times, when she remembered, the events became a feature of the present.

She had never spoken to Ben about this. He was critical of her, after all, and would have wondered if she might not be imagining, thinking uncontrollably in a style of metaphor, which was how he often claimed she thought.

It was possible that these things of Melbourne, of Australia, a nation somewhat more open regarding its colonial history than the United States, came back to Erin, there in the Parisian turret of an anointed expatriate midwestern man, but it was such a small room, in spite of the view, and it was possible that there was not room enough for all the lives that seemed to pertain to Erin, hopelessly insignificant as each one was, the bouquet of them, when they were held together, jostling, full of sound and smell.

"You're not sure?" the Midwesterner repeated. There was a twinge of disbelief.

"I thought we were just going to look at the dictionary."

"The dictionary!" The Midwesterner began to seem ancient, eerie.

"Yes," Erin whispered.

"Did you *actually* think I had a dictionary? Who the hell thinks that?"

Erin wanted to say that if there was not in fact a real dictionary, then the dictionary of which the Midwesterner had spoken had sounded very interesting and he had a good sense of detail as well as those effects that lead a reader to a sense of reality, which could no doubt be exploited to remarkable ends in the novel he was writing.

"I," Erin paused, "thought that."

"I was just saying that so you'd come up to my room!" the Midwesterner exclaimed, as if this were not a full admission.

"OK," Erin told him. She did not want him to be upset. She did not want to ruin the business opportunity.

It was late and the transit system had shut down for the night. She stayed with him until dawn, at which time she had trudged down from the tower and boarded a train that carried her across the river and back to her host's lodging, where she saw that she had missed several messages from Ben, having for some reason left her phone by the sink in the bathroom.

But that was not the end of it. That was not the end of it because Erin was unable to permit this to be the end of it. Erin did not know why this was so. She felt nothing but contempt for the Parisian midwesterner, and yet she could not stop it. She felt she could not stop it.

Erin's husband, back in New York, sent her an email containing a photograph he had taken of himself using the camera built into his desktop computer. The photograph showed only Ben's crotch, in jeans, as well as his hands and wrists. In the image, he was standing and had removed his penis from his fly (he did not wear underwear, as a rule), and had wrapped it, flaccid, around his wrist, as if it were a watch. This was a visualization of a set phrase between them, a readymade or meme. It was called Dick Watch. It had originated in Ben's adolescence, a prank played on him by a friend or an older male relative, Erin could never entirely understand. (Perhaps it was a prank played on a friend by that friend's older male relative?) In the story Ben told, the scenario went as follows:

Knowing party:	Hey, guess what time it is?
Rube:	What time is it?
Knowing party:	[*holding hands in front of pelvis,*
	shaft of penis wrapped around wrist]
	It's dick o'clock!

This story and the meme, Dick Watch, pertained to a series of stories and memes explained to Erin by her husband, Ben. They came from his childhood. They were steeped in unknowable fears and lusts. There were others: Irregular Sit-Up and Evidence Room. In Irregular Sit-Up a naive individual was asked if he had ever done a sit-up with his eyes closed. The naive individual would, of course, confess that he had not. The naive individual would then be told that it's actually nearly impossible to do a sit-up with your eyes closed, because of certain peculiarities of the human body. The naive individual would be told that such a sit-up was called an Irregular Sit-Up. It was part of military training regimens. It required incredible core strength as well as preternatural spatial awareness. One did an Irregular Sit-Up lying on one's back, knees bent, hands crossed over one's chest, as if dead. Another person would sit on the sit-up doer's knees so that the sit-up doer could not cheat by using his legs. If you could demonstrate that you could do an Irregular Sit-Up, word was you could skip certain portions of US basic training. By now, the naive individual was very excited. He would almost certainly have the suspicion he would be able to execute an Irregular Sit-Up with greater skill than any person who had ever lived. He would gamely assume the position. "You have to really close your eyes," he would be told. "If you don't really close your eyes, you won't really be doing it, and we'll be able to tell." This was a world, of course, in which vision and blindness were two completely separate categories and never intermingled. The naive individual would assume the position. The naive individual would be forced to swear that his eyes were closed. Someone would lower his pants and undergarments and sit on the knees of the naive individual so that, when the naive individual triumphantly and forcefully executed the Irregular Sit-Up, his nose would enter the ass of his tormentor.

Evidence Room was more personal. This was a story from the history of Ben's family. In this story, Ben's older brother, Colin, was angry with their parents, probably because the parents had forbidden Colin to do something he wanted very much to do, such as go to a concert or stay out late. Colin's response was to take swift revenge by exhuming from the back of his parents' closet a pornographic VHS tape in which a female "police officer" assaulted herself with a side-handle baton on an evidence-room table. Colin fired up the media stack for a screening. He'd apparently left it playing, until the whole family had gathered, summoned by top-volume moans.

Ben talked about what Evidence Room had revealed less than he talked about the effects of Irregular Sit-Up. He'd told Erin that Irregular Sit-Up was how he had learned that men were violent and afraid of physical contact that was not either violent or sanctioned by sports. Of Evidence Room he said only that he had begun crying shortly after he had walked into the room where his mother and father and three siblings were all frozen in the brilliance of an auto-erotic primal scene.

"Were you afraid?" Erin asked.

"No," Ben said. "I was sad. I knew I would never be able to watch that tape again, and I wanted to be like, 'Colin, why did you *do* that to us?! We don't have Evidence Room anymore!'"

"Did you say that?"

"No! My dad was all, 'Look what you did to your brother!'"

"To Colin?"

"He was speaking to him, yeah. I was crying a lot."

"They were mad?"

"I mean, I think my dad wanted to kill him, nonmetaphorically. But what could they do? He was telling them they were hypocrites."

Erin was never sure exactly why Colin's actions had revealed

Ben's parents' hypocrisy. What the screening seemed to reveal, foremost, was that everyone in their house was masturbating to the same blue movie in which a woman used a historically charged anti-riot paraphernalium as a dildo. They were all coming, the girls and the boys and the adults alike, to the image of a woman coming, as she rubbed against a club. Was the hypocrisy that they kept this cherished tape hidden? Or was the hypocrisy that the parents had accepted the perversity of their own pleasure, while denying their children theirs? Had what Colin really been asking for been permission to go out and have sex—only, he had cloaked it in polite terms? Was he not, in some sense, imitating them? Had he not learned? And, when they refused him, did they not, in some sense, "out" him, showing him that they understood exactly why he wanted the permission he wanted? And did he not, in turn, out them, demonstrating that they, too, operated under the auspices of a contract that allowed much of what went on in their home to go unremarked and that there were consequences when such a contract was broken?

It was, as people say, a tight ship. No detail was unaccounted for, all tabs were kept, and yet the score remained eternally unsettled. Erin preferred to think of this domestic world as existing in an alternate dimension, much like the ThunderCats, Mr. Snuffleupagus, and Cobra Commander, to name but a few of the avatars of her youth. Ben's family didn't have to be very real, at least, not to her. At any rate, she hardly ever thought about children.

She must have replied to that email of Ben's in a sweet way, mechanically. Perhaps she had even been relieved to see it, good old familiar dependable Dick Watch!

The Midwesterner, meanwhile, sent her a message after the elapse of a sensible twenty-four hours, in which he recommended several bookstores. He noted that he believed these retailers carried dictionaries.

Because Erin seemed not to comprehend what anything was, was incapable of comprehending in these days and months and years, she had replied. She and the Midwesterner had made a date for lunch at a remote café in the 13th. She sat with him and observed as he ordered himself blood sausage: a petite purple tusk. She drank tea.

He was telling her how hard it was to find *boudin noir*, which he pronounced in a luxuriantly pretentious way, particularly around the vowels. One did not see it on menus. Such regulation! Such risk! It's rawness and thickness! It was also an ancestral delight of certain Wisconsin communities. He said nothing to her of her refusal of food.

It had occurred to them both, Erin thought now, at this moment, during that lunch, that they were both gifted and high-functioning and probably insane. They were both bent under the weight of pasts they could not remember, knots they wished to untie but, as in a dream, their hands were numb.

They were saluting each other along the road. That was what this was.

The Midwesterner with his chiseled jaw, his improbably flattering turtleneck sweater, his medieval fare and frenzied laugh: even he was not immune. Even if he had been pulled from the flames more times than he could narrate, even if he had been saved and preserved and repeatedly groomed, still he was chattel, no one's child, a servant from birth, a bastard. An invisible, intangible, unspeakable hammer fell upon him.

He described his upper-class Parisian girlfriend and their impending breakup.

Later, after they had rolled around on a city bench, grunting, and then parted, and after Erin had packed and boarded a plane where she drank more wine, and increasingly more, as the flight hit turbulence ("This is going to be a bumpy ride, sit tight" was the ominous intercom advice), she only thought: So, I have felt this. She did not require herself to wonder what it meant.

She said nothing to Ben.

She felt relief as the distance between what she took to be the Midwesterner's madness and her own receptivity to it increased.

Life in New York went on. But, of course, it was already over.

Even if she had wanted nothing from the Midwesterner. It was a sign, if not a symptom, glaring. Ben cheated. He must have viewed it as leisure.

Ben had been cheating for a very long time.

Tonight Erin, here in the present, was going to her parents' home.

Erin's mother knew about the Midwesterner.

Erin had told her mother about the incident a few weeks after she had come home.

"So?" her mother had said.

Erin had of course not explained the feeling of coercion, the feeling of being dragged into the sway of something that had already taken place, long ago, and that was, nevertheless, dumbly demanding her participation. She might not, at the time, have been able to name the feeling, its insistence notwithstanding.

Erin had asked, by way of answer, and a lovely set of verbal tennis it was, too, "Should I tell Ben?" She was clarifying, for her mother's benefit, the reason for the conversation.

"'Should you tell Ben?'?" Her mother snorted. "Not if you want your marriage to continue!"

Although this turn in the conversation had been eminently foreseeable, Erin was still surprised. She would not have been able to say this to her mother in the moment, but another version of Erin, participating in a dialogue that occurred only in Erin's imagination, wanted to say that it did seem like marriage should be a relationship of deep and abiding trust. For this reason, it might be sensible to loop Ben in.

And, of course, Erin had never said anything to her mother about what had happened in Australia.

What Erin understood now was that the relationship with Ben had been a relationship in which trust had been an entirely one-sided affair. Or, rather, that Ben trusted, and trusted strongly, that Erin had no idea what sorts of things he got up to outside the house. He trusted that even if she intuited, all but unconsciously, that he was unfaithful to her, she was too frightened of the vagaries of single life, combined with society's rampant misogyny, to ever, ever leave him. Erin, meanwhile, trusted that Ben had her best interests at heart. But this, Erin now saw, was a relationship to a concept. It was not trust and never had been.

In this sense, Erin's mother had been entirely correct. If Erin had told Ben what had happened in Paris, he would have called her all sorts of names. He would have told her that she was a faithless woman. He would have said that he could no longer trust her. He would have forbidden solo travel, probably forced her to drop out of school. All the while, he would have continued his own activities, attempting to establish the reality of some liaison or other, such that he could, in a final burst of rage and glory, leave Erin, heaping the blame for the devolution of their love on her head. She could then walk on through life with that mark.

Now let *him* wear the mark, Erin thought.

Erin's mother, whom Erin also loved, was a covetous person, treacherous and clever. She liked to read expensive gardening catalogues and kill houseplants. Her home, which she shared with Erin's father, contained a quantity of sofas.

Erin's mother did not exactly have Erin's best interests "at heart," either, but as she was of the opinion that Erin was an animal who belonged to her, there were limits to her violence. Erin's mother needed Erin alive.

So Erin hadn't. She had lived on with Ben and attempted to love and honor her mother and tried to tell herself that many things were unreal or, failing this, only slightly real.

Erin walked up a hill toward the building where her parents lived.

She made plans with herself about what she would and would not say. She told herself not to drink too much, to eat as little as possible, not to become enthusiastic or disordered, not to be beguiled into arguments, not to become uncontrollably enraged, not to shout or stammer or say things that made no sense. Her heart beat and she compulsively checked her email, along with Facebook ("Cold-ridden and in-transit in NY, but really looking forward to 'Sublimities' at CU later this week. In the way of shameless acts of self-promotion, I'm speaking on this panel:"), several times before going indoors.

Erin's mother was a stockbroker and believed in bourgeois systems. She did not give a shit about Freud or Marx or Nietzsche or anyone else who had attempted to dismantle this way of life during or after the nineteenth century; she had not read them and never would. Erin's mother did not as a rule read much, although Erin could remember a period of years when Erin was in high school during which her mother had labored over *Anna Karenina.* Erin's mother liked to display the book at beaches and on terraced evenings, when she moved *en famille* among various other families whose acquaintance Erin's mother dryly tolerated in acquiescence to social norms. Although Erin's mother had no friends, she was unconfused enough to see that people who had no friends were generally looked down upon. Erin's mother therefore maintained carefully manicured proximities that no one, even the most discerning sociologist, Erin's mother felt, would be able to distinguish from genuine affiliation and affection.

The building where Erin's parents lived had doormen. It had been erected in 1921, the same year in which, coincidentally perhaps, Erin's paternal grandfather had arrived, in April, in the United States by boat. The building was thick, brick and granite, with an echoing lobby full of blackish-yellow light. Erin entered alone, as she usually did these days, and experienced the sensation she always felt upon such entrances, as of feeding a coin into the earth, a toll she was helpless not to accord to certain powers that she did not understand but that seemed to live beneath the building's threshold, sealed in in the course of construction.

The man on duty nodded. He had fled "political revisions" undertaken by Albania's Communist regime in 1991, when he was in his midtwenties, if Erin was guessing correctly. He was tall and handsome in a conventional way: long eyebrows, straight nose. His name was Armend. Erin had known him for more than half her life.

"Hello, Erin," Armend said.

"Hi," said Erin. "How are you?"

"Very well," Armend said. "Good," he reiterated, looking down at his podium and seeking out the correct switch to permit Erin access to the floor on which her parents' apartment was located. He indicated a preference not to expand the conversation.

Erin speed-walked to the elevator, mashed the plastic call button.

There was a whir of cables and a woman with violet lips emerged with a small brown dog. "Here we are," the woman breathlessly informed the animal, averting her eyes.

"Hello," Erin said pointlessly.

She let the duo pass. The elevator smelled of synthetic pine and various canine emanations. The mirror in it was bad, and Erin knew not to seek confirmation of her humanity in it as the box gingerly elevated itself.

There were three apartments on the floor where her parents lived: a very big one and then two others, which had been created through the division of a formerly very big apartment. Erin's parents lived in one half of the reapportioned former palace. Erin's mother had mysteriously assumed responsibility for decoration of the hallway that gave onto the three front doors, perhaps during the time when the very big apartment and one of the divided apartments (the smaller of the two, not the one belonging to Erin's parents) were in between owners and she had been able to convince the building's board that she was in possession of an all-important aesthetic authority. The walls were now papered in the classic colonial banana leaf (as seen in the world-famous Beverly Hills Hotel, *Golden Girls* TV Show, *Niki Hilton's Pad*, *Friends* TV Show, and many celebrities' and dignitaries' homes. Designed by Don Loper, 1906–1972; clients included Lucille Ball and Ella Fitzgerald . . .), and a slender black table supported a glass jug of artificial eucalyptus.

Erin knocked on her parents' front door. She wasn't sure what she could possibly be interrupting, but she always knocked before opening this door, which was (also always) left unlocked. Erin did not ring the bell. She had never done this. She eased the door open, saying, "Hello?"

"Hello?" came a reply from another room.

A small tortoiseshell cat with a two-tone face and bulging, unblinking eyes arrived to stare at Erin before it retreated behind the feet of a decorative wood and brass elephant.

"Is Ben there?" the same voice called.

Erin looked down at the cat. "Pss pss pss," she told it.

"Meroawr," remarked the cat, departing for alternate zones.

"Hello?" went the voice.

"Hi!" Erin shouted. She pivoted to the kitchen.

"Where's Ben?" Erin's mother wore the jacketless remains of her day's pantsuit and a lime-green apron embroidered with blue salamanders. She was in the process of inserting a large piece of fish into the black jaw of the oven, where it was first to be warmed and then, as per Erin's mother's personal specialty, aggressively desiccated.

"Hi," Erin repeated.

"Hi yourself. Where's your husband?"

The oven door groaned.

"He can't make it. He's really sorry. There was a work thing. They're raising money for that," Erin rummaged, *"digitization project."*

"Hmm," remarked Erin's mother. She was conveying a bowl of broccoli into the microwave.

"I thought I told you," Erin lied.

"'I thought I told you,'" Erin's mother trilled. "'He can't make it,'" she muttered.

Erin was looking around for something to eat. She saw a peeled clove of garlic sitting on the counter and put it in her mouth.

"What's a digitization thing?" This was Erin's father. He had crept up behind Erin.

"Oh hi, Dad," said Erin's mother.

"Where's Ben?" asked Erin's father. He was wearing a flannel shirt tucked into matching flannel pants and was freshly showered, powdered, gleaming.

"Ben's not here, Dad," said Erin's mother. "Can I get you a glass of wine?"

"I don't know, can you?"

"White?"

"Is that what's open?"

"It is what I have."

"OK, then." Erin's father received his glass of wine. "Where's Ben?"

"He's working," Erin's mother whispered.

"Why's he working?" Erin's father persisted, languidly consuming wine.

"He's working on a thing that involves money!" Erin's mother seemed at once enraged and pleased.

"Oh really?" Erin's father observed. He was about to withdraw into the living room, Erin could tell. Now Erin's father withdrew. "'He's working on a thing that involves money,'" Erin's father repeated as he went, limping slightly.

"Mom, may I have some wine?" Erin asked, spitting the garlic clove quietly into her hand and setting it back on the counter where she had found it.

"We're drinking now?"

"Since when have I not drunk?"

"Suit yourself," said Erin's mother. She turned back to her mixing bowl.

Erin dumped what remained of the white wine into a juice glass so as not to have to get any closer to her mother by interacting with the cabinet in which her parents' wine glasses were stowed. She went into the living room and sat on a couch.

Erin's father was in his chair. The particolored cat was crouched under the coffee table, its eyes closed. It looked like its bones were bothering it.

"So," said Erin's father, "no Ben tonight."

"No," said Erin, "no Ben." She began to drink her wine. It tasted floral—curly and wispy and paisley. There was a hint of garlic on her tongue and hanging from the insides of her cheeks, and the wine slid over this taste, turning peculiar and vile. Erin put the wine down.

"Well," said Erin's father, "I guess we will have to make do."

Erin nodded. She touched the surface of the couch. It was upholstered in an apparently hard-wearing patrician fabric that nominally resembled velvet but possessed no luster or give. Erin brushed the couch, feeling its prickle.

"Testing out the furniture?" Erin's father asked.

Erin's mother appeared. "Let's start with salad," she announced, "since Ben is not here."

They went to the table.

Erin understood that the original layout, when this apartment was new and whole and palatial in the mid-1920s, had been different. It had been new in January of 1921 and still new five months later when the United States closed its borders in accordance with the May 19, 1921, Emergency Quota Act. This legislation would be surpassed, in its nativism, by the May 26, 1924, Immigration Act signed into law by Calvin Coolidge in order to "limit the immigration of aliens into the United States" by means of annual quotas of "two per centum of the number of foreign-born individuals of such nationality resident in continental United States as determined by the United States Census of 1890." These restrictions were intended to return the nation to a bygone time of supposed ethnic and racial homogeneity. The 1890 census gave license to dramatic restrictions. For example, a colonial construct called "South West Africa (proposed mandate of Union of South Africa)" was allotted the minimum quota of one hundred persons, for descendants of enslaved Africans living in the United States were not counted. Other large nations receiving this minimum designation included India, China, and Persia. Erin had researched these matters only this morning.

Her paternal grandfather had arrived in New York on April 30, 1921, from "Urmiath, Persia," by way of Southampton, England. He was, from what Erin understood, then nine years old.

In the original layout of the apartment, the room in which Erin now sat with her parents had been classified as a "den." In the reconfiguration, part of this "den" was taken up by the kitchen, and the rest became a dining room. Beyond the back wall of what was now Erin's parents' kitchen were three other rooms, composing the third apartment on the floor. These rooms had originally been intended for occupancy by servants. Currently, they housed a twenty-five-year-old with a trust fund and a fiancé. ("She will move out as soon as she is married," Erin's mother said.)

Erin sometimes tried to imagine the first owner of the apartment. In Erin's mind, this was a blond woman in early middle age, a divorced woman benefiting from the relative liberalization of society as well as family money. She wore a long dress and stood at a window. She smoked and drank, moving through her large home followed by a pale gray whippet. There might also be a man or a woman whom she employed as a companion. Erin attempted to imagine such a life.

On the one hand, Erin thought that this was possibly a very good life. On the other, Erin felt that the imaginary woman was probably incapable of considering her own life good. She was probably sad and frequently drunk. The woman was "tight." She got tight. She pickled her gums with cigarettes. She went to the movies in a fur coat, not bothering with a girdle. She carried a slender metal flask and possibly a small revolver. She was paranoid, but (and, again, possibly) not without reason. She was one of the ones who were being made an example of. She was a "New Woman," but not precisely by choice. She was enthralled to a series of images. It was easier that she be maintained in this state than remarried. She kept herself in

a condition of extreme thinness, and, in exchange for this labor—
along with the modicum of work necessary to the maintenance of
her dwelling, which mostly required dusting, while the laundering
and occasional scrubbing of it could be bought for nothing, and the
companion dusted and opened doors and occasionally transported a
tray, according to Madame's sparse instructions—the woman was
permitted to live. She lived too far uptown for real fashion. She was
an aunt of some sort at family gatherings.

Of course, the woman would need to turn to some good work
and pursue it with single-minded mania, but indeed Erin felt that
the woman had the opportunity to become a great poet, philosopher,
painter, theologian, or social worker. Although the woman, the tight
and thin white-blond woman, was entirely imaginary, Erin sometimes
criticized her for her lack of fame. The woman had not employed
her separate and nominally liberated life to accomplish anything of
worth. Beset by insecurities and the frailty of addiction, the imaginary woman had wasted away, dying in her early fifties, her funeral
attended by ten people.

When Erin was a child, she had known some of the initial, if not
original, occupants of the building. They had moved in in the early
1940s. They were called Garari, a distinguished Jewish surname of
eastern Latvia. Erin never knew their first names; they were simply
"Mr. and Mrs. Garari," and she could recall elaborate herbaceous
prints, maybe a Persian cat. Mrs. Garari had a high voice, strongly
accented. Before she and her husband became infirm and passed
away, she seemed to have taken quite a liking to Erin. They were
each, from what Erin understood, only a decade or two shy of being
a hundred years old, or perhaps less, certainly increasingly less.

They were from Dvinsk, or modern-day Daugavpils, also the
birthplace of the abstract expressionist painter Mark Rothko. In fact,
they were likely around the same age, born at nearly the same time
as this painter, the turning of the nineteenth century. Their families
were in manufacturing, owning several factories between them. The

match had been a natural one and also apparently happy, although they seemed to have had no children.

Presciently, fatedly, who understands why, Mr. Garari had begun traveling to New York in the late 1930s to explore the textile and garment industries in the city. In summer of 1941, in late June, when the Nazis invaded Daugavpils, he and his wife were, apparently by chance, staying with business associates on a small farm on Long Island, a seasonal home. For the rest of their lives, the Gararis did not return to their birthplace, which from 1941 to 1944 pertained to the Reichskommissariat Ostland, being briefly renamed by the Nazis Dünaburg. Just under .2 percent of Daugavpils's Jewish population survived this period.

The Gararis said nothing about this. There was of course no reason they would have shared their story with a four-year-old girl. Erin visited them once a week and then no longer visited them. Her memories of Mrs. Garari are, however, quite strong. It was not just the interior of the apartment, with its browns and whites and greens and pinks, the edges of gilt on certain objects and geraniums everywhere. It was the physical presence of Mrs. Garari, her thick scent of jasmine and the great bosom retained within blouses and cashmere, against which Erin was lovingly held. "There she is!" cried Mrs. Garari, with her irreplaceably accented American English. A clock made shuffling noises. Mrs. Garari played the piano. Erin ate a cookie topped with almond slivers.

In her ignorance, Erin had thought that the Gararis came from Italy. They had both died by the time Erin, age eleven and in the fifth grade, learned of the Holocaust. She and her classmates, many of whom were far better informed than Erin, wept. They were given texts written by actual children who had suffered and died during the 1940s at the hands of Nazis. They read these texts in class and at home. Erin could remember that one of her classmates, Jenny Marks, had become inconsolable one day. She remembered Jenny beginning to scream during a class, screaming about how she did not understand it, how you could have to die without having lived and there could be nothing you could do about it; you could die without understanding what was happening to you.

Erin had looked at the surface of her desk. Months earlier, at the beginning of the school year, she had been assigned this desk by a teacher, and a sticker with Erin's last and first names written in turquoise marker had been affixed to the upper right corner. Now, as Jenny cried inconsolably, and as the class descended into a stiff silence that made Jenny's cries all the louder and more urgent, Erin began to worry the sticker. She scraped at its edges with the metal top of a pencil whose eraser had been rubbed away.

Later that same day, Erin would be disciplined for defacing her desk, but before this happened, Jenny was taken away. Jenny was sent home. She needed to rest. There had been some upheaval in her family.

Erin could not recall so precisely when she and her classmates learned of the enslavement of Africans by Europeans, or of the genocide of Indigenous people throughout North, Central, and South America by Europeans. She thought that this might have been covered earlier in her education, at which time her teachers, subscribing to a theory of their pupils' immaturity and pursuant lack of imaginative or emotional control, had leaned heavily on narratives of abolition and survival.

We are not bad people, the teachers had said. We are appreciators. We exist beyond history. We look down on it from our seats in the balcony.

Erin had not lasted long in that school.

This morning Erin had tried again. She sat at her computer and pushed against a mental presence, a bad content. It was sludge: wet ash, inky cream of uneven consistency. Or, perhaps the substance looked white. It was deep, viewless white. The repulsive, fascinating substance was extremely dark and very pale.

She used YouTube this time. She forced herself not to forget to enter the simple terms, to scrub the substance off these little gestures. Actually type the words now, Erin. Her search turned up a documentary (3.8K views) detailing the extermination of Assyrian Christians during the first years of World War I in Turkey and later Iran, by the Turkish state. The Iranian Assyrian population—who lived in a region called Urmia, with a famous saltwater lake so large it is visible from space and, in present day, a site of ecological collapse—attempted to survive by means of an alliance with the Russians, enemies of the Ottomans. The association furnished these Assyrians with arms, but in early summer of 1915 the Russians fled north rather than face the advancing Turks. Although it seemed the Iranian Assyrians fared somewhat better than those in modern Turkey, still they were raped and slaughtered, skinned and burned alive, cornered in European missions and fed bread with metal shavings baked in such that they (who, in the case they were sheltering in these missions, were mostly children) died unimaginable slow deaths.

There was aerial footage of a trek into Russia later that year, during which tens of thousands perished crossing snowy mountains, on foot without food or water. A poetic voice-over: "There was no water, only snow." This moment faded into a montage of photographs describing Urmia's volunteer militia, villagers in felt hats. Then another litany of different kinds of rapes, of different kinds of stabbings; who was made to die how, who refused to die in one way and therefore died in another.

But now Erin's mother was speaking in Erin's general direction. Erin could not determine if these words were addressed to her, but nevertheless she permitted them to come into focus, to grow edges and take on distinct form.

Erin pressed the points of her fork into the spine of a lettuce frond.

Erin understood that her mother was debating playfully with her father about whether they should tell Erin something.

"Does it even matter?" Erin's mother wanted to know.

"Does what matter?" Erin's father said.

"I thought it was such an incredible move."

"What was an incredible move?"

"The letter!"

"Which letter?"

"The one in the elevator. That had to be the icing on the cake."

"Which cake?"

"In the expression!"

"You mean, Memorial Day?"

"What else am I referring to?"

"I have no idea!"

"She probably has no idea who they are. She doesn't remember them."

"But I'm telling you, I think I saw one—had to be the brother. He came into the building. I thought it was him. It had to be the brother."

"They look so alike. Like twins."

"I was never able to tell them apart. When I was on the board I figured it out, that there were two of them, and the mother, she was hardly leaving the house, and there were some issues with how she was getting help, but she had the second husband."

"He was a miserable person," Erin's mother said.

"He couldn't stop touching her money," said Erin's father. "I guess in some way he was there for those boys."

"She was on drugs," Erin's mother said.

"That's what she did," said Erin's father. "She got here around the same time as us, during the first marriage."

"I remember him. He was cold."

"He was fine."

"Of course he seemed fine to you."

"But then she made a bad choice. It's not everyone's husband who's writing a notice about I'm sorry if your Memorial Day weekend was interrupted by these events. I'm extremely sorry for the disruption. It must have been such a strain for your family."

"I thought someone should have taken that sign down."

"I think Lekë did."

"Someone must have asked him to. They should have given that sign to the police. I'm surprised there was no detective!"

"What do you know about a detective?"

"I know that nobody asked us any questions," said Erin's mother.

"Why would anyone ask you?"

"I live here!" Erin's mother exclaimed. "Maybe I heard something!"

"I'm extremely sorry if your Memorial Day weekend was interrupted!"

"We weren't even here!"

"They said he couldn't kill her. They said that was what the 911 call was about, that he stabbed his own mother but she isn't dead."

"Did they make Armend go up to check, is that true?"

"No, that didn't happen."

"That's a relief."

"Not for her!"

"At least he called 911."

"No," yelled Erin's father. "He did not call 911! It was the husband. He's locked in his study. *He* called 911 and said my stepson is killing his mother but she's not dead yet. I'm afraid, he said. She's lying in the kitchen, bleeding out, I can't stop it. He said I locked myself in a room. He was apparently going on and on about 'He has a knife.'"

"How do you know this?"

"I read it in the *Times*," Erin's father said.

"And what happened?"

"She was dead. He killed her."

"But the husband, he didn't do anything? What is his name?"

"He made the call," said Erin's father. "John."

"Horrible," said Erin's mother.

"I heard," said Erin's father, "that you could hear it. There are people in the building who did hear it, her final screams."

"But how is the other one here?"

"Who?"

"The stepbrother."

"No, it's just the brother."

"I haven't seen the husband again," Erin's mother said.

Erin was attempting to recall a configuration of faces corresponding to this tale. She remembered, briefly, the recent news story of the psychologist whose life had been ended by a patient wielding a hacksaw; how the psychologist had reached out to colleagues beforehand, talking about warning signs and fear. This psychologist's office was only a few blocks from her parents' building.

"What do they look like?" Erin asked.

"Who?" asked Erin's mother.

"They're not twins?"

"No," said Erin's father. "They're not twins. They look like normal people. They don't talk but they look normal. They look exactly the same."

"So," said Erin's mother, "enough about this. What's Ben up to these days?"

Erin recalled one of Ben's numerous lines of observation concerning Erin's parents. The particular line that Erin was recalling concerned Erin's gender, which Ben said had come as a surprise to her parents. He had told her that Erin had obviously been supposed to be a boy. He said that he could imagine it was very difficult to figure out what to do when you had a girl but you wanted a boy, and he could see that it had not been easy for Erin's parents.

"They didn't know what to do with you," Ben said.

Erin wondered, briefly, if her parents were concerned that she might one day stab them. Certainly, she would need to bide her time. They were currently far from infirm.

Erin regretted that there were two of her parents and only one of her, as far as such a crime was concerned, since she would almost certainly fail.

In the story of the woman who had died horribly in Erin's parents' building on Memorial Day weekend, there were at least three people in the family in question who were not being murdered. The odds were on the side of the majority, as the killing proved.

Erin considered the fact that at this moment, as she sat at this table and as a fish hardened in extreme heat in the next room, Ben was possibly at the apartment that she and he had shared, if he had seen her message. There was a sense in which her email was a way of lashing out, and lashing out was something that Erin did not believe in, because she felt that he who strikes the first blow is usually at a moral disadvantage. Still, Erin had composed and sent it, this message, because she needed something to happen; she needed for this thing, whatever kind of thing it was, to get started.

Four days ago she had written, "Attached are book photos. Send a list of what you want this week before 10 a.m. on Thursday and I will leave these for you that eve in the hall. Please in return bring me back Hilton Als's *White Girls* and my heart-shaped pie dish, as well as copies of all tax documents you have. Also, when you come, which you are welcome to do anytime between 11 a.m. and 8 p.m. on that day, please leave behind the key to the front door." The subject line was "Books." Ben had not replied.

What Erin had not written in this message was that before composing and sending it, she had gone down to the local avenue to the locksmith's, an establishment she had passed many times without entering. In the locksmith's, she had spoken to a man behind a counter emblazoned with a number of nationalist and sometimes racist stickers and slogans decrying terrorism and celebrating the United States' military, as well as the country's lenient gun laws. She had said to the man, "I need to change my locks." The man had explained to her how she could remove the top lock on the door herself, using a screwdriver, and replace it with a new bolt he was happy to sell her. Erin had accepted this proposition and purchased the mechanism. She had gone home and installed it that afternoon. She was claiming the place.

The apartment was large and cheap, but moreover Erin had been living in it for some time, and as she understood that she had only just begun to suffer, as far as Ben was concerned, she planned to keep it, in order that she might have a place to exist once the suffering met her full force. She could feel its momentum building. The suffering wanted her.

And so what Erin had meant, in sending this email, was that Ben was advised that he no longer lived in the apartment that she and he had shared. Although he had been the first to leave, she was the one who would be so magnanimous as to accord his action a name. This was why she mentioned tax documents. She imagined it would flummox him. He seemed to have left with an odd assortment of objects in a large overnight bag, and she was still in the process of ascertaining what exactly it was that she did and did not have.

She had no idea what she needed. Maybe, she thought, she needed to sleep. Almost certainly she needed to become successful. She needed to sleep and to work and not to become distracted. She was going to have to live, and she had to prepare for that, because triumph required that one go on living.

Erin said to her parents, "Nothing much." She had promised herself that tonight she would not drink to excess, but at this moment she drank from her glass of wine.

Erin's mother, who must have decided that she wanted something from Erin, refilled Erin's glass. Erin's mother said, "But I bet he's doing a lot!"

Erin nodded.

Erin's mother said, "How are his parents?"

Erin's parents did not communicate directly with Ben's parents, but Erin's mother liked to cultivate an air of engagement.

"They are good," said Erin. She was unsure what it was that Ben's parents knew. Perhaps they knew everything.

Erin's mother asked, "I guess they're enjoying their house?"

"Yes," Erin said. "They like it." Erin held herself in place. She would not tip and she would not splinter. The room in which she sat with her parents was bright and flat. She wanted to remain inside it, not because she wanted to be here, but because she needed to prove a point. She needed to prove that she was capable of simple, wholesome existence. This was still a unified, normal life conducted by Erin, and she was not about to be dislodged. She was not going to crumble in madness. Erin could judge what was real and what was not.

"Are they coming down to the city soon?"

Erin felt a tremor in her mouth.

Erin recalled a certain scene from a film that had frightened her as a child, *Return to Oz*, in which Dorothy (actor Fairuza Balk) briefly becomes a mental patient before being transported to an Oz in which a magical, shape-shifting despot named the Nome King tyrannizes the populace. Although the Nome King is eventually defeated through his accidental consumption of a chicken egg (poisonous to nomes, apparently), while he is still viable, he proposes a test: He has the power to transform living beings into objects and he has transformed at least one of her friends. If she can guess which of the objects within his lair is in fact her transmogrified companion, he will release her. If not, he will transform her, too.

Erin remembered the movie as unbearable. It played cannily upon the natural fears of children (becoming lost, being disbelieved, not understanding a given symbolic system) and, since set in a post-apocalyptic magical kingdom, partook of a baroque relationship to real estate and ruins: evil entities were encased in elaborate hybrid castles; meanwhile, everyone else was imprisoned, homeless, or dead.

Still, Erin had been fascinated by Dorothy Gale's successful guess. She had watched as the soft, small guesser developed a series of first principles, by means of which she could distinguish among the many tchotchkes assembled in the Nome King's den. Whatever else the movie depicted, including, perhaps, an allegory for the advent of an insane president, it was also about disinformation and excess, how one should behave if one finds oneself in an alternate world in which there exists a single, unpersuadable source of power and, therefore, events.

And Erin answered her mother, "I do not know."

And Erin's mother said, "Well, that's good." She said, "They haven't rented another van?"

This was a cue. It meant, Now we shall discuss the ways in which Ben's family are beneath us.

Erin's father, as a rule, did not participate in this discussion. The reason Erin's father did not participate in this discussion was that he had grown up in a working-class home in which languages other than English were spoken, having been born in the Bronx to a Polish American mother and an Iranian father pertaining to a stateless people of the Middle East. For this reason, Erin's father was not considered fully qualified to unpack the failings of persons of Western European stock who lived, if in comfort, in a backward northern suburb. According to Erin's mother, Erin's father might not fully comprehend what was wrong with them. Erin's father might, given their long pertinence to the nation, even be intimidated by this tribe, aka, Ben's parents and siblings.

Erin's father was often out of control and was, in actuality, intimidated by Erin's mother. Therefore, Erin's mother's speculation, through the power of transitivity, became true.

Erin, granted the power of speech, spoke. She said, "I don't think so."

"I love," said Erin's mother, "how they all travel together. I love how they can't go anywhere alone."

"Yes," said Erin, who did not like Ben's family, anyway.

Erin's mother was turning now to the dietary preferences of Ben's family. She wanted to articulate just what it was they didn't eat. She wanted to be exact, sociological.

Erin's father did not like this. It was not just that he abhorred lists, parataxis, any scenario in which items gathered, free from hierarchy; he was not invited to this topic and therefore he did not matter.

Now Erin's father said, "Erin doesn't know anything about what they eat."

"Yes, she does," said Erin's mother.

Below the table, the tortoiseshell cat wound itself around legs and feet. Erin thought, the mouth of a cat is used for cleaning, eating, breathing, yawning, self-defense, abstract vocalizations. Erin thought, the mouth of a human is used for eating, breathing, yawning, speech, along with other emanations, and sex. Cats carry their young in their mouths, thought Erin.

"No, she doesn't. She's making that up."

"Why would she make that up?"

"I don't know," said Erin's father, shrugging. "Why does anybody make anything up? People lie."

"Do you think Erin's lying?"

"I don't think Erin knows anything about those people. Why should she?"

The cat made a honking noise and sprinted abruptly out of the room, its claws clattering against hardwood.

"Because they are *unusual* to her."

"They don't seem unusual to me."

"Well, to her, *darling*," said Erin's mother, performing a tonal curtsey.

Erin's father blinked. A limit within his internal cosmos had apparently been surpassed. "Why," he paused and then bellowed, "*should they be unusual?*"

Erin had known this moment would come. She had been preparing for it for the past twelve hours. She felt a chill across her shoulders and the front of her body vibrated slightly.

She recalled that she had promised herself that she would remain calm. She recalled other versions of this scene, neatly labeled and stacked in her mental representation of the past. In the past, perhaps Ben would have been present. Ben would have gathered these events in like a deck of cards, redealt them. He would have told Erin that she was wrong. He would have attended to matters.

Because of her promise to herself, sworn with great solemnity only this morning as Erin rode an elevated subway, clacking and swaying, and then again only this evening, Erin did not protest. Instead, she said, "Dad, you are shouting."

"What?" said her father.

"You are shouting. You're raising your voice."

"I am not raising my voice!"

"Yes, you are."

"You have no idea what I am doing!"

Erin saw that she was too late. In spite of her promise, she had already failed to deviate from her established role.

"You're shouting," Erin repeated, helplessly. Something disintegrated. Erin heard the *glug glug* of blood, going somewhere. She wished to be able to turn to her left or her right to discover a friend. She very nearly shook her head from side to side, but she was not yet so confused that she had begun to see things in the air, even if this was, historically speaking, not out of the question.

In a sense, everything was already over, but Erin's father was still screaming. He was screaming about how he would now do what he wanted. He hit the table, screaming about how murder happens all the time. Erin's mother smiled. She was removing her napkin from her lap and appeared to be preparing to clear this course's plates.

Erin observed as her own body stood. Erin's mother stood, too.

"I'm leaving," said the front of Erin's head.

"I'm sorry?" said her mother.

"Get out!" Erin's father bellowed. "Where is your husband?"

These are the events, to the extent that any human events are knowable, that led Erin Adamo to stand alone on the street in upper

Manhattan at approximately eight p.m. on a Thursday evening during the second decade of the twenty-first century in the midst of an unseasonably warm autumn.

It was important that Erin had landed here, but it was hardly apparent to Erin that this was important. Instead, as we may well imagine, Erin was disoriented, distressed. She felt folded and jostled, but also numb. In her haste to exit her parents' dwelling, she had taken her bag and her phone, but she had left behind her coat, which was home to her all-important house keys.

It wasn't really so cold that Erin was cold, but all the same, Erin shivered. One option was to use the phone to call her landlord at home. Her landlord lived with his wife and small child in an apartment underneath the apartment Erin had shared with Ben. Erin contemplated their probable conversation.

She imagined greeting her landlord, whose name was Gerry, short for Gerald, and explaining the situation. She knew that, in making this phone call, it was possible that she would wake not only Gerry, who worked long hours as a contractor and tended to die and be reborn over the weekend, but also Gerry's son, who was frequently beyond consolation and about whom Gerry was extremely sensitive, particularly now, as the child had recently been diagnosed with autism.

"Gerry," she said in her mind, "I've forgotten my keys."

She abruptly revised "forgotten" to "lost." She considered claiming to have been robbed.

Erin paused this scene. She recalled that a year earlier, when Ben had for some reason dropped her key ring down a sidewalk grate and disappeared for thirty-six hours, she had gone home in the middle of one particularly morose Sunday to beg for Gerry's assistance. Gerry was friendly, especially so given it was before five p.m., but said that he didn't have a spare set. He said he'd given them both his sets and why hadn't they made a spare? Also, he wanted to know, where was Ben?

Erin had had no answers. All she could think was that Gerry was an eminently reasonable man. Indeed, having posed this question once before, now he would be well within his rights to ask . . .

Here Erin remembered that she *had changed the locks*. Or, rather, the top bolt. And had made no duplicate key.

She would need to call a locksmith.

She would also want to undertake this project when no one else was home, which could mean first thing on Friday morning, but definitely did not mean tonight, as nocturnal discussions in the hallway often led to Gerry's annoyed appearance.

Above all, she did not want Gerry to know. She did not want to have to explain why Ben could not just let her in, why he had no keys to the upstairs door, why the current lease was probably no longer valid.

Of course, it was also the case that Ben might have already shown up loudly for the project of the claiming of his books, but in this moment Erin saw, too, how much she doubted this. Ben wasn't coming for anything, because at the moment Ben did not care. Ben was not involved with whatever had happened to their relationship.

Erin had a debit card. In her account were sixteen dollars and thirty-eight cents. She had a Metrocard, too. The Metrocard was unlimited. It would expire in a week. She had a university ID and a working phone and a bag that contained a book and several documents.

Erin attempted to think. She decided to send out an exploratory text message and began walking. The thing was—the main thing was—that she hadn't told anybody, not about Ben. "hey, sorry for the silence. can i ask you something?" she wrote to a female friend. She walked down the hill.

It felt like it was hers, this situation. It pertained overwhelmingly and exclusively to her, a fate or chemical pattern. She was afraid in a low, ambient way, but she was not struck by terror because she had arrived at that which belonged to her and to which she belonged. Here she was, stupidly outdoors.

She came to Lexington and descended before boarding a train headed downtown.

People on the train were either leaving work or on the way out for the evening. Those leaving their jobs were service industry workers; there was the flash of white clogs, scrubs. Men carried cases for tools. There were security guards in uniform. Someone filed her nails.

Erin looked at those who were coming from work and at those who were moving toward the part of their lives where they mated. Those who were coming from work appeared to be concentrating now on distracting themselves; they were in the process of traveling between states that were not merely geographic in nature. They wore headphones, all but universally. They crossed their legs, closed their eyes.

Those who were headed out for the evening, on the other hand, twitched and giggled. They preened their very voices, combing them with unseen combs, combing their faces with these combs, too. They were awake and idiotically present. They seemed to anticipate and long for all the sight in the world, that it should be turned upon them.

Erin was not sure where she was going. She permitted her thoughts to be detained by one woman's narrow, symmetrical face. She tarried on the woman's false eyelashes, her superfluous puffer coat in winter white, the fur of a coyote that had no doubt been starved before being dismembered, a fragment of its pelt stitched into the hood of the garment.

There was a way in which Erin desired something like this for herself. She understood the deception waged by appearances, that the woman she examined augmented the hair on her eyes and wore an item of outerwear that had been manufactured in dizzying quantity and that was, therefore, ubiquitous in this city and elsewhere, not in order to externalize her self, but rather in order to externalize a quality that was instantly recognizable and therefore pertained to no one.

Erin believed that this woman was safe, and this security was what Erin envied. She also believed that the woman had a conception of her own worth such that she did not feel compelled to manifest her true self on the sidewalk. This woman might someday show you who she really was, but she would show you that on her own time, thank you kindly, when she was ready.

Erin did not have this ability. Erin simply was. Erin was like a chair or shoe or rock. The reason Erin simply was was that Erin's self had no real value, as Erin understood it. This self was useful mainly insofar as it seemed to coincide with her consciousness, and, for the moment, consciousness was a state from which Erin preferred not to be separated, except through the occasional workings of drugs and sleep.

Erin's self sat there, mediocre and actual. It could be seen, but no one looked at it.

Erin did, if we are being honest now, have the sense that this was not the first time she found herself in a predicament akin to the current one. Although she was too exhausted and frustrated to cry, she was not incapable of pitying herself—or, failing that, of perceiving that a narrative stubbornly clung to her feelings, in spite of her attempts to be free of not just this narrative but also the feelings to which it was ineluctably sticking.

Internally, Erin swam away from what she was always beginning to feel. The world was actual. The world was composed of petrochemicals and political economy, not of what Erin felt or longed for. Erin, too, was in the world and available to it. Erin made use of a self-imposed method of discipline to deal with these facts.

When Erin was a teenager, Erin had cast a spell on herself. She had not known enough about the world at the time to know that this was possible, but she had known enough to try and was surprised to have succeeded. The spell went as follows: *It does not matter how you feel.*

Erin had been seated in Central Park. She had gone to a bench on a lawn near a baseball diamond. It was the end of winter and there were still little lips of ice on things.

Erin was casting this spell because she found herself stupid. She felt that she possessed intelligence but was squandering it on account of drifting despair. The despair would settle on her and she could not move. She would remain in her room, unable to stand or speak, watching as minutes unfurled, setting sail into the present, traveling away from her.

Erin was seventeen.

She had fallen in love with a boy in her class at school. They had become acquaintances and then friends through his frequent teasing of her. He made comments about her body, which in her mind she converted into a style of amicable advice. Later, the comments about her body ceased and she was invited over to his house to view his CD collection. During the visit, he told her that his mother was very ill. Shortly thereafter, his mother died.

Erin had felt completely uninterested in this boy physically or romantically, and yet she had accepted his friendship because he spoke to her frequently of her intelligence. Erin's intelligence had been remarked on before, but it had never been described in such detail, including but not limited to exegeses on its relationship to common sense. This boy marveled at the way in which Erin perceived, how she spoke of what she saw. They kissed one afternoon.

Erin told the boy that she wanted them to date, that she wanted them to be together, that she loved him.

The boy twisted away. He grew attenuated. He told Erin that he knew that when she was an adult she would have a house and a room in the house that she would go to in order to be alone, and that if he were with her in the house, her husband, she would always leave him for that room.

"But I would come back to you!"

"We can't get married," the boy told her.

Erin did not know what to say. Even in telling the boy that she wanted to be his girlfriend, she felt that she had been lying a little. Probably she did not want him so much. Yet, when he refused her, it was as if some net inside her had broken. Something rushed out. She was losing something. She couldn't seem to get this thing back, whatever it was. Life became unpleasant.

She tried pleading. The boy laughed at her and told her more things about herself. He told her that she would be successful and live a wonderful life.

Erin begged him to reconsider. She told him that her happiness was bound up with him, a thing she would not have believed possible even several weeks earlier.

The more Erin said, the more became true.

This was how Erin arrived at her plan. Seated on the bench, she vowed to herself that she would become that person, that pleased and successful person, whom the boy believed her to be. She would not lie down under his thumb. She would not think of him with aching need. He was a boy of average gifts.

It does not matter how you feel, Erin told herself. From this moment forth, it no longer matters. In this moment, your feelings have become separate from your thoughts and you are free and healed. There is the bad life you may abandon, and there is the clear, rational, good life in which feelings do not matter. You can go through the day and feel fine about what is happening, because there is no reason to be unhappy. Everything is still here. You have not lost anything.

Good things will happen to you, because it does not matter how you feel.

Erin had staggered a little getting up from the bench. Perhaps she did feel a little better. What was true was that she no longer felt like screaming. Perhaps she had become someone new. She went on a long aimless walk in the city and returned to her parents' apartment dehydrated, cautiously satisfied.

The spell stuck. Of course, Erin did not know for many years that it was a spell. She believed that it was a conviction.

However, it was not long before Erin began to experience the effects of the spell. It began during Erin's second year of college. She began losing blocks of time. It was usually no more than a few hours, but she would come to, unaware of what she had been doing, which was also to say, who was doing it or what they did. Sometimes she looked at her email and saw that she had composed messages during one of her episodes. At other times it seemed she merely slept or stared at things. Erin wasn't always sure.

Erin told herself that she needed to be more organized. She told herself to get going and work harder because feelings aren't real. As if in response to the growing vehemence of these self-exhortations, the spell tightened its grip. Erin began to hear voices at night as she waited for sleep. The voices were not addressed to her. They sounded like people encountering one another in a train station, discussing the weather or plans for home remodeling. She followed the specifics of their chatter. They enumerated facts about maintaining one's gracious life in America. Erin had no idea who these people were.

After the demolition of the World Trade Center, which Erin had happened to watch occurring live on television, things deteriorated more rapidly. Erin began to lose the power of speech sporadically. She could no longer depend on herself to comprehend the order in which basic life tasks needed to unfold in order to benefit from the laws of cause and effect. If I put this shampoo in my hand, will I then be able to raise my hand to my scalp? What does placing the shampoo on my head do? Should I rub my head or look for soap? Should I turn off the water now?

Somehow, Erin managed to graduate. Erin's adviser was a poet, and during some of her episodes, Erin seemed to write poetry. Erin was not sure if she had a strong interest in poems. Erin went along with it, the poetry, because she passed these classes and was not regarded as a problem.

Erin once, during this time, was convinced that she had seen the ghost of the American poet Marianne Moore, b. 1887, d. 1972, striding across the college campus. Marianne Moore was extremely tall and wore her signature mortar cap, traversing the greensward with stentorian dignity in a flapping cape. Marianne Moore's ghost had the aplomb that comes from death. It knew where it was heading.

Erin told her adviser that she had seen the ghost of Marianne Moore strolling around the quad.

The adviser was interested. The adviser wondered if Marianne Moore was attempting to send her, the adviser, a message. The adviser said, "I should reread her work this weekend."

"Whose?" asked Erin. Erin was thinking about the fact that soon her conversation with the adviser would end and she would be forced to return to her own wrecked subjectivity.

"Moore's," the adviser murmured. The adviser rearranged her hair. "She can be very urgent."

"She seemed a little annoyed."

"Oh really?"

Erin nodded. She attempted to feel pleased with herself, as if she had seized some exclusive opportunity.

The adviser began speaking about a Nobel laureate who had offended her during a cocktail party.

Erin graduated and went to a master's program and there she met Ben. Erin had feelings for Ben. It was the first time she had had feelings of this type for another human since the incident with the boy in high school, and the feelings for Ben were very strong, stronger than before with the boy whose mother had died. Yet Erin's spell continued. Erin had feelings for Ben but still she believed that her feelings did not matter. In a way, this was useful, because Ben often behaved strangely. He would wake up in the night and berate Erin for perceived offenses Erin was barely able to comprehend. Erin was accused of coming between Ben and his family, whom Erin had never met. In the light of day, Ben apologized. As his rages consisted only of words for the moment, unpleasant words, jellied with delusion, Erin did not consider Ben's rages important. She had feelings for Ben, but in the end it did not matter how she felt. She let herself be guided only by the feelings she "might have" "for" him. She did not ask herself what this might mean.

So Erin lived. So she rendered her place in history habitable. She looked down from the balcony.

The train reached Union Square and Erin got off. It was 8:30 p.m. on the dot. She began to tell herself, with practiced impassivity, that she was simply a brainstem on legs, destined to shepherd a certain awareness around until such a time as she would be defunct, but she found that as she went within her mind to articulate this thought, to bite it off from the tilting mass of memory and language, she could not. She made the familiar move, the little lunge with the small knife of articulation, but it would not take place. She could not think it.

Erin drifted. She sank. Erin was walking, and Erin's heart beat in her chest and hurt her somewhat.

Erin had nowhere to go and her text message remained un-answered. She attempted to convince herself that this was an opportunity. Erin tried to say, in the voice of her mind, Now I can work. Now I am free. It does not matter how I feel! Now I will work harder than ever I have worked before! Yet even these vows were puny.

There was, for the moment, no one to whom Erin could turn. She felt the abstract vastness of phenomenal reality.

As if stimulated by these epic apprehensions, Erin's phone began to vibrate.

Erin looked.

It was Ben.

Reflexively, Erin answered. She was standing in front of the university library now. The world shivered. It became a twig on the ground.

She was breezy. "Hello?"

"Erin?" Ben seemed surprised that she had picked up. Or, per-haps he no longer recognized her voice.

Erin was afraid, but part of her welcomed this. A nonminor part of her wished now to encounter the truth of her own life, along with the epistemological violence that seemed to pertain to it via the person of her husband.

"Yes?" Erin said.

"It's Ben," Ben said stupidly. He sounded annoyed to have to speak his own name.

"Hello," Erin told him. Then she said, "It's Erin."

"I know!"

Erin did not say anything. She did not laugh. She waited. She hurt very much, but also she felt that she did not need to move. She did not have to make a thing happen, at least, not for the moment.

"Hello?" said Ben, who seemed to expect Erin to explain the subject of their conversation to him.

"How can I help you?" Erin asked.

"I saw your message," Ben said.

"Yes, I wrote you a message."

"But you didn't give me very much time. I couldn't come today."

"When can you come?"

"That's not what I'm calling about."

"What are you calling about?" Erin asked, remembering, although she did not wish to, when he might have been calling about what they might eat or a movie they might see, all the insignificant exchanges that established a comfort that was no more.

"I need," said Ben, "more than books."

"OK?"

"I'm going camping next week, so I need my tent, my sleeping bag, my boots, and I need a bunch of other things. There's a lot I need. I don't even know what all of it is because I'm not looking at it. I need to come into the house and see things," Ben said. He said, "To find them."

"No."

"What?"

"I'll leave them for you."

"That doesn't work."

"No," said Erin. "It does. It does work." And Erin said, "You left. You left stuff in the house? Too bad. I don't want you there."

"No—" Ben was starting to say.

"I'm not finished! You have some of my things. I want those back from you. I don't want you to have anything that belongs to me. I need you to give me those things, and then and only then, when I have those things, will I give your things to you."

"You're talking about the book and the casserole?"

"I'm talking about my book and my tart pan that you took with you for some reason. I need those things back!"

"Wow," said Ben. "You're insane."

"These things are important to me. It takes a lot of work and it has taken a lot of work to move all of your crap. I'm going to be doing this for a long time, moving all of your crap around and setting it out on the stairs so that you can come take it away."

"Maybe you should have thought about that earlier."

"Me?"

"Yes." Ben was bold.

"When, exactly?"

"You always knew!"

"I never knew!"

"You say that."

"Ben, I truly, truly wish I had! Unfortunately, you were fucking," she stumbled, realizing her gerundive might be mistaken for a participle, and that she was, meanwhile, ridiculous and weak, "lying your ass off."

"I was doing," said Ben, "what I had to do. Maybe it doesn't occur to you, but you are not the easiest person to live with. You're not exactly anybody's idea of an easy person to live with. You know that now I don't even have anywhere to live?"

If Erin could have pitied Ben, she would have. Erin would have pitied Ben in the moment and also she would have asked him to meet her back at the apartment so that they could deal with the lock situation together and make a snack. The next morning, when they woke up, they would have looked into a rehab for him and gotten a restraining order against the other woman he was sleeping with (Erin was not so sure how this sort of thing worked), and Ben would have called his parents to disown them and found a therapist. They would have gotten through this together.

But Erin knew now the extent of Ben's laziness. His was a torpor of stupendous, infernal proportions. Although he appeared to be a fully grown man, in fact he was an early pupa, a limbless slug basking in the broth of some spiritual incubation tank, a feeding tube plugged into his neck. Ben was The Matrix (trademark). He was a being of almost pure projection: He went around on two legs and was recognized as a legal adult, but this was mere appearance, a trick done with light and vapors. It was an infinitesimal mass that dwelled among the living as "Ben," a mere mote; the larger part of Ben, the great lugubrious reality of him, was tied back into the labyrinth of his ancestry, into the pipes and roots. He did not really live, having chosen to receive all of his cues, beliefs, and nutrients from the ancestral system. He was a hologram, but here he was yelling at her about his suffering. He strove, at least in words, to be a righteous citizen of the present. He wanted her to save him, was crying out from the last place that had not been colonized by the past, but she could not save him, not because she did not want to, but because it was too late: he was already enveloped. If she went to him now, she would only be participating in the archaic reality, nursing it through his body.

Ben had not always been this way. All the same, it seemed now that he was always going to become this way. This was her husband, a horror.

Erin felt the wanting of a home. It was like being dragged a city block against her will. She wanted all that had happened to be forgotten, and for there to be a home to which she could turn to be held by the person she loved and who loved her in return, but there was no use pretending. Erin could not embrace The Matrix (trademark). It was from this conviction that she progressed.

And there was more to this story, because this was the story that moved alongside the story of the spell, sometimes contradicting it. Erin struggled to make sense of these two personal narratives: First, the one in which she had no feelings, in particular, even if she could feel; the one in which she was subject to tugs and pulls and even a precipitation, as if out of doors, exposed to elements that pertained to an ecosystem constrained by its own cycles and laws, but that was fundamentally separate from her, a landscape or environmental installation she basically accepted but did not esteem. And the second narrative, in which Erin was a doll on a leash: She fell into a hole and could only experience need she had no idea how to meet. The need swam through her. She could not work, and she could sometimes only barely speak. She felt so *without*, without qualities, faculties. There was nothing to maintain, or nourish, or be, given she was crucially in deficit of something she was powerless to identify.

The second narrative had asserted itself, Erin understood, via the lost time. It had followed quickly on the heels of the spell against feelings. Erin was not sure if the spell had caused it, or if it would have shown up anyway. It felt like it might have, like it had always been there, latent and grumbling. The spell was merely something Erin had done. The need was something she had been given. It soared toward her, out of the past. It leapt up and threw itself upon her in the present, its ugly speckled belly blotting out the sun.

In the throes of this need, Erin panicked. It would occur and last for days. She could still only feebly identify its presence, so subtly did it match itself to her surroundings, becoming what was actual instead of an aspect of her subjectivity. When it came on, Erin bought things she did not want, carried around bags of books she would never read, stared for hours at photographs of strangers on the internet, pondering their social lives. This was if Erin was doing well. If

Erin was not doing well, she might become caught in a loop—sitting somewhere, she'd spend hours simply trying to decide to stand up. Her brain would natter; Erin would ping in and out of narrative time.

Ben, when they had met, had seemed like the solution. Erin had not understood how this was possible, but in the initial months of their intimacy, the need had disappeared and Erin had experienced herself as a plain organism. There was nothing wrong and Erin was not to blame. Erin and Ben met in many locations. She had not thought this kind of happiness was possible.

Of course, it had changed. Erin had tried to ignore the changing, particularly because when the need came back, as it seemed to have been fated to do, it was far, far worse. While in her early twenties the need had been a cosmos she unpleasantly inhabited, now it seemed to be inside Erin's head, an aspect of her own will. Whereas in the past she had become disoriented or entertained auditory hallucinations, now, when the need came on, Erin sometimes struck herself with her fists or with objects, punching shallow holes in walls and one time sticking a knife into her leg, an act she successfully hid, pouring vodka into the wound as she had seen, she later supposed, in films about frontier gunplay. The excruciating throb Erin's folk remedy produced elicited an animal moan from Erin's body, and after the throb had ceased, Erin wept with relief, hopping to the bathroom for a compress and Band-Aids. The cut closed, eventually. Erin was chastened, even satisfied, and did not explain what she had done to Ben, who, although increasingly subject to his own violent bouts, was critical of Erin's difficulties. "Why are you so insane?" he sometimes asked, as she slapped herself in the face. "What do you want to do? Why are you crazy?"

When he was feeling nice, later, whenever it was, he would hold her and tell her about moments he treasured from his childhood. Erin attempted to be charmed. This was different from before, when Ben had spoken of the suburban community from which he hailed as backward and segregated, plagued by recurring environmental catastrophes due to nearby industry. Now it was a place where people did not have to lock their doors.

So, Erin now recognized, things had continued. Things had developed, even, richened in their sickness. Erin drank, in order to keep up with Ben. She became worse at living. She cried, sometimes, attempting to park their much-keyed car when it was late and spots were hard to come by. She would come close to losing consciousness in subway cars paused in tunnels. If unsupervised, she had a tendency to live on gummy candies and slices of processed cheese. She alarmed dental technicians. She sometimes threw her clothing out the window and did not do the dishes.

Maybe she was impossible to live with. When Erin could manage it, she retired to her study at the back of the apartment, closed the door. After a few hours, Erin might feel better. She might re-emerge. She might cook for Ben.

In all of this, Erin clung—like a little rat, she thought at least once a day, staring down at the weaving, scuttling, tumor-beset denizens of the subway tracks, as they sought out discards from humans above—to history and to school. She had books, and, when feasible, she had contemplation. Although she was increasingly a source of tragic disappointment where her parents were concerned, at least she was enrolled in a degree-granting program. Even if she could only flee to and from sources of calories, Erin could move, for escape was still movement. Life was not dignified, yet it was not absolute stultification. Erin suffered and was very poor, but she was not dead.

Ben, for his part, had often yelled at her about what he perceived as her parents' excessive wealth. He wanted to know why he and she had to struggle to get by when her parents could easily do something for them. "And your parents never help us! They never do anything!" he'd scream, at the close of a series of what he seemed to believe were brilliant strikes, sentences that exhaustively condemned her.

Other problems exhibited by Erin included: lack of authenticity, reluctance to reproduce, confusion regarding the greatest good attainable by a human female as opposed to a male human.

In the presence of her parents, Ben was jovial, polite. He made frequent reference to Erin's (enduringly endearing) foibles. He got very drunk.

Having learned during the course of one of his performances that Erin's paternal grandfather had arrived in the United States as a child, Ben developed a fascination with what he perceived, unreasonably, Erin felt, as Erin's exoticism. It had, of course, taken many years to develop this level of intimacy with Erin's parents, such that they would reveal this fact. It was not something they had ever been willing to discuss with Erin, and in a way she was alarmed that they would so blithely open up to Ben. She was not precisely jealous of their pliancy in relation to him. It was actually something more ancient, a sedimentary part of her that was vaguely roused.

Ben could not stop talking about it. "You're really lucky you got your mother's nose," he pointed, "at the end there. It's big but like a ball. I always wondered about that ball! I was looking at your father during dinner, and you could have gotten that long hook. But you didn't," he mused. "It missed you, Little Dewbie," he concluded, employing a pet name that bespoke infantile informality, soon to become a mess.

Ben told his friends about Erin's ancestry. He told them not to mistake her last name. It was not Italian. He told Erin that if she wanted to be authentic and a decent human, she needed to live up to who she really was. He found the manifest testifying to her grandfather's arrival aboard SS *Aquitania*, passenger number 105138060455, in the company of a "Cousin." Ben emailed the list to Erin and printed it out, put it on the fridge.

He emailed it to his family, who also printed it out, put it on the fridge.

At the top of the now grease-spattered document was bureaucratic boilerplate:

*I, _____, of the _____, from _____, do sol-
emnly, sincerely, and truly _____ that I have caused the
surgeon of said vessel sailing therewith, or the surgeon employed by the owners thereof, to make a physical and mental examination of each and all of the aliens named in the
foregoing Lists or Manifest Sheets, _____ in number,
and that from the report of said surgeon and from my own
investigation, I believe that no one of said aliens is of any of
the classes excluded from admission into the United States by
section three of the Immigration Act, and that also, according to the best of my knowledge and belief, the information in
said Lists or Manifests concerning each of said aliens named
therein is correct and true in every respect.*

The blanks were completed by one "J. T. W. CHARLES, MASTER," using inked stamps applied at wild diagonals. Erin memorized the words, standing in her kitchen.

At first, at the very first, when Erin had begun, several months earlier, to know that Ben was betraying her, she had tried to feel that he was a loving person whom she had wronged. She labored, insofar as she could figure out how to labor in this direction, to correct her mistakes. She repeatedly apologized, offered to do more to make him happy, whatever he said.

Ben suggested that she drop out of school.

In these early times of the thing, Erin asked, "If I drop out of school, then will you come home?"

After a long pause, Ben said, "I don't know. I don't know if I can. But you have to do it."

Now, over the phone, she told Ben, "I'm sorry that you don't have anywhere to live." In a sense, Erin meant this. She meant, "I don't have anywhere to live, either." She meant to say, "I understand how that feels."

Ben was, however, beyond consolation. Or, he seemed to have

heard Erin a little too well. He seemed to have become imaginative and elaborate in his reasoning, where Erin was concerned.

His voice was even. "You know you never loved me, right?"

Erin did not respond.

"Yeah," he said. "So I'm just trying to, like, make sure you understand. Like, for the future. So maybe you can have a fighting chance. Love," Ben said, "isn't about Dewbies, and Dewbears, Dewbutts, and all that. You know? Love is something you do. It's something you do for another person, not something you feel. I know you're confused about that."

Erin was confused. Or, rather, Erin was clear. She said, "That's not true."

"No," said Ben. "It is true. That's why we're here. It's why we're talking like this."

Erin slid. Erin stood on the dampish sidewalk in the too-warm late-autumn air in the upper portion of lower Manhattan in some early section of the century, and she was upright, but there was a forty-five-degree tilt. She slid and slid. The ocean was present. Her nostrils burned.

A wave had crashed, rolled on.

Erin said, "I want a divorce."

Ben spoke instantly. "That's great," he said.

"Yes," said Erin.

Ben was increasingly unrecognizable. His voice grew tender, striving and melted. "I just thought it was so crazy! How you thought I wanted you to be like my mother? I never wanted that from you!"

"Goodbye," said Erin and hung up her phone. Shaking, she used her thumb and middle finger to turn it off. Next it fell on the sidewalk, screen up, and she stood looking down at it there. She moved through space to retrieve it. Space functioned as a thick hood.

Erin cleaned her phone and put it into her bag.

She wondered if it was broken, but she did not really wonder about this very much. She walked over to a wall and touched the wall. Careless, she pressed her face against the textured stone. Her face could feel the stone. Stone could feel her face. Phenomenal reality bobbed. It bounced, jiggled.

Erin unstuck her face from the surface of the wall. The bridge of her nose hurt. She might have cut it.

Erin adjusted the strap of her bag on her shoulder.

In Erin's bag were, in no particular order: an unpaid utility bill, printouts of two word-processed manuscripts written by Erin, a page belonging to Faith Ewer, and a library book.

2
Interiors

I now propose the bottle as hero.

—Ursula K. Le Guin

A.

Maison Close
A Novella

by
Erin Adamo

HORATIO.

Re-enter GHOST

[. . .]

. . . if thou hast uphoarded in thy life
Extorted treasure in the womb of earth,
For which, they say, you spirits oft walk in death,
Speak of it.

What everyone fails to remind you is that since the early eighteenth century Hamlet has, very often, been portrayed by a woman.

And, in fact, I had a childhood friend. *Her* name was Hamlet. Her full name was Hamlet Voorhees, but her last name hardly registered, given the first. Even her family came to be called "the Hamlets," due to the power of this name. Hamlet was their middle child. She was older than Rose, her sister, who may have been either a secret Rosenkrantz or Rosemary (for remembrance), and younger than her brother, the achingly predictable, as well as unfathomably violent, Will, who was alleged to have pleasure-killed four koi, three gerbils, two guinea pigs, and one cat.

I was an only child. My father was a veterinarian. My mother worked in real estate.

*

Here is how Hamlet appeared: This much is traditional, Hamlet was a blond. Hamlet was a beauty as a child, but this beauty would not see her through to adulthood. Somehow I think, recalling her face now, that she will be a beautiful old woman, if she is still living when she is old. But when she was little, this Hamlet was a walking flower. Her pointed face held yellow eyes; her hair was gold. A barrette secured it. She laughed, receiving a compliment or food.

Hamlet had chosen me. We were in school together. We were six years old.

There was a game with Hamlet, who was never taunted for her name, somehow, even if the literary reference meant nothing to the other children and rhymed with *omelet*. In Hamlet's young world, everything was already known and had simply been forgotten through disuse. And by disuse I mean: Hamlet's inexperience. Although there were many, many things that Hamlet had not lived and did not know, for the girl Hamlet these new things were all ancient acquaintances, objects relegated to a closet or the bottom of a box, their faces turned away by collective neglect. Hamlet rescued these items by means of her attention. She restored the world, merely by passing through it, by speaking and naming, by smelling, seeing, indicating. So Hamlet, a girl, restored me. She was the one who gave me something like a memory. Thank you, Hamlet. With you, my history begins.

*

There are three famous dreams from the time I first met Hamlet. I tried to tell Hamlet, too, but I think I repeated myself too often, and Hamlet hated repetition.

The first dream was a dream about escaping crucifixion, although I do not fully understand what sense I could have had at the time regarding the reality of crucifixion, a premodern capital punishment. I was a child living in the West and dead Jesuses were everywhere. I believed that these Jesuses were only shriveled men, disappointed, ancient, and unwell. I did not understand that they had been executed, as I probably would have known had I received any education in religion. I think I thought they were sick. God had made them sick. They were what sick people looked like to God. My dream was distinguished by its interest in crucifixes—nor were these merely decorative. They were arranged along the crest of a hill that formed the backdrop to what I can think of as a town, though maybe it was just (or, merely) a crossing of roads, a reviled place that desperate consensus caused to appear as a corner of civilization. Everything was lumps. The sky was a gray dish. Nothing worked. We were in a broken taxi; it vibrated and you smelled gasoline. We had to get away, my parents and I. Something was drifting into the landscape, nonchalantly consuming human lives. It was very swift, this thing. Maybe this thing was other people. I've never known what it was. This was just a dream full of slippery mud. My heart was racing. I wanted to run when I woke but instead I stayed in bed. This is the first of the dreams I have never forgotten. The bodies droop from the wood. They have been pinned there, peelings.

The second dream I have never forgotten is set in what I take to be a European forest. Maybe a black light is being used to give special illumination to this place. Many things are black, shining, as if patent leather, black glass. There is a febrile green here, too, a chemical lawn, wild strawberries. White, like lace, edges things. Bright white is used for the seeds of strawberries; also for glints on things. I walk through the European forest. I have just escaped from a building I take to be a hotel. There they warned me that I would not be able to see at night. There in the hotel blinding lights shone. Tables were always being moved—round tables, rolled on their sides. I ran away to the forest where for a short period I was indeed blind. Now I have begun to see. I walk and gaze at the alarming strawberries. They are like thoughts. Maybe there are violet pansies, too. This is when I find a thing. The thing has long, black hair. It rests on the forest floor. I approach. I am looking over it and looking at it from the side, and I can see what it is, although I do not want to know what it is. I know what it is, but I do not want to know. The thing is a severed head, very white and very silver, with long black hair. The hair is like grasses and gets everywhere. The hair is sticky. The head knows that I have seen it. It is dead and also alive. Its mouth is open, its painted gray mouth, and I think that the head is moaning. It makes a continuous moan. A film covers all things and I cannot speak. I can't move. I am lost in the scream of the head.

In the third dream I have never forgotten, I lie in bed, unable to sleep. As I lie in my bed, unable to sleep in the dream, this is what I dream: that I am lying in my bed unable to sleep. I dream this all night long: lying in my bed, unable to sleep, under a comforter with a pattern of blooming roses. I am thinking, in the dream in which I lie in a bed identical to my own, of a red-haired chef. The red-haired chef wears a white, buttoned uniform, carries a spoon. The red-haired chef is substantial. What is it, I think, during the dreamed period of sleeplessness, during which I am in fact sleeping, to be a chef? What is it to stand behind a wall and create in order to serve? I don't know why I think this, in my dream. I don't know why I contemplate the dark-gold skin of the red-haired chef, what seems to be his rage and also his genius. I want to know what a chef is. I am dreaming, but I am awake. The chef stands in my mind, bearing his spoon. He stands in a mind that is part of my dream. It is not my mind. It is a mind that I dream I have, while I am dreaming that I am not asleep.

*

I try to tell Hamlet about the dreams. I feel that she will appreciate them. They are so vivid and pointless and strange, and I think she will admire my style, although we are only eight years old. Hamlet knows a lot about style. She understands fine things and will comprehend the rarefied nature of what I see when I'm unconscious.

But Hamlet does not want to know about my dreams. She tells me not to talk about them. Her little face seems to get littler for a moment. She appears to be washing something away.

Hamlet says that she has a story to tell me and this story will amaze me. "OK," I say. I don't want to show how eager I am to hear Hamlet's story, but, yes, it is true: I am eager.

Hamlet raises her hands and makes the world disappear. I'll never know how she did it. At this time, Hamlet had powers that, as far as I can tell, were never hers again and that no one else in the world had ever had or would possess. I sometimes have to ask myself, How was it, really, that I came to know her? How did I stumble upon her: she who was the temporary greatest prodigy of all of human history? I was the sole witness to this. I knew and was alone.

But Hamlet, as I was saying, raises her hands. She raises her hands and she proclaims, "This is a story about what would happen if both of my parents died and we are orphans."

Neither of Hamlet's parents are home at the moment, and I don't know where her siblings are.

"We are orphans?" I ask.

"Yes, you're living here too, now," Hamlet says. "Imagine it."

I try to imagine. There's a way, anyhow, that Hamlet's house looks—as if it has just been robbed. Each room has only one or two items of furniture in it, and these items of furniture, although usually upright, are always in a different place, from day to day if not hour to hour. They seem tossed aside, as if they at one time stood in the path of someone who was looking for something. I can see how I might be called upon to be responsible for this home—this home that daily, nightly, some invisible force ravages. It's like a ship, I think, attempting to dwell more warmly in Hamlet's words.

"We're here and my parents are dead and they want to separate us." Hamlet pauses, permitting the accumulation of gravity. "But we're not going to let them, and the way we're not going to let them is to fool them into thinking that they are alive."

"Your parents?" I ask. I mean about the counterfeiting of them still being living. "Don't they already know they're dead?"

Hamlet does not like it when I interrupt her stories. I should not have asked these questions.

"No!" Hamlet exclaims. Her face goes crooked for a minute and I think that she may cry. "You need to have someone living with you who is over eighteen and who is your guardian and that is what we are going to do. Because we have to because they want to separate us." Having said this, Hamlet seems relieved. She was right all along, she understood which story she was trying to tell, while I, stupidly, doubted. I'm very lucky that she is still willing to talk to me.

But Hamlet doesn't really care about justice, and this is why she cannot stay mad at me for long. She knows that she has made it past my misgivings and that we are already in the story. I am captive. Hamlet is free.

"These are going to be our problems," Hamlet says, adopting a grim, conspiratorial tone. "We have to get money and we have to get food, and also we have to keep the orphanage away, because they are going to keep sending people."

"They are?" I am predictable, which is why I am permitted to participate in Hamlet's life.

"Yes," Hamlet says. This interruption does not exasperate her. In fact, it excites her. Now I am indicating the ground upon which the story must be built. "Yes," she repeats. "They are extremely persistent. In particular, there is a woman. She is evil. Her name is Mrs. Stick. She looks like a stick, too, and she has weaknesses, diseases, things she has to hide. She might be one of those people who," Hamlet pauses, "has to wear a mask over their face because their face isn't something other people can look at. Mrs. Stick," Hamlet repeats, "has weaknesses. Her face is just this goo, like, that covers these scales? And she doesn't really have a nose or any lips and half her tongue is missing, so she has to have this specially made rubber mask to wear over her face to make her look normal and actually the worst thing about it is it really hurts. And Mrs. Stick doesn't have any hands or feet, either, and her body is completely shapeless, so she has to wear this case around her body like a cast, to hold her up and make her look like something. It's really uncomfortable and she is always itchy, and she has to use these motorized wheels to get around because she can't walk, but her suit and mask and everything that holds her up are very advanced, so it all looks really natural."

"Where did she get this from?" I ask.

"Where did Mrs. Stick's skin come from?"

"Yes," I say, because I want to know. In a way it is horrible, but Mrs. Stick would also seem to be overcoming quite a lot in order to chase us, so much, in fact, that it occurs to me to admire her.

Hamlet is happy now. The story she is telling is causing a new story to form. "She's not actually married," Hamlet begins. "That is for starters. Her name is just a lie to make her look good. She's not very old, either. She's going to live for a long time yet, particularly if she can keep on fooling people into thinking she's a good person. She is very rich. That's how she gets away with things. She doesn't even need her job at the orphanage." It looks for a moment as though Hamlet is remembering something. "She's completely silent when she moves. You can't hear her coming. She could be standing outside this apartment right now. We would have absolutely no idea. And you know the way the peephole in the door lets you look out into the hall? One of her fake eyes has the power to let her use the peephole to look in, so she can see into the whole apartment and she can know what we are doing at any time. She isn't always there, but we have to be ready."

"Her eyes are fake?" I ask.

Hamlet does not have time for my background queries. "There are a lot of ways that we can do this," Hamlet says. "The main thing is that I'm going to be able to go to the bank. My mom has this fur coat, it is fox, which is the softest fur, and I know that it is not the most valuable but if you buy a coat that is a better quality of less valuable fur, then that is the best thing that you can do."

"Yes," I say.

"Fox fur softens a harsh woman. It gives an air of plush sophistication. It makes me look older than I am. I can wear sunglasses on a high-pressure day in winter. I feel like people will notice my dignity."

Hamlet's vocabulary is remarkable. She knows the names for all things, all states.

"I will get us all the money we need. We will keep it in a shoebox and when we have to use it, we will. And we can use coupons, judiciously. And if anyone ever calls the house from the school, I will pretend to be my mother over the phone, and if they ask to see me, I will say that I am going away on a very long business trip but I signed all the permission slips."

"What about Mrs. Stick?" I ask.

"What about her?"

"Doesn't she know it's you in your mom's fur coat?"

"I have been thinking about that," Hamlet says, as if she truly has. She contemplatively plucks a Dorito from the family-size bag between her legs, nibbles at its edge. "I do think Mrs. Stick could end up inside the apartment."

"Are you sure?" I am genuinely concerned.

"I'm starting to think it's the only way." Hamlet makes an impressive face, primordial and sublime. "I think one day I would let her in and say, 'Oh Mrs. Stick, it's so nice to see you,' and I will sit her down and serve her fancy tea, but it will be poisoned and after this I will take off her mask and bodysuit and make them mine and I will be able to go anywhere in the world."

I say, "But what will you do with Mrs. Stick? Won't the orphanage want to know where she is?"

"No one trusts her," Hamlet tells me. "She's already double-crossed everyone she knows. It will be a mercy killing."

I don't know what a mercy killing is but I say nothing. Instead I say, "What will you do with the body?" hoping that the answer to my question is not already contained in the concept of a mercy killing.

"What are *we* going to do with the body? That's easy. She is all soft and slimy so we can flush her down the toilet. We'll have to stop using that one for a few days, of course, but after that no one will be the wiser."

I consider this. "What's going to happen?" I ask.

"What do you mean? I'm telling you what's going to happen."

"I mean, once your parents are dead and you find out how to live."

"Then we'll be free."

"Won't it be sad?"

"You won't be sad because it's not your parents."

"It's true," I admit.

"And maybe I'll be sad, but I would have had to have been sad anyway. If my parents died, I would already have had to have been sad."

Probably Hamlet knows that I don't always understand why she says what she says and why she feels compelled to talk about the world we live in and the people we're supposed to love in the way she does. Sometimes I feel a coldness when I'm near her. Maybe that's just the fact that we are different, but it could be something else. I look in on Hamlet's life and I see knowledge there. I see what I think, based on movies and TV, a human life is supposed to be. I don't know if Hamlet knows that this is how I see her. Sometimes I think she is aware that she has power over me. Hamlet often asks if she can hit me. Usually it's my arm. She says that it's a game. She says that she is going to hit me on my arm as hard as she can so that I can know true pain. She tells me when she is going to do it, how many times, and then she hits me. "Ready?" she will ask.

I think about the pain. The pain has never been unbearable. It did surprise me at first to find out that the pain Hamlet could inflict on me wasn't so different from pain I'd already felt, or, for that matter, a certain level of my feelings, my basic everyday feelings, which were like weather and simply hung there, the name of a day of the week, part of my breathing.

The pinkness of my arm, the heat of my skin, the faint bruise: these qualities remind me of the qualities of the complex social and familial world to which I believe Hamlet pertains. I celebrate them. I believe that Hamlet is making me more real.

Hamlet is still talking.

"You get over things," Hamlet says. "You have to, to survive. So I would be sad about them dying, but the freedom would make up for that and also knowing that it's not my fault, that will help me. They just died and that's how it is. I could not stop them from dying and now I have to go on and do everything that I can to survive because that is what is important. Not everyone can get through a thing like this, which is why it is a story, and when it is done I will write my memoir of the time and it will be published with my picture on the cover and then I will have a dog and be married and probably I will live in England and have horses."

*

The kitchen in Hamlet's parents' condo is centrally located. It's not very big, but Hamlet's mother, who is also a real estate agent, like my own mother, has known what to do. Contractors have ripped out some walls and we can see into the dining and the living rooms, both of which seem to have recently suffered the passage of small storms. A pile of clothing sits on the dining room table. The clothing looks unclean, but I imagine it is there because someone washed it. Someday someone might put it away.

Sometimes I do feel as if Hamlet's parents have died. It is a surprise, in a way, that I am not compelled to live here and dodge the predations of Mrs. Stick, even as I plot to murder her, rob her of her valuable technology, and flush her down the toilet. Anyway, Hamlet and I have not spoken of the roles to be played by Rose and Will, who would surely be difficult to manage, to say the least, under these circumstances.

This is not even the first time that Hamlet has told me this story. Often, her parents die. Their deaths result in triumph for Hamlet. Hamlet's life becomes an endless vacation, a site of wealth and leisure, involving cruises and mansions with elaborate gardens and husbands and horses, always horses.

I do not like horses. I like bears. I would like to have a conversation with a bear, in fact. I believe that bears are wise and that they know all about sleeping, which is an activity I am not good at and which scares me.

Hamlet's mother will come home soon. Hamlet's mother looks a little like a horse, herself. Although there's no way I understand this at the time, she wears all the latest fashions and even is a bit ridiculous, in her leather pants and loudly printed blouses; her long, frosted hair. She and Hamlet do not resemble each other, but I see some of her in Hamlet, all the same. Everything Hamlet's mother says seems already to have been written out in the scripts of television. She is always giving us tips about how we can expect that other human beings will act, what is normal and not normal, what is valuable and not. "I was so fascinated by that," Hamlet's mother frequently confesses. She knows all about the city, all its parts and people. She knows all about the right sorts of things and wears a blouse with a frill at its neck. Her voice goes up sometimes, very high.

Hamlet's father writes for a well-known magazine. This is why I am permitted to be friends with Hamlet.

What Hamlet's father writes about is theater. I have never read a thing that he has written, but sometimes what he writes is popular. He and Hamlet's mother seem to be agreed on certain things— mainly what is right and fascinating. Hamlet's father is overweight. He wears a blazer with his jeans. He is an aggressive person. He has many responsibilities and perseveres in spite of them. He has often let us know that he does not wish to be disturbed. He says he wants to work from home, but due to us he cannot.

Watching Hamlet's mother and father together is like watching a fake swordfight. Probably no one is going to die, but that does not mean they do not want to kill each other. It is also like staring at two fake swords hanging on the wall. I am afraid of them and know, at the same time, that I fear them needlessly. Their life is detailed and they seem unaware of most of it. I see, too, that they are not important characters. They bicker and make strange claims about the meaning of the city but, at base, they are about as conscious as a pair of shoes—or, as mentioned, plastic swords, dull tips.

*

My parents do not have many children. They do not have a chaotic house. They have an orderly house and they even let me name myself.

Therefore, my name is Amethyst.

What my parents, the parents of Amethyst, do have in common with Hamlet's parents is that they are almost never home. My father works as a veterinarian—a fact that has the potential to make me popular at school, although so far I seem unable to turn this to my advantage. You could expect him to be a warm man, a funny man, a man who sees the humor in the world, given his proximity to dogs and cats and other small creatures with miniature organs, the speechless beings unaccountably beloved by humans, but in fact he is a quiet person, difficult to speak to. He is small and he is bald. I have his long, thin nose.

My mother is the one who meets with other people. She is the one who connects us to the world. I can't understand her, and I am not sure if, in fact, I want to.

My mother is in real estate, but actually she has more than one job. It's not that my mother is frightening, but that she is the background to all things. She seems to be the person who taught me what words in English mean. Even now, after my nearly ten years on this earth, she is still compelled to correct me. My mother works part-time for a school. I do not go there. My mother has an office and people are often with her. The school is a school for boys. It is nearby our house and so sometimes we go there, in order to see the plays they do. I get the sense that seeing the plays is a part of my mother's work. I meanwhile like to watch the dust moving in the spotlight beams. Girls' schools visit to act. I stare at the students, boys and girls, acting and try to see them as real people. I wonder if they feel proud.

Hamlet does not like my parents. She simpers at them when they are around, but privately, when we are alone, she wonders why I have not talked of killing them. She says it, in so many words. I haven't had to give an answer, but I want to: I would say that if they were to die, I would be entirely alone. And I don't think that I could convince anyone of anything, then. Mrs. Stick would be the least of my problems.

Hamlet wants to know why I obey my mother when she tells me to get off the phone.

I can't give a good answer.

Hamlet is angry. Hamlet cancels on me about coming to see *Macbeth* at the boys' school. She stops asking me to come over to her house.

*

It is the weekend.

My mother is responsible for all the furniture in the apartment, while my father cleans the windows.

My father is standing on a chair to reach the outside of the top pane of the living room windows. Then, he falls. I am not in the same room as him, but I am in our home. I hear a loud crash and there is moaning and then the sound of my mother's feet and her voice, calling to me, but I do not come. I stay where I am in the bedroom. She is interrupting me. She wants from me something I cannot be compelled to give. I do not know why I think this, as the upsetting noises go on, as pigeons flutter upward, cooing in the airshaft.

Later, my father has a concussion, and there is something wrong with the bones in his shoulder, although, as is repeatedly said, there is nothing wrong with the bones in his hands. I can guess why the fate of my father's hands is important, although I have never been to

16

his clinic and know next to nothing of what he does. He looks at me gravely from the bed in my parents' bedroom the next day, a Sunday. He is grayish, a newt.

"Papa," I say, because this is what I call him, "does it hurt?"

"Why did you let her in here?" my father asks. Obviously, he is not speaking to me.

"So she can see how you are." This is my mother. She is carrying a glass of orange juice. "It's the concussion," my mother says.

My father groans and closes his eyes.

I walk somewhere. I think it is the kitchen.

My father gets well.

My father continues to make his living.

But this does not last.

The next time my father falls it is seven months later and he is at work and there is a wet floor and something happens to his back.

It takes longer this time before I see him again.

This time my mother says, "Don't try to speak with your father."

*

I turn eleven years old.

I ask my mother, "Am I pretty?"

"You are attractive," my mother says.

I think about this, then I say, "Can I be pretty, do you think?"

"Being pretty is a lot of work," my mother tells me. "It's a big responsibility. Is that something you would want to take on?"

"Yes," I tell my mother. "I want to be pretty."

My mother looks up from her needlework for the first time. She is cross-stitching a front for a pillow. A pattern is printed on a plain-color lattice and she trains yarns through it. The pattern shows a basket of spear-like lilies. You can also buy the pillows finished instead of making them.

My mother examines my face, putting down the pillow front, which trails its yarns like a beard.

"You are going," my mother says slowly, "to have to work very,

very hard." She pauses. "Your father and I shouldn't have let you name yourself."

"Why?"

"It gave you ideas."

"I want to get a haircut," I say.

"A haircut?"

"I will look prettier with my hair short."

"Are you sure?"

"I am sure."

"Most people do not look prettier with short hair. Most people look uglier with short hair, except people who are naturally pretty."

"Maybe I am naturally pretty," I say.

"Maybe you are," my mother replies, looking back at her yarn.

"If I get short hair, then we can find out."

"It's true," my mother tells me.

We go to the hairdresser and I get my hair cut very short and when we come home my father who is still in bed rolls onto his side. He croaks, "She looks like a boy."

I try to smile. I run to the mirror. I can see my round face. I stay there with the mirror for a long time.

*

Later, I go to my mother and I tell her, "I looked for a while and I decided it's true, I am naturally pretty."

My mother is somehow microwaving pasta. She reads instructions for this process from a book. She tells me, "You look very natural."

I have to leave the room in order to think about this.

*

There is a poem I wrote when I was learning how to read and I still know it now. The poem is about my father, and also it is about a joke cover of the magazine Hamlet's father wrote for. The cover showed the back of a man's head and all around him dogs and cats were falling through the air as if they were raindrops. It was a visualization of that common phrase about the weather.

I wrote:

> This man must look about
> Himself, for pets are raining
> In the sky.
> It may be a change in the weather
> Or a sight for you and I.
> But regard his look
> For it is carzy!

You could not see that man's face, and I could not spell that word, and maybe this was what made this a poem. I went and looked at the poem, which was inside a clear protective sheet. I could see my painstakingly printed letters. What had I meant by this?

I went into my parents' bedroom, where my father was snoring. I looked in the mirror opposite my parents' bed.

My father was right about me. I did look like a boy.

*

However, my haircut did have the desired effect, because everything changed. I have, anyway, to assume it was the haircut.

I don't know if Hamlet believed it was a message. She began to see me again. She spoke to me.

Hamlet had changed. Hamlet was no longer beautiful. Hamlet's face was now graced with a sheen, an oil. Her blond hair sat in unattractive dark blond coils that seemed never to fully dry. She wore heavy eye pencil, as if her face required a decoration, thick emphasis. She chewed her lips.

It was a single-sex school and there was something rude and heavy about Hamlet now, something lazy and disliking use. Hamlet had a kind of hood or mask. She had to draw her eyes on. She was something more than twelve.

It was as if we were meeting again after a long journey. Hamlet returned to me. I told her what had happened to my father.

"It's a good thing," Hamlet said, "that you don't have any pets."

I had never thought of this before. Leave it to Hamlet to see right through the mists of human affairs!

"Are you mad?" Hamlet wanted to know.

"Why would I be mad?"

"Aren't you going to be poor now?"

I considered this proposition. I went home and asked my mother.

My mother was standing in the kitchen in her work outfit. This consisted of a skirt and jacket, along with matching headband. She was looking through her book about the microwave. Perhaps she was contemplating creating some bread.

"What makes you ask that?" My mother eyed my hair.

"I thought Papa can't work anymore."

"Who told you that?"

"No one," I said.

"Who have you been talking to?"

"Hamlet," I admitted. "Hamlet was warning me."

"You're speaking to Hamlet again?" My mother raised a carefully painted brow. "You'll probably have to be surgically separated from her."

"Hamlet says that if Papa stops working we could lose all our money." It felt like a reasonable summary.

"That's not going to happen."

I examined my mother.

"Hamlet doesn't know anything about you or your family. She's just a girl. Stop embarrassing yourself."

"What's going to happen?"

"You really want to know?" My mother was flipping through her cookbook again.

I nodded. I felt I could be brave.

"Since you ask, nothing is going to happen. Nothing is going to change. Your father enjoyed being a veterinarian, and everything is taken care of."

"OK," I said.

"Hamlet wouldn't understand."

"Mom," I said, "what exactly is your job?"

"I am an agent and an administrator."

"So if Papa isn't going to work, why do you do those things?"

"Why am I an agent and an administrator?"

"Yes."

"Because these are my passions."

"Oh," I said, feigning awe.

*

Hamlet had acquired new predilections.

Now she liked to throw things out of windows. Usually, we made packets of iceberg lettuce with ketchup and mayonnaise. We also dropped pennies, which we had heard might be fatal.

We stood over a toilet in her parents' apartment, smoking a cigarette.

"Do you want to do a makeover?" Hamlet asked me. "You should look like more of a slut."

It did not occur to me to refuse.

These days there were no books on the shelves in Hamlet's parents' living room. Rose, who had gone feral, used the bookcases as a climbing structure and as storage for partially consumed snacks. The sofa was missing all its cushions. Hamlet's parents had a damp-looking unmade bed.

The bathroom, all mirrored, was streaked and sprinkled with Mrs. Hamlet's cosmetic leavings. A bleak beige, apparently the color of her face, was everywhere.

Hamlet sat me on the toilet. She began her work. She wet my hair and combed it back. Various kinds of pressure were applied to my eyes and eyelids.

"Now go look at my brother," Hamlet commanded me. "See what he does. Oh wait—" Hamlet seemed to remember something. She fetched a sequined tube top from her mother's closet and made me put it on. "She can't wear this anymore. Now go," she said.

Will's door was closed and I did not really want to knock.
"Will," I said.

*

I depend on Hamlet. I always have. It has always been true: I believe Hamlet when she tells me the difference between right and wrong. I believe her because I believe I have to.

Hamlet and I steal. We aren't above the law, but the way this system works, no one wants us to fall below it. We are not even unusual in our proclivities. It is just that now security cameras are ubiquitous in retail. Evidence accrues with every step.

We talk about kidnapping girls we know. I guess I could say that we "joke" about it, but we are too limited for that. There is no humor in our speculations. Everybody has things we don't know how they got. No one tells us anything about hard work and rewards. There is something called "the market."

We think ransom would be a good way to get a lot of cash.

I don't know what Hamlet and I need this money for. Hamlet wants to run away, but I could not go with her. Hamlet wants to cover her neck in jewels. She wants to get a tattoo on her thigh and become a crime lord. She might like to lose an eye or take a familiar. She rants to me, at all times, about the things she could become.

I walk in the city. I have to go to school, of course, but whenever I am not at school or listening to Hamlet monologue about her coming transformation, I take the subway down the island and walk back up it again. I don't know why I do this. The only people who notice me seem not to have homes. It is mostly men. I am thirteen and a girl, and they are not afraid of me. I don't always stop to talk, but when I do, most of what they say makes sense. I carry change, stale candy, plastic toys I no longer want. I quickly stop with the candy and toys because the candy scares or angers some recipients and one man attempts to return a plastic cocktail monkey I've dropped into his cup along with seventeen cents. It's an enormous

mess and I'm embarrassed for days. I've disturbed the natural order.
I don't know how to live.

Everyone in the city who has money could give money to those who
do not have it, but they don't. It could happen any day yet never will.

*

My mother tells me to go in and visit my father. "His colleague bought
him out of the practice," she says. "He's very happy."

"I thought you said we did not have to worry about money?"

"I did. And I was right!"

My mother does not sleep in the bedroom with my father
anymore. There is a room behind the kitchen that she used to call
"the den" that now she calls "the maid's room." After dinner she
says, "I'm just going to the maid's room." She keeps on telling me
how happy my father is, given his sale of his practice to a younger
man I think I met once on Long Island. The man seemed so clean
and dynamic.

My parents' bedroom is painted pale green. The carpet is pale,
too. There's a buzzing sound from a humidifier and a smell like stale
popcorn mixed with animal reek.

The door, hung with a heavy mirror, is ajar. I knock, producing a
ringing. The mirror is loose, vibrates in its attachments.

"Yes?" my father says from the bed.

"It's me," I say.

"Who?"

"Your daughter," I say. "It's me."

"I have a daughter?"

I am pushing the door now, so that I can go in. Is there any other
direction in which to go?

"How are you feeling, Papa?" I ask. I think of myself as a character
in a movie, an image, something that is a shadow and therefore casts
no shadow. I hear the sound of my own voice. I sound bright, I think.
I sound female. I am dutiful.

In the case this is a movie, the audience is duly won over to my side. I am apparent to them as a responsible style of being, one for whom they should feel sympathy, even a general human pride.

I think about the audience thinking about me. I give myself extra points. I am a hero.

But then the vision fades. We are right back where we were. There is the low-pitched stink of humanity, the sighing bedsprings. A bedside lamp is on.

"I almost didn't recognize you," my father says. He is lying on his back atop a tangle of blankets that somehow looks like another body underneath him. His back is slightly arched and he does not look at me.

I decide, again, that it does not matter if he knows me. I have, I think, the audience for that.

I consult the audience again. I had been ready to abandon them, just moments ago. Thank god they are still here. They admit that they adore my stoicism.

I cover the smell with thematic music. The audience holds its breath.

I am walking around the bed now. I can feel my father's eyes connect with my form. He is wearing a loose-fitting pair of cotton pants and a T-shirt.

My father does not move, but his eyes follow me. I am walking toward the light. Next to the bedside table there is an antique chair that is never used. It was designed for the malnourished of the previous century. It creaks, accepting me.

My hair has grown since the time of the haircut. Also, I do things to make myself appear more recognizably female. I wear clothes that are too small, as well as makeup.

My father's head turns. "I really would not have recognized you," he repeats, with a difference.

The audience examines my unchanging face. It applauds.

I am trying not to look at my father's body. I know that he knows that I am making an effort. In a different family, this would be because I do not want to make him conscious of how decrepit he has become. In our family, it is because I do not want to look at my father's body, precisely because he wants me to.

I wonder how much the audience knows about all of this. Can they reconcile it with what they formerly took to be the plot? Do I still meet with their approval?

Unfortunately, the bedside lamp is blinding me. I can no longer tell what's going on, out there in the crowd.

There is, by the way, no question for me as to whether my father knows the revulsion that I feel. He knows it. It is a force that can sustain him, a metaphorical milk.

I say, "Mom said that you were happy. You sold your practice."

"She's talking about me again?"

I don't know how to answer. I'm working hard not to breathe through my nose.

I say, "It's good we don't have to worry."

"Why would we worry?" My father is louder now. I do something quick with my mind where I see an image of myself doing exactly what I am doing now and I cause that image to be the scene playing on a television set that I am watching. The scene in which I am watching this television set now becomes the scene inside the film.

Some members of the audience yawn. Others settle in for metacommentary. This is, after all, art.

I'm glad that I have thought of this, that I'm in touch with the audience again. I'm not answering my father's question.

I remember how, two years ago, before the first of my father's twin injuries, we had gone on a family vacation to Italy. It was a long vacation. I ate endlessly. In the moments when I ate, then I could think and feel. I was alone in the universe. I could think, and I was free. My thought seethed out over infinite fields. I understood the intelligence of birds and the music of insects. I was pacified. I walked in the heat and viewed the chiseled intricacies of great cities of the time of Shakespeare, the culture he sought to imitate—their mournful, fated, urbane Christianity and the many drapes depicted in paint. I looked forward to meals.

We were in the country, soon. We stayed in a hotel, in a single large room into which, to my deep chagrin, a small supplementary bed was wheeled. The room had a piney smell, sugars and dust.

Doves rustled beyond the shuttered windows beside my cot, out of which I could make out the hard, pill-like form of an Italian moon. It slid across the night, seemingly pleased with its progress.

In the mornings here, I woke up feeling ill. I hoped for quantities of bread. The area was picturesque. We ate out of doors and observed a fashion shoot, models in ball gowns wading in flower beds.

I snacked and watched. I often felt ready, now, to swoon in my desire for food. I asked if one day I would be a model.

My mother looked shocked but my father was quicker. "You're getting fat!" he shouted.

I did not know what to do. I pulled the bun from my mouth.

"You're going to be fat, is what," my father continued, now quieter, snide but invested. It seemed my innocence regarding my own metabolism was doing him personal harm. "You're fat already, the way you eat." He paused. "You can't eat that! That makes you fat!" Then my father got up and went away to do who knew what, pay a bill or consult a newspaper.

I resolved, meanwhile, never to eat again. In my mind's eye, I envisioned tearing my own stomach out, grilling it, serving it to models, who consumed it with electric relish.

Here my mother spoke. "You know your father's right."

So perhaps it was that day. This might have been when I stood alone in the large room in the Italian hotel and breathed on the mirrored doors of the incongruously modern closet, and, in the condensation, an oval at the level of my face, wrote the words FUCK YOU. Then wiped them out.

That afternoon, after tennis, my father found me.

He was thin in his fresh clothes. He looked glad. He seemed to have forgotten all about my eating. Perhaps he was even inspired.

"I have something I need to ask you," he informed me.

I was still deep in my resolution never to eat again, and this made me resist speech.

"Do you know anything," my father said, as we stood beside a swimming pool, "about some writing in the room?"

I already knew exactly what he was getting at and cursed my earlier self. I continued, however, to look at my father. "Like letters?" I asked. I added, nonsensically, "We ran out of stamps."

I observed as it dawned upon my father that I might be devious. I thought of him holding down a cat as he injected it with a blue serum.

"No," my father said. "Not that kind of writing. It's something that surprised me. I took a shower after my game. On the closet door there was some writing. I don't think it was there the other day. Do you know anything about it?"

I could feel all the incoherent pieces that made me up.

"I don't know," I said.

My father appeared confident. "So you don't want to know what it said?"

Some months earlier, back in the United States, driving up the West Side Highway past graffitied boulders, I had asked my mother the meaning of a word. It was a little like I had asked her the meaning of life, in the most offensive fashion possible.

The road was crowded with people going over sixty miles per hour.

"It means to hurt someone."

"So when they write that they're saying, 'Hurt you'?"

"Yes."

"'I want to hurt you.'"

"Something like that." My mother was annoyed. "Don't ever say that." She stared ahead in the front passenger seat.

"Because that's the worst thing that you can say?"

"It is the worst thing you can say."

My father did not say anything.

Now in the countryside in Italy my father stood beside me above the spangling pool. I was worried that models might appear and begin swimming.

I must have been taking too long, because my father said, "You must already know what it said, if you don't want to know."

I tried to keep my face blank. The five or six different people I was in this moment grew restless on the hillock or stage; they shuffled around. I was afraid that some of them might run away. I shook my head.

"So you don't know anything about this?" My father was languid. He could take his time. His dominion was, after all, complete.

I signaled wordlessly that I did not know.

"You want me to tell you what it said?"

I did not move.

"Do you?"

The pool was burning.

"I didn't recognize you," he tells me again.

It is night. I go to bed.

*

I speak about some things to Hamlet. Maybe in truth I don't speak about very much. I think I say to her, "A boy winked at me."

"I bet," Hamlet says. She says, "You have a mustache. You're young to have that."

Hamlet is slightly right, in that I do have a mustache. No one else seems to notice. However, Hamlet likes me best.

Hamlet says, "Too bad about your dad."

"Yes."

"Anyways, you should help them out. Get it over with."

I ask Hamlet what she means.

Hamlet says, "Maybe you'd be happier if you were free."

We are in a diner on 79th Street when Hamlet says this. I am looking at the burnt part of a fry.

Hamlet is, again, slightly correct. This is why she is my friend.

"Your dad can't move, right?"

"I don't know," I say. "I don't really know what's wrong with him."

"He's not paralyzed but he can't really move?"

I nod. I slowly eat what I perceive to be the smallest fry. I have read in a magazine that a way to eat less is to eat more slowly. To count the number of times one chews. To count one's breaths. To be mindful of the hands' movements toward utensils and, if possible, to count that, too.

Hamlet is speaking to me. "You're saying he can't, right?"

"Yes."

Hamlet says that she recently learned on television that many old people are smothered with pillows by their relatives. You can't tell that they didn't die in their sleep.

I do not say anything. I look out onto 79th Street, which is a pointless place. It is a clear day in February, milk blue. I look at the remnants of a bicycle, chained to a post. I feel the hairs at the back of my neck stand up. Perhaps I need to defecate.

Hamlet says, "You have options as far as your mother is concerned. In a way, I don't know if you could handle being on your own. That's not for everyone. In a way, I doubt you genuinely could. But you have to think about what happens after. What is she going to do? Think hard. Could the same thing happen again?"

I don't know what Hamlet means. Still, we sit in the diner until it is night. The food is terrible and the only reason they stay in business is they don't kick anyone out.

Later, I don't walk home. I take a couple of sighing buses. I make some black tea and carry it to my desk.

I walk by my parents' room, now my father's room. He is asleep.

All the lights are on. I look at the pillows on my bed.

*

Hamlet has grown disgusted with me again. She doesn't talk about it, but I know my hesitation does not sit well with her. It's not that she feels I am disloyal. She sees I lack imagination.

I do not want to carry out her plans.

People used to say that Hamlet was a genius and a beauty, but they do not say this anymore. She sits at a weird lunch table and wears a safety pin through one ear. I'd term this derivative, but nobody is asking me.

In school plays, she's somebody who waits along the roadside, a crone. If I had to imagine her inside a painting, she would be a blue horse or the distant pasture where it stamps along. She is a fleck at the horizon.

Hamlet sits with a girl who always wears galoshes and does not wash her blouse. She sits with the rodent girl who irons her hair and pencils in her brows too much. I sit with all the nerds. The nerds pity me, but they only want to talk about the homework. They basically look fine.

Hamlet isn't speaking to me. For days, then weeks, then months, then almost a year—which is when it happens. Within a six-week period, both of Hamlet's parents die.

Her father has a heart attack. Her mother dies of cancer. It is extraordinary. Everyone says so.

I can't help thinking that Hamlet made this happen. She has made a wish.

Hamlet leaves. She goes to another school.

I hear, when we are sixteen, that Hamlet has a baby. I don't go to see her. It's not because I'm not allowed.

By this time, my father is in a home. Meanwhile, my mother goes out every night.

I get my mother to let me buy a toy poodle and for some reason I name it Hecuba.

*

But even before this, before he is gone, my father and my fiend, I began.

His closet smelled of shoe polish and loose tobacco, the shirts in bags from cleaning, pressed flat. He slept, drugged. I crept. I embraced the pants on their hangers, folded myself into jackets. The garments were shelter. They were architecture, curtains. A horizon and the province of men. They were tombs, sorrow and safety. A business. I took them away to my room. I tried and wore them. They fit me. My father was, you will recall, a small man.

B.

THE GOLDEN FLEECE

Démocrite Charlus LeGouffre
and the Search for Reconnaissance

Roger Herbsweet

_____ University Press, _____, _____
1978

Library of Congress Cataloguing in Publication Data

Herbsweet, Roger, 1941–
  The Golden Fleece : Démocrite Charlus LeGouffre and the search for
reconnaissance / Roger Herbsweet

  Bibliography: p.
  Includes index.
  1. LeGouffre, Démocrite Charlus, 1829–??—Life.
  2. LeGouffre, Démocrite Charlus, 1829–??—Writing.
  I. Title.
  PS ⸺   ⸺   ⸺
  ISBN ⸺

ACKNOWLEDGMENTS

This study had its unnoticed conception more than ten years ago with my purchase, aged fourteen and a half or so, from a secondhand bookshop on _____ Street in Cambridge, Massachusetts, of a two-volume collection of the poet Paul Éluard's correspondence. The two august volumes were read, pondered and underlined, and, then, retired to one of my fashionable mother's neglected book cabinets—among the very few truly secure spaces in that rather porous house—to be all but entirely forgotten until the second semester of my doctoral course, when Professor A_____ von D_____, through his interest in the pleasures, games, and innovations of the Parisian avant-garde, communicated some of the same spark to me. It is to these two encounters that I owe my own discovery of and interest and pleasure in the life and writings of the man known as Démocrite Charlus LeGouffre.

The strangers who inhabit the country of the past are always in motion, and it is nineteenth-century figures who, to my mind, seem to change the most radically over time. I would therefore like to thank Professor F. A_____ B_____, now of the University of _____, and Professor L_____ P. S___, _____ State University, for their allowing me to engage in the studies that led to this book. I am under special obligation to the *fonds* Démocrite Charlus LeGouffre and the late Laël Edelbrot-Mélaton who scrupulously maintained it and selflessly made herself available to provide this researcher with invaluable *reconnaissance*.

Lastly, it is necessary to record here that my former fiancée—now enviably capable wife—produced a flawless manuscript copy. Beginning from an irregular assortment of pages and notes, she made sense of near-madness. She is to be lauded by the reader and by scholars everywhere who lack the finer skills of typing.

CONTENTS

THE GOLDEN FLEECE

INTRODUCTION

By the 1830s, cross-dressing had become, if not *de rigueur*, then a subject of tabloid fascination and frequent speculation among the fashionable in Paris. As is only natural, those who scrupulously pursued the fashionable were also swept up by this craze.

I shall return to this matter momentarily. In the chapters to follow, the reader will find a study of the life and works of Démocrite Charlus LeGouffre, sometimes known as Charles or "Charlie" LeGouffre, poet and author of narrative prose, born in 1829 in a Parisian seraglio and deceased at a later date in an unknown location, thought by some, inclusive of the author, to be Mexico City, where he is conjectured to have journeyed at some point previous to the *Expédition du Mexique*, or *Segunda intervención francesa*, of 1861, which, as we know, was Napoleon III's poorly conceived military incursion undertaken to secure loan payments.

Evidence for LeGouffre's presence in Mexico City in the 1860s is mostly if not entirely due to limited correspondence with his contemporary, the painter Édouard Manet (1832–1883), who in 1867 began work on a large-scale history painting depicting the execution of the emperor of Mexico, Maximilian. This puppet ruler was born, coincidentally, in the same year as the painter, making this something of an unconscious self-portrait. In two letters dating from the year of the emperor's death, LeGouffre, who at this time had taken mercenary work as a professional photographer, recounted events to the artist, with whom he was not personally acquainted but with whom he had begun an exchange of letters at the urging of an old intimate of the woman who was probably his mother, LeGouffre having been recommended to Manet as a reliable source of information, due to the former's presence in Mexico City probably dating from the early 1850s.

Amazing though it may seem, it is this pair of letters, rather than LeGouffre's quietly celebrated novella, *Passe-partout*, that secured the author's place in history. Beloved to at least one historian of art for their precise descriptions and visionary insights, these two briefs are also in part, if not wholly, responsible for the surrealists' resuscitation of LeGouffre. In 1925 or '26, while researching an article later published as "Manet raconté par lui-même," the late scholar Laël Edelbrot-Mélaton (1901–1977) conferred with the surrealist poet Paul Éluard (1895–1952), who was then entering his Communist period and keen on political imagery of the past. Éluard's youthful interest in the poetry of Walt Whitman provided the originating spark that led the pair to retrace LeGouffre's path in reverse: from Mexico City back to New Orleans, where he had journeyed with Whitman in 1848, after Whitman had accepted the offer of a position as editor-in-chief at the *Crescent* newspaper; and thence back to New York City, where, in dialogue with another magisterial poet, Whitman's doomed rival Edgar Allan Poe, LeGouffre had composed *Passe-partout*, destined for highly specialized publication in January of 1857 in the first and only edition of the Parisian journal *Le Loup charmant*, which serialized fiction and presented accounts of *flânerie* and bizarre events at the theater. Éluard was able to obtain a copy of this rare *feuilleton* by way of an extremely resourceful antiquities dealer and shared his discovery with G_____ T____, the book designer, binder, collector, and poet, who, together with Maurice Heine, was then engaged in recirculating the works of the Marquis de Sade. Collaboratively, these three produced a limited run of *Passe-partout*, published as a novella and *livre d'artiste*, with illustrations by Joan Miró, who had recently joined forces with the surrealist painter and collagist Max Ernst (a rival of Éluard's) on designs for balletomane Sergei Diaghilev. When, in the following year of 1928, André Breton's *Nadja* appeared, there were some who would say that Breton's book could not have been written without the precedent of the "sheen of magic cast upon time by the strange, pre-historical movements of objects," as imagined by LeGouffre.

Thus, although this study does not encompass LeGouffre's rehabilitation by the surrealists, it owes something to them, and, beyond this, it must also disentangle itself from the LeGouffre they created, a figure of liberation and synthesis, somewhat in the mold of Claude Henri de Rouvroy, the comte de Saint-Simon's reading of the utopian social philosophy of Charles Fourier, in which the androgyne is seen as key to the end of all of society's woes. Éluard, who could not resist appending a preface to the 1927 edition of *Passe-partout*, referred to LeGouffre as a "rare Janus," someone who lived forward and backward and in more than one world at once, who was "reputed to have been born a woman before he became a man." The strange rhyme with the plot of Virginia Woolf's uneven experiment *Orlando*, published in October of 1928, is too pronounced to be omitted.

I have endeavored to bear in mind the myths of the 1830s in light of which biographical information may have become bent or skewed. We recall that when the novelist George Sand—who still went as Madame Aurore Dudevant—first left her husband's château to come to Paris in 1831, she began wearing men's attire because it was less costly and made movement easier (male footgear, in particular, enabled her to traverse Paris's cobbled thoroughfares more easily, as she wrote in her letters), but also because it conferred notoriety. Sand's decision, as we must understand it, was not merely personally pragmatic but necessary for her professional success, particularly given the shocking nature of her work. Yet, when her prose began to appear in 1833 authored by "George Sand," she was always reviewed in both the French and English press as a woman, and it was not until 1837, four years later, that her cross-dressing also became part of the response to her writing. When this did transpire, it took the following uncertain and suggestive form, as we read in the British journal *Atheneum*, in a piece by Jules Janin: "George

Sand, in his own home, is, by turns, a capricious young man, of eighteen, and a very pretty young woman of from five-and-twenty to thirty—a youth of eighteen, who smokes and takes snuff with peculiar grace, and a grand dame whose brilliancy and fancy at once astonish and humble you."

As we see, Janin's interest is not merely in the clothing worn by this figure, but in the novelist's apparent dual nature, which he attempts to account for by reading her as at once male and female, young and old; a stylish rake and learned genius. Sand was not, in fact, both male and female, but her way of living made her appear so, superficially speaking. Janin, one must own, seems extremely entertained by Sand; she is a harlequin: a changeable, checkered being; a walking scandal.

Given that not one but three major novels dealing with transvestism and androgyny appear in the late 1820s and 1830s— Latouche's *Fragoletta* (1829), Balzac's *Séraphita* (1834–35), and Gautier's *Mademoiselle de Maupin* (1835)—it seems timely that a legend might grow up around a precocious child raised in a fashionable house. Although the record of LeGouffre's birth is not extant, a supplementary document, created when the boy would have been about seven years old and acquired by Edelbrot-Mélaton in the course of her researches, testifies to his true sex. It is fully in keeping with the imaginative tendencies of the surrealists to have propagated the legend of a holy androgyne. Éluard's preface, which sometimes slides into "automatic writing," the poet's brand of inspired language, is fanciful and self-interested. Éluard saw himself as particularly concerned with the eternal feminine spirit, due to his status as a bard in search of a muse. It is quite possible that he chose to continue the fiction surrounding LeGouffre as a way of exploring his own creative identity and strengthening public perception regarding his own gift.

In Gautier's relevant fiction, *Mademoiselle de Maupin*, published just six short years after LeGouffre's birth, the title character proclaims, "It often happens that the sex of the soul does not at all correspond with that of the body, and this is a contradiction which cannot fail to produce great disorder. . . . Beneath my smooth forehead and silken hair move strong and manly thoughts." Based on the real historical figure, La Maupin, a seventeenth-century French female aristocrat who had learned fencing as a child and traveled in men's clothing with her lover, a fencing instructor, before eventually becoming a celebrated opera singer who died an early death, Gautier's Maupin lives only for love. An exercise in following an absurd premise to a titillating conclusion, Gautier's novel was banned for its salacious content in various quarters, no doubt causing the book to be all the more widely read. I cannot but imagine that this oft-repeated tale of the woman who disguises herself as a man—certainly more possible in the theater than in everyday life—which was reaching a frenzied peak of popularity during the third and fourth decades of the nineteenth century, shaped the rumors surrounding LeGouffre.

But *why?* Throughout the nineteenth century, as during every other epoch known to human history, artists and writers were obsessed with the image of such a person. This obsession owed little to biological or scientific realities, and even less to life as it was lived. Is this not reason enough to account for the popularity of such a conception? I would wager that it is, and that it is not therefore necessary to seek explanation further afield. In spite of certain fads entering the academy, the reader will find that in this study, at least, the possibility of pure imagination is respected.

Thus, the present work seeks to illuminate more relevant aspects of the life and times of Démocrite Charlus LeGouffre. Our tale begins with LeGouffre's early childhood in Paris, moving through his adolescence in the second chapter, and on to the trials he faced in the first moments of maturity, his flight to America, the composition of his grand novella, and the crucial correspondence with Manet. I conclude with a summation of the themes broached in these chapters, demonstrating that

LeGouffre's oeuvre, although slender in the extreme, is nevertheless worthy of our attention.

This has been my quest, and we shall turn to the quest of another man, whose unusual fate was to carry him far in his search for a usable sense of self.

1

THE ACTRESS WHO COULD NOT ACT
AND "L'ENFANT DOUÉ"

The century began with the devolution of reason into revolution. It was then marked by the rise of industry, urbanism, technology, and, above all, capital. It began as a time of promise and terror, republicanism and knives, and concluded as an epoch of images, publics, moral panics, pandemics, mobilizations, fads.

At the dawn of this century, in the English port city of Brighton, in 1806, an Eliza Maria was born to a Mr. and Mrs. William Waast. Waast, listed as a "Concert master" in public record, had fathered some seventeen offspring with his wife, twelve of whom survived past early childhood, a number only mildly remarkable for the period. Eliza was the eleventh. Her home was full of shouting, singing, and dance, with siblings "to suit all tastes, nut brown and blond and of all other varieties, so myriad that it is no longer possible to recall their exact characteristics," as she later wrote. In this same account, the author maintained that her father, a "serjeant-trumpeter" known by the nickname Crispy, had died when she was five. However, it seems that Bill "Crispy" Waast in fact abandoned his spouse and legitimate dependents and emigrated to the United States (probably around the conclusion of the 1810s), where, according to one source, he went on to remarry four times, fathering no fewer than eighteen additional children.

Eliza, meanwhile, benefiting from the resources of a maternal grandmother who maintained a mysterious independence in London, was sent to a boarding school outside Boulogne at the age of ten. Here she learned passable French, as well as other skills appropriate to a girl of her standing. Upon her return to London, rather than the place of her birth, she lived with this grandmother, a Mrs. Neckcloth, taking work at a milliner's. In her memoir, Eliza tells of this fateful era: One afternoon, exiting her place of employment, Eliza, just fifteen, encountered a middle-aged man who offered to accompany her to a pastry shop. "'Care for a sweet?' said he. I shyly acquiesced." Leading the girl instead to a tavern, this opportunist plied the innocent with grog, taking her to bed once she was fully incapacitated. Eliza awoke to a stack of bills, and thus began the career of a *grande horizontale*.

Eliza Maria Waast wasted no time bemoaning her state. The satyr's payment had the redeeming quality of being generous, and she knew "there was no return." She did not consult the grandmother, instead rented a modest furnished apartment, and, with the lustrous complexion, good figure, and cunning verbal skill that would later earn her the title of La Scintillante, obtained the affections of men of means, although she avoided her first despoiler: "I have never again seen the man who played wolf to my Little Red Riding Hood. He was, it appears, a diamond merchant."

There are, as is so often the case with autobiographical writing of this genre (usually composed with the motive of profit), reasons to doubt this account. Reconciling various dates, it would seem that Eliza would have been at least nineteen during this period and therefore of an age to recognize a carnal proposition. Secondly, and more seriously, there was a strong connection between girls in milliners' shops and prostitution in mid-nineteenth-century London. In Paris, these pliable young persons were known as *grisettes*, for the coarse gray fabric from which their costumes were constructed. Working-class women, even in skilled trades, earned less than a third of what their male counterparts did. They might take a wealthy older lover to supplement their pitiful income before they married, usually with a man of their own class.

Eliza Maria Waast never received a marriage proposal. Operating under the name Mary Walter, she took briefly to the stage. Her typical English brashness served her well there. In the eighteenth century, abductions were not uncommon for actresses in London, and, even in the early part of the second decade of the nineteenth, one was not out of the way of such things. Yet, the theater was also a means of social mobility. It is known that a personage of no lesser nobility than Charles II condescended to take mistresses from the stage. It was also the case that so-called She tragedies were coming into vogue. Actresses elevated themselves by playing more refined male roles. In 1776, that liberal year when all bets were off, Sarah Siddons portrayed the Dane Hamlet in Birmingham and, in 1777, in Manchester, going on to reprise the role in Liverpool in 1778, Edinburgh and Bristol in 1781, and Dublin in 1802. Although Edward Vining's argument, advanced toward the end of the century, i.e., that Hamlet is actually a princess in disguise ("She has been secretly raised as a boy for reasons of state and is trapped in that fiction"), is preposterous, some perverse desire for originality on the part of audiences had long resulted in transvestism in this hero. Usually this was for benefit nights (a "benefit freak"), and in 1796, at Drury Lane, Jane Powell was probably the first woman to act Hamlet in London. (In the mid-century, several Americans walked the boards in breeches: Charlotte Cushman and Fanny Wallack. Sarah Bernhardt did, as well; we also know her profane history.)

While all this is mostly irrelevant to Waast/Walter, her brief and somewhat shadowy career as a thespian, glossed over in her memoir as private readings of abridged plays, has been the focus of some critics, if for ill-advised reasons. A series of unrelated facts hardly amounts to a zeitgeist. Nor does it signify, as has also been put forth, that "The Player Queen, a male actor in drag, recalls the fact that both Ophelia and Gertrude would at one point have been mere performances of femaleness." Waast/Walter encountered, at some point in this period, an individual whom she names "Mr. Petrie," a man she claims had "a heart like a pumpkin fricasseed in snow." It was a match of convenience, although the two seem to have been well suited. Traveling together to Paris, probably in early 1827, when "Mary Walter" would have been approximately twenty-one, they came to the mutual agreement that "Mary" would be better off alone and "Mr. Petrie" must return to London, after seeing to her comfortable establishment.

One might well deduce that Mary/Eliza had become a specialist of some sort. Either she held secrets that "Mr. Petrie" trembled to think might be revealed, or she had promised him future delights, should his affairs bring him back to France. In the aforementioned memoir, "Mr. Petrie"'s actions are treated as a matter of course. Subsequently, in this second city, soon to be the first city of the ongoing century, the site of the Bourbon Restoration and a magnet for immigrants from the French countryside, both Eliza Marie Waast and Mary Walter disappeared. They were replaced by "Henrietta Diamond," a courtesan of considerable ingenuity. She was sometimes called Heni Diamond, a pun on her native tongue, *any diamond*. Common and rare, *douce* and cruel, crude yet unreachable, free yet ever for sale, she typified the contradictions of a growing *demi-monde*, a term that did not reach polite ears until 1855, via Alexandre Dumas, *fils*.

Prostitution's history in France is hardly remarkable. By the 1900s, it had its own well-established vocabulary, mostly stemming from the barnyard. In one sense, we translate *grisette*, a word we have seen just above, as a "warbler, lark, duck, weevil, butterfly"; yet we already know the other meaning. A *cocotte* is a hen. A *biche* could be a doe or female dog, and a *chameau* may be a camel or cow, as well as a heartless bitch who exploits credulous men. The humor implied by these sobriquets is possibly related to the nation's reluctant tolerance of its oldest profession. Although prostitutes and those who sheltered them had been subject to banishment and seizure of property since Charlemagne's day, such prohibitions were almost always followed by periods of tolerance, during which special neighborhoods were established.

By the fifteenth century, it was more common to see the institution of sumptuary laws governing the dress of prostitutes, as well as clipping of ears and noses, than more extreme remedies associated with the ever-unfinished *projet de règlement pour les prostituées.*

After the revolution in France, the *laissez-faire* attitude of the eighteenth century was replaced by a new concern. In 1791, abortion became illegal, even if Napoleonic law did not generally punish women who self-administered drugs. In 1802, free facilities for examining prostitutes for venereal disease were generously established. Meanwhile, the Napoleonic Code of 1804 mostly avoided discussion of the legal status of women, save for those who were married and therefore received sensible guidelines. Divorce, which had been briefly permitted from 1792 to 1816, was outlawed and the filing of paternity suits prohibited.

Even with attempts to regulate a complex industry, rates of infection from venereal disease leading up to the 1820s were extraordinary. In Paris, a formal registration of prostitutes was undertaken. Those registered were known as *filles soumises.* They had "submitted" to the state, which would assume their care. We must recall, as well, the rise of the love-marriage during the nineteenth century. Wives were coming into possession of elevated moral ground and demanded, if passively, that appearances be maintained.

There were multiple classes of prostitute in Paris at this time. There were women owned by brothels and there were independent workers, known as *filles en carte.* A *fille en carte* might have a program by means of which a *clique* of male clients purchased her favors *en bloc*, deciding among themselves who would go to her on which day of the week. This pooling of resources was thought to be a prudent safeguard against the scourge of syphilis. The *fille en carte* received the complimentary *contrôle sanitaire*, which took place at the prison-hospital of Saint-Lazare. Above the *filles en carte* were the *femmes galantes.* These were true courtesans, kept women, and they were always unregistered. It is to their *rang* that Balzac's creation Valérie Marneffe pertains, she who is so interesting for her revival of eighteenth-century fashions.

Although one did not join the *demi-monde* by choice, a woman did have certain privileges once she was there. Foremost among these was the ability to copy the *haut monde*. It was frequently stated, by the middle of the century, that it was no easy task to distinguish between genteel ladies of birth and well-compensated courtesans. Although the two categories almost never conversed, they imitated each other, with courtesans taking the lead in the course of their golden age, 1852–70. A wise woman, who avoided the amorous profession, once said, "A professional lover requires two digestive systems and the strength of four seamstresses." A courtesan was indubitably employed and, in a sense, worked hard, although one might say that she had little enough to do. It was her role to lavish, rather than scrimp and save, the funds provided by a wealthy protector on luxuries such as fresh exotic flowers, quantities of champagne, and refined dress. The age demanded that the kept woman stand as an ostentatious symbol of her benefactor's status. She was not just a vessel but also an artist of publicity.

In spite of the relative privacy maintained by courtesans, they were not entirely immune from Paris's ambition to improve itself. There were several well-meaning attempts made during the Restoration to submit *femmes galantes*, the prostitutes who served the upper classes, to the gratis health exam. In 1817, the police hired a "M. V_____" to assist. His project led to the arrest of about five dozen individuals, who were subject to rigorous exams. Spoiled rich men protested, and the police were powerless to continue. However, in the fall of 1820, *les gendarmes* came up with the clever notion of *petite* dispensaries, which were somewhat more secluded examination chambers. Unfortunately, even this plan was suppressed by 1822. Further attempts were made up until about 1830, when, for unknown reasons, this was deemed no longer feasible. Despite scrupulous records of their movements kept by the authorities, courtesans remained, in effect, largely un-policed for the rest of the century, even as venereal disease spread wildly.

The common prostitute was sometimes affected by a "*maison close* policy," which kept her indoors, at the mercy, beck, and call of a madam, but not so the courtesan, who, even as she worked constantly, was constantly free.

This was the situation of Heni Diamond. She had apparently chosen the right side of the Industrial Revolution. Certainly, it was unusual for prostitutes of any length of experience to have children. Perhaps this was due to the pioneering efforts of individuals like Francis Place, disseminator of birth-control pamphlets of the 1820s, who wrote with a monomaniacal enthusiasm about prophylactic sponges, "large as a green walnut or small apple," which do not "diminish enjoyment." Perhaps folk remedies or rudimentary diaphragms, a squeezed half lemon, did the trick. Or, perhaps most prostitutes had undergone so many abortions that they were no longer able to conceive at all. And perhaps Heni's dream of discovering a male child inside an oversized cabbage in the Jardin des _____ holds some grain of truth.

Thus, it was just before yet another revolution would transform the political shape of Parisian life that Heni's unconventional household came to include a child of significance for our purposes, one Démocrite Charlus LeGouffre.

But who was the child, and to whom did he belong? Easier to reply to the first question than the second. Born, as stated in a late document, in 1829, young Démocrite entered the world at a time when the liberalization of the French family and the institution of marriage was, as has already been intimated, definitively on the wane. In 1820, the influential idealist of Heidelberg, Georg Wilhelm Friedrich Hegel, published *Elements of the Philosophy of Right*, in which the philosopher gave an account of the individual's relationship to family, nation, history, and God. History, Hegel argued, moved inexorably toward freedom. The citizen participated in this process through two dynamics:

recognition and exchange. Even as every man wants something different from a given exchange, a common will is constituted by co-existing differences. Most perceptively, Hegel showed that processes of exchange must be mediated by the family, where individuals are seen and truly known: *recognized*. So began the era of the "two spheres": private love, public profession. It is not clear to which sphere Démocrite, possibly the offspring of someone whose bed was her office, belonged.

His name offers further clues: In the years after the revolution, names evoking the right of the people to self-governance were *à la mode*. Whether indicating the "laughing philosopher" of antiquity or the simple fact of democracy, the boy's first name memorializes the recent history of France, while his second name might be a reference to his probable mother's Englishness. *Charles* is related to German *Karl* and other Anglo-Saxon terms for "ruler," and it suggests the history of Britain's monarchs. It is difficult not to observe the aspirational latinization, via the *-us* suffix. Whether Heni was the boy's biological mother, it seems certain that his name originated with her pretensions. And here we come to that surname, most anomalous of all. As we know, a *gouffre* is a natural feature of the world: a gulf, chasm, maw, abyss, pit, ravine, hole, mouth, or trap. It is a void that consumes (bodies, money, light, time, meaning, and so on). It is not, the reader will hardly be surprised, a family name of any sort of commonness. It is scarcely a name at all.

It has already been noted that it was not particularly common, during this time, for the ostentatious homes of courtesans to contain natural progeny. As the nineteenth century progressed, it became possible for these unfortunates to be married to one another, in a sort of shadow dynasty, and, via these means, to obtain a modicum of exotic respectability within Paris's ongoing modernization. Such a fate was probably foreseen by LeGouffre's benefactress, even if it was not to come to pass.

Démocrite Charlus represented, we can easily believe, an extravagance on the part of Henrietta Diamond. She lavished education upon the boy, who was said by Éluard to have spoken both ancient Greek and Latin, after a passable fashion, perhaps in the spirit of the education of the essayist Montaigne, although "Madame" Diamond could only have had a vague idea of the great humanist and must have hired a young, energetic tutor to guide the upbringing of Démocrite Charlus, thus unknowingly permitting many gleefully esoteric enthusiasms to run their course. The boy was renowned for his suppleness of limb as well as his eloquence. It seems that an imitator of the cartoonist Honoré Daumier used LeGouffre's likeness for a sketch. The high-bourgeois existence in Paris held great interest for that artist, who depicted an elegant and slender, beribboned adolescent who blushingly informs a customer who seems to have come at an inopportune hour, "Oui, ma mère, elle travaille . . ." This piece was titled *L'ENFANT DOUÉ*.

Yet, it is difficult to say if, talent and comeliness aside, young Démocrite, or "Charlie," as he came to be known, perhaps in deference to the fashion for all things British, would have considered his existence a gift.

2

A BRIEF STAY IN THE HALF-WORLD

After the July Revolution of 1830, which brought to power King Louis-Philippe, Paris held the mecca of gambling in Europe, the Palais-Royale. This pleasure dome was but a gateway to others. He who won here went on to win. The city's celebrated covered walkways of iron and glass, built over fifteen years, roughly 1822 to 1837, were the hiding places, the nests of a secret life. The Parisian gambler converted the arcade into a second casino, a gambling den, where now and then, if he were feeling providential, he could place a colorful *jeton* of emotion on some public woman, a rouged face that appeared lovable in artificial lighting. Fate and chance were beginning to play new roles under the July Monarchy. The emphasis on rational chains of causality and the description of events from this point of view that so characterized the Enlightenment were being revised for a new age, one that concerned itself with, above all else, the interests of an autonomous individual.

LeGouffre would have understood implicitly what lay behind the face paint worn by the woman who claimed him as her dependent, as well as what it meant to be the client of such a woman. It comes as no surprise that he himself might become the author of similar illusions. We might also say that he was the type of person whose luck was of the sort that was perpetually threatening to run out. And, by the time he noticed what a lucky person he was, that he was at once gifted and free, it may have already been too late for him to capitalize on these facts, an irony that of course haunts his solitary masterpiece, *Passe-partout*.

Here is a thumbnail sketch of the boy, a *croquis*, as he would likely have appeared in the year 1844, when he was fourteen or fifteen years old:

> His face strongly resembles the curtains in theaters: it rises to reveal a pre-ordained scenario. When it falls, one has the sense that one should take one's leave. "Charlie," as they call him, is an irreplaceable fixture of a certain set. His round face is never more childish than when he is at the table, betting prodigiously against the bank. A sprig of black hair points upward, past all chandeliers and toward the celestial firmament, communicating incessantly with the goddess Fortune, who is doubtless inexperienced with the young and therefore easier to command than the boy's own mother. His feet, however, are firmly planted on the ground. One is given to strange fantasies, regarding possible political careers.

As the author of this column, provided to me by Edelbrot-Mélaton, knew only too well, Charlie LeGouffre would need to make his own way in the world. Society planned to test him and perhaps to make an example of him, should he fail.

It is also the case that Charlie, or "the Young Democrat," as he was also occasionally termed when one comes across a sighting of him in print or in correspondence from this era via the *fonds* LeGouffre, now far from being the bashful child depicted by Daumier's imitator, was protected by the contemporary *demi-monde*'s enthronement of the inexplicable. He was permitted to gamble while underage not simply because he understood the rules of the game, nor because of his "mother"'s wealth, but because society recognized that gambling is a celebration of the present, a bacchanal continually renewing its rejection of history as well as one's personal past. It is also related to an infantile pretention to omnipotence, which we might additionally describe as a desire to give birth to oneself.

Here we must again turn to the rumors regarding the boy's

sex. It may be helpful to note at the outset that Parisian hedonism had come to such a point that it was now, perhaps paradoxically, the height of refinement for a prostitute not to undress. Given the historically dialectical function of payment in the practice of prostitution—in that it pays for what cannot be purchased and always fails to compensate the vendor—it is no wonder that secrecy was a key component of the trade. In this environment, in which all has its price and money gave life to a number on the gaming wheel as well as to the cool flesh of the *cocotte*, secrets grew like vines.

Various references to LeGouffre's "impossibly" pale and "fine" complexion, the "softness" of his "figure," in Éluard's introduction, are to be considered of a part with the milieu in which he was raised and educated. Nor is it possible to overstate the influence of Henrietta Diamond's reinvention of herself in the late 1830s and '40s as a practitioner of *les tables tournantes*. Perhaps even more feminine than the art of seduction, the art of communion with the beyond, with its ectoplasmic excitements and adroitly disguised wires and surreptitious movements of the feet, would have permitted the inexperienced LeGouffre a front row seat to a remunerative blurring of the line between life and death. No doubt it made him a great skeptic.

It would have been enough, had the mercurial Heni contented herself with levitating furniture or secreting alarming quantities of bodily fluid in semi-public. For reasons that are by no means easy to discern, she did not. By piecing together contemporary accounts, one arrives at the following menu for a séance she might enact: The clients are gathered into a salon on the second floor of the *maison* she maintained on the rue des _____. Seated in a hemicycle at the center of the room, beneath dim lighting, these visitors are told that someone who is no longer with them wishes to communicate. It is entirely possible that during the course of this transmission one of them may be overcome by a force beyond his or her control. This sensation, which may be enough to produce temporary paralysis, the visitors are told, begins with a pricking feeling, by means of which the Spirit informs us of its presence. After this, numbness follows. It is not unusual for a participant to spend as much as an hour in a state of incapacitation, although such possessions may be more brief, depending on the sufferer's susceptibility to the ancestral plane. Individuals of finer sensibility are more likely to receive the touch of the beyond. During this period of contact, Heni would enter into a trance-state and, as such, would be unreachable by any other human. She would speak in the voice of the ghost, explaining its wishes and movements.

It would seem a non sequitur here to explain that these performances occurred in the days before pasteurization. Yet, as H_____ Y__ has shown, improvements in food-preservation technology were of great significance to an artist like Diamond. In a longer study of charlatanism of the time, Y__ demonstrates that a courtesan such as Mlle Diamond would have found it nearly impossible to beguile women of means into her establishment without a highly convincing display of supernatural ability. Indeed, as Y__ is also at pains to demonstrate, no respectable woman would ever admit that she had been enticed into the domain of *any diamond*. It is for this reason that accounts of what occurred here are at second hand and stretch the imagination with their ludicrous claims of soul-wrenching professions of love from beyond the grave. Society mocked those who paid—and, as word had it, paid dearly—for such ghoulish conferences, but it seems that there was hardly a person who had heard of Mlle Diamond's talents in these matters, and who possessed the means to purchase them, who did not avail him- or herself of a cautious visit, usually in the company of a trusted confidante. For some *habituées*, the practice could become quite extortionate and, thus, was as perilously impoverishing as it was bizarre.

Y__, who began the arduous climb toward tenure as a scholar of the history of agriculture, has been able to demonstrate that a pseudo-shaman of the July Monarchy such as Heni Diamond must have become aware of the inventions of Nicolas Appert

(1749–1841), the father of modern canning, who began, around the turn of the century, investigating means by which food could be preserved through its enclosure in glass bottles that were subsequently heated to a very high temperature. As Appert's techniques demonstrate, there was a general understanding of food's tendency to become inedible when left enclosed without precautionary cooking. Having studied Diamond's movements after her arrival in Paris through a meticulous consultation of private records and bank statements pertaining to wealthy men, as well as the records of the police, Y___ maintains that it is more than likely that Appert, who, in spite of his humble beginnings, had grown prosperous through his inventions, became one of Diamond's earliest protectors. Y___ argues that the apparently miraculous paralysis recounted by visitors to the Diamond salon can in fact be explained by knowledge, on Diamond's part through her former customer, of the effects of certain food-borne bacteriological toxins on the human organism. Y___ maintains that Diamond might well have dosed her visitors with minute amounts of *botulinum* toxin, a highly deadly substance but naturally occurring and nonfatal when received in very small amounts. These pricked subjects would have experienced a numbing sensation that, as Y___ argues, could even have had a relaxing or elating effect for some, further increasing the pleasure they felt in their supposedly supernatural communion.

Whatever our disposition to Y___'s finely argued history, it is certain that Heni capitalized on her knowledge of the human body as well as her status as someone who remained eternally outside of good society. Yet, the agency accorded to a woman of Diamond's standing is difficult to characterize. Here we must ask again: What of LeGouffre's origins? What, crucially, of his father? We know from his one piece of extant juvenilia, a reasonably accomplished sonnet in the British style, published in a journal of extremely limited circulation in early 1846, "Les Vagues à l'âme," again retained by the eponymous *fonds*, that LeGouffre was capable of writing in the lyric mode about a distant parent who had knowledge of the sea, even as the author compared himself to the mythic hero Jason, one who must travel far in order to claim the singular key to his identity.

Albatrosses rustle throughout the jagged iambs of the poem, and, indeed, it is enough to make one feel a keen longing for a clear sense of nation and, perhaps, patrimony. Still, it seems unlikely that Heni Diamond would have lowered herself to the level of consorting with a mariner, if indeed she was LeGouffre's mother. The sonnet probably speaks more eloquently to a household myth, i.e., that one's father is loving if absent, unreachable but thinking always of the forsaken child. English was spoken, after a fashion, in this home, and LeGouffre was fed a limited diet of anglophone literature. Books were an all-assuaging comfort. It is, for example, known that he read Tennyson.

But before we can come to LeGouffre's subsequent triumph, first we must arrive at his defeat. He was precocious, particularly in relation to pleasures typically reserved for adults. He did his best to keep pace, to maintain his faith in the light of his own genius, even when the recognition he sought was denied him. It is also a well-worn certainty that, in constantly raising the stakes, in hopes of getting back what is lost, the gambler steers ever more surely toward absolute ruin—if, for example, we trust to the metaphor of the boat and the waves that come to rock the soul.

3

IMMORTAL GESTURE

What, in truth, was LeGouffre's crime? Was it to have seen that money's relationship to effort was hardly one of parity or justice? Was it to have grown up within a world founded on the edges of sobriety and respectability? Was it to have lacked a normal family, one in which love, that sacred and priceless substance, was not for sale? Was it to have trusted to chance? So much fell upon his head that it seems a miracle he survived.

It is also possible that the boy LeGouffre, seventeen years old in 1846 and '47, those years leading to another revolution, foresaw, if instinctively, a career for himself. It would have been (and, perhaps it was) a fugitive, if not subterranean, career, given the regulation of gambling in France at this time, but, again, one learns through imitation, and the model set before this sensitive and even studious (in spite of his capers) youth was hardly one of earnest toil.

We must remember above all, given the widespread and spectacular nature of gambling during this time, the way in which it was viewed socially. It was mandatory to participate, yet not to honor one's debts was to utterly destroy one's reputation. To do so was to exclude oneself from any part of Parisian *grand monde*, even its lowest ranks.

What we know of LeGouffre's debts comes to us by way of several ambiguous lines in Heni Diamond's memoirs. As was the case for many courtesans of her time, Heni lived primarily on credit, and the larger part of what her son had wagered must not even have been in her possession. Her séances had for a time made it possible, it seems, to have some ready cash, but this new debt went beyond all previous, given it was common in many houses to win or lose tens of thousands of francs in a single night. Diamond began to sell off her household. While she was not at first destitute, by 1846 her financial situation had become dire. Late that year, she sold her rue C___ home. By 1850, she had returned to common prostitution, renting an apartment above the shop of a coach builder on the avenue C___-E___, where she received clients. In July 1852, she was forced to sell her château in the Loiret.

Diamond's desperation did not abate her passion for fine tailoring, horses, jewels, and drink, among other illicit expenses. Habituated to elaborate luxury, she was now restricted to modest pleasures, which led to her experimentation with the pursuit of easy money. J___ A___, an old acquaintance, claims in his own memoirs, which I discovered through Edelbrot-Mélaton's kind suggestion, to have encountered Diamond outside a casino in Monte Carlo, where she had journeyed with the idea of taking the waters and attracting new clientele. He wrote: "I found the woman seated alone on the kerbstone and weeping dolefully. She appeared handsome but much bedraggled. She told me that she had been turned out of her lodgings, her belongings seized by the landlord in lieu of rent. She had no place to go, was hungry and in misery. I confessed that there was little I could do on her behalf."

The *Mémoires de Henrietta Diamond* had been greatly anticipated when it became known that this infamous personage was composing her autobiography. The book was published in 1853 in Paris and subsequently in London. The author claimed, as many eighteenth-century British actresses were known to have done, to have sent relevant pages to former lovers, offering to alter their names if they paid her—although, of course, most names have now been identified. Soon after the publication of her memoirs, Diamond became seriously ill with an unknown cancer. She died on the 9th of July, 1854. Obituaries appeared in London and Paris. Diamond left only mountainous debts, in spite of her salacious publication, and her remaining possessions were liquidated in a two-day sale in October of 1854. She was interred in Batignolles Cemetery, in a grave leased for five years. After this juncture, whatever fragments of her corpse remained were transferred to an ossuary and the grave resold.

Impossible to say with perfect certainty, as any researcher worth the name knows, but it seems there is no record of LeGouffre's presence in France after 1847. We conjecture that he sailed for London and then New York in late summer of that year, and we begin to sense his presence in Manhattan and the Bronx in late 1847 and early 1848, through the social calendar of no lesser personage than Edgar Allan Poe. Unless he began to move under an assumed name at some point after his presence in Mexico City in the 1850s, we must assume that his life's trajectory was from Paris to New York to New Orleans to Mexico City, where he would have lived out his days.

Paul Éluard, writing of this period of LeGouffre's life in a late essay published in 1950, speculates that LeGouffre left France in search of an alternative to the decadent society into which he had been born. As evidence of LeGouffre's youthful obsession with gambling had not yet come to light, Éluard can be forgiven for overlooking the obvious pragmatic reason for his subject's flight. LeGouffre would have been all but forgotten in France in Éluard's day, save for the surrealist resuscitation of his writing; those among whom LeGouffre had been raised were long since dead, and it was only through the intervention of a curious scholar that he came to the attention of twentieth-century writers.

Éluard imagines LeGouffre as a sort of feminine national spirit, tending ever westward in search of true democracy. The late 1840s were a time of transformation, once again, in France, and, in spite of LeGouffre's extreme youth, Éluard reads him as a politically nuanced and susceptible being, one who seeks an autonomy unavailable to him. It seems likely that Éluard's interpretation owes something to the surrealist's own transforming political commitments in the years leading up to his death: Éluard's purism led him to embrace Cold War fascism in places, to such an extent that at the time of his passing it was not politically feasible for him to be accorded a state funeral. To paraphrase Éluard in this essay, even after a time of great folly and upheaval, some part of us may remain that struggles to learn. In order to teach this estranged part of ourselves, this part that refuses to turn either left or right and that seeks after extremes that would seem to unite the two, one must travel far. There is no cure (*remède*) for this emotional and philosophical malady, save distance.

It is also the case, as Éluard notes in brief, that in July of 1847, around the time when LeGouffre would have begun to formulate his plans regarding a transatlantic voyage, on the third of that sweltering month in a journal called *La Démocratie pacifique*, a translation by Isabelle Meunier of an important American author appeared. Edgar Allan Poe's "Colloque d'Eiros et Charmion" was among the first works of the American poet to appear in French, and 1847 is also the year in which Charles Baudelaire became acquainted with this master of gothic tendrils, mourning, and suspense. Although we do not know with certainty whether LeGouffre first encountered Poe's work through this early translation, we do know that, in fall of 1847, the young Frenchman sought Poe out at his dwelling at the "cottage at Fordham," a secluded spot some fourteen miles from the bustling city. If LeGouffre was inspired by Poe's apocalyptic dialogue between two spirits, we must infer that there was something in this piece that summoned the young man to the older writer's side. It is, of course, also important to bear in mind LeGouffre's allegedly charming English-speaking abilities, given Henrietta Diamond's British origins, as well as the mysterious matter of the identity of the boy's father. It seems possible that a fantasy of uniting with a kindred soul spurred LeGouffre on, furnishing him with a satisfying pretext to escape his debts: it is likely that, in Poe, LeGouffre saw something of himself.

A moment must be expended here in discussion of the content

of Poe's fictional dialogue, a work that was popular in its day but that cannot fail to puzzle us, given its stilted language and risible premise. In the 1830s, the destruction of the world was of particular concern to Americans. William Miller, a Baptist preacher residing in New England, calculated that Christ would return to Earth in 1843 and was astonishingly successful in recruiting adherents after his prediction was published in a local Vermont newspaper in 1832. Miller's claim was strengthened by the advent of several meteor showers and later a succession of comets in 1833, manifestations that many considered forerunning omens of the world's impending obliteration in flames. At this time, comets aroused much popular interest: Halley's Comet, for example, had returned in 1835. Although Miller was subsequently disappointed by humankind's continuation, Poe was clearly taken with the preacher's vision of a generation of people whose deaths would be the last to occur, given the finality of the apocalypse. When Poe first published his story in the Philadelphia *Saturday Museum* of April 1, 1843, he titled it "The Destruction of the World."

One wonders, if indeed LeGouffre saw the July 3, 1847, translation of this piece, in which the recently deceased Eiros gives an account of Earth's demise to one Charmion, another denizen of the beyond, what he could have made of it. Did it remind him of Henrietta Diamond's signature séances? Poe's beloved wife had passed away on February 1 of 1847, leaving Poe alone in the Bronx cottage with his mother-in-law and aunt, Mrs. Clemm, a décor in a "fine floral taste," several tropical birds in cages, and a peculiar cat that sat on the author's shoulder. Indeed, it was not to be many years before Poe, a heavy drinker who was frequently publicly mocked in the press for his dipsomania, would succumb to "delirium." This was the time of the composition of his great poem of repetition and grief, "Ulalume," about two lovers who are inexorably drawn toward a mysterious grave site, only to discover that it holds the body of someone they both know. As Éluard wrote in his essay, it was a time of mourning for the American poet as much as rebirth.

It is difficult to account for LeGouffre's movements during late summer and early autumn of 1847, until he appears at the Fordham cottage. Poe, in spite of his wrung psychological state, was engaged in multiple love affairs. Although certainly chaste by today's standards, they help to explain "Ulalume," a poem that famously puzzled all of Poe's acquaintances in its day and led some to question the author's much-vaunted abilities, along with what were increasingly seen as the last vestiges of his sanity. "These were days when my heart was volcanic / As the scoriac rivers that roll," Poe's speaker confesses. In the poem, the then-sylvan environs of the Fordham cottage, the banks of the Bronx, Poe's favorite ramble, are transformed into "the ghoul-haunted woodland of Weir."

The Poe and Clemm household kept an active schedule of visits, and in the diary of an elocution professor, C_____ P. B_____, who was in the habit of spending at least one day of his weekends with the author and his faithful aunt, we find, thanks again to the meticulously maintained LeGouffrian *fonds*, precious evidence.

> At Poe's for Sunday. Pleasant exchange regarding the necessity of chromatic touches and even "perfume," as he tells me, within the poetical symbol. I find him ever jovial. Mrs. Clemm, on whom he depends, scolds me amiably for my persistence. We sit for tea only to be disarmed by the appearance of a young man who, pausing shyly in a slant of sun, manifests the handsomest hazel eyes, filled with a racy lightedness, one may hope to see. He is a citizen of France, that voluptuous nation. Poe calls him "Charlie" and stands to take his hand. The boy is of so clear and bright a complexion it seems to me he can be no more than fifteen years of age, yet I am told he is nearly eighteen and a pilgrim here in search of poetry. Well, says I, you have come to the right place. How strange his voice is when he makes his reply. And you have learned our speech, I tell

him. He owns his mother was his instructor she not having been born to Paris as he was. Poe exclaims that the boy has met Whitman but is loyal to our cause. It is very much to be hoped, I say. I would have done more on this particular, but Poe walks with Charlie his friend to the threshold and they vanish. Mrs. Clemm tells me to pay no mind. It is their way, she maintains. Does the young gentleman visit often? I would say so, she nods in that sparkling fashion that never fails to endear her. I would say that he is with us every day.

This entry, dated the 24th of October, 1847, gives some sense of the familiarity that had grown up between LeGouffre and Poe. It also provides important evidence of LeGouffre's acquaintance with the Brooklyn-residing Whitman, who seemed currently to be auditioning for the role of archnemesis to the inhabitant of the charming cottage at Fordham. Whitman's work as a newspaper editor at the *Brooklyn Eagle* included tabloid-style reports of literary goings-on about town, and he was not above detailed accounts of Poe's *mania-à-potu*, as it was sometimes termed. This was a time of shockingly unvarnished personal attacks in the press, and the literary world was no exception. In that summer of 1847, the novelist Herman Melville was subject to a scathing career review in the *New-York Tribune* by one G. W. Peck. Peck's public analysis of Melville's sexual pathologies was scorching enough to put at risk Melville's prospects for marriage. Rumors of homosexuality and other unspeakable tendencies were to follow Melville for the rest of his life, and his novels never again attained the glittering success of *Typee* and *Omoo* until after the author's death, at which point adulation was of little help.

There can be no doubt that, howsoever LeGouffre survived during this time, he benefited from the guidance of both Poe and Whitman. One sees the hand of the Bronx-based master in *Passe-partout*, which first appears some nine years later, serialized in early 1857, in the Parisian journal *Le Loup charmant*. LeGouffre seems to have taken inspiration from Poe's musings on mortality, decay, and the hereafter in writing his strange tale. Although we do not know when the Frenchman would have composed this narrative or what inspired him to cause it to be conveyed back across the ocean to the young editor, about whom little is known save that he perished at an early age in the collapse of a dance hall, we may speculate that its obsession with seemingly opposed entities—the dynamic movements of a traveling commodity and the stillness of marble—were a reflection of aspects of LeGouffre's own experience.

Marble was, in the mid-nineteenth century, a significant medium. We are so accustomed to the image of the female nude in white stone, the labor necessary to the counterfeiting of softness around her breasts, thighs, and pubis, as not to require a lengthy rehearsal of these conventions. What *is* significant for our purposes is the symbolism of this material, as well as its apparent purgation of sensualism from the naked body. Marble was used, not merely as a matter of convention, in other words, for its association with classical and Renaissance art, but because of the moral necessity to transform the feminine form into art through transubstantiation of the flesh.

A useful touchstone, if the reader will forgive the pun, for the central figure of LeGouffre's *Passe-partout* is a celebrated statue of the 1840s. Hiram Powers (1805–73)'s *Greek Slave* was seen in London as early as 1845, and the third version of the sculpture delighted masses in the United States in New York, New England, Philadelphia, Baltimore, Washington, Louisville, and St. Louis between August of 1847 and July of 1851. It is quite possible that this work would have been viewed by LeGouffre himself, perhaps in the company of one of his protectors, whether Poe or Whitman. While the statue would likely have appealed, in both its style and its subject matter, to Poe more than to Whitman, yet the spectacle of the crowds that came to inspect this plastic image of bondage, cruelly ironic in the America of the time, would likely have conformed to the tastes of the bearded man-about-town. Whatever the case may have been, it is worth lingering for a moment on the left hand of the statue, with its simultaneously restless yet passive gesture, its concurrent acquiescence to chains and strange liveliness, as if it possessed a dreamy face of its own. Contrasted with the visage of the figure, the gesture of this centrally placed body part is in some sense more evocative of the situation of the adolescent Grecian, unclothed and manacled beside a plinth decked in an artfully rendered swirling tasseled scarf. She bears the hand before her, using it to shield herself, even as, with this gesture, this antic hand seems to pass beyond the confines of the narrative implied.

Whitman, whose predecessor at the *Brooklyn Eagle* had died on the 26th of February, 1846, from a mysterious ailment diagnosed as "congested liver," had been working since March of that year at what he would later term "one of the pleasantest sits of my life." For this influential paper, a Democratic organ, "Walter" Whitman devoted one to two columns of the front page to literary affairs. Although he was later let go for being "slow, indolent, heavy, discourteous and without steady principles," he oversaw the implementation of a fresh new typeface and innovations in "phonographic reporting," by means of which whole sermons by the famed mass manipulators of the American pulpit could be reproduced in print. In the early 1830s, Alexis de Tocqueville wrote, "The inhabitants of the United States have then at present, properly speaking, no literature. The only authors whom I acknowledge as American are the journalists." Whitman was of course of this type and would popularize a visionary mode. It is no wonder that he was to become a fellow traveler and figurative *camerado* to LeGouffre, as we shall shortly see.

4

HIS ERRANCY

On March 5, 1848, in the *Daily Crescent*, as editor of which he was now ensconced, Walt Whitman published a serialized account in three parts of his travels south from the state of New York to Mississippi and the great city of New Orleans, then legendary for its "vicious people" and lax morals. Whitman, that mythic "great tender mother-man," journeyed in the company of his younger brother Thomas Jefferson Whitman, and "our young chancer, Charlie, the ur-Democrat," as we can imagine Thomas Jefferson, writing in a volley of plaintive and half-literate letters back to the Whitman household that February, might have maintained Walter was wont to call the youthful Frenchman. Whitman's own public account of that journey, which lasted from the 11th of February to the 25th, when the trio arrived in New Orleans, is more concerned with the routes, mountain relay stations, hotels, baggage procedures, vehicles, and meals in question than with intimate company, although strangers come in for careful consideration, particularly those "tall, strapping, comely young men" who gathered at places of commerce and repair. "I can tell you," Whitman writes, "these stoppages were not without interest." He additionally notes:

> And here I may say, once and for all, that, though expecting to find a shrewd population as I journeyed to the interior, and down through the great rivers, I was by no means prepared for the sterling vein of common sense that seemed to pervade them—even the roughest shod and roughest clad of all.

Whitman, under thirty years of age, not yet the magus of *Leaves of Grass*, was just beginning to discover America, a place of "tartar encampments of white-canvased juggernaut-wheeled Conestoga wagons by the hundreds loaded with freight," where the transients "warmed themselves by stupendous fires of soft coal." He watched the leisure activities enjoyed aboard the steam packet he and his companions boarded in Wheeling, Pennsylvania, with the acuity of a journalist and publisher. It was a twelve-day expanse of social monotony on those yellow-brown waters, during which "a late newspaper is a gem almost beyond price," and where, "[i]n the evening . . . the passenger spends his time according to fancy." One can only guess at the ingenious games LeGouffre convened. We obtain little intelligence of these more personal goings-on from Whitman's columns; however, the younger Whitman, in his first letter from the city of New Orleans, could have written:

> We have (I think) got along very well for such a long journey, not a single accident occurred on the way. Walter's friend went off very pleased. He says he will call on us at our new place, just "around the corner" from a very fine public park. We take our walk in it every night. The price of a good apple here (such a one as you could get in New York for a cent and at some places two for a cent) is the small price of ten cents. You will remember too that I said that we were to have a balloon ascension opposite our boarding house. The thing was tried five or six times, but as just enough persons got inside the thing would manage to burst. The persons that paid thought it was nothing but a suck in (which I think was the case). No sooner was it on the ground they all laid hold of it, and dragging it over the fence tore it all to pieces, they did not leave a scrap a foot square. So ended that.

The LeGouffre of this time and place would have been a capable young slip, someone who departs, "pleased," perhaps on account of his success aboard the steamboat with the captive gaming audience—remarkable to imagine it! He does not appear in either Thomas Jefferson Whitman's or Walt Whitman's letters, nor in the elder Whitman's reportorial prose. But in *Leaves of Grass* we read a glancing likeness, near the beginning of Book II:

> What are you doing young man?
> Are you so earnest, so given up to literature, science, art, amours?
> These ostensible realities, politics, points?
> Your ambition or business whatever it may be?

Indeed, the reader must wonder: What was LeGouffre's ambition or business? His liaison with Whitman necessarily provokes more questions than it furnishes answers: Was LeGouffre among Whitman's numerous *camerados*? Or, was the meaning of the briefly shared time and journey something more?

Shortly after the "Excerpts from a Traveler's Notebook" series, Whitman composed a pair of passionate editorial notes on the not entirely expected topic of nude models. On March 8 and March 14, Whitman wrote in defense of employ of the natural human form, "the *human* master-piece," as a basis and inspiration for art. It is difficult not to see a rhyme here with LeGouffre's staging of the luscious scene in which the sculptor makes one last barely clad likeness of his dying wife on the occasion of a royal commission in the opening scene of *Passe-partout*. Given LeGouffre's noted handsomeness, it is additionally possible that he himself, still under twenty years of age, took work as an artist's model, when he was not able to support himself by means of his talent for cards and dice. Perhaps Whitman wrote his two editorials as a sort of wink between himself and his former traveling companion, in hopes that the latter might become responsive, wherever he was now within the teeming, lively city of New Orleans. It was likely a challenging going for Whitman, acting as his younger brother's tutor and caregiver. But here we must bid farewell to the bearded nurse-poet, as he will return to his beloved Brooklyn in short order, and in spite of his special interest to us as an influential acquaintance and literary lodestar, here at his side LeGouffre's trail turns cold.

It is now early 1849. LeGouffre is attaining his twentieth year. Let us visualize him: He is not a tall man, but by the standards of his day is likely not distressingly small in stature. He is well formed, with a pale olive complexion that tends to freckle in the sun; his eyes light, slate gray or at times nearly yellow; his hair black. Perhaps he wears a small mustache. He keeps his collar clean and has but a single suit. He is fluent in English and French, along with the other languages of his education, and this is useful to him in the thoroughfares of New Orleans. One cannot help but admire the spirit of adventure that animates his subtle and judicious movements. He survives by means of his wits.

It is not clear precisely how long LeGouffre lingered in the southern port city, a noteworthy gateway to Central America in those days, with its "strange vivacity and rattle," as Whitman wrote. (Whitman was to quit his position at the *Crescent* in late May, celebrating his twenty-ninth birthday aboard a northbound steamer, *Pride of the West*, returning to Brooklyn where he eventually became embroiled in the anti-slavery politics of the Free-Soil Party.) While 1848 had been a significant year for democratic nationalism, particularly in the city of LeGouffre's birth, events of the summer of 1849 are important for the United States' politics where the South is concerned, in that this period saw the first and, to date, most extreme flooding of the city of New Orleans in early May, as well as the signing of the Treaty of Guadalupe Hidalgo in early July, if I am not mistaken.

The flooding of New Orleans resulted from the failure of a levee at a plantation owned by one Pierre Sauvé in Jefferson Parish, upriver from the city. The water moved at such a rate that it proved impossible to contain it, and the flood itself was named "Sauvé's Crevasse," after the fatal breakdown at this location. Several picturesque illustrations of boats floating peacefully along the streets of the city during this time are extant, which give a sense of the willingness of residents to make the best of what was in fact a severe situation, for the streets were not clear again until June 22. Given Whitman's opportune flight, it is certainly worth asking if by the time the treaty between the United States and Mexico had been signed in Mexico City on the Fourth of July, LeGouffre might himself have been ready to relocate. Perhaps he lacked the funds and connections that had permitted Whitman a speedier exit; certainly he was without the family obligations and political commitments that would have motivated his elder.

What at last inspired LeGouffre's journey south and in what year this finally occurred are historical realities concerning which we must be content to remain ignorant. It is the case that in no less than one year, in 1850, an advertisement appeared in *El Universal*, a Mexico City newspaper:

GRAN ESTABLECIMIENTO
DE DAGUERREOTIPO
DE H. CUSTIN,
Situado en los dos altos de la casa núm.
2 de la calle de Tacuba

El público tiene libre entrada de 8 de la mañana
á 4 de la tarde.
Los precios de los retratos son de 3, 4, 5, hasta
25 pesos, segun el tamaño de la lámina,
y la clase y adorno de la caja ó del cuadro.
En este establecimiento se venden por mayor y
menor todos los enseres de este arte.
La instruccion con todos adelantos se da por 250 ps.

Henry Custin, an American daguerreotypist, had begun plying his trade in Niagara Falls in the 1840s, arriving in Mexico City and establishing a photography gallery there probably in late July of 1849, a few weeks after the signing of the treaty between the United States and Mexico. Significant for our purposes is Custin's offer of instruction and the technical appurtenances necessary to "this art." Given that photography was at this juncture only entering its second decade of existence, it is reasonable that professional photographers would present themselves not only as portraitists but as missionaries of this new mode of popular image-making. They fed the growing hunger for realistic likenesses, creating inexpensive and widely circulated *cartes de visite* that brought the masses closer to a new sphere of detailed pictures. Such was the culture of Mexico City, as was that of so many urban centers of the era.

If *Passe-partout* would necessarily have had to have been completed at the very latest in early 1851 or 1852, given the rate of transatlantic correspondence during this period, this is also when LeGouffre would have been realizing or perhaps refining and completing his fantastical tale. For this reason alone, it is an important moment in his life. Certainly, one notes an air of the American South in the blasted landscape where the novella's action concludes. As the Civil War was not to begin for another ten years, the conflict to which the prose alludes must either be entirely imaginary or in some way inspired by the war with Mexico; it is one of the great mysteries of the text that it seems to predict the devolution of social order in the land that it describes.

It is likewise not entirely clear what the intended meanings of the grand time scales imagined by this short work are. The nineteenth century was a time of imaginative sermonizing and lonely, rigorous books. Authors often crowded years of unrequited passion into a word, rendering their writing the more ornate, like a snake-like walking stick carved with figures one uses to prod a poorly maintained road. We, as contemporary readers, must take care not to underestimate the depth of the allegories entailed. I would however venture that there must be a connection between LeGouffre's choice to describe the afterlife of a fragment of a statue and his own education in the possibilities of photography.

Photography, supposed to have been "born" in August of 1839, was still in its infancy when it became all but ubiquitous. Its mechanisms were portable and, although this art was flexible, it froze life, not unlike the marble of neoclassical statuary. Where Mexico was concerned, many of the first Daguerreans were, fittingly enough, French. A chemist named C. Théodore Tiffereau was, in 1842, the first to bring a camera to the country, and, during the 1850s, an archaeologist, Claude-Joseph Désiré Charnay, made a series of journeys, collecting images he created into an album published in 1863 under the title of *Cités et ruines américaines: Mitla, Palenqué, Izamal, Chichén-Itzá, Uxmal, recueillies et photographiées par Désiré Charnay avec un texte par M. Viollet-le-Duc, architecte du gouvernement, suivi du voyage et des documents de l'auteur; ouvrage dédié à S. M. l'Empereur Napoléon III et publié sous le patronage de Sa Majesté.* There were nearly fifty photographic reproductions of ancient buildings included in this volume.

It was to a fellow countryman that LeGouffre was eventually apprenticed: François Aubert. Born in the same year as LeGouffre, 1829, in Lyon, Aubert had purchased his studio from another Frenchman, Jules Amiel, who went by Julio Amiel in Mexico City. By 1863, Aubert's business was in operation at the former Studio Amiel. But this leaves a decade of LeGouffre's life unaccounted for. Dissatisfying although this is, we comprehend that LeGouffre published his slender novella and somehow subsisted during this time, an international flâneur. Aubert, meanwhile, was handy and socially gifted; he had quickly made himself indispensable in bourgeois circles and was becoming a favorite at the ephemeral imperial court of Maximilian (1864–67) for his large-format portraits, which were subtle, detailed, and flattering in the extreme. It was through his lucrative connections that Aubert was able to expand his business and extend an offer of employment to his expatriate acquaintance, whom he probably encountered upon arriving in Mexico City in 1854, which helps to confirm LeGouffre's presence there. Aubert had arrived in the great town a painter, intending to insinuate himself among the throngs of Europeans increasingly in residence in the capital but— learning of the profitability of photography, the ease of obtaining accurate and affecting images—wisely redirected his career.

As LeGouffre wrote to Édouard Manet in late July of 1867, "Chez Aubert, on peut parler de réalisme." And here I shall continue, in my own translation:

Sir, I am told that you are a painter and of a most unusual and original sort, at that. The word "genius" is employed, and I am informed that you would paint the true present of the modern world, life itself, every breath and breathing color. They say that each of your canvases is completed in a single day, that you do not linger over your forms but rather sculpt them directly from the very moment as it is given you. This is the truth of what you paint and its significance.

Where Aubert is concerned, one can speak of realism. He is a first-rate photographer. As a portraitist, he drives at the essential, ignoring the florid temptations of artificial décor and placing all his attention on the face and hands. No affectation, just the essential; he makes one see the individual and society as a whole in a single glance. He has made photographs at Monterrey, Morelia, and Guanajuato, selecting an elevated place and producing elegant and symmetrical views. In spite of the encumbering equipment, he is nimble and determined. I think often of how the unadulterated material of history meets and is absorbed in the time of exposure, and this has informed his entire artistic practice, nowhere more so than in the task of capturing these infamous events at Querétaro. When he photographed the ruination left by the final days of fighting or the field in which His Majesty the Emperor and his comrades were executed, he no longer employed a distant and elevated point of view. He put himself practically into the soil, in order to make us feel the chopped and uprooted cactus and disturbed mounds of earth, those derisory tombs.

I am told that you wish to know what it was to be in that place on "that day." First, I must inform you that it was never a single day. France's forces left Mexico City on the fifth of February and all has transpired as in a play in which actors have been replaced with mechanical figurines, given the length of the siege of the imperial hold-out at Querétaro, which you must by now well understand, as I have heard that there was no small measure of disbelief in France. As foreigners, we have been treated as well as can be expected and perhaps better. Aubert had insisted on joining the court after the end of the blockade and particularly during the trial of the emperor and his generals Miramón and Mejía, which was to conclude so poorly on their side. We imagined that this, too, was a manner of playacting and that all would be resolved through the rectification of debts, but this was not to be the case. The executions went forward and I attended these sacrifices.

As LeGouffre reveals, Aubert was not permitted to document the execution itself. The group of soldiers tasked with dispatching Maximilian and the two generals were exceedingly young, and perhaps it was feared that, as did in fact occur, the process would be faulty. We do know that at a point before his death, when the two generals had already been ushered from this world, Maximilian's vest caught fire and had to be extinguished while the former emperor, who lay writhing in pain after having been shot in the right lung, attempted to tear it from his own body. Several misfires ensued before the *coup de grace* was delivered by a noncommissioned officer.

As LeGouffre argues in his first letter, the photographer "establishes a standard; he performs an accounting of reality and bears witness." LeGouffre assisted Aubert in making images of the firing squad at ease before their task, revealing, as he writes, "eight very young men of honest character, all of whom were dressed for the occasion and whose white cartridge belts startled me." The writer informs Manet, "You must describe, above all, their shoulders. These are the shoulders of young men. They are decent and inexperienced. All of the thought of that day is in the shoulders and the backs of their necks. You must make their backs, in the dusty blue uniforms, seem like faces."

LeGouffre begins the conclusion of this letter with a series of meditations on the adobe wall before which the three men were shot and from behind which Aubert and LeGouffre bore witness to the proceedings. "The bricks of adobe are long and flat and, while soft, provided some security. Aubert strode backward into the countryside, seeking a hill, while I lay on my stomach pressing my eye to a gap in the structure several yards from the determined place of execution. Later, we made a landscape of the three meager graves before the wall. It is a fateful site, loathsome in its insignificance."

But Manet does not receive these tidings entirely without an expectation of recompense. LeGouffre is frank:

> Monsieur, I believe that you understand that I was originally and by inclination a writer. As quite an immature youth, I was fortunate enough to see some verses of my own devising appear in print and fifteen years ago a fanciful tale of mine was circulated, with quiet fanfare, by a highly selective journal. I am becoming an American and it is not much to be hoped that I shall return to France during my lifetime. I beg of you, would you take the enclosed copy of my tale and convey it to an editor whom you trust? I am sure that once the first step is ventured by a man such as yourself, the work cannot fail to receive greater attention. My first poem concerned Jason, that adventurer of myth, and it is also true that I once believed that I was, like him, to find glory. Alas, I am abroad now and have not found my home. Please do as I ask and I can assure you that in some way <u>you</u> <u>shall</u> <u>be</u> <u>rewarded</u>. I should be happy to provide

introductions were you to make the voyage to Philadelphia and New York and am not without connections there. It is in certainty of future correspondence that I take my leave of you now.

So writing, LeGouffre concludes his message. It is likely that the letter was not read by Manet, as Edelbrot-Mélaton informed me, until he returned from his summer holiday for Charles Baudelaire's funeral in Paris on September 2, 1867. It is around this time that Manet seems to have set aside the first *ébauche* upon which he was previously at work, concerning the depiction of the execution of Maximilian (a muddy, bluish affair), here beginning a new canvas, hoping to complete it, one assumes, for the next salon, which was to open the following May. Manet seems also around this time to have ventured to compose a second letter to LeGouffre (now missing), to which the writer, in turn, replied that autumn.

I reproduce this second letter here in full (again, the translation is my own):

My Dearest Monsieur Manet,

I am grateful for your reply and for news of life in that metropolis that seems to me the absolute center of the world, the more so as I am distant from it. It gratifies me to learn that I have been of some assistance to you in the arrangement of your new work. I was able to say little enough of what occurred at Querétaro, in truth, but perhaps there is something in "my details," as you write. It is a wonder that there has been such amazement at our friend Aubert's images, but perhaps this is, as you write, due to the embargo on language that has not been extended to photography. I suppose we have both realized that it is quite a piece of luck that my first letter was able to reach you. I view it as a sign and should be very glad if your painting is a great success and serves to convey to many men the spirit of that day, which now seems more and more to me like a cursed thing that haunts me wherever I am, something insistent and living, rather than an ephemeral moment increasingly given over to the oblivion of the past. Is it possible that there are some events which do not take place only once, but rather multiply themselves across future time, always and forever seeking and insisting to join the present. I feel certain now that this is so. I hope only that I have not made of you one of my kind, but perhaps you are a more formidable presence than I. At times I seem to myself so mutable, I hardly know what I may be.

Please allow me to understand what you may have heard regarding my little history. I trust and depend upon you and think of you frequently.

With admiration and most profound thanks,

This missive is the last evidence of LeGouffre's existence. Nothing more is known concerning his whereabouts or the length of his life. Two years later, in 1869, his former employer or partner, the photographer François Aubert, was to return to France. Édouard Manet realized three additional paintings depicting the execution of Maximilian, along with a lithograph. While it is clear that these works were greatly influenced by LeGouffre's account, it is not known to what extent Manet made efforts in the direction of LeGouffre's request regarding re-publication of *Passe-partout*. Manet died in spring of 1883, after having had his left foot amputated due to gangrene. His demise seems to have been hastened if not caused by this operation, as well as by circulatory difficulties that made the intervention necessary, among other complications stemming from the painter's advanced syphilis, the curse that had withered most of his adult life.

CONCLUSION

It is the height of unusualness for a scholarly title to avoid literary interpretation and analysis. I, however, wanted to avoid the pitfall into which so many writers stumble when they assign to imaginative prose the burdensome task of explaining the mystery of a life as it has been lived. As we know, the value of literature arises precisely from its lack of perfect representational accuracy! As LeGouffre's reputation has rested, until this time, entirely on his own anomalous literary production, it seemed at once necessary and fitting to treat him as a full human being, a living and striving man, rather than as a myth or character invented by avant-gardists between the First and Second World Wars. To leave LeGouffre in that state—or, what would assuredly have been far worse, to continue to promote that manner of reducing a complex figure to a sort of corroboration of the musings of an influential and headstrong but nevertheless limited group of readers—was not my design, and given that I had other goals in mind, it has not always been possible or necessary for me to turn to LeGouffre's writings in order to say what has needed, and for so long, to be said of his life and his search for recognition.

Where we left him, in his final letter to the doomed Manet, LeGouffre once again turned to the matter of *Passe-partout*, evidently hoping that the painter would be struck by some of the same urgency that had animated him to compose those sentences. We cannot know what Manet made of that plea. Did the painter perhaps share LeGouffre's tale with influential friends? Was it received with incomprehension in those rarefied circles? Or, was it the case that Manet himself, having perused the musical sentences detailing the peregrinations of a fragment of statuary, set the copy of the *feuilleton* down in a state of enchanted distraction and merely returned to his own work with renewed energy?

Manet had, only a year earlier, in February of 1866, been introduced to the novelist Émile Zola. Manet began work on a portrait of Zola after the latter produced a long and very positive review defending Manet's paintings; this portrait was later exhibited in the 1868 Salon. The image in question shows Zola seated at his desk, on which we perceive an example of the pamphlet praising Manet. Above the desk hang a lithograph, likely the work of the painter and engraver Célestin Nanteuil, mimicking Velazquez's *The Triumph of Bacchus*; a Japanese print, entitled *The Wrestler Onaruto Nadaeman of Awa Province*, by Utagawa Kuniaki II; and an etching and aquatint version of Manet's own *Olympia*, completed some four years earlier in 1863. The figures of *Olympia*, the Japanese wrestler, and the Bacchus all gaze directly and intently at Zola, who seems to refuse to look back at them. Here we see the stirrings of a lack of affinity that the painter and engraver Odilon Redon, a man who would most assuredly have felt sympathy toward LeGouffre had he known him, remarked upon in his Salon review of the summer of 1868, when he called the portrait "rather a still life, so to speak, than the expression of a human being." It is said that Zola was no great admirer of this likeness, even if he continued to support Manet's efforts, more generally. (The novelist and critic Joris-Karl Huysmans was to observe that Zola had sequestered the painting within a remote room of his dwellings.)

I mention this painting not merely to underline Manet's relationship with the significant writers of his era—and, as a realist of stringent political views and even empiricist sociological leanings, Zola was not likely to have expressed much enthusiasm for LeGouffre's work, so we may well wish to discount him from the start—but to explore a strange feature of the image, which, over the years during which I have pursued the faint trail of LeGouffre's life, has never ceased to give me pause. The writer's right hand, so pale and bulbous and prominent in Manet's depiction, hardly appears to be the hand of a living man. It is less that it is poorly painted, than that it gives the impression that the author is in possession of an artificial fist, one which has been fashioned, of course with great care, from pale pink marble.

We might see this as a commentary on the relative liveliness of Zola's writings, his subtlety or lack thereof, but I prefer to view this anomalous hand as a lingering trace of the Parisian writer who remained all but unseen and unknowable from the vantage of Paris itself: here is a portrait, not of Émile Zola, but of Passe-partout, that strange spirit-object of LeGouffre's one cherished work of fiction, and, by association, of LeGouffre himself, whom Manet could not have seen and whom he would therefore have been incapable of painting in the flesh. It is a bright flash, a moment of true *reconnaissance*, gone all too quickly, and yet this image lingers: insistent, faithful, beneficent. Here I have found LeGouffre, at last; here he sits alongside the literary lights of his day.

NOTES

Introduction *pages 9 to 14*

1. See Alfonse's major study as well as S. de Gauita, *Essais de sciences maudites*, I, Paris, 1890, and Jules Bois, "La femme nouvelle," *Revue encyclopédique*, Paris, 1928.
2. For a more detailed discussion of these epistolary exchanges as well as the original letters, see Laël Edelbrot-Mélaton, "Manet raconté par lui-même," *Revue du Salon*, Paris, 1927.
3. Ibid., 87–89.
4. I have consulted R. Cradson's celebrated biography of Éluard almost exclusively.
5. For example: S. Charléty, *Histoire du saint-simonisme*, Paris, 1932, p. 125; L. Cellier, *Fabre d'Olivet*, p. 345.
6. M. Thibert, *Le Féminisme dans le socialisme français de 1830 à 1850*, Paris, 1926, pp. 35f.
7. Quoted by L. Abendsour, *Le Féminisme sous le règne de Louis-Philippe et en 1848*, 2e éd., Paris, 1913, p. 8.
8. Th. Gautier, *Mademoiselle de Maupin*, Nouvelle éd. Paris, Fasquelle, 1922, p. 224.
9. Thibert, *Le Féminisme*, p. 36.
10. Quoted in Cradson, p. 89.
11. Quoted by Thibert, *Le Féminisme*, p. 37.
12. Charles Yriarte, *Paris grotesque. Les Célébrités de la rue, Paris (1815 à 1863)*, Paris, 1864, p. 93.
13. J. Erdan, *La France mistique. Tableaux des excentricités de ce tems.* Paris, 1855, p. 623. It will have been noted that Erdan employs at times a highly personal phonetic spelling.
14. The reader is advised to avoid such anomalies as F. Tristan, *L'Emancipation de la femme ou le testament de la Paria, ouvrage posthume de Mme Flora Tristan, complété d'après ses notes et publié par A. Constant*, Paris, 1845.

1 THE ACTRESS *pages 15 to 23*

1. Quoted in J. Jeannel, *De la prostitution dans les grandes villes au dix-neuvième siècle et de l'extinction des maladies vénériennes. Questions générales d'hygiène, de moralité publique et de l'égalité. Mesures prophylactiques internationales. Réformes à opérer dans la service sanitaire. Discussion des*

réglements exécutés dans les villes principales de l'Europe. Ouvrage précédé de documents relatifs à la prostitution dans l'antiquité, Paris, 1868, p. 401.

2. See M. Cod's painstakingly researched and extremely useful critical biography. I have consulted Diamond's own *Mémoires* as little as possible, given their questionable veracity.

3. Ibid.

4. Ibid.

5. Ibid.

6. J. Jeannel, *De la prostitution*, p. 399.

7. Yves Guyot, *Études de physiologie sociale: la prostitution*, Paris, 1882, p. 53.

8. Here Cod throughout.

9. The reader is advised, if at all possible, to pass over E. P. Vining, *The Mystery of Hamlet*, London, 1881. We will recall that Vining was a railway systems expert, not a literary critic.

10. Ibid.

11. Again, Cod.

12. Yriarte, *Paris grotesque*, p. 94.

13. See J. A. Bondage, "Prostitution in the Medieval Canon Laws," *Signs* I (Summer 1976): 825–45.

14. P. Dufour, *History of Prostitution*, 3 vols., Chicago, 1926, III, pp. 1–276.

15. J. P. Glutton has observed that enclosure was regarded as a "miracle solution" for vagabonds, thieves, and other roamers in the sixteenth and seventeenth centuries because of the intriguing possibility of extracting work from inmates while simultaneously administering religious instruction. See his recent *La Société et les pauvres: l'exemple de la généralité de Lyon, 1534–1789*, Paris, 1970, p. 305. I have also wondered at related discussions appearing in the publications of commentator Michel Foucault, even as I have found these sometimes concerning in their liberality. See also C. Paultre, *De la répression de la mendicité et du vagabondage en France sous l'ancien régime*, Paris, 1906.

16. Guyot, *Études*, p. 110.

17. Quoted in Dufour, *History*, p. 2.

18. Jeannel, *De la prostitution*, p. 400.

19. See A. Williams's forthcoming study, *The Police of Paris, 1715–1789*, Baton Rouge [1979].

20. H. Mireur, "Historical Note" to N-E Restif de la Bretonne, *La Pornographe, ou idées d'un honnête homme sur un projet de règlement pour les prostituées*, Brussels, 1879, p. xix.

21. More Cod.

22. Ibid.

23. Quoted in Guyot, *Études*, p. 111. See also Parent-Duchâtelet's monumental account.

24. Quoted in H. M. S. Sinford, *The Different Systems of Penal Codes in Europe*, Washington, D.C., 1854, p. 30.

25. Cod is particularly useful in this arena.

2 A BRIEF STAY *pages 25 to 30*

1. L.-J. Cavelety, *Les Jeux de la société*, Paris, 1978, pp. 186–87. See also D. Oldguy, "Chance and Skill: A Study of Roulette," *Sociology* 8, no. 3 (1974): 407.

2. For an overview of these notions, see I. Hacking, *The Emergence of Probability: A Philosophical Study of Ideas about Probability, Induction and Statistical Inference*, London, 1975. I have also been inspired by a number of intriguing remarks appearing in F. Semrau, *Würfel und Würfelspiel im alten Frankreich*, Halle, 1910. Nor can I neglect to cite P.-S. Laplace, *Essai philosophique sur les probabilités*, Paris, 1814.

3. Here I have taken care to indicate my influences within the body of the text itself (in fact, my preferred mode of citation, since it is less obtrusive and tends to evoke truer feeling). I was—to speak, in a sense, of fate—the lucky recipient of the hospitality of the scholar in question, and it is through a series of intimate conversations that I have come to absorb the full import of this history. In such instances, there is something more than mere intellectual endeavor at stake.

4. My colleague I. C. Freakes, author of a forthcoming exhaustive study of doggerel of the early to mid-nineteenth century provided invaluable assistance here. I am eager that he should find a publisher for his very unique twenty-six-volume work.

3 IMMORTAL GESTURE *pages 31 to 39*

1. Cavelety, *Les Jeux de la société*.

2. Here I have made extensive use of Cod.

3. See Cradson.

4. The reader is advised to consult the forthcoming watershed publication *Collected Works of Edgar Allan Poe*, ed. Thomas Olive Muppitt, 3 vols., Cambridge [1978].

5. I recommend, although without great enthusiasm, S. Bliss, *Memoirs of William Miller*, Boston, 1853. For a more entertaining treatment of these episodes, one may distract oneself for a day with F. D. Nichol, *The*

Midnight Cry: A Defense of the Character and Conduct of William Miller and the Millerites, Who Mistakenly Believed that the Second Coming of Christ Would Take Place in the Year 1844, Washington, D.C., 1945.

6. Again, consult Muppitt's compilation on these several points and citations. Muppitt's introduction is also quite worthwhile, as I understand.

7. I am also very pleased to be aware of the forthcoming publication of *The Edgar Allan Poe Scrapbook*, ed. P. Hating, New York [1978]. I anticipate a review copy and plan to honor this critical occasion with reverence and respect.

8. Here a crucial aside that I am unable to treat elsewhere: Although LeGouffre places the goddess Diana at the poetical center of his imagined sculptor's work in his singular novella, it is important to note that the primary female figure of neoclassical speculation in the early nineteenth century was not, in fact, the goddess of the hunt, but rather Psyche, that mortal beauty turned goddess of the soul. This belated entry into the Olympian pantheon, a truly modern female deity, is known to us primarily through the early novel of North African author Lucius Apuleius, who relates her story as an aside within his larger tale of one man's transformation into a donkey. Psyche, an ordinary human girl born to an unremarkable family, is so famed for her beauty that she excites the interest of the god of love, Cupid, the son of Venus. Psyche and Cupid are married on the condition that Psyche never know the identity of her husband, who will come to her bed only under cover of night. She experiences him as a shadowy and, one is given to assume, pleasure-giving presence. However, Psyche, being mortal and quite imperfect, takes it upon herself to illegally inspect her mysterious husband while he is asleep, using a lamp. Clumsy in her manipulation of this item—perhaps shocked at her discovery—she spills hot oil onto the love god's wings, waking him. Betrayed by this investigation, Cupid leaves in a rush of grief. Psyche must then make a petition to Venus, who dislikes Psyche instinctively and only agreed to the marriage with great reluctance. Venus sets Psyche four monumental tasks. Somehow, Psyche manages to accomplish these and is reunited with her husband and also deified, becoming, as John Keats was to write in his "Ode to Psyche," the "latest-born . . . Of all Olympus' faded hierarchy" and, therefore, "too late for antique vows." That LeGouffre employs Diana in the place of a more modern goddess, one particularly popular in England throughout the Victorian period, suggests either that he was uninterested in trends in contemporary sculpture or that, well aware of such trends, he instead elected to comment upon the trend with a radically traditional choice. In either case, I view his choice as judicious and illuminating.

9. It is certain that Whitman was with the *Eagle* by the third of March. On this date there appeared a characteristic editorial decrying a bill to suppress licentiousness that had just been introduced in Albany. And on the fifth of that month the paper contained a review of Keats's poetical works generally agreed to have been penned in Whitman's early style. I have often wondered at the lack of classical motifs in Whitman's own poetry.

4 HIS ERRANCY *pages 41 to 52*

1. I have received useful guidance from G. W. Allen, *Walt Whitman Handbook,*

[*Subsequent notes/pages missing; ripped out. —Ed.*]

C.

Hypergraphia
A Novel

by
Erin Adamo

Contents

The symptom is transient, subtle, and can easily be overlooked.

—Yamadori, Mori, Tabuchi, Kudo, Mitani (1986)

One: Resurrection

In the story that is repeatedly told, Elliott is in prison. He is probably twenty-six, at the time. He is at lunch in the prison cafeteria and there is a disagreement. As the story is told, a leader defends Elliott because "we don't hurt our [mentally disabled individuals]."

In the story, Elliott's offense is to have openly consorted with nonwhite inmates. This is the reason for the disagreement, and it is also what leads to Elliott's salvation: a tautology, miracle, or plain social fact. The leader considers Elliott developmentally challenged, slow, or, possibly, stark raving mad. As far as the leader is concerned, there can be no other explanation for Elliott's willingness to be kind to people who are not white, as they are. Elliott, son of a rich man, survives prison for a second time. In the story, it's just dumb luck. He returns to his parents, gets clean, relapses, dies.

Elliott was my childhood acquaintance, a cousin or pseudobrother. His story, the story of his goodness and innocence, is now told at Thanksgiving and at Christmas and at New Year's. It's the last story told by a living Elliott, if at second hand. All the other stories rehash what people said about him at his memorial. Elliott died of a methadone overdose two years ago. He bought it on the street in lower Manhattan and shot it there, where he also died, and where his body was discovered, ten hours later.

In the story as it is told, which may or may not be Elliott's version of events, Elliott is the only decent person in prison.

We're in a loft on Spring Street and tonight it's Christmas. The loft is rent-controlled and Elliott's mother, Barbara, has lived here forever. It's the most precious thing she owns, although she does not own it.

Getting here has not been easy. My mother, father, and I rode down from the Upper East Side in a taxi. I am in part responsible. It's true that I begged Barbara to let us come here, that I wrote some emails explaining why what's happened in the past won't happen again. I've asked her not to make me spend the holidays with them alone.

What happens in my life is not Barbara's responsibility, but there seem to be few people I can ask for help.

My mother and I are in the back of the taxi, dishes on our laps. My father, who is nearly eighty, rides shotgun.

I'm lying when I make it sound like we spend all our holidays with Barbara. That's not really true. We used to spend the holidays with Barbara, but we don't do that anymore.

My father, up front, is speaking. What he's saying does not make sense, but I'll repeat it now. He says, "I'm bringing bathrobes for the guys."

He clarifies, "I told all the guys I'm bringing bathrobes."

I can tell that there's a way in which, each time he speaks, he's waiting, once he's done, for laughs.

No one's laughing.

My mother maintains a bustling good attitude. She seems busy and content, even if she's sitting here in silence.

This is not actually a taxi. It's not an Uber, either, since presumably my father's rating is so low he can't order them anymore. This is a car from a 1980s-era livery service that, for some reason, still exists.

Before we left my parents' apartment my father got on the phone. He called the service up. He'd made this reservation in advance, is what he said. The car was coming.

On the one hand, this felt old, a resurrection from my childhood; it resembled preparation for a journey to an island nation during the course of which I'd be asked to wait in various locations while my parents attempted to withstand being in each other's presence.

Here, in the kitchen, in the present, I asked why my father used a car service. Didn't he understand the notion of an internet of things? Did he not comprehend that even within our nation's border labor could be rendered up so swiftly and exactly it was as if slavery were legal?

My father did not say anything in reply. Pressing a button and dropping the handset into its cradle, he concluded his interaction with the cordless phone.

My mother, nearby, laughed in an unbalanced way.

It took a while to think: Oh yes, my father has certainly yelled at Uber drivers. He's certainly berated Lyft drivers. He's probably asked them to stop the car in the middle of a trip, to let him get out on the highway. He's definitely refused to pay. He's certainly been on the customer service line for hours, yelling, yelling, yelling.

My mother knows that, (a) because my father is very bad, she, in turn and by contrast, must be very good, but (b) it is by no means clear why somebody so good would be married to somebody so confused and awful.

Everything is on the surface. Nothing is hidden.

I am an adult woman in her early thirties. I am in a livery service car with my parents. I write it all down. Not in real life, I mean. I mean, in my head. In life, I am not allowed to write. But in my head, I can. I can't write anything down, but I can describe the world— silently, privately. I put words to it.

I will say more about this later.

Now, I think, *I lean back into the slippery black leather. Now the sound of the tires and the mutter of the driver speaking low into his headset an Eastern European language [note somewhere in this passage that he has three cell phones, one Samsung, one Motorola, one iPhone] and all the broken-off pieces of the din of the city even at night [reflection of streetlights and for once it's seasonably cold] and on Christmas.*

When I was a child, my first sentence was *The moon is peeking through the trees.*

We were in the car when I said it, and I was two. It was a practice of mine even then, while illiterate, an unformed blob, etc. My earliest writings were a picture-language, a rebus. And I still write that way now.

Even as I write nothing.

I ask my mother, "What is he talking about?" I mean the bathrobes. She says: "How should I know?"

My mother intends to make this a game.

Because it is Christmas and because I, too, wish that my mother loved my father, I acquiesce. We can have a volley. We can pretend.

"What do you think he means?"

"Have I ever understood what he says?"

I would like, very badly, to answer yes. However, if I say yes now, I will lose the game, and I do not want to lose. I would like to say, "Yes, you have frequently and possibly even without exception understood what this person says. I am, for one, so convinced of your understanding that I have created a fantasy version of you who acts upon her intelligence regarding the meanings of these scary utterances. This imaginary parent is someone whom I respect and love. I keep her around to help me in my interactions with you."

I have to assume my mother knows that I would like to say this. I also have to assume she understands my obsession with success. So instead of saying what I want to say, I say, out of what I take to be my love for her, "But why bathrobes?"

Fortunately, for the purpose of the game, at least, my father steps in. He starts embroidering.

He tells us, in his heavy voice, "I called ahead and let everyone know that I've got bathrobes. All the guys can put them on. We'll hang out. I got them for us guys."

I ask my mother, "Is this about Harvey Weinstein?"

It's not my turn, but I'm going anyway. I feel I've served an ace.

"Hahaha," my mother trills. "Anything is possible," she says, losing.

The driver gets off his phone. He interacts with my father.

We're getting close.

Elliott, while he was alive, was about two years younger than I was, maybe a little less. The moments I remember most vividly from his life are two, too, maybe a little less:

First memory: It is a holiday evening in the loft and I, with my parents, am shown Elliott's drawings. Elliott is ten and maybe I am twelve. The drawings are pictures of men in a landscape expressed by means of a single line. Handguns float in the air. Limbs have been severed. Blood flows out in ribbons and jagged bolts. It spots the air. Someone jogs with an axe.

Elliott is an amazing artist, Elliott's mother, Barbara, and father, Kris, say. Elliott's half sister, Magdalena, is somewhere else. She's almost twenty. Elliott's mother and father talk about Elliott's style, his expression, his brilliant lack of inhibition. They're getting some of his works framed. I don't know where Elliott is at this moment. Maybe he's with his sister. Elliott is a sweet-faced kid, round and apparently gentle. He looks like a schoolboy in a French film and smiles a lot and cries a lot and speaks with a lisp. He also has a stubborn side. Somewhere in this evening Kris his father is yelling at him. Or maybe Kris his father is trying to get him to stop screaming.

Second memory: I am sixteen and it is the weekend. My mother is remarking to me and perhaps my father that if she were Elliott's mother, which of course she is not, she would not so easily let him go. She would not permit him to be what Elliott's mother, Barbara, is permitting him to be, the ward of a private institution for troubled boys with addiction issues. My mother does not like it when Barbara, and sometimes Kris, from whom Barbara is now divorced, come over to our house and speak solemnly about the fate of Elliott and what they are learning about how to behave toward him at the home for boys. The home has a strict philosophy. In a decade or so, those who run it will lose whatever license they have that permits them to conduct whatever program of reeducation they're currently conducting. My mother says that if the sorts of things that are happening to Elliott were happening to me, she would quit her job and move with me to the country. There I would be safe. There she could look after me. My mother does not say anything about where my father would be at this point. Anyway, a year earlier I was kicked out of school, but I'm still with them in the city.

These are the two clear memories I have. I see Elliott's face as a child and also I see him as an adult, very tall and slightly overweight, his head shaved. He became a very large man, what I think is called a "scary man," but he was always young and part of what made him scary was that he looked unambiguously like a child no matter how old he got.

Rewind. Let us go back a handful of months. It is not yet Christmas. No cab ride yet and no bathrobes. It is the fall and my mother tells me a story. We are in the kitchen of the apartment she shares with my father. "I saw Barbara this summer—and Palmer," my mother says.

Palmer is Barbara's third husband. He lost all his money in the financial crisis; at least, this is what I have been told. I remember Palmer from when he was supposedly rich. He seems kinder now. More inclined to look directly at other people's faces. Less interested in golf.

"You know we were renting a house in the Hamptons?"

My mother has to mention this in a strange way because when she had invited me to the rental over the summer it was during a time when I had blocked her email address and cell number and therefore did not receive the message. We're speaking now but not of this.

My mother is still talking. "And so they were able to come out. But it was very *strange*." She describes how Palmer asked her to buy him a tank of gas one afternoon. I can't tell if she actually bought it for him. I know I shouldn't ask.

Here I have a vision of the backs of Barbara's and Palmer's heads. It's bright and somehow, although this is a vision, I can tell the air smells sweet. Barbara and Palmer are moving humbly around the kitchen of a modest but elegant home through the windows of which the teal edge of the Atlantic is visible. They seem worried that they may be asked to pay for groceries.

"I don't know what happened," my mother says, but of course she knows. Barbara is in her late seventies and who knows how old Palmer is. There are few ways they can generate income, and I don't imagine either of them plans on picking up a job in the service industry anytime soon. I assume they both have a lot of debt.

Fast forward. Later, after Christmas, after we have been in Barbara's loft, now painted entirely dove gray, with some bright pops, soft accent lighting; after the meal during which my father remarks multiple times upon the beauty of Barbara's seven-year-old granddaughter, Magdalena's second born, a daze on his face like a song about it, little girls and their unwavering stares; after the failure of any sort of pleasant feeling to arise; after weeks pass and then a month; after my mother has been cruel to me again and my father has kicked me out of the house during a dinner arranged a month late to celebrate my birthday, I write to Barbara to ask her if she will have lunch with me. I tell her, although I do not know what this means, that now I need the real story, please. I need to know what happened.

I'm not asking about Elliott, by the way.

I am asking about my parents. But I'm not sure what I am asking.

I'm not planning to pay for lunch. I want Barbara to understand that it's time to bring an end to all the secrets and unkindness. I want her to understand that I can offer absolution. It's not fair of me but in truth she's the most vulnerable individual in this system and I'm too desperate for mercy.

We select a mutually approved macrobiotic location, and I wear a heavy, hut-like Dolce and Gabbana skirt I found at Goodwill with a tear in the lining and the tags mostly cut out. I've taken the afternoon off, trained in from Jersey. This could be a film.

Barbara sees me coming.

"I didn't know your job was so glamorous," she says, by way of greeting.

She's moved by a mixture of jealousy and an ancient form of curiosity that sometimes doubles as concern.

I say I am taking a little time off today.

"How was the trip?" She means, into Manhattan.

"Fine," I reply. "Trip-like."

"You don't miss living in the city?"

It is as if we have not seen each other for years, as if Barbara knows nothing of my fate, not the bouts of mental illness nor my divorce, not my unrelenting practicality when it comes to my exceedingly average job and personal finances.

All the same, there is but one answer to this question. "Ha!" I answer. "No!"

We are both flipping through our menus.

"How is your mother?" Barbara asks.

The other thing you have to understand about Barbara is that she looks like a retired model. She's a beauty for the ages, tall and lean, eyes like headlights. She's had work done, but it's very good.

"I don't really know," I say. I'm letting Barbara comprehend I'm no one's emissary.

"Ha," says Barbara. Then, "I know what I want, do you?"

But Barbara keeps on talking. She knows we have not come here to eat.

Barbara says, "This summer we were out in the Hamptons with your parents. Your father," she says, "is a miserable man."

I wait.

"He has led a miserable life. He is brilliant but he took a job that he hated for money and he has always been miserable. He doesn't know how to be any other way. Your mother at least found something interesting."

"Yes," I say.

"But safe. This was too safe." I think she is referring to my mother's job. "Anyway, your father doesn't respect me, never has. He's a miserable man. Whenever he sees me," Barbara says, an incomplete sentence.

The waitress comes and Barbara asks for almost all the elements of her dish to be placed to the side. I realize that I often find myself at this particular restaurant with people who make me uncomfortable.

"We went to Laynie's house and when he was greeting Laynie," Barbara is telling me, but the waitress comes back and asks Barbara if she is OK to substitute wakame for hijiki, due to a shortage of the latter.

Barbara wonders if maybe they might just give her a little side salad but without tomatoes as it is too early.

The waitress says she has to check and departs.

"He grabbed her ass, I could see it. He always does this to me when he hugs me, he always has. Grabs my ass. And Palmer saw it, too. And I saw Palmer's face."

The waitress reappears. She says it will have to be a very small salad.

"Fine," Barbara says. "But maybe not too small?"

I don't ask Barbara any questions. I don't ask how long this has been going on or who knows about it. I don't ask what Laynie did when my father grabbed her ass or what her face looked like. I don't ask what Palmer thought.

Instead, I start talking about Christmas, which is the last time I saw Barbara.

I'm thinking about the matter of the bathrobes. I'm thinking about the way my father spoke about the little girl.

I beg Barbara. Other people start to look. I've already lost control.

"Fine," Barbara says. It's like I've asked her for money, which in some sense I have. "I know I shouldn't be doing this," she tells me. It's like I'm getting more than I deserve or too young. I almost hear her say, "I'm going to do this just this once, but after this you're on your own."

In the story Barbara tells, she is still on her first marriage. She's living in a loft on Canal Street with Tom, her first husband, who is Magdalena's father, although they haven't had Mags yet. To give a bit of context: About seven years later, Tom will be shot in the head in a deli near Prince Street when he goes out to buy the paper on a Sunday morning at ten a.m. He won't die. The bullet will perform a miraculous transit around his skull and exit, finding its destiny in a nearby wall. Tom will leave Barbara after this and he will leave New York and he will remarry with a woman named Celeste on the West Coast, but this hasn't happened yet. There is no Celeste, and Barbara and Tom are still together in their loft on Canal Street and it is the mid-1970s and they have a party.

My mother is out of town on a business trip but my father comes to the party. My parents have been married for almost a decade at this point. Barbara and Tom are my mother's two closest friends in New York. Although my mother is out of town, my father, Barbara maintains, comes to the party and he brings another woman with him. This woman, I repeat, is not my mother. My father and this other woman go home together.

Again, I don't ask Barbara any questions. I don't ask who the woman was or how my father knew her.

Barbara is saying, "Tom and I were very kind of shocked, you know. But it was the seventies. And I can remember asking him the next day if that really happened, like, Tom, did you *see* that? But you know a lot of things happened in those days. And even the other day I was talking to Tom on the phone and it just came up and I said, 'Oh, do you remember that?' And do you know he made me swear I would never tell Celeste? He said it would break her heart, he said, 'Oh, she idolizes their marriage!'"

On the 12th hospital day when she had been talking with a nurse who had a pencil and a writing pad, she asked for them and started scribbling. On the first sheet of paper she wrote, "It is fine since morning. Twenty-ninth, October. A doctor quoted a haiku for me the other day. [The haiku was fully quoted but is omitted in this translation.] But I wonder if a baby can understand the meaning. I wanted to raise my child with joy."

—Yamadori, Mori, Tabuchi, Kudo, Mitani (1986)

Two: Memories of the Future

I've never tried to tell this story. I've told plenty of other ones—and, to almost anyone who would listen, especially once I got divorced—but never this one. The reason I haven't tried is that I'm not sure that it's a story. It's like I've removed myself from so many of the scenes, and so effectively, that although I know what happened I'm not sure what relationship I myself have to the events. It's like I'm floating on the ceiling, I'm sitting on the bookshelf, I'm laid out underneath the kitchen table, I'm tucked into a drawer—and I'm not that person, I'm not that person there who lives and speaks the words.

The other major problem with the story is that it does not begin. I'm going to try to talk to you about it, but it doesn't have a proper beginning.

Anyway, I have a theory about human development in the contemporary era that helps to explain this. I don't entirely understand who I am in the larger system of inheritance and imitation, but I have some idea of how it works. The way it works is through repetition and also through forgetting. While you are a child, you will forget some of the things that happen to you. When you are an adult, what you cannot remember is what you do. The result is that the world is an inversion of everything that has already happened to everyone, an imprint in reverse—the original details of which no one recalls.

Of course, I'm not saying that it is exact. The repetition is significantly flawed, wonky. It's like how the camera lens, that device that organizes light and distance, necessarily distorts that which it at once reveals: the picture or repetition, what comes to pass, is lossy, flat and inexact. Perhaps it's uglier, perhaps more beautiful. I've never been particularly photogenic, except when very young.

This is how newness enters the world, by the way—and why anyone can have memories of the future.

Speaking of youth, my life was extremely eventful, when I was fifteen, sixteen, seventeen. When I was seventeen, I wrote a novella. That is how much there was to say.

I made the classic early error of showing the novella to my mother, and now that novella is gone. Its title was "Expectancy."

I wrote the novella for my high school English teacher. He was fifty-one, a charismatic burnout with whom I was in love. We called this "independent study." The teacher's name was Graeme Bird and I know how old he was because once it was his birthday and he told me—about his age, I mean. I remember the number because I had recently learned that Honoré de Balzac was fifty-one when he died, of caffeine poisoning. Balzac would stay up all night and write, corrosive breakfast beverage by his side, a massive pot.

I suppose at the time I knew that I, too, would be a coffee addict. That there was, in truth, no other high that I preferred.

When I told Graeme Bird, on his birthday, that Balzac had been this very age, fifty-one, at the time of his death, I think Graeme thought I was offering an optimistic compliment. Perhaps there was some chance that he, Graeme Bird, might yet himself become a Balzac—alchemically and analogically, through vague association. Graeme referred to himself as a "failed novelist."

"Why are you failed?" I asked him once.

"There are things I could not write about," Graeme said.

"What kinds of things?" This was when I was still bold and proud.

"Things," Graeme repeated, "about me."

What Graeme probably did not know was that I already considered myself the Balzac in this relationship. I was only talking to Graeme in this way because I wondered if I would be as emotionally and morally corrupt as him when I was fifty-one—or if, like Balzac, I too would have trashed my body chemistry with Starbucks and Earl Grey and therefore be defunct.

But I wasn't just in love with Graeme. Graeme and I never really did anything, anyhow. We'd just talk about old books after school in his classroom and sometimes go canoeing north of the city. One time, in the boat, I looked up his shorts and saw one of his testicles, and one time I caught him gazing, mesmerized, at my undepilated crotch when I was in a swimsuit. We both seemed too in awe of our vaguely competitive, if unlikely, emotional connection to fuck.

Graeme Bird was extremely tall. His classroom was full of infantilizing desks for students and he, too, sat at one of them. His long legs stuck out with a pointlessly jaunty, Abraham Lincoln air. He clutched a paper coffee cup and laughed as I spoke about Chekhov. He grew pensive, explaining to me, as if from on high, that the countercultural movements of the 1960s and '70s had been almost immediately "sold back" to America's youth.

In the Middle Ages he would likely have attempted to impregnate me (using wiles, as I imagined it, rather than brute force). But for now, for the short duration of this modern life, he examined my language. His mind was a soup he lavished on us all. We were his students. He had not become a novelist.

But there was, as there always is, someone else. This someone was in my grade at school. His name was Jamie Cullinan and I could never remember how to spell his common and admittedly phonetic last name. This was just one of the strange things about the way in which I knew him.

Jamie sat behind me in AP chemistry. My shirt rode up and he made a comment about the hair on my lower back, which was excessive in his opinion. Why I loved this insult I do not know. Later, we were lab partners, and later, after his mother died, I came to his house and listened to all his CDs with him, one by one. Then, one night, we had sex on the couch in the college adviser's office. It was an event at the school. Not the sex. I just mean, everyone was elsewhere and distracted by an official school function, which was how we were able to make use of the office.

I did not know I loved Jamie until after I had sex with him. Before we had sex, I would have used the term "best friend" to describe Jamie. Given the existence of Graeme Bird, it was not even my first time falling in love.

Jamie had a certain proclivity. The longer I knew him and the more I loved him, the more pronounced his proclivity became.

This proclivity was that Jamie liked to remove his clothes when he was around friends. At parties, at casual gatherings, in his bedroom at home. He didn't want to be touched in a sexual way. He didn't want to be looked at sexually. He wanted people to be with him, when he was like this. He wanted witnesses.

The reason that he liked this and that he did this was that when Jamie was naked, the ghost of his dead mother appeared. I know this because once I heard him talking to her.

Jamie's mother died when we were in the eleventh grade. About fifty people from our class came to the funeral. It was a warm day in the fall, and Jamie seemed not to mind so much being sad, as long as he didn't have to be in control. He walked with the casket and spoke during the service and afterward in a living room was given a chair and girls from our class sat around him and put their hands on his knees and legs and sometimes on his shoes.

For a few months after, Jamie seemed to love people, without caring too much about them. I observed him. Thoughts of his mother crept by. Sometimes he saw her floating above him near the ceiling when he took a bath: She wore a black wool skirt and jacket, gold buttons and a thin white line up the front. She had on pantyhose but no shoes. Her eyes blinked continuously, her hair blowing across her forehead.

Girls in school gave him hugs; boys nodded solemnly.

When he changed his clothes his mother sat on the dresser. It was high so she had to bend her neck to keep her head from striking the ceiling. She wore running shorts and a red sweatshirt. Heavy socks. Her sneakers looked clean. He wanted to ask her where these clothes came from. The suit was familiar, but not this athletic gear. Sometimes it looked a little like she was laughing, which scared him, but not enough for him to want her to go away.

I mean, I have to guess about the above. I have to guess that at night Jamie did not dream about his mother much, that instead he dreamed about amnesia. He would stand in a furnished room or walk the length of a crowded avenue thinking how he should know exactly where he was, what was the next step, what his own name was, but he could not recall. He would see a commonplace object on the table but be unable to retrieve the word they were using to refer to it "these days," which in the dream he put to himself as "this time," examining the turquoise digits of a clock radio someone had left on a couch. In other dreams he ate. He ate mixing bowls of milk and cereal, heads of lettuce whole like apples, poured boxes of sugar into his mouth and listened to his (living) mother and father talking, weighing the advantages and disadvantages of going into the city or buying a convection microwave.

In the dream he became sleepy. He fought to stay awake until the last word.

I'm not sure if I put this in my novella, but Jamie did not love me. That fundamental fact of our relationship was somehow inadmissible, even in fiction. To Jamie, I was a dear but experimental entity: a pattern, style, or pretty girl. He once sent me a photo of himself looking moody at the edge of an Irish cliff in summer. He wanted me to understand that he took life and himself seriously. But I didn't need a snapshot from his month abroad to know that.

I forget where he went to college. I forget everything about him. He, like me, had a scar on his lower lip. His eyes were an impossible substance: blue coffee, black like ocean foam, sometimes green as cloud or the stinging edge of the sun. His small face was perfect, beautiful and perfect. He wanted to be an actor but could not act.

"This isn't working," I remember him saying.

Meanwhile, Camila was also my best friend.

I don't remember the day Camila and I met, but there was a feeling I got that she believed she already knew me, had chosen me for one reason and one reason only: we were already acquainted. This would happen to me again later in life, when I met the man who would become my husband, but with him there was a kind of hard twist to the recognition, followed by a rush like drugs.

For Camila and me, it was just that we had more in common than either of us could have predicted. This unforeseen commonality expressed itself through collaborative writings, inscrutable poems and fragmentary stories we liked to inscribe on bathroom walls.

I say "expressed itself," as if there was an impersonal or mystical dynamic at play, because that might even be slightly true. Camila's mother was a spiritual healer who meditated for an hour or more each day. Camila had information about medicinal herbs and other substances one immolated or consumed that I, in my radical ignorance of magic outside of cheeseball TV scenarios, was too dull to display much curiosity about.

Camila and I were only in high school. We weren't really formed enough to maim each other, as women sometimes do—or even to establish, with any specificity, what pertained, strictly speaking, to one of us in the relationship, but not the other.

Camila lived in the South Bronx with her mother and a younger sister, who looked more like their mother than Camila did. At this time, the area was still reeling from the 1970s, something that my father, who had himself been born there before the Second World War, did not feel inspired to explain to me on the few occasions he acknowledged me in conversation, although he did seem to find it interesting that my closest friend lived in the district of his birth. Camila did not invite me over, but she told me stories about her neighbors, two or three of whom became her lovers and one of whom twice impregnated her, necessitating a pair of abortions I attended. Almost everything we both wanted to understand concerned love. We thought about it as a kind of limbed and featured wind, what I would not have known to call a spell. It was a rare and partly invisible animal. We went to the Cloisters together and stared at the unicorn tapestries.

This unicorn is male. His garden is red. How red. His earth. And all the flowers zombie flesh, growing out of the crimson . . .

What I'm trying to say is, we were both convinced that it would happen: One day each of us would espy love, sitting on its small, symmetrical hill. We would be initiated into the mystery.

Camila came to my house and stayed, sometimes multiple nights in a row. An acquaintance of my parents, present for dinner, inquired about the relationship between something called "the D.R." and the sport of baseball. He was a man with a well-groomed beard. I watched Camila receive his line of questioning.

Later I took this up with my parents. I didn't think it was a good way to speak to my friends.

"She's Dominican, right?"

This was my father, child of an immigrant.

It was as if the subject of this conversation were irretrievable.

As I was saying, the novella I wrote during this time is lost, but that does not mean that I don't remember it. I recall, certainly, the way in which I wrote, the difficulty. I can't imagine it was more than twenty thousand words, but I agonized, sitting on the floor, terrified by the liquid ease with which time fell, as if down an infinite stair, into the future-present. It was an anemic work with a first-person narrator. I did the best I could. I'd manage a single sentence. I knew nothing about what the novella was about, had no idea what I was saying.

But I have to specify this nothing: This was not the not knowing of a great artist. It was, I believe, a more basic, primal ignorance. There was a significant portion of my own experience—let us say, the sensory data, the events and actions to which I had been privy in my brief lifetime, but also, and perhaps more pressingly, the origins of the names of things, the ways in which things were judged and called—that I did not understand. Thus, if I was writing a novella, it was a sort of warily executed drawing of something that I had concluded did not exist but in fact existed. I was, given these conditions, more suited to the composition of fiction than I ever could have imagined—but I did not understand that then.

Although I can't be entirely sure, I think the novella began with an account by the narrator, an adolescent girl maybe sixteen years old, regarding what seems to the narrator to have been a fatal accident on the West Side Highway. The narrator was in the car and her mother was driving. Someone was walking down the highway in the right lane, moving in the same direction as traffic on the southbound side. This person was simply there, walking without hurry. It was either very late at night or early in the morning, and I am not sure that reasons are given for the unusual hour of travel.

In the novella, the mother, driving, hits this walking person. It's a full-on collision at fifty-plus miles per hour. After this, the mother does not stop. The mother keeps driving, and, presumably, from this point on, the mother keeps on with her life as well, much as before, except that now the narrator is aware that her mother is reasonably adept at vehicular manslaughter.

I think I can also say with certainty, having hovered over these faint memories of plot, that the narrator was not in the car, not literally. Yes, I remember it now. The novella begins with an account of the mother's appearance in the apartment where she lives with her husband and daughter. I can't remember if the mother comes home at night or in the morning. I can't remember where the husband—the father of the narrator—is, either. All I remember is the mother comes home and announces that she has hit someone with her car on the West Side Highway. After hitting this person, she did not stop.

I believe that the narrator waits for something to show up on the news, but nothing does. The narrator is uncertain.

Into this ambiguous household come other events.

This household is adjacent to other households.

In fact, there is a boy. *In fact*, there are two boys.

The first boy is the son of a friend of the narrator's mother. He is a troubled youth. The narrator is fascinated by him, for she, the narrator, is not troubled. She is good. She watches this boy's glowering movements from a safe distance. The narrator is, meanwhile, in love with a boy she knows at school. We are eventually given to learn that the narrator is having sex with the troubled son of the family friend, but not with the boy at school whom she loves.

The narrator has become pregnant.

Perhaps she has been pregnant since the beginning of the novella. The end.

I turned the novella in to Graeme Bird. After he had read it, he told me that it was not very good. I might, according to him, want to reconsider my ambitions. I was probably not really capable of this work. He gave me an A- and made some wistful pronouncements regarding the playwriting of one of my classmates, the scion of a powerful political family who was unlikely to avoid a life of public service. "*That* was interesting to me," Graeme Bird confessed, of the scion's recent one-man show.

Then Graeme Bird handed the novella back. "I'm not going to keep this." The sentence was stuffed with meaning I could not make out. "I won't be keeping this for you," Graeme Bird repeated.

Something else I need to mention: My mother—my real mother, now—is a devotee of *The Red Shoes*. By this I mean, the demonic Pressburger and Powell film of 1948 that inspired Aronofsky's hackneyed thriller, and I also mean, the shoes themselves. I remember, too, when I first heard, or, rather, *saw*, David Bowie's "Let's Dance" as a video on MTV (red shoes in the Australian dust below a cloud produced by nuclear testing).

"The red shoes are not tired," says the vampiric Boris Lermontov (Anton Walbrook, also of *Gaslight* fame), director of the fictional ballet company in the film. He is paraphrasing the central problem of the Hans Christian Andersen fairy tale. "Put on the red shoes, Vicky," he tells the heroine. The shoes never stop dancing.

Lermontov, to the extent we understand him—his only friends are cavernous, thickly appointed apartments in Western European cities where he lounges in improbable smoking costumes, usually enraged—desires the work of an obsessively committed dancer. When he first meets Victoria Page, played by Moira Shearer, at a party in her wealthy aunt's home, the two strike a Faustian bargain.

It's not clear if they know what they are saying to each other. "Why do you want to dance?" Lermontov asks, feeling himself cornered by pushy aristocrats. "Why do you want to live?" Vicky counters, admitting, perhaps prematurely, that suicide is never off the table, as far as she is concerned.

We nearly hear the gears clicking in Lermontov's head. Meanwhile, Vicky is internally confirming a certain logic, previously unacknowledged. Dance = live. But also, live IFF *dance*.

It's the meeting of a sadist and a masochist, although ambition veils everything—and quite effectively. Shearer's exceedingly white body, a spray of freckles between her clavicles, the unreal redness of her hair; Walbrook's powdered face, the rabbit pink of his eyes and bloodless glossy lips, his proto–Kurt Cobain bubble tortoise sunglasses. There is a feeling, too, among the actors, as of corpses reanimated after battle. A desire to reclaim youth lost to bombs. Men wearing more makeup than the women. Shearer, if a doll, still the only living person; the impossible smallness of her starved and muscled back.

In 1948, my mother would have been five years old. She lived in California, in San Diego, near the naval base there. I doubt she would have seen the film till later.

Still, I think about what she could have seen, Vicky's final leap into a plume of steam produced by a locomotive, her death as a hideous painted twig bundle on the tracks.

I had taken Latin and I knew: In another era, this body would have been transformed. Gods or muses, moved by pity, might have made of her a seagull or attractive lichen. But here Vicky only dies. Film is a late-industrial art form, after all. Vicky's last words are a request that her idiotic boyfriend, an insecure composer, remove the red shoes.

Here the film cuts back to Lermontov. He emerges, grief-stricken, from between crimson curtains to announce the death to all of Monaco. Walbrook's performance is inspired. His acting is so modern that for a moment one feels one has slipped into a David Lynch film or something by Paul Verhoeven.

In the Vicky-less "Red Shoes" that ensues, all the dancers are in violent mourning. They are automata and spin nearby an empty spot that slips across the stage. The weeping of the black-clad priest is real. At the ballet's conclusion, the shoemaker once again offers us, the audience, the red shoes. Perhaps it's recycled footage from the first performance, also depicted in the film. Nothing in his gleeful expression seems to have changed. The shoes are not tired.

In 1949, in a strange follow-up to this allegorical masterpiece, Metro-Goldwyn-Mayer rereleased another film about red footgear and the coming globalization of American mania, 1939's *The Wizard of Oz*. I watched this film so many times as a child. I had no idea it had been a flop when it first came out.

These were written without hesitation and in a careless manner. The first sentence and the date were written in the right upper half of the sheet starting from the middle and proceeding laterally to the right corner then going down vertically along the right margin of the sheet. The second and third sentences started again from the top middle but this time going down vertically and each vertical line proceeded from right to left until the left margin was reached. Then she turned the sheet 90 degrees to the left and started writing from the left upper corner just below the first sentence. This time the sentence was written laterally, shifting the head of the line slightly to the right each time the line was changed. [Note: In Japanese writing, lateral rightward writing and vertical downward writing are in current use. Generally speaking, the former style is employed for scientific matters and the latter is employed for literary purposes. In handwriting the style depends on personal liking.] Thus spatial arrangement of sentences became chaotic. Letterforms were clumsy and letter sizes were irregular. Some letters were so clumsily written that they could not be identified on later reading. But there were no omissions or substitutions of letters. Grammar was also without problem, although the meaning is loose and difficult to grasp. She continued writing in a similar fashion consuming two more sheets [fig. 1].

But the behavior was never observed again even with prompting. A tendency for inappropriate use of any other objects was not observed.

—Yamadori, Mori, Tabuchi, Kudo, Mitani (1986)

I wrote things down by hand so that the mediated experience might impart something to me.

—Hanne Darboven (1989)

This page intentionally left blank.

Three: Happiness

Oh, and there is another thing: the last time I saw Graeme Bird. By this time, I was married.

I was twenty-five. I had been married for a year.

I took my husband with me. It must have been a weekend. Graeme still lived in Connecticut and had the same wife he'd had when I was in high school, his third, a fact that, for some reason, surprised me. Anyway, she was no fool, Graeme's wife. Beth Bird: She was an ugly woman with a voice so beautiful she seemed beautiful. Thus, Beth Bird was beautiful. She was a beautiful and intelligent woman and Graeme was a weakness she permitted herself.

My husband's name was Cody. I know that's a bad name, a name invented in America, and he was a bad person, Cody was, but I was not aware of this, not then. Someone who didn't know him might have said that Cody was a drunk with a remarkable sense of humor. I just thought of him as my soul mate. I had met him in the early days of my work in standardized testing.

An aside here regarding my life and what had become of it since high school: I think I was in college when the problems started. I can't remember the first time I had the feeling, although believe me I have tried. I've tried, too, to think about how to describe the feeling. During the day it expressed itself via a series of sensations analogous to the experience of being seated in a darkened theater, watching a movie unspool on the screen. Everyone I encountered had been written into the plot. Only I had nothing to do with the scenario. There was a distance between anything that took place and me, between the world and my thoughts and feelings.

I often went for long walks. I did this because it seemed to be the only behavior I could engage in that brought relief. The feeling, which is to say, the feeling of the feeling, was not good. It wasn't like the relaxing detachment from one's personal narrative a person in a cinema undergoes. Rather, it was, paradoxically, a feeling of extreme and unrelenting closeness: I had trouble breathing and sometimes wanted to scream. The detachment I felt, which was in fact or at the same time a constriction, expressed itself as a problem of scale: things were either too large to touch, or they were too small. People I was required to communicate with in order to purchase coffee, lunch, or groceries were aware, I believed, of the difficulty in which I found myself. I would go to lectures and make sketches of the professor's hand gestures. I ignored the lesson. I believed it was, overall, better not to listen to anything other people said. Their utterances were either unintelligible, since germane to a plot in which I had no role, or they were threatening augurs, warnings that I did not belong.

On my walks I was able to calm myself by means of silence and repetition. I studied the light.

Most things were a lie.

At night, when I closed my eyes, I seemed to hear all the voices I had heard during the course of the day, replayed at random behind my ears. They nattered endlessly. It was always as if I were not there, as if I were *not* their host. No voices "told me to do things," in that cliché. None of this mass of phantasmagoric discourse was addressed to me.

There was a distance.

Still, I believed myself sane.

If I had been raised differently, I might have understood that I was undergoing the early stages of what is known as a psychotic break. Instead, I chose to see my condition as historical and as, therefore, a feature of the real, actual world. It was a product of events.

Part of what made my delusion regarding my state of mind difficult to recognize, never mind dispel, was that I was not, strictly speaking, wrong. My psychosis *was* a product of events. I just did not know which events it was a product of.

Thus did I do pretty poorly in college. And thus did my mother, who did not believe in psychotherapy, inscribe to me a number of emails in which she cautioned me not to lose my mind, not to "go and kill yourself." I had, above all else, to "stop writing."

I was lucky, however, in that, in spite of my affliction, I had always been good at making friends. People my own age were, generally speaking, excluded from the alienation. It was through one such, the female offspring of an industrialist clan, a strict fan of facial masks and twinsets skilled in the abuse of prescription medication, that I became employed, reporting two weeks after graduation at Paulette, a Canadian standardized testing conglomerate with offices in mid-Manhattan. I was to deal in American regionalisms beyond the ken of extranationals. It was perfect for my background, particularly as I did not have one.

It was, for example, beyond the pale to compose a question involving a phrase like "slow cooker," because "slow cooker" is, in fact, dialect. A test taker in the Midwest might not understand that a slow cooker is what is properly, from her point of view, termed a "Crock-Pot."

I weeded out shibboleths.

I was good at it, too, and this was how I met my coworker and later spouse, this young blond man, Cody Peters.

We were in the office and he was always offering me things. He never once approached me, but if there was a chance for us to speak, he offered: advice, coffee, water, string cheese, amusing recaps of the culture, choice internet video. It was I who first walked over to his cubicle, who lingered after Friday drinks.

Cody wore sneakers with his work clothes. His pants were too large. He lived in a FiDi loft, an apocalyptic hovel whose nightmarishly frail dividing walls charmed me. This is real life, I thought. I myself resided primly in Cobble Hill with roommates. This was happening during a historical period when one could still do this.

I knew Cody drank heavily, but I did not know this had a meaning. I drank with him and mistook this activity for a bond. Or perhaps it was a bond. It was chemical for sure. "Dewbear," he called me, meaning the dew of the morning lawn, a clawed mammal's vestigial digit. He was from upstate and happiest in winter. He was constantly erect.

His eyes were small and deeply set. He allowed a beard to come in.

We got married on a whim and told no one for months. Then we told everyone, and everyone took us out drinking.

My parents were introduced the last. I tried to think of all this as epic, as a story I would one day tell. It did not occur to me to wonder to whom I might one day be telling my epic. I was banking on an increase of happiness in direct proportion to years. All I cared about was mutual understanding. Money, children, home: none of these things factored into my decisions.

I felt mostly sane.

Cody's gaze was soft, buzzing.

My parents demanded to know if I was pregnant.

"I guess it's your life," my father said.

I do remember an edge of fear creeping in, even then, in a moment I took to be one of great happiness. I noticed that still, at this time, as an adult, I did not know who my father was. He kept his distance. I had the sense he was of a mind to believe that Cody owned me now. And there was something else I could not identify. Something my father seemed to smell, a way his eyes moved.

A song seemed to play, but I could not hear it.

Everything was normal. Everyone was sane. It was a story about the normal formation of sane families.

I fell asleep quickly now and did not dream.

There was nothing more to know.

Cody would come home late and scream about his love for his parents and siblings. He wanted me to comprehend that under no circumstances was he going to abandon his family for me.

Yet, in the daytime, he loved me. And New York was harsh. We planned to journey to the center of the country for a while.

It was this, the plan to travel, that caused me to look up Graeme Bird. It—our plan—somehow reminded me that I wanted Graeme Bird to know that I was married now.

Cody and I rode the commuter rail. "So this guy was your English teacher?" Cody inquired, as if I had never spoken of Graeme before.

It was August, one of those days when it is impossible to imagine a changing of the seasons.

We rode backward and I began to fall asleep, even as I began to feel slightly ill. Cody put his arm around me, and I touched the denim on his thigh. It felt correct.

Graeme came alone to pick us up. He was as tall as ever and squinted in the parking lot.

Cody was not tall. He and Graeme shook hands.

Graeme drove. He asked for news of my classmates, but I had lost touch with everyone, including Camila.

Graeme seemed vaguely impressed. It was clear he had not expected this of me.

We careened into his driveway. His small house sat on a hump of land. Water shimmered blackly behind it.

Beth Bird greeted us with what I now remember as a plate of cured meats. She set these on a table in a shady room. She returned to her cooking.

Graeme seemed determined to ingratiate himself with Cody. I remember listening as Graeme posed questions carefully designed to ensure consensus. I observed as the feeling of consensus grew. Cody was impressed by Graeme. Cody wanted to know how such a man as Graeme came to live such a life as Graeme lived.

Graeme suggested a quick sail before dinner.

Beth was consulted.

The three of us trooped out through the back screen door, down the lawn.

The day was old already and the light like a syrup and a mist, both at once, indeterminate. The boat curved away from the land, as if on a track.

Here I was, or so I felt, with all questions answered. I was only twenty-five, but I knew my entire life. Here I was, telling Graeme Bird about it. My whole life. I did not even have to speak.

I should say that there had been a death in my family, back when I was in college. It had nothing to do with the condition of my mind, so called. It had little to do with me.

I had only known her as a child. There are photographs of me, brown in a sundress with crossed straps, squatting on a lawn near white birds. But I do not remember being there.

She was alive but we never went to see her.

I have been given some of her life because of this.

I have some of her sins. I cart them around. It is my job to expiate them. My mother gave them to me. It was a sin on my mother's part to have done this, but it's too late to go back now.

The weight, by the way, is enormous. I sometimes have to carry heavy things for no good reason, just to make it seem more real. Otherwise, the burden does not make sense. I'll take sample textbooks from the office. I don't need them at home. But I tote them with me, senselessly, to and fro, never reading them.

I'm grateful to these objects. Their sharp edges and piney, gluey scent. How they fit neatly into bags and seek a destination near the center of the earth.

I do have a story.

This is the only story I have to tell you. I used to like to think that things might work out differently. That is youth for you.

And as I'm trying to say, I had a husband once, too. A great love. Where you find me is in the midst of an immense act of interpretation. I was wrong about him in every way it is possible to be wrong about a person. But this, you see, is part of the story. It's how I know I have a story. It's also how I know the story is a test.

When I was in college, when my mother's mother died, I did not know what to think. It took some time, the dying, and it happened mostly out of sight, in that large place called California.

I considered it unimportant. I know that's a terrible thing to say, but I didn't have much choice.

My mother, still recouping a certain gross emotional debt she felt was owed her, mentioned, in an offhand way one day, that her mother had been discovered collapsed outside her home.

I imagined the body, "discovered collapsed," atop a pile of neon decorative gravel.

I must have been speaking to my mother by phone. I was nineteen or twenty. Or, maybe I was twenty-one or twenty-two. I do know that I was twenty-four when my mother's mother, at last, died.

My mother's mother had been avoiding the presence of other human beings for at least a decade at this point, although it is possible that she had been avoiding the presence of other human beings for something more like two decades—or, more than this.

Who, after all, was counting?

My mother's mother lived in a modern wooden house on the side of an eroding hill. You could see the naval base and bay and observe the airport from her deck. The house was, perhaps, most conspicuously modern in that even in the arid climate it had begun to rot. The floors and deck were particularly unstable. It did all those who encountered it the strange service of acting as a reminder that modernity had come and gone. Whatever it was we were living in now, we were not modern.

We had, in fact, no word for ourselves.

This might even have bothered my mother's mother.

After her collapse, she was discovered by someone delivering groceries. I'm not sure how many days it took. She had apparently for some time been living on scotch and cigarettes. At the hospital, given that she weighed just eighty pounds and was additionally suffering from advanced throat cancer, the doctors were amazed she was alive. There were noises about doing a study.

In this scene, I imagine her as a sea creature, a relic. She was, at this time, apart from my parents, my closest living relative. I had not seen her for more than fifteen years.

My mother's mother had been existing, forever, it seemed to me, in a state of extreme solitude, a suspended animation. This was how she had lived out the 1970s, and the 1980s, the time of my birth, and the '90s, too. She kept her distance. She medicated diligently as the ads in magazines of her youth instructed, hand around a glass, plume of smoke directed at the ceiling. She had a proper living room.

We went to see her in the hospice. My mother and I did. My mother's mother wore dainty black sweatpants and a black sweatshirt and black cotton slippers in a wheelchair. I don't know if I have ever seen someone so thin. Her hair was short, elegant somehow, someone's drawing of a cloud. She was lucid yet insane in her determination.

"You are so beautiful," she told me. "You are so beautiful, you can't even help it."

Having spoken these two sentences, she asked to be wheeled away, and my mother reappeared.

"I had to get more pads," my mother said.

I thought that this might be a reference to incontinence.

My mother continued, "She goes through them very quickly. The staff are in awe." And my mother produced a set of yellow legal pads contained in plastic. She zipped the wrapping off.

This was how I began to understand.

I don't know if it was before or after my mother's mother's death that it became clear what the pads were for. I don't know if I asked my mother then, although I have a memory of being told that my mother's mother made use of the legal pads for writing. Always in pen, she transcribed conversations and events from her bed. She wrote down everything that happened. I think my mother said something about how her mother claimed that in this way no one would be able to deceive her.

I am starting to come to the conclusion that it must have been on this trip. My mother had been in San Diego before me, staying in the decrepit modern house that her mother would never return to. Maybe, after the revelation about the legal pads, I asked her. Maybe I said, "Did she always do this?" It's possible that I wanted to know if there might be more of them. But it's also possible that I did not come to this information by way of inquiry. I may simply have been told: "I threw away all of my mother's writing."

The living room in the modern house, dyed tea color by its occupant's dedication to cigarettes, had been full, stacked high, as I was told, with my mother's mother's writing.

"You could barely walk around it."

I must have asked what it was like.

"The living room?"

"Her writing."

"Her writing? It was nonsense." My mother paused. "To be frank, it was terrifying."

"Oh," I said. "All the same, I wish you hadn't thrown it away. I would have liked to have seen it."

"You would say that."

"Say what?"

"You aren't listening. It was gibberish. It was disgusting."

I did feel something, then. It was cold, as if someone had opened a flap at the back of my head.

A hypergraphic tendency was observed for four days from the 22nd to the 25th postoperative days. For instance, one day when the patient was asked to write down her address, she wrote it correctly. But instead of stopping there, she took another sheet of paper and continued writing sentences such as, "My disease is called cerebral palsy. Pain is so severe every day that I feel like crazy. My doctor's name is so and so [actual name was written]. I wish I could be better soon." These sentences were written without hesitation, not paying much attention to the people present.

—Yamadori, Mori, Tabuchi, Kudo, Mitani (1986)

At home, the girl was considered "too intelligent"—the characterization did not only stand for Hanne's keen perception, but was also supposed to secretly excuse her personality traits, which were making her parents increasingly uncomfortable.

In the following months, Hanne became ill. The doctor discovered a serious middle ear infection. Then came the seizures.

—Verena Berger (2015)

Dostoyevsky and Flaubert were both epileptics.

I sometimes think there is something wrong with my brain, too.

When I was in the ninth grade I had a gym teacher who said he'd never met anyone with as much energy as me. Too bad I couldn't aim for shit.

Hypergraphia is a behavioral condition. It is often associated with temporal lobe epilepsy—in fact, only 10 percent of individuals with temporal lobe epilepsy exhibit the condition—but other circumstances contributing damage to the hippocampus and Wernicke's area can bring it on. Strokes. Something the literature calls "chemical factors."

Hypergraphia not caused by epilepsy usually occurs in the right cerebral hemisphere. Lesions to the right brain disinhibit language function in the left.

Thus hypergraphia cannot be isolated to any single cause or portion of the brain.

Some hypergraphs write in legible sentences and lists. Others: not. They scratch and scribble.

The condition was first identified and studied in the 1970s. I love the researchers' names: Waxman, Geschwind. The first you will have to do your own work on, but the latter: from the Old High German *swind*, from the Proto-Germanic *swinþaz*, meaning "quick."

During his lifetime, Lewis Carroll wrote over 98,000 letters.

You might be tempted to think of this as a genius's disease (did I mention Van Gogh was also a sufferer?), an ambiguous productivity miracle, but I am not so sanguine. From what I've read of it on Reddit, pronounced and recurrent hypergraphia is debilitating. It creates shut-ins who on some days are compelled to commit to existence tens of thousands of words.

In 1999, a man in Georgia was acquitted of the murder of his wife, who had died after having eluded the public eye for twenty-seven years. It was her massively verbose and detailed diary that saved him (over a million words). It testified to her epilepsy and unwillingness to go outdoors, along with an abnormal fervor for setting things down on paper.

Yet, I doubt that the majority, or even a large minority, of those with a chronic inability to leave their homes are hypergraphs.

In a way, hypergraphs are like ancestors, or like an idea I have about ancestors that I struggle to articulate in other terms. I also think that it's possible that my own mother was right, I mean, about her mother's writing being disgusting. However, my only certainty with regard to these scripts is that I'll never know.

I thought for a while, too, that the way I got my adult life—my job and husband—was through my determination not to become a writer. If, I sometimes used to think, I had started writing during the times when things were bad, when I, for example, would soothe myself with aimless walking, then perhaps I could have become a happy member of society, which, perhaps I really mean: I could have become a visionary.

I did not become that, although I have never been devoid of thought. I'm still thinking.

Instead, as is now clear to me, I got a job at which I display stolid competence. I was promoted twice.

Also, I got Cody.

Cody was, in a way, the right person. He was the wrong person, of course, but he was, in addition, the perfect person, as I doubt that there is anyone else on the planet who could have offered me a more thorough disillusionment. The disillusionment offered by Cody was a powerful dose; it was timed release, a joyful capsule, and I savored its tasty, awful disintegration over the course of a decade.

Cody and I moved deep into a borough. We set up a fragile house then went away for a month to reconfirm the ecstasies of early marriage. We traveled and camped in the Upper Midwest and returned to find New York unchanged.

I was not surprised by this, New York's unchangedness, but it seemed to set Cody back. There was a spin under his eyes, a minute whirlpool, who knows how deep it went.

But if I saw this then, I didn't care. Everything about Cody seemed true and fitting, even the basic, gentle flatness of his eyes.

Cody quit his job at Paulette. You shouldn't work at the same office as the person you were married to, he said. It led to tension.

He took work as an art handler. We shared my health insurance.

I learned, to my surprise, that Cody was an artist. This was the reason that Cody's work clothes were too big, that he knew so much about YouTube, carried a notebook into which he dipped a much-gnawed pencil, photographed everything. He cut his own hair and did not shave.

It seems insensitive, bordering on delusional, of me, when I look back now, not to have recognized this fundamental fact about the person I was married to. But to me Cody was the man I was always going to know. He wasn't anything more or less than this. His proclivities, interests, dreams were fundamentally unimportant, in the sense that they could not sway me. My plan was to leave him free.

Cody purchased a bag of cement and brought home scrap wood.

I fretted about the state of our apartment.

Cody said he'd get a studio as soon as feasible. He said he thought he had some leads. He was cooking pasta and demolishing a six-pack, baseball on the radio.

He was not devoid of charm.

In my conception of the world, which was in fact a conception inherited from my parents, the meaning of one's interest in art was summed up by one's ability to avoid (1) making art, and (2) identifying as an artist. If one could not avoid the first, it was at least necessary not to do the second. I was, in the meantime, fairly proud of myself. I, quiet and mediocre, did neither. For this reason, the meaning of my interest in art was that I was a good person. I was so much better than Cody. I didn't have to be an artist, because I was already—and so extremely—perfect.

I clung to this notion, unconsciously sniffing and lightly licking it—polishing my sorrows as if they were a charm.

Cody had no such pretensions.

His repulsive desk was now stacked high with paint-filled yogurt containers, jars of screws and bitty litter he had collected from New York City sidewalks, a rusted hacksaw and an assortment of weary pliers, cloudy plastic sacks of colored sand, acrylics and cans of enamel, unusable brushes, broken pencils, plywood fragments, balls of twine and coils of salvaged wire, sculpting clay, copper mesh, candle wax, bags of blond hair covered with candle wax, gouache and charcoal sticks, faux bois paper, newspaper, pots of black ink, cardboard covered with white paint, tacks, deconstructed leather bindings, boards, cutout endpapers embellished with pasted papers, pasted-on cloth mounted on wood, partially painted wood, painted plaster and cork mounted on canvas but abandoned, a stuffed silk stocking suspended in a wooden frame, several plaster heads with painted cloth, googly eyes, two steel rods, part of a wooden chair hung on a board, a piece of a door covered in hessian, laminated plastic bits, Masonite, oils, unidentifiable plastic objects, a neon tube, a plastic rod, felt, cord, cotton, a dented pail, a sack, dust, cassette tapes, papier-mâché on a rubber hose, a broken tree limb, white tape, duct tape, galvanized metal, fiberglass, toy motors, a section of artificial turf, a Formica pedestal, a nonfunctioning surveillance camera, a dish of green glitter, felt markers, muslin, printouts of various websites, mirrors, several live flowering plants, corrugated cardboard, oil wash, rags, painted foam core, pornographic DVDs in a paper bag labeled PRIVATE.

I did not know how the heap had arrived. One day it was a desk; now it was something else.

Because I was continuing to work full-time I was seldom in the apartment when Cody was not and for this reason was never truly alone with the desk. In the morning I would pass it by on my way to the door and would note that it had a funny, knowing look. The lips on the smile it did not have curled back. It seemed to want to let out a bestial cry.

The desk was a double. It was the malingerer Dostoyevsky (though not Flaubert) would have encountered on an urban street. In the twenty-first century, it had moved inside our home. Like a dune, it shifted. It had something to do with the internet.

"What's in the bag?" I asked one Sunday.

"What bag?" Cody emerged from the kitchen.

"The bag on your desk."

Cody was holding a spoon, presumably because he was fixing pancakes. "Which bag on my desk?" He ran his tongue around the implement.

He had a point.

I indicated. "The PRIVATE bag."

"Sometimes a person," he told me, "needs *space*."

"Is this your space?" I asked. Perhaps I was flirtatious. Perhaps I edged toward the PRIVATE bag.

Or perhaps this scene did not take place. Instead I looked inside the bag one day. The titles of its contents had things like the word *cum* spelled with a *k*, the mention of youth, stuff about butts.

It was pretty standard issue.

When I mentioned my discovery to Cody over our latest repast of carbs and beer, he was abashed. He seemed to expect me to mete out punishment. Maybe I would set fire to the apartment.

This was the first time I had an inkling of the strength of Cody's ongoing attachment to his parents.

But all I wanted to know was why we could not share these interests.

In my defense, I had now for several years been working at a standardized testing company and had long since ceased to be a subtle reader.

Later, Cody would tell me that he had recounted this conversation to certain of his male friends. He claimed that he had touted the wonder of having a wife like me, a woman who did not disapprove of sex.

We must have watched the DVDs, the PRIVATE ones, but I don't remember anything about them now.

It's possible, anyway, that I was curious about the wrong thing. With regard to the desk, I mean.

Cody's first show was to be held at a Chelsea gallery that had been interesting and successful in the 1990s but had long since lost its way. It represented the estates of several dead and worthwhile artists and meanwhile paid its rent through sales of hideous fantasy paintings of *infantas* and other heavily decorated child-women dreamed up by an oil painter who was selling out like selling out was going out of style, which of course it wasn't.

The gallery, perhaps in an attempt to reclaim relevance, had hired a very young woman as its director. She was beautiful and small and loud.

This young woman, the director, was dating a boy who was even younger, who was in the process of being radicalized by the online right, which at this time (2008) passed for being a "post-internet hipster." Both of them came over to our house.

The director, whose name was Alexis, liked the desk.

I don't know if the PRIVATE bag was on display.

In a matter of days Alexis had whipped her bosses into such a frenzy that Cody was signing contracts. He had become the putative next thing. It was a coup.

A little later, Alexis's boyfriend, Zeke, was always around. Zeke was so attractive that minor fashion magazines ran features on his aimless life. They dressed him up in avant-garde suiting and asked him questions about his disaffected Twitter. He'd flash a couple of hazy stick-and-poke tattoos.

We'd go to a bar where I sat on the sidelines. Alexis and Cody schemed. Zeke's well-formed eyes ping-ponged pitiably, I thought, from wall to wall.

This part is the most difficult. I did love Cody. I loved him, and also he loved me. I'm not sure I've mentioned this. This was a reality and is contained in some segment of the history of the world, like an insect sealed in amber (iridescent hairs, frozen mandibles). We in the present no longer have access to these events, these conversations and glances and embraces, along with the more or less viable beliefs they might or might not have aroused and been expressions of—except as an image. A simple figure glitters in fossilized resin. It looks more or less OK back there.

It would be easier had I not loved this person, if my not loving him had been a key factor in our misunderstanding. However, this was not the way things worked.

And I remember, after things got bad, how hard it was to comprehend the decay of intelligibility, the way in which it no longer mattered that we could perceive each other's thoughts in all their dappled, pebbled, mixed familiarity, that they were always close enough to bite and touch. It wasn't that we stopped understanding each other. It was that we stopped caring about what we understood.

I remember one weekend Cody had been away, and when he came back we fought. At the end of the fight, when we were tearfully acknowledging our continued love, he told me that I fucked him up. I said, "How?" He said I fucked him up for being around other people. He said that when he spoke to me I analyzed every word he said as if it had a million different meanings. "I forget," he said, "that when I'm with other people if I say something it's just going to be a thing. If I say a word it's just going to be a word. I forget that when I'm around other people."

I tried to understand this as a compliment.

Cody's first show took place at the beginning of our third year of marriage. He was renting a studio by this time, so I had a less nuanced sense of what was going on with his desk.

In fact, I did not see the objects in the show until the night of the opening. The gallery had a truly massive, rangy space on the fifth floor of a former warehouse on 24th Street, a block from the water. The old wood floors were full of gaps. Through the windows, blackened by night, you could make out feeble stars.

It was warm, unseasonable as was becoming more common. I arrived alone. In black vinyl on the first spotlit wall was the exhibition's title:

DON'T WORRY ABOUT THE TRACE

It looked really good. I stood with my arms crossed, probably longer than was absolutely sane, contemplating what I was about to behold. I'm not sure if I would have admitted to myself at this time that I was afraid.

There was also part of me that knew exactly what Cody had done. After all, he knew every detail of my life. And I fell into the warm arms and bodies of friends and acquaintances under a luster of sweat that was not altogether a product of the air temperature.

The gallery's rooms were filled with re-creations of my grandmother's notebooks, ingeniously fashioned from inappropriate materials, plaster and wire and wood and sheet metal. They had been shellacked in some cases, in others slathered with house paint.

They gathered hugely in stacks. They massed. They were bright and slick and ugly. The effect was fantastic.

I encountered another artist, Scott, who for some reason began explaining in detail what it meant to give an "elevator speech." Over his shoulder, I could see Cody on the other side of the room.

Cody was staring at me, and I could make out that, much as I had never dreamed that he and I would meet in such a setting, he had not quite thought through what it would mean to see me in the midst of these materials. I can't say that he looked ashamed, but I also cannot say that he did not look ashamed. What he looked like was what it looks like when someone is enjoying their own fault. He had on a hard little smile. His eyes were like two bits of candied foodstuff, balls of polished dough.

PRIVATE, the bag had read.

I brushed past Scott and went to bury my face in Cody's shoulder. He held me very tight.

Here, now, is a list of dreams dreamed during my marriage:

Dream One

I stand near a window, high up in a building. I am at a cocktail party in its early, nervous stages. It is not a cruise ship but "as if" it were a cruise ship. Everything a bright Versace violet.

Dream Two

I am in Paris and go into a store that sells mass-produced, designy items. I am apparently looking for something to eat and afraid to ask questions.

Dream Three

I am somewhere with girls. A man offers us a credit card. This turns into transport to a Caribbean vacation, with routine violence in the hotel complex. It begins, incongruously, to snow. Smell of blood. As it becomes late, we gather in a room with picnic tables. A vampire holds a microphone.

Dream Four

There is a cat I have been given by a fairy. It is a difficult animal and dark yellow, the Garfield color, with tufted ears.

Dream Five

Swans, television.

Dream Six

Am held hostage by a mafia. Much time spent prostrate on carpet. Attempt to escape via a wicker tower.

Dream Seven

Meet Cody in an airplane hangar with many levels. Later we are discussing something in a bathroom, and he approaches and kisses me. I kiss him twice and lick his upper lip. Later I walk distances across a Swiss town, trying to find him. It is a sad time, but my hope knows no limits.

Dream Eight

Cody and I live in a much larger apartment than the one we in fact live in. White walls in several rooms we never visit are peeling, and I keep reminding him how much space there is. I want to move into other rooms but feel they are cursed. I try to appoint rooms in minor ways, pretending one closet is a kitchen, one corner a place of contemplation. Damp fertile smell. We discuss how we could invite hundreds of people over in the two back rooms, each larger than many theaters I've been to.

Dream Nine

I am in Scandinavia. I stay in a great house with ancient, much repainted moldings. There are corpses that are our responsibility. We find a cellar, hoist them down.

Dream Ten

I am with someone I love. It's a hilly suburban area, granite masses. Local highways have been blasted in. In some room, in some small manor, I am with a man whose face I cannot see. There is something about his voice, not his words, that tells me to keep coming forward. The room is in shadow, and I feel quiet excitement because it seems that he is asking if we can live together. I say that I thought that he had told me years ago that we could never live together, and we drive in a car by large lawns. It is either just before or just after it has rained, hours that would have no content except for this strange hope for love that has been resurrected. Later, I encounter an agent of the CIA who shows me how to leap from wall to wall.

Dream Eleven

I am on vacation with Cody in an equatorial country. We go for a walk/hike in some sandy, swamp-like region, and Cody climbs over a dune to look at a black pond where an alligator is. Then he gets into the pond with the alligator, and the alligator eats him. The alligator is very green, with a flat head the size of a truck tire. Later I am on a telephone at a hilltop café speaking to my parents, and I say something like, "I'm just going to tell you something that happened. My husband is dead." I have to hold my face together to keep from laughing. Yet it is as if someone is beating me with a shovel.

Dream Twelve

I have my old heart. I am the one who looks into rooms where people are together, while I am alone. Again, Cody is gone, for eminently rational reasons. I am a girl. I have to live in the corners of others' apartments. It is crowded and there is a lot of bedding and people are handsome poets. The others are young, too, even if they are older than I am. And they are impatient even if they spend most of their time lying around, taking slow walks, imagining ways to pay less rent. I have been away in another country where someone said I was Jewish. There is nothing anyone wants from me.

SELF-ASSESSMENT

1. Do you worry about how much someone drinks?

2. Do you have money problems because of someone's drinking?

3. Do you feel that if the drinker cared more, he'd drink less?

4. Do you blame the drinker's behavior on his family?

5. Are plans frequently upset or canceled because of the drinker?

6. Do you ever make threats, such as "If you don't stop drinking, I'll leave"?

7. Do you ever say, very quietly, once you are at home, "I'm worried about your drinking"?

8. Do you immediately leave the room before you can hear the response to your statement?

9. Do you find it chilling if there is no response?

10. Is there a response?

11. Have you ever been hurt or embarrassed, especially professionally, by the drinker's behavior?

12. Has the drinker ever publicly shamed you while drunk?

13. Have you considered calling your parents for help but abandoned that impulse, realizing you would face criticism?

14. Do you ever ride in the car with your husband who is driving and who has not only been drinking but is at this point completely blacked out?

15. Is he sleeping with the director of his gallery (to whom he keeps swearing, unbeknownst to you, that he's just about to ask for a divorce) and getting blow jobs from a college acquaintance, plus that random intern who texts him photos of her ass?

16. Has he moved on to something more serious?

17. Why don't you get rid of that car?

18. What will you do if he locks you out of the house again?

19. When will you stop locking yourself into the bathroom?

20. What is your definition of harm?

21. Do you ever feel there is a way in which damage to the skin lets out a word?

Five: Myths

My mother liked Cody, even very much. At first she merely condescended but subsequently, after some years had wriggled by, he became her ally.

Perhaps my mother believed, early on, that Cody was a ploy on my part at escape. This would explain her initial intolerance, the pursed lips and outings to restaurants elaborately adhering to conventions of nineteenth-century *haute cuisine,* the buttons of aspic and humorless waiters; her curt, shocked stares.

My parents glowered as Cody fumbled with forks. They glowered but internally they glowed. My error was a boon they had not expected; it left me open to an infinite reserve of resentment, which they might otherwise have felt for each other and which they had been stockpiling since my birth.

I had made that classic American miscalculation, in attempting to come home. *There's no place like home,* sang a reedy voice I attempted to ignore. Meanwhile, my parents batted lazily at Cody's gaucheness. They served each other damning proofs of his weak vocabulary. They chuckled at his mangled grooming.

Then Cody did something extraordinary. He went over to their side.

This isn't how it's supposed to happen, by the way. At least, not according to the movies and TV. In popular narratives, the spouse never fails to see through the in-laws' cruelty.

In real life, it did not work like this. In real life, the victimized party might be, before all else, determined not to be a victim.

As was Cody.

And here I need to say something about Cody's family, too. I've left them out so far because I wish they did not matter. However, they mattered more than anything else when it came to my husband's actions, and this was extremely unfortunate.

Cody was the youngest of four children. He was probably an act of revenge. Cody's parents' escapades in child creation had begun in high school, resulting in a shotgun wedding and the almost immediate stunting of Cody's father's pretensions to become a freewheeling member of the Merchant Marine. Instead, Cody's father, who was born to the upper class in an upstate suburb, became a lawyer. Cody's mother, whose family was not upper class, became what I have just termed her, which is to say a mom.

By the time I encountered these people, they had grown thick from sedentary life. They spoke a nasal accented English, something like the chewy, tinny vowels I associated with the Kennedys.

It was confusing because my first instinct was to see them as a genre of person I had never met before: true souls, gold-hearted tribalists who disliked cities. I looked at them across their dining room table among their chunky decor, their large family, and I wanted to believe that this was good. I wanted to believe that this inefficient way of life was inherently better and good. That it was OK to devote oneself to family, to shop exclusively at big-box stores. That careers *could* really not matter, if one had love.

They welcomed me only insofar as was absolutely necessary. There had already been one divorce, of the eldest daughter from her triathlete CEO. They were not fools, and they quickly came to comprehend that I did not represent an asset. I was DOA but too naive to notice.

Among the things I learned at Cody's home was the traditional myth of the original treaty between woman and man. It was not entirely clear where or when this treaty was signed and which woman it was—clothed only, perhaps, in a sash of daisies—who'd accepted the proposition. We munched pretzels from the head of a bear-shaped plastic barrel and lounged around a sticky den, cradling beers, as the ancient myth of this treaty was impressed upon us.

Once upon a time there was humanity. Humanity was mainly figured in its rightful, truthful form, which was male. The male form had electric thoughts, and thank goodness it did, because otherwise nothing much would ever have happened, and we certainly would not have so many varieties of motor or bomb or frozen entrée. The male form with its throbbing and important thoughts approached the female form, which, too, was there. To the female form, the male form said, "Stand behind me and see if you feel something." The female form obliged. "I don't know if you're far enough behind me," the male form commented, after a moment. The female form started to reply. "No!" exclaimed the male form, "I am not interested in your thoughts. I only want to know what you *feel*. You can't even listen to my instructions!" Here one might suppose that the female form pondered these instructions. It was getting to be a pleasant day. The male form stretched his limbs, reveling in the luscious confusion and ambiguity that now attended all his movements through the world, although this confusion and ambiguity had nothing, at base, to do with him. He strode forth with clear assertive steps, unambiguous thoughts. Somewhere else, a mystery foamed and trembled. It gazed upon the being that went before it, a being endowed with certainty and purpose. Mystery sang a little song. She did not know what else to do.

I listened to the myth. I kept waiting, but there wasn't any more to it. Probably I frowned. I might have said something about how I'd never heard anything like that before.

We were sitting on the couch. Cody's older brother, Jason, was present, too.

At my remark, they must have exchanged a glance. The sun was setting, and all things seemed filled with a muscled, airless mood. This was, to my mind, the mystery: The mystery is that anything exists. The mystery is that things have names and we believe in them. But for Cody's family the mystery was not that there is something for us to stand on. The mystery was that there is no strength without weakness, no presence without weakness, no good without weakness.

In their unfailing belief in the necessity of weakness, they had me.

You can be weak, they let me know. Around us, you're going to have to be. It will be a good idea to get used to that now.

Later that evening everyone watched some old home movies. These showed suburban interiors in the early days of Cody's parents' marriage. Here were the first blond children.

I sat on the couch and made sounds of appreciation. One could see how the elder daughter's heart had been repeatedly broken by the addition of each new child. A ten-year-old, she turned away from her younger sister to attend to a tangled necklace. Her face held a strangled agony.

It was harder to understand the two middle siblings by way of the footage. They were vague and also blond. Then came the final reel:

It must have been shot in 1982, when Cody would have been just over three years old. It was Easter Sunday and all four children had been posed on a thawing lawn, or perhaps simply discovered there—it was hard to say. The three eldest children wore coats, hats; you had the sense the weather was still wintry. Only Cody stood in bare legs and a shirt just long enough to cover his genitals. He wobbled on a stone at the garden's edge. He had a large head and a mild, dazed look. He was not an attractive child.

The camera began to be attracted to dances performed by abler children in weather-appropriate attire, but it did not pull far enough away from Cody's rock to miss the moment when he abruptly fell backward and disappeared, headfirst, behind it.

I jumped off the couch. I had perhaps already commented on toddler Cody's lack of pants, but this was a step too far.

No one else in the room seemed surprised by these images. No one in the images took note of Cody's fall.

When the lights came up and I continued to exclaim at what I feared was brain damage, Cody's mother shot me a warning glance. She was ensconced among her offspring. She was in her late fifties. Her dyed hair and succession of neatly starched sweatshirts worn with polo shirts, collars popped, attested to her sense of triumph. She was Machiavellian, one had to understand: which, I did not. She went to a secular church and voted for some Democrats and no one could say that she had not been flexible, at least where Cody's father was concerned.

Thus there was no conversation about toddler Cody's fall. There was some talk from time to time about his childhood asthma, his whimpering around doctors' needles, that youthful white-blond hair. But one could not discuss his mother's smoking, a habit that had attended the term of her pregnancy with Cody and apparently resulted in his challenged breathing, his stunted body and strangely bulbous fingers.

As time went on and we were married longer, even Cody seemed to be forgetting these events. I alone retained them, as if they were a feature of my own past.

My mother had no interest in Cody's family. But she did like to talk about marriage.

"She has been very successful," she said, of Cody's mother.

I requested clarification.

"She's had a very successful marriage," my mother repeated.

What about the lack of a life outside of her home, I wanted to know.

"She never had those expectations." My mother, a retired professional, was not in a good mood.

I told my mother that this was crazy.

"Good," my mother said. "That's good. You married him, and when you marry someone you get the family, too." What she did not say was that she knew that Cody and I were increasingly living separate lives. She did not have to say this. All she had to do was to invite us over for dinner. It would sometimes take me a month to pin Cody down.

This could have been year five or six. It could have been year seven.

When my mother saw Cody, she hugged him and smiled. She ushered him into her home.

Cody did not make much money, but that was OK with my mother, because she saw him as a wife in our relationship. I was a wife, too, of course, but only when convenient.

Cody's first show had been a critical success, but nothing sold. The art handling continued.

Cody had devised a pet name for me, a shortening of my first name into a single-syllable diminutive. He used it around my mother, saying he was sure that she, too, had used to call me this when I was young.

My mother had never used this pet name to refer to me at any point, but she liked to tell Cody that it was true, that she had used it. She liked to say that she could not imagine how he could be so intuitive, that it was really quite amazing.

She refilled his glass.

Cody and my mother agreed that it was true, I was very sensitive. I did not have a good ear. I was always taking everything too seriously.

My mother asked Cody, "And how are your parents?"

Cody spoke about renovations to their home, a dental surgery.

My mother asked Cody about his sisters, both of whom were now divorced.

Cody said something brilliant for its deft sifting of the truth.

My father, in a chair, watched. He seemed to consider this conversation an art form, like the dance.

"Those years, when a person has closed their ears." That is a rhyme. It's a phrase that's been starting to come to me, to describe a time and to describe myself, during this time. I remember vividly, for example, the women's bathroom in the bar we used to go to. It was Cody's bar, not mine. I'm sure it's still there. The bar, I mean, but of course this would entail the basement restroom, too.

The bar was not really a bar. Or, at least, it had not always been one. It was at one time a cultural association that pertained to a small ethnically Czech but German-speaking community that had relocated to northern Brooklyn from what was then the Austro-Hungarian Empire to escape pre–World War I difficulties. They were Christians and over the years organized numerous beauty contests and fishing excursions, commemorated in beady-eyed photographs that lined the walls. There was a moldering quality to the space: a banquet hall in back and a warren of empty, wood-paneled rooms upstairs. It would have been great as an impromptu interrogation facility.

Cody befriended the bartender, who was Polish. The bartender lived in Europe for half the year and had a girlfriend back home whom he tended not to invite to the United States, a fact that fascinated Cody no end.

The bartender was not prone to effusion. His English was fluent and thoughtful, but his face did not move. I supposed this had something to do with his work, which required that he interact with alcoholics. My husband was merely the youngest man pulled up to the bar.

I liked to think there was a modernity to our relationship. We did not have children, my husband and I, and my husband did not drink without me. I joined him. He was already two beers in.

He'd asked the bartender, who went by "Patrick" while stateside, to change the channel on one of the TVs to a Knicks game. My husband was drawing on a paper cocktail napkin in blue pen.

"Hi," I said.

Cody looked up. Alcohol softened him. It lent a litheness to his small, crowded features. An invisible hand seemed to press a smile onto his lips.

"Hello, Dewbear."

I hugged him on his stool, and we kissed.

Patrick extracted himself from a codger's monologue. He wanted to know what "the lady" would be drinking.

Cody pointed to his own stein.

"Very good," said Patrick.

"Thank you," I said and touched Cody's cocktail napkin. "What are you doing?"

"The Knicks are on," Cody told me.

On the napkin was a drawing of the twin towers. Cody had made two rectangles and was currently attempting to articulate the windows. There was, additionally, a pair of Beats (trademark) headphones so large that the towers appeared to be wearing them, each building a monolithic ear. Around this crude illustration, Cody had inscribed a border made of words:

beats by dre never forget 911 was an inside job everyone in the newspaper is a leopard

"Wow," I said.

"Just an idea."

We were different people.

He was becoming increasingly different.

I could feel the frozen mass of all I did not know about him.

My beer came. Again, I thanked Patrick.

I'm trying to recall what we would have spoken about, Cody and I. How would it have worked, given that Cody had devoted an hour or more of his day—the day that preceded this meeting, whose labors we had allegedly retired to this hole to recover from—to sexual intercourse with the woman who rented the studio next to his? We must have spoken about something.

Here, then, is a list of topics for conversation with one's beloved husband, who has, for the past 1.5 years, been having unprotected sex with a woman you have on five or six occasions encountered socially, who is also an art handler; who has also slept a handful of times with the director of the gallery that represents him; and who has been unfaithful to you on other occasions during the course of your eight-year relationship; bearing in mind, for the purposes of the list, that you are, if not blissfully then agonizingly, unaware of this long-standing pattern of infidelity, a pattern that is only going to continue, that, if one is frank, in fact defines your relationship with this person, in spite of or perhaps because of (who can say how interpersonal knowledge really operates) your inability to see it:

1. The Knicks
2. Difficulties at work involving a colleague who may or may not suffer from hypertension as well as narcissism
3. Pet names for players on the Knicks and professional athletes more generally
4. Others (ancient men) seated at the bar
5. Beauty contests of the past

6. Immigration during the early twentieth century
7. Poland
8. Jobs one can do without thinking too hard
9. The impending end of capitalism and how (whether?) to limit the outbreak of violence at this time
10. Ways to drink one's own urine

INTERPRETATION

For the following questions, select at least one answer. If more than one answer appears to be correct, you may select more than one answer. However, only responses for which you select a single answer will receive a score. Incorrect or unanswered questions receive a score of zero. You are advised to select a single answer and, where necessary, to guess.

The quotations included in between the chapters serve what purpose in relation to the novel overall?

a. It is most likely that they are intended to refute claims made in the novel.
b. They do not serve a purpose in relation to the novel.
c. They show that hypergraphia is a more widely experienced condition than the reader might previously have believed.
d. They show that truth is, as ever, subordinate to the form(s) and media via which facts are received.
e. None of the above.
f. Answer c, although not exclusively.

Hypergraphia is <u>best</u> defined as:

a. A pathological form of a normal human impulse to create and record.
b. A normal human impulse to create and record.
c. Compulsive writing.
d. A and b are interpretations of c, which is merely a description of a symptom. C, too,

is unsatisfactory. Therefore, there can be no definition.

e. A question about origins begins to enter here. In other words, how is it possible that a specific technology could become the unique means of the expression of a human disease? Is it not necessary that hypergraphia be expressed otherwise, elsewhere, without, or beyond writing?

f. Could it, therefore, be understood as a kind of involuntary desire to relive one's life?

The narrator's grandmother was likely a hypergraph. What can the reader infer from this?

a. That the narrator's grandmother suffered from temporal lobe epilepsy, the symptoms of which she hid from public scrutiny by remaining indoors and drinking heavily.

b. That the narrator is frightened that her grandmother's condition may have been passed down to her, through DNA.

c. That the narrator is frightened that her grandmother's condition may have been passed down to her, through learned behavior.

d. That the narrator's mother is afraid that her daughter shares some of the grandmother's traits.

e. That the narrator's mother caused the narrator to exhibit symptoms of hypergraphia.

f. That the narrator admires her grandmother.

Which series of adjectives best describe the narrator's mother?

a. Loving, wise, admirable
b. Observant, concerned, thoughtful
c. Lonely, confused, flirtatious
d. Paranoid, vindictive, ill
e. Fearful, reactive, blind
f. Odd, jealous, weak

Six: Weakness

I'm not interested in how things begin. I never have been.

Consider the "before" of that set phrase "before and after." Talking about "before" is not the same thing as talking about beginnings. Even if you try to pose the question "Where did this begin?" you don't really mean it.

"Before" is when I meet him. At the time, I don't understand why he's so obsessed with photographs. I don't realize that later on, after, when he's gone, I'll be the one in possession of the images. He's apparently made the archive for private use, but what I don't understand earlier, before, about the images, is that he is taking and collecting all these photographs for me.

He's getting all these photographs so that later, after, there will be something for me to look at. Because I won't be able to look at what has occurred, of that much I am sure. I look at them now because I can no longer understand Cody. I look at them because he isn't here and I need something else to see to understand what we were doing in those days and who we thought we were. I know somebody believed something, then. I must have believed. I'm still trying to figure out what that belief was. Or, I'm trying to develop some compassion for a person in the past, who is me. The person in the "before" is someone I feel I ought to know. The problem is that whenever I encounter her, I want to run up to her and shake her. I know violence is never a good plan, but I want to slap her in the face. "No," I want to say. "No, no, no, no." Stop what you are doing. You know there has to be a better way. He is going to deceive you. He is not a good person.

But even in my fantasy, she will not listen.

I haven't told you everything. I mean, I meant to. I meant to start off speaking in a full and earnest voice, but it turned out not to work that way. It seemed like Elliott's overdose and resulting death were clear events that I could point to, there in that first awkward chapter, but it's harder than I thought to explain what they may mean. In truth, I didn't know Elliott that well. He was someone I saw often. But did we ever play together? Did we ever have a conversation? Or, was everything we said to each other filtered through the speech and glances of our parents?

A bubble sat around me.

I had bad information, is what I am saying, and when one has bad information, often one is desperate. And when one is desperate, one attracts bad actors. My desperation was, for example, something Cody found alluring and subsequently groomed. It hung around me like a brilliant jacket mostly only he could see.

I remember, too, when I was in college, several years before I met Cody, when my madness was at its zenith, when everything had come un-knit, standing one night outside a bank. This bank for some reason had a television suspended from its awning, and all night long this television played CNN, sound broadcast through speakers. On the night in question, one of the features of this broadcast was a bizarre noise, high pitched and troubled, its delicate contours obviously beyond the capacity for fidelity of recording devices used. It sounded like a billion glass pins dropping. Like the dried pine needles of millions of dead Christmas trees falling to millions of floors. The city pictured was green; it flared in night vision. It was a cold late March. I was on fire with fear. There were booms and then that uncanny whir, so musical and harsh, a precipitation. It was the sound of all in the windows in all the buildings in the capital breaking, as the city was bombed. Find it now on YouTube.

I lingered. Presumably, there was some delay. With the video, I mean. How much delay is there? I wondered. What is the time difference between Boston and Baghdad? Did they gather all the children and hide them in the country and tell stories about the origin of the world in which one part of creation smiles to another? No one is harmed in these images, I thought. No one dies or is lost. If someone is harmed, then the world splits in two. If a child dies, miserably and in confusion, then, I thought, I live at once in the historical time after their murder and in the historical time in which their murder is as yet unknown, perhaps never to be known by the residents of this suburb. Here is time. But all time is not here. Passersby vaguely slowed.

I recall a passage from Sylvia Plath's *The Bell Jar*, in which the protagonist ceases to be able to read. She can't read anything that is associated with the proper activities and interests of a member of her class. All she can read are the headlines of tabloids.

I had problems with the news, once upon a time, is what I am saying. But the problem was not exclusively with that.

The problem was with something I was unable to remember. It kept cropping blankly up. It was a psychic lump, a fine calcified ridge. I was so in need of something.

One day on a walk I went to a museum and saw for the first time an artwork by a female German artist, born in the first years of the Second World War. This artist liked writing, but although she liked lines and the idea of letters, she did not seem to much like words.

She draws a line, I thought, staring at her objects.

I returned to my dorm and began a paper:

> In her *Cultural History (1880–1983)*, the artist Hanne Darboven illustrates a fundamental quality of the historical record, that the event is a construct, a fiction. The items she uses to indicate this are (1) written loops, and (2) certain readymade objects. With her loop drawings, she makes a daily abstract gesture, indicating the kind of inscription it is possible to enact in a single day. When this nonhierarchical writing is displayed in a gallery setting, the effect is of being out at sea: What shall we look to in order to discover a significant event? How will we know it? Is the event the sum total of the installation? Is it a page of loops? A line? Do these nearly identical units (perhaps arbitrary, but nonetheless) allow us to usefully parse the human world? Time seems discontinuous. It is flickering, dialectical,

ambiguous—a *relationship* rather than an identity; it takes the form, impossibly and at once, of "or" and "both."

Into this space in which narrative is not composed of extent but rather of conjunction, Darboven inserts found objects and print ephemera. These feel at once like artifacts and then like signposts, pointing a way into the neither perfectly discrete nor perfectly continuous field of markings, of cipher-like loops. But these indexes trouble their own referential offer. They reveal that it is just that, an offer, an arrow made of dotted lines. As I am set adrift . . .

After this, I must not have been able to go on. I failed or nearly failed a number of classes that semester. It wasn't that I was incapable of the work, objectively speaking, but rather that I would come to a point in my thinking, in my expression, and experience agony. There was a piece of metal in me and at these moments it cut. There was a voice that shouted and I could not hear. These are only metaphors, of course, but how else can I tell you about these unreal things?

I should come back to the present.

Most of the vast trove of photographs I destroyed or deleted. There were analog photographs and digital images.

The great joke about all this is that although Cody accused me of not loving him many times, in the final analysis I'm the only person on earth who still cares that this occurred. Perhaps this is why I've become an archivist of these experiences. People talk all the time about the relationship between memory and photographs, but is that really memory? Isn't that just looking? To tell the truth, I don't remember anything now. The reason I don't remember is that, in the present, Cody is still alive. But he does not exist. The reason he does not exist is that he is not the person that he was, then, now. I'm not even sure if he was the person he was, then, *then*.

He was mostly gone on the very first day and even in the first minute. This was how I recognized him. He was out of sight but left decoys in his wake. Even the unimportant things were lies.

I do remember, by the way, the final date we went on. This was after the relationship was over. It was perhaps the cruelest night of my life. I remember walking by a Catherine Breillat marquee, *Abus de faiblesse* (*Abuse of Weakness*). Her autobiographical film about a con artist who was her lover. Later, over the phone, Cody would tell me, "You'll always be a victim." An incredible thing for someone who has told you that he loves you countless times to say. I know I need to put things in an order here, to get to the photographs, not to talk to you about the feeling of his hard-on through his pants. I could see that I was standing in the path of a slow assault that had lasted a decade. He had primed me for these moments. It wasn't just that I should know that he had lied to me, that he had been inside other women and inside me. He needed me to understand that he had meant it. He needed me to recognize that he would not have lied to *just anybody*. I was unique in the world and knowable to anyone at all only insofar as I was capable of inspiring such deceit. This was a communication style, and I had desired and requested it. This door, as Kafka wrote, was intended only for you. And now I am going to close it.

There aren't many photographs from the year of our separation and divorce. The only photographs of me taken during this time are by acquaintances, posted on Facebook. I am exceedingly thin and curved in these, a crescent. I was on a lot of speed.

It was how I managed to walk out of the house in the morning. Sometimes now I want to be high like that again. With my earbuds in on the elevated train, aware that there is no longer any life ahead. I'd stopped wearing my wedding ring, and I would look at the hands of other women in the car to see who was now possessed, safe and possessed, unlike me. I was sure that I was in the gravest danger, although I was, in spite of the drug use, probably the safest I had ever been. I found a therapist and sometimes I'd go to see her slightly high. I was sensitive to Adderall and could divide the tiny pills, which I'd come by via the same friend who'd gotten me my job, into quarters to make them last. It went on for about six months, this flirtation. I came down and gained weight. The car crash was over. I'd managed to remain in motion along with the metal body until the metal body stilled. I survived. There is no photograph of that.

The first of the last photos (analog) was taken in South Dakota. When I look at it I think Cody was teaching me something about how to take pictures. He held the camera out in very late afternoon, an evening of summer when we were near a lake, and photographed our faces. I am looking at him in the image. He is smiling and his eyes are half closed. He is completely happy, as if he is just about to begin laughing. I can only use simple language to describe how this looks. The forest behind us is blue. There is cool gold in the sky. I am wearing a borrowed sweater. I'm about to kiss him. Even looking at this image now, I can feel a kind of happiness. Even knowing what will happen. It's like a thought about time travel: How can this happiness not exist somewhere in the world, if these two people are so happy? How can this moment not be saved? I feel all the simultaneous strangeness and familiarity of that place and time. Something seems to have begun there, but it also feels true to say that that thing always existed. We always loved each other that much, even before we met and even before we were born, as in all the sentimental literature. If we no longer love each other, it must be because neither he nor I continue to live. But I am here, with these words. Nothing that has come to pass as far as Cody and I are concerned is possible, yet all of it has come to pass. Happiness somehow fits into the strange causal structure of the world.

The next picture (analog, again) was taken in a forest in Iowa. It is still our honeymoon. We are with his friends from college who stayed after they graduated. Behind us, they attempt to swing from vines and drink seltzer they have brought with them into the woods. Cody is touching my face. He's holding a small video camera. Soon I will take the camera from him and film him. Everyone, except for the person who is taking this photo, ignores us. The photographer is a young woman whom Cody knows well. She is having an affair with one of the men pictured, who is older than everyone else and married. In the future, this man never tells his wife, to whom he remains married, what happened between him and the photographer, although, for many years, he promises the photographer that he will leave his wife. This adulterous relationship, which is not really pictured in the photograph of Cody and me, but nonetheless indicated for the person who knows how to look, could contain a message. I remember thinking, at the time, that I was glad that I was not in a relationship like that. I believe this is what is called irony.

In the third photograph (analog), we attend a party. We are back in New York, in Brooklyn, and someone has captured us through a doorway, looking from the living room into a kitchen where a vintage clock is visible above my head. Cody has his hands in his pockets and seems in the midst of completing a sentence. His mouth is open and maybe he is making a sound like "ehh," or "hehh." Across from us, someone is standing with his back to the photographer. You can't make out his face, just his dark shoulder and hair. This person is tall, and perhaps this is why Cody's chin is lifted, why his body seems to perform a *puff* in the effort of articulation. Meanwhile, I grasp my plastic cup. I'm hanging out inside a world of men. My body is slack, but you can see around my mouth, darkened by wine, something forming. I'm looking at the tall man and listening with what appears to be appreciation, yet I turn away. I don't know if I would have felt this, then. Somewhere a fragment was hardening; it dropped to earth.

The fourth photograph (analog, too): it's in a park. I am in the foreground, out of focus, and beyond me a man, sharp, does something to his bicycle. I don't understand this image, which is why it is among the few that I will keep. I may even have it enlarged. I have the feeling that in this image, this one image, taken in the desperate middle of our marriage, I am beginning to appear.

I haven't let on how many of the digital images I've dragged to the recycling bin. An electronic approximation of a crunch rings out. *Crunch crunch crunch*, all morning. Now there is but one pair of photographs remaining, before and after. I place them on the desktop, side by side. I open them in Preview. I will destroy them soon, I tell myself. They are taken within the period of a single week, before and after I have sex with someone who is not Cody for the first and only time during our marriage. Cody took both of these photographs. The "before" photograph exists in a series that suggest to me Cody knew all about what was going to happen to us. He was lying in wait. He was watching. He could not wait to see what I would do. Because, when I did what I did, I was only imitating him.

Cody was a person who liked to be imitated.

I wasn't even alive, then, but look at me, so thin and clean. I was hollow and would float on anything. Now I am filled with a ballooning, thundering life, but then, back then, while I was frail and dead, I had love. I was a loved object, a floating mote, and did not know it. And, here, look at me, after I have found out. Cody photographed me and I am all eyes. In this photograph, I still do not know that he has been unfaithful to me, because I cannot believe it. I imagine that what has happened to me could not be possible for him. I can't imagine how he could go on living if he were to have done to me what I have done to him. It's in the photograph; I see it. Admittedly, my imagination, normally so wild, has failed. At the time when this image was taken, he'd been sleeping with someone else on a daily basis for more than three years.

Could I have been a better person? This is what I want to know. I don't pose that question in the sense of wanting to gather all the faults and heap them on myself. I know that's not possible, anyhow. I just wonder, thinking back, did I even live any of those eleven years, did I know him well, what was true? In those days, I was often unsure which one of us I was, and maybe that was the case for him, too. That we "shared a brain," as they say. Or, maybe it wasn't. Maybe he always knew that he was only himself, and that was the whole problem. I was the stupid one who didn't know any better than to be both of us. Oh well.

I wonder if it means anything to him that we lost each other. He remarried so quickly. I pity him for that. It suggests that he still knows very little about who he is. I guess I used to believe that there are lots of kinds of tragedies in this world, but now I know that there is just one kind. And it is available to all of us.

I was talking to my therapist, trying to tell her what I've learned about grieving since losing Cody. I was telling her that what is painful is not the loss of the person. This loss is basically an intellectual event and if you are able to look at it, you will be OK. The problem is the fact of the affection you bear this lost person. The affection will still be there, long after the disappearance of its recipient, and here is what happens: the affection dies. You must sit and keep watch as the affection dies. You watch as the corpse of affection softens and opens and begins to be reclaimed by the earth. Every night you dream that you possess the power to reanimate it. You place a magic tablet under its tongue, and its face is smooth and whole once more. Affection laughs in the dream and embraces you. However, come morning, it is the same ragged skeleton, slowly picked clean by scavengers, the same abject carapace you despise yourself for cherishing. Soon, with spring, there is nothing. The grass is just a bit lusher where affection once was, and you understand that you are probably the only person who would perceive a difference.

I have lived this. It is now a thing about me, something that took place. I have lived these things and kept watch. I stayed here, staring at what once was and staring at the present.

It was good for a while that I did not look away, but the benefits attained seem to diminish in direct proportion to the amount of time that passes. I should stop looking, should dispose of the photographs entirely, but I don't know if I can.

I read somewhere that the past is at the service of the collection. I guess that's true. I wish that this were true of the present, too, sick though that probably is.

What is most remarkable now is that he is like anyone in the world, on the street, in a building, in a house, on a bed, in a chair, at a table, anywhere, anyone, a living person. He walks to a window, touches a door. He is no longer the mate of my soul, nor is he my tormentor. I could pass him by, my great love Cody, and it would not matter.

A person, scattered in space and time, is no longer a woman but a series of events on which we can throw no light, a series of insoluble problems.

—Proust, *La Prisonnière* (1923)

Hanne radiated a catatonic energy. I'd already observed something like it in my youth, when I worked in a psychiatric unit for three months. There were patients who suddenly switched from extreme physical arousal to utter passivity. I also experienced such variability in Hanne. In her case, I sometimes asked myself what kind of relationship to her own body she actually had.

—Kasper König, interview with Verena Berger (2015)

To return to the matter of art: Hanne Darboven was born in Munich, in 1941, the second daughter of three. Her father, Cäsar Darboven, was a member of the Nazi Party and heir to the J. W. Darboven coffee roaster and general store (1895–1972), not to be confused with the J. J. Darboven coffee company, a better-known firm that has since expanded across northern Europe. Hanne's mother, Kirsten, was Danish. Early on in the war they were living in the suburbs outside Hamburg. Later, there was an adolescence involving boarding schools and social dysfunction. The father seemed unpleasant, uneasy. Although originally trained as a concert pianist, Hanne entered art school, the Hochschule für bildende Künste, as a young adult. She was thin, yellow blond, pretty, yet with a kind of sacred circle around her: unteachable. A comment by a teacher, Almier Mavignier, sent her packing her bags for New York. In Manhattan, after two years of relative isolation, Hanne met Sol LeWitt in 1968, along with, among others, artists Lawrence Weiner and Carl Andre, whose name I cannot write without adding that of another artist, Ana Mendieta. Hanne's father's illness and eventual death brought her back to her childhood home; here she set up a studio, along with a daily routine.

Although she had begun her career in New York with drawings that fit rather neatly into the minimalist paradigm, now it became the time of something the artist described as *Schreibzeit*. It was Writing Time. This began in 1975. There was a strict schedule but no hurry. Hanne woke at four a.m. She kept goats and thus fed them before smoking a bit and returning, with coffee, the ancestral elixir, to the rooms she used as studio space. At tables loaded with kitsch objects, commercial mascots, souvenirs of others' travels, tokens of European colonialism, newspapers, magazines, toys, bourgeois decorative items, Hanne wrote. In letters to other artists, a voluminous correspondence often undertaken on postcards, she said, "my novel

[is] a real book," and "there are no aesthetic tricks no research just writing," and "i learned where i came from by doing it."

But Hanne, save in her letters, was mostly not writing words. "i don't like to read i do like to write," she wrote to LeWitt. Hanne wrote loops. *uuuuuuuuuuuuuuuuuuu* . . . They were a system to mark time, a calendar. They were a log, an accounting, and they were writing, just writing. The artist reached up through time to enact a loop in pen or pencil. A wave rose, crested, fell. It was pure writing, not a trick. It was always writing, not meaning. Perhaps Hanne lived in a permanent trance. The *Schreibzeit*, or Writing Time, lasted for some eight hours, until noon. At which point, Hanne, who did not drive, went, by car, to a local café with her mother, who did.

Hanne had her own math, a math that she had invented. She wrote out sums for each calendar day. Let us take the day of my birth, for example: a German would write it as 10.1.80, and Darboven's summing of it works as follows: $1 + 0 + 1 + 8 + 0 = 10$ K, with K as her unit of measurement, what she termed *Konstruktion*, construction, or *Kombinationsmöglichkeit*, combinability. But she did not merely add days. She summed months, decades, centuries in her ledgers. She wrote music, converting numbers into musical notes, e for 1, f for 2, etc.

All of this was Writing Time. All was collected into binders. Sometimes she wrote in the names of historical figures, artists, and writers: George Sand, Rainer Werner Fassbinder, Marie Curie, many others. Darboven said in an interview in 1989, "I wrote things down by hand so that the mediated experience might impart something to me." It was the experience of being, as writing, that counted. This was what was intelligible. Not the content of the words.

I am not an artist. As I have said, this is probably irresponsible of me and has likely led to madness, but I have learned, more and more, about this woman whose art I once saw, when I was twenty. I never discussed this with Cody. I only thought about Hanne. I listened to Cody talk about his art. And, as he talked, I thought about Hanne. Cody and I are no longer on speaking terms. Now I'm speaking with you about her.

In the summer of 1943, when Hanne was two, the Allies bombed Hamburg. It has been said that this attack, code-named "Gomorrah," was a turning point in the war. The aerial campaign began on the 24th of July, a time of unusually arid and hot weather, and lasted for eight days and seven nights. Blockbuster bombs hampered the movements of firefighting crews and subsequent assaults created a firestorm, a 1,500-foot tornado, with winds of up to 150 miles per hour and temperatures of 1,470 degrees Fahrenheit. Asphalt burst into flame and fuel spilled into the harbor, causing the surface of the water to ignite. Many people were pulled into the conflagrations, "like dry leaves," as one description has it, as, below the earth, those in shelters died of carbon monoxide poisoning, suffocation, and extreme heat. Overall, the attack is thought to have killed some 42,600 civilians, wounding another 37,000 and decimating the city. Given the bombings of Hiroshima and Nagasaki in late summer two years later, one cannot refer to the destruction of Hamburg as the most brutal bombing of the war. That such a superlative must be reserved is a crime that human history has not fully digested, or so I believe.

But I digress.

The destruction of Hamburg was made possible by means of a radar-jamming technique known as "chaff," or "Window," as it was code-named in early use. Chaff/Window were clouds of tinfoil strips dropped into the air. The reflective foil interrupted radar images, creating false echoes, a fuzzy abstract array not unlike a painting by Mark Rothko. Chaff is a block in the flow of information generated through excess, a wordless propaganda campaign. The Germans called the metal ribbons *Düppel*. The tool was known to both sides but for some time unused, for fear of retaliation.

Earlier, in mid-July 1943, initial bombings had already begun. The Allies haphazardly released excess armaments as they returned from sorties over Hamburg, and these detonated in the suburban landscape. The Darbovens' neighbors' farm was one such site. Shortly thereafter, the Darbovens fled to Lower Saxony, thus avoiding

Gomorrah by a matter of days, although their home was still standing when they returned in 1945.

I mention these events less in an attempt to inspire pity than to point out a series of historical events for which Hanne Darboven was effectively present without the capacity for conscious memory or comprehension. Whatever else she lived before she began to make her "writing"—which was, by the way, the term she used for all her art—echolocations and bombings, the repeated hollowing out of vast architectural spaces, consumed her early youth.

In 1966, when Hanne embarked for New York, never before had so many people in the United States been under twenty-five; the baby boom was bearing fruit and the future of the world appeared American. Information and information technologies proliferated: mass communications, soft power. Hanne met artists. But a changing family structure at home called her back.

Hanne in some sense took up her ailing father's place. She investigated the unintelligible side of information flows. She inverted information. She inverted the number, the one thing, she said, that humans have created that actually exists.

I think of Plath and her tabloids. I think of chaff and abstraction, of how little I know about my dad. I think of American suppression of Iraqi air defenses.

In my own way, I am a clerk. I perform functions, actions, that cannot be accomplished, during my lifetime as I understand it, by an algorithm. I labor as a handmaiden to automation, a process that is not, and will never be, complete.

I am the one who determines the actual legibility of a word. A computer can tell you if a word exists within the array of known words, if the word has been formed correctly and how it stands in relation to others, but only I can tell you how it means and appears to someone who has been born to life on earth, what its lived history is. For meaning is eccentrically distributed.

I lay claim to this narrow strain of intelligibility. No one shall deny it. Meanwhile, I am overseen by a manager.

I don't know everything, of course. I don't travel the highways and byways of the United States collecting language—although, perhaps I should. I read some journals, lurk on Twitter, watch TV. I am told I am good at my job. I am told that certain subject-matter tests for which I am responsible create "less friction" than they used to.

But I am no scholar. I could have been, maybe. If I had not lost my mind, then become enmeshed in marriage and New York City. If I had not begun, as a college student, to regularly forget who I am.

Sometimes I wonder, *Has someone "edited" me. Has someone chosen my words. What has been elided, without a trace. Why can I not stop thinking about writing, and why can I neither forget nor remember.*

I promise myself that, again, I will not write today.

Two months after the end of my relationship with Cody, I received an email from my mother, who was on vacation in Mexico. It was winter and I was pretty deep in grief, taking speed, preparing for my move to Jersey, where I believed I would obtain some needed distance. The subject line read: "thinking in Ixtapa."

> Hello, dear~
>
> You are probably feeling a whole lot better now than when we spoke on Friday, but our talk upset me a lot. You're making great progress freeing yourself from a bad situation and it seems you've pretty much gotten over Cody but not, I fear, yourself.
>
> You're trying real hard to figure out what happened to bring the blowup, but to my mind, it's not helpful to forage overlong for ways in which you might have failed to foresee disaster. Okay, so maybe you'll learn something, but after a while you'll be spending your precious time and energy for little reward.
>
> You'll probably never forgive Cody, but make sure to forgive yourself—for not seeing, knowing, or throwing conniption

fits when you should have, for not throwing out more bottles of booze, for not making cheese sandwiches, or for whatever crime or misdemeanor you can dredge up. That kind of stuff can make a person not only miserable, but weird.

I know it's HARD, and I'm here to listen, sympathize, and (goddammit) share your pain (yes, I do!). But at the end of six months, I'm going to tell you in no uncertain terms: "Get over it!"

I want back the lovable, witty, charming, spunky, invincible you. And so does everyone else we know.

I absorbed this message. I did not reply.

I thought a lot about this sentence: "That kind of stuff can make a person not only miserable, but weird."

I think all the time about the lost writing by my grandmother. But I don't know if it would have explained anything. For all I know, it might have made things worse.

My grandmother was older than Hanne Darboven. In 1943, she was eighteen. In April of this year, three months before Operation Gomorrah, my grandmother gave birth to my mother. At this time, she was either married or unmarried. If she was married, she soon divorced. I know nothing about my mother's father. I don't know even what she knows about him. My mother and her father never met.

One thing I do know about this time, this year, 1943, and perhaps some portion of the previous year as well, is that my grandmother was prescribed a form of synthetic estrogen, diethylstilbestrol, during her pregnancy. DES, as this drug is sometimes called, was supposed to prevent miscarriages and other complications in pregnancy. It was developed in 1938 and prescribed from 1940 to 1971 in the United States. However, DES, an endocrine disruptor, does not in fact have salutary effects during pregnancy and has been shown to pose serious health risks to children who were exposed to it in utero, including increased risk of vaginal clear-cell adenocarcinoma, vaginal adenosis, T-shaped uterus, uterine fibroids, incompetent cervix, breast cancer, infertility, hypogonadism, intersex defects, and depression. It is no longer prescribed.

My mother, who was exposed to DES in utero, suffered vaginal clear-cell adenocarcinoma, a rare form of cancer. In this type of tumor, the insides of cells look clear when viewed under a microscope. Women with vaginal clear-cell adenocarcinoma die at a rate of roughly 25 percent in the United States. My mother did not die.

When she was sick, Cody and I were still married. We were, I suppose, in the thick of things. My mother never explained her illness until after it was over. She did not relay the statistics given to her by doctors, the chances she faced. I do not know if she understood the link to artificial estrogen—although, who am I kidding, she must have known. I wonder why, after it was over and she at last named the cancer to us, she chose to leave out its origins. I sometimes think that it was because to do so would have implied that her mother had had a lasting effect on her life, that something inescapable had in fact been passed down. Or perhaps it was that the cancer implied that my mother was unlucky, much like her mother before her. Or, that to be female was itself unlucky. Possibly weird, as well.

But, again, I don't really know.

Could hypergraphic tendencies also be associated with those who have not been believed? Is it possible that events involving the organism as a whole, with its name and sentiments, could inspire such behavior? That it is not merely damage to some specific organ that sets the hypergraph in motion but rather the strictures of a world into which she has, unwillingly, fallen?

For isn't it clear to you already? I say that I do not write, that I cannot do it, yet I have long had a practice of writing out my own tests.

ANALYSIS

For the following questions, select the best answer. You may not select more than one answer. Responses including more than one answer will be marked as incorrect. Incorrect or unanswered questions receive a score of minus one.

The narrator has said, "I write it all down. Not in real life, I mean. I mean, in my head. In life, I am not allowed to write. But in my head, I can. I can't write anything down, but I can describe the world— silently, privately. I put words to it." The narrator has also said, "I do not write . . . I cannot do it."

The best explanation of what motivates such statements on the part of the narrator is probably:

a. The narrator views writing as a dangerous activity because it can introduce falsehoods and duplicity into the world.
b. The narrator cannot prevent herself from thinking about the world in a certain way— which she analogizes with the activity of writing. In this way of thinking about the world, the world (composed of both sentient and nonsentient things) has an existence that is distinct from descriptions of it. The narrator is attempting to make the world visible and intelligible to herself, within her own mind. This activity is not an activity she feels compelled to share with others. Thus, she "writes," in her way of speaking, internally but for no one else.
c. The narrator has internalized a prohibition.
d. The narrator is aware that she has internalized a

prohibition, but she struggles against it. What she says here means more than one thing. She feels guilty because her early life has been much easier than her mother's was.

e. None of the above.

The narrator has said, "It seemed like Elliott's overdose and resulting death were clear events that I could point to . . . but it's harder than I thought to explain what they may mean." What should the reader infer from this statement?

a. The narrator suspects that her parents' friends secretly wished their child harm.

b. The narrator believes that it is possible that her parents' friends were unconsciously endangering their child. As she is able to identify this possible interpretation of her parents' friends' actions, she wonders if her own parents' actions could be interpreted in a similar way. Sometimes friends—and, who are we kidding, members of a given generation—have things in common.

c. The narrator does not have a clear idea of what the death of her childhood acquaintance Elliott means. She has given up trying to interpret it, but all the same, it lingers. Elliott is not alive anymore. He is not here, in the present. Once the narrator heard Barbara, Elliott's mother, say that "the world was too much [for Elliott]." The narrator thought about this statement for a long time. The narrator thought about how we are each born into a situation that is like a net or maze. It holds us. It confuses us. It presents false paths. And yet it holds us. It is part of what keeps us alive. Everyone who has ever lived was born into something that was already taking place. This happened to Elliott, to Barbara, to the narrator's mother, and to the narrator. It happens, very possibly without exception.

d. The narrator is withholding information from the reader. The reader will have to wait and see if the narrator will share this information at a later juncture.

The narrator's interest in visual art serves what purpose in the narrative?

a. The careers of other artists—that of the narrator's former husband and that of a German artist primarily active during the twentieth century—are described in order to explain parts of the narrator's own experience that she clearly does not know how to narrate in any other way.

b. The narrator fell in love with an artist unknowingly and is currently attempting to learn from that mistake by thinking about another artist she became very interested in as a young person. Contemplation of visual art, in this story, seems to be a mode of problem-solving.

c. All people have some interest in visual art and other forms of physical and aural representation of the world. It is unfair and probably reactionary to characterize the narrator's interest in visual art as something that sets her apart from humanity. It's a mean political strategy you see deployed all the time.

d. It does not serve any purpose. It is included in the narrative because it exists.

e. All of the above.

The artist Hanne Darboven famously maintained, "I write, but I describe nothing." What is it likely that this statement means to the narrator?

a. It suggests that Darboven was suspicious of the ways in which her statements might be interpreted.

b. It shows that Darboven was not very ambitious when it came to composing meaningful texts.

c. This statement is a key that helps the narrator to interpret Darboven's artwork, since it suggests that Darboven, like the narrator, may have grown up in an environment in which there was a taboo around certain kinds of descriptive language. In Darboven's case, it turned out that, as an artist, she was able to make beautiful works by taking the implications of this taboo regarding naming as far as a human being could possibly take them. Rather than attempt to describe events in the way that a witness or historiographer might, Darboven decided that she would simply show up each day for the act of writing. She didn't want to say things. She wanted to show what the saying was doing. She created a graphic environment, rather than a message. She liberated herself into this field of loops.

d. The narrator claims she does not write, but she seems to want to describe everything. Perhaps the narrator wishes that she had the sort of relationship to writing that Hanne Darboven did. Too bad about the grandmother.

"You do not support me," Cody used to say.

Often, when he said this, I was on my way to work. I had already read my email, and the panic these missives produced (so much to attend to) caused my thinking to become patchy. "Yes," I muttered, because I was not listening. On the floor there was a small sculpture made of plywood with metal staples, painted safety orange. I had to hop to avoid catching the tip of my shoe inside one of its angles.

Cody was testing me again.

Once, in the back room he used as a second studio, he began drying a dozen peeled and cored apples, and, as the fruit began to decompose, moths took up residence. They filled the house, making fibrous white nests on the ceilings. I was afraid, not precisely of the moths, but of the disarray they engendered. The darker bodies of their caterpillars hung there, then burst forth.

"Cody," I said, "you have to do something."

"About what?"

"Our house is full of moths." I opened a cabinet. Gray bodies traipsed across a bag of lentils.

Two days later Cody went out and bought some poison and went around spraying the nests. The moths disappeared but I did not feel better.

It had already been going on for years, was the thing. There weren't always sculptures underfoot or moths, but there were other things. Cody tested me because it was a way to justify his actions. He tested me because he wished to show that I did wrong. The more he tested and the more I failed, the more correct he became. Cody ran a tight ship. His life was a shambles but his conscience clean. He always came home at some point in the evening.

Often, he returned and knocked things over in the dark. He spoke in tongues. He uttered gummy, piney disquisitions concerning the North American continent and man's free will, the need to go alone into the desert, the ancient command to lose one's mind in order to find one's liberation.

I was not free. Cody told me. "You are not *free*," he muttered, rummaging in a pile of clothes at three a.m.

I told him I was glad that he was home.

Cody started describing the necessity, for me, of discovering my freedom, of getting to it by any means. These recommendations always stopped short of disclosing the reason freedom was most necessary: that I lived with a man who loathed me.

Indeed, it was by no means certain that there had ever been a moment during the course of our relationship when Cody had not been unfaithful.

It took so long to hear what he was saying.

Now various constructions of Cody's were scattered around the house.

I did not desire freedom, as far as I knew. I did not even desire that Cody appear at our home with any regularity. What I desired was to go to work where, in return for funds, responsibilities were meted out. These duties I metabolized by means of email. I did not write and yet I wrote, voluminously.

At home, Cody created a mock version of his impending exhibition in the eat-in kitchen and small living room. I was sometimes afraid that I might tread upon one of the groupings of painted twigs he had wired together or one of his dishes of colored sand. Like the moths, this was a dare. Cody wondered just how still I could remain, just how careful I could be in my movements. He wanted to know if I could share this space with him, given the complexity of the life he was currently living. He wanted to know if I could navigate a structure I was mostly not permitted to see.

Years earlier, as I have said, Cody embarked on an affair with the young woman, Alexis, who was the director of his gallery. This was in fact how he had secured his first show: he'd offered her his penis, and she, in turn, had given him some rooms in which to show his art. It was the traditional arrangement. As I think of this now, I wonder if part of me did realize that the relationship was taking place.

I remember there was a night when Alexis came to dinner. I had a feeling I would later on become better able to name, which was the feeling of having arrived late to a drama. Perhaps this was the second act. No one bothered to catch me up to speed, but I could perceive by the way that Alexis took her seat at the table that she must have been in our apartment before. This puzzled me, as I had not been aware of her existence at this point for more than a week. These two pieces of evidence—(1) that I had not previously seen Alexis in my home, and (2) that Alexis was not someone known to me for very long—were enough to convince me that, whatever Alexis's movements seemed to tell me—the way she touched a chair or balanced on the edge of its seat—I could not treat these intimations as meaningful.

I was a little dizzy, but I settled in to eat and drink.

Every time I met Alexis from this point on she seemed annoyed by me. I assumed that she must be annoyed because I was not an artist, and, therefore, although I possessed some modicum of intelligence, was unable to fully comprehend what she, through the gallery, and Cody, through his works, were getting up to. I thought that perhaps it was fatiguing to have to speak with somebody as dense as me. I did not know that Alexis was annoyed by me because I was sleeping with her boyfriend-of-the-moment. And I was taking up a whole lot of Boyfriend-of-the-Moment's time.

I remember once, during some post-opening drinks, Alexis put down her vodka and began ranting about marriage and the art world, how you could never tell what anyone's position on the institution was anymore, that it didn't mean anything if somebody was obviously married, they might still try to fuck you.

"They might try to *date* you," she sputtered.

"It's crazy," an acquaintance confirmed.

I was quietly working on a beer. I was thinking that I was glad that I was traditionally married to someone and could depend upon that person. I was thinking about Cody. He sat to my right, sousing himself and whisper-shouting with an obviously independently wealthy Austrian journalist who for some reason kept telling everyone that he was going to make them famous.

Not long after this Alexis met Zeke. Alexis and Zeke began dating. It was a thing. And Zeke and Cody became fast friends. There was a certain lessening of tension, where Alexis was concerned. Now she had someone she could depend on, I thought.

And even later, even when Cody began asking me, did I maybe want to sleep with Zeke, he was so young and attractive and even slightly famous, I did not grasp it. I did not get that what Cody was telling me was that there was a score to settle, that things were not even, not by a long shot. I knew that what Cody said meant that he was feeling insecure—I just did not realize in what sense this was true. Cody felt unstable, vulnerable, because he knew that he had done things that could hurt me, that had probably hurt me, would hurt me, were I to find out. This wasn't empathy. Cody had grown up with many siblings. He knew what politics was all about.

There was an interim, years when I don't know what Cody did. Maybe he still slept with Alexis from time to time. Doubtless, there were others. The art-handling company had high turnover. It was a business designed to catch the dregs of liberal arts curricula, those who hadn't moved on to law school and a hobby.

In the offices of the company Cody met Sophie. Sophie was an artist, too, although I didn't find that out until much later.

It's hard, even now, to talk about this. And maybe I have become "weird." I do sometimes think that I sacrificed my life to something I still cannot see or touch.

Intellectually, I can recall and narrate how it felt to know Cody at the very first: how it was like drinking water. Everything softened. It was not that we said or did anything together that was so remarkable, but in knowing him I forgot what had come before. Water seems like the correct metaphor. To look at him was like water, to touch him was water, to hear his voice. It's hard not to feel bitter looking back on those early days, but at the same time I am in awe of what takes place there. I know now that I risked something.

I did have an idea for the future, was the strangest thing. But I wasn't thinking about houses, or children, or jobs: I was thinking about a kind of intimation of liberty. This was what I, incoherently, believed that the future was for. The future was a field where one might go to seek one's liberty. It was light on plants but mostly it was horizon. The past was washed away; our bodies were about to become beautiful.

It was just a meeting in an office. It was just walks in the financial district, that blue cavern empty on weekends. It was just a touch of his thick hand, his yellow-copper eyes, his nonchalant sneakers, the way he handled Metrocards and money, how he liked blossoming trees, the way a hangover produced a visionary daze. We went to the carousel in Central Park. The subway was cold later, and we slept on each other's shoulders. We didn't say we were lucky. The mystery of those days and nights was greater than that.

We moved and we rested and we ate, and knowing each other was the most important work that either of us could do. I could say that I don't know why this changed, but I am not sure that I do not know why. This turned out not to be that field and not that liberty. It turned out to be a rehearsal of something rather more antique, something inherited and cruel.

It took a decade-plus. That was the temporal cost. That was the life that I fed to this repetition, what had presented itself as a way out. I have to try to put things in an order here, but it is hard. I think back to that late moment in the marriage, when Cody has filled the apartment with his constructions. They are made of painted wood scraps and large staples. They are like small tables without tops and they lean around our home. There is one in the bathroom, between the toilet and the sink. There are several in the kitchen, they ring the bed, they wait just beyond the front door: when I come home at night, there they are, condemning me, bright red, orange, yellow, green, with crooked angles. They do not resemble people and yet there's something they seem to know. I could easily crush them. I have the sense that if I do, if a single one is damaged or even slightly moved, I will never see Cody again.

The thing was, Cody never showed these things. They didn't turn out to be part of the exhibition he was putting together. They were a bluff. What Cody showed were charcoal drawings done on tan construction paper. They were images of a bed with a figure in it. It seemed to be an entombed body, colored darkly in. The bed appeared to have a cast iron frame; the draughtsman's hand had lingered over detail here.

At the party after the opening, one of Cody's gallerists approached me and asked if I thought that the pictures would sell. She had not been drinking, and, although I had, I was yet conscious enough to recognize this as a puzzling question. There was no reason, as far as I could tell, why my opinion could have any bearing on the show's commercial outcome. The gallerist's face was undersized, canny and candid. She had grown up in the city and in her fifties had become divorced.

It felt, for a moment, if I can explain this, as if I were a funny clock, maybe a metronome. Tick tock. *Tick*, I could say. *Tock*. I was being handed the baton.

I searched the crowd for inspiration. Alexis, who had long ago been fired for some opaque reason, was present. Her expulsion had not dissuaded her from attending Cody's opening, nor had it kept her from this more intimate gathering. She was bold, I reflected, bizarrely so. She held her glass to her cheek, offering some gossipy notion to a tall sculptor dressed in hunting camo. I felt Alexis's belonging. Even if she had been made redundant, still she was needed.

I memorized her movements.

The longer my response took, the more interested the gallerist became.

Then, because it was now the only answer available, I dredged up, "No."

The gallerist raised an eyebrow but did not seem altogether displeased.

I watched as, at the other side of the room, Cody inched along the wall toward his coworker Sophie.

I was right, too. The drawings did not sell. I think Cody made a total of $250 on the show. It was kindly reviewed in one or two publications, and then the world rolled blindly on.

Cody was enraged. He did not smash his constructions or invite additional vermin into our home, but I could perceive that the nonresponse undid him. If I had been wiser—if I had been less deceived, for example—I would have understood that my own reaction meant something. I did not care about Cody's fate, and that I did not care about his fate was meaningful. I, too, was drifting.

Cody was, if this was possible, absent even more. He began attending conferences associated with art handling on the weekends. He claimed he needed to be practical. He needed to make a future in the industry. When it came to creative work, somebody was out to get him. He was thinking of switching galleries. Mistakes, he told me, had been made.

I asked if maybe Cody felt like going to the beach. It was summer now and hot.

"I'm going out," he said.

I lingered in the kitchen.

I listened to him tramping down the stairs to the front door, the clicks of hardware, the swish and clap as the door swung shut again. I heard him on the sidewalk for what seemed to be a long time. These were footsteps or the efforts of my heart to move my blood.

In my inbox was an email from someone at my office who wondered, winkingly, if I would have a drink with him.

If I had been brilliant, I sometimes think, if I had been a great reader of novels and philosophy, if I had been a friend to many clever women, if I had gone to grad school, if I had lived in other countries, if I had been good at math, if I had been an early investor in internet currencies, then, and then, and *then*, I tell myself, I would have known. All the signs were present. Anyone with half a mind could see that Cody, my husband of nearly ten years, despised me. Cody, my most beautiful friend, the person who had long ago rescued me from the gyre of insanity, who had seen me where I struggled and kindly said my name, my confidant, my savior, my unacknowledged twin.

It doesn't really matter how I found out. It doesn't matter that I thought Cody and I were the same person, that maybe we had been born into the world together. It doesn't matter that I had to figure out that I was wrong.

What matters is such things are possible.

We are frequently taught that humans deceive one another for personal gain, but what we are not taught, what has largely been withheld, at least from the canon of American common sense, is that people lie without motivation—or, to be precise, that they lie with the primary motivation of deceiving, and thus controlling, only themselves. People wish for entrapment. They wish for restraint, true bonds. They are everywhere, eager and smiling. I used not to believe in them, and then I feared them, and now I encounter them and lightly step aside. I don't need them anymore.

Cody fell from a rock when he was a child. Everyone saw him fall and no one came to pick him up. He was discarded in full view. I have to imagine that at this time, and at other times like it, Cody did not so much wonder why he was neglected by his family as invent versions of events in which this neglect made sense. He developed a style. The name of this style was delusion, and the name of this style was truth.

I don't know if I neglected Cody. He was not an infant when I met him, but then again, neither was I. He did sometimes confuse me with a child.

When I found the photographs of Cody and Sophie, of Cody by Cody, of Sophie by Sophie, I tried to pretend to myself that this was an event like many others. Yes, I had been deceived. Yes, now my life would change. But what I could not account for at the time, and what I am still living in the wake of, was the bizarre familiarity. Given this familiarity, extraordinary and insistent, I could not claim that this was an event like many others: it was rendered unique because it seemed, paradoxically, to have already taken place.

She showed viscosity, circumstantiality, soliloquy, euthymic mood and normal cognition. She wrote profusely, e.g. lists of various categories and letters to eminent clerics and politicians. Her diary was scanned for illustrative purpose.

—Gil, Ponte, Marques (2016)

Nine: Saturday

There is a famous story about a man who ate his own children. Perhaps there are many such stories, but you must know the old one. In the old story, the man is a god, but he seems to have the wrong kinds of power for the era in which he finds himself. He has a wife, who provides him with offspring, and after each birth he ingests the infant like a sandwich: eyes hideously open, pupils turned back in his head; mouth vastly empty, filled with blackness.

(Obviously, here I am influenced by Goya.)

In at least one version of the story of this immortal nightmare father, the children he swallows remain alive inside his belly. When he is overthrown by the youngest child (who has been switched out for a rock during snack time), the previously devoured emerge from his stomach like passengers from a bus. They are adult gods, variously gifted. These are the deities of the modernity of the classical era. They bring to a close the archaic preclassical time—those eons of cannibalism, the patriarch's heinous jealousy, his weird pregnancy. The new gods bring about new politics; the family is no longer the sole governing body within the human sphere. We like, now, I think, to believe that the rescued gods are our gods, too. They seem to approve of capitalism and perhaps they even invented it. According to them, consumption of other people's children is preferable to consumption of one's own.

The ancient child-eater was a Greek god or a pre-god. Possibly he was an ancient deity of Asia Minor, a creator of worlds. The Greeks cast him as a madman, a self-defeating slayer of the future, a delay. The Greeks' magic is, I think, the closest to our own, and I have often wondered why they saw this Titan as a stop on the road to civilization, a sovereign deity but from a time no longer actual. I don't think that they were wrong. It's just that I don't see the cannibal as a creature of the past. He seems to me a fixture of empire, a familiar and gigantic dad, always hovering.

115

The Romans, in their way, recuperated him. Their god Saturn, from whom we have the name of the seventh day of the week, bore some of the old god's legends, quirks, and qualities. Saturn was a dissolver as well as a begetter. He presided over the changing of the year. His consorts were Lua Mater, goddess of the loosening of bonds, and Ops, associated with wealth, both of whom had beautiful names and were obviously fantastic lovers.

It's the Greek doubt, by the way, that I identify with—what I perceive as their herb-tinted melancholy, their respect for dust and slaughter. It's why I'm trying to claim them for us, in spite of the far more obvious parallels between the Roman Empire and America.

I grew up in the United States and of course we have our new gods, too. The problem is that we haven't bothered to name any of them and meanwhile go around worshipping some principle, even as the gods are present and continue to demand sacrifices of us. We have kinetic images we call cartoons. On Saturday morning, children all across the land drug themselves with fructose- and glucose-infused dairy (and/or dairy substitute) and lounge before a screen, upon which humanoid animals and animated inanimate objects struggle and love. Violent deaths are part of the repertoire, as are scenes of seduction. Sometimes the characters encounter a witch or other hermit-like, self-taught chef, someone who would like very much to eat them. A child could find herself imploring the moving fields of color on the screen, "Don't go in there!" It is meant to be fun and funny, but, as all projections do, these scenarios contain lessons.

I sat there, as a child, and I am not sure what I learned. Could I even truly feel the moments when, watching, I was transmogrified into a dancing cow, for example, or a female cat pursued by an amorous skunk? I know that there was dread in these brief plays. There was joy, too, but the joy was fragile and entirely without permanence (if not mixed with awful cunning). "I love you," I whispered to the gray rabbit, as he bent his tall frame over a fence or leaned against a shed. *Life is everywhere*, silently I prayed, knowing this animal's powers of self-transformation, the certainty of his success, his ageless elastic ubiquity. All things were living. All things contained the secret music of the world, its possibility; the objects, winds, waters, and animals. Vast, intricately informed hours rolled through my extremely young life. I watched. The brain strained atop its stem; it became a smooth-walled theater.

Meanwhile, my parents had discovered neighbors who resembled them. These were a man and a woman who were married with a single daughter. There was also a divorced man with two children who relentlessly pursued my parents' friendship. I want to talk about them.

It is terrible to talk about them, too. The couple with the only daughter, the Lerners, were intelligent and rich. My parents felt that they deserved the Lerners' friendship. The Lerners' daughter, Caroline, was older than I was. In fact, she *is* older than I am now, of course, since she is still alive. She has never married and has no children. One weekend, several years ago, I was invited by her mother to the building she and Mr. Lerner, Richard, had owned together. By this time Mr. Lerner, Richard, was deceased. I went to eat with Caroline and Caroline's mother, Mrs. Lerner, who was also named Caroline and must therefore be referred to as Caroline 1. Caroline 2, my supposed peer, was meanwhile very nice but had lately developed a tendency to not look me directly in the eyes when we spoke. I got the sense that Caroline 2 had been informed by Caroline 1 that I was a career woman, due to my apparently stable office position. What I did was either shameful or intimidating, perhaps a mix. Caroline 2 had begun adulthood as a software engineer on the West Coast, but had abandoned this life in her early thirties when her boyfriend, a presumed husband, pronounced her ultimately uncompelling. Caroline 2 returned to New York City where she took odd jobs, abandoning IT. Her existence was largely subsidized by her parents and she seemed to have determined never to date again. She was over forty but looked much younger, particularly after her father's passing. I have puzzled over the case of Caroline 2 for some time.

I can't imagine Caroline 2 found it comforting or delightful to be handed taxi fare by her mother at the end of the night, but perhaps

I am wrong. I can't imagine Caroline 2 liked living alone and waitressing. I can't imagine why Caroline 2 put Caroline 1 at the center of her perfectly good life but, then again, this was happening. Caroline 2 dwelled in a deep margin if not a pit.

Most of what I knew about Caroline 2 came, by the way, from the mouth of my own mother. Even as I observed Caroline 2 with fascination, I could not bring myself to form an alliance with her. Perhaps this was because I, in turn, understood that everything that Caroline 2 knew about me came from the mouth of her mother. We looked at each other from across a very long view. We grimaced and mimed. We liked to talk as little as possible, to be in the same room, if possible, not at all.

The last time I saw Caroline 1 and Caroline 2 was at the residence of Caroline 1, for that dinner. As I walked up the stairs of their narrow building where the kitchen was for some reason on the third floor, I considered, as I always did, Caroline 2's position. She was bound to inherit. Was her lack of a separate existence from that of her mother therefore a form of preemptive penitence for unearned wealth? Or, perhaps Caroline 2's renunciation wasn't even the result of personal feeling: Maybe Caroline 1 required it. Maybe it was a simple exchange.

Richard, husband and father, had died in a velvet armchair in one of these rooms. He was, to my mind, the only bearable person associated with the Lerner enterprise, but he may also have been a pathological liar, if not a career criminal; I just don't know. Richard was a short man, extremely charming. He had that premodern habit of being always very drunk or very high, but seeming sober. He smoked cigars among other things and carried a distinguished scent, was forever tanned and twinkling vaguely. I looked to him for avuncular advice, even as that impulse that had rendered me demented since the age of thirteen led me to try, perfunctorily, to sleep with him.

About that impulse: I know this is something I have so far left out. I've always been like this: by turns manic and catatonic. Of course, perhaps you've seen it anyway; I don't know. It has defined my life, even as I have tried to escape it. I've tried, too, to think about the way it feels. In simple terms, it occurs to me as a vague hope for love—that someone will love me. Yet, in practice, particularly in the earliest time of its onset, it expressed itself via off-color remarks at dinner parties and weddings, etc., short skirts and carefully applied makeup, the cunning deployment of my vivid face. I was thirteen when I did what my mother would have considered unspeakable things, things I somehow felt compelled to experience: the apartment with that boy whose parents were never home and whose friends seemed to make their own money. The wall above the bed spray-painted in a crimped-seeming checkerboard pattern. The incompleteness of the place. I wonder even now if our acts live with us forever.

My mother's hatred of me prevented me from enjoying my unusual teenage beauty. I was not thin (a point my mother strove to keep foremost in my mind), but I was shapely and, given what I vaguely understood as my father's paternal Middle Eastern heritage, exotic, apparently. An acquaintance asked my mother once, indicating me, "How did she get so *exotic*?"

"She is not *exotic*," my mother replied.

"Mom," I wanted to know, "why did [X] say that I am exotic?"

"She was just trying to find something to say," my mother told me coldly. "[X's daughter] is so plain."

My mother was, at best, I think, unfriendly. However, I knew how to make her laugh, and it was this ability that made it possible for us to be in each other's presence.

My mother, of course, recognized the impulse. She said almost nothing to me about it. If ever I used the noun *sex* or adjective *sexy* she would become enraged and warn me, speaking in stiff bursts, about "your language." It was not, she seemed to intimate, that I was bound for hell but, rather, that I was disgusting, and no man wants a disgusting woman. I was likely, because of this, to be poor.

My disgustingness was, fortunately or unfortunately, a facet of myself I seemed helpless not to pursue. I pursued it variously: I kissed and felt up my female friends, slept with people whose names I did not know, maintained a catalogue of conquests that attained three digits by the time I finished high school.

I'm sorry that I haven't said anything about this until now. I've tried to admit it, but I haven't known how. It somehow doesn't fit with everything else I know about myself. I suppose Richard makes me remember, in a way. I wanted him to take me far, far away. When we spoke he sometimes discovered a complex and distant region in his mind, and I enjoyed having a look at it with him. Also, my father adored Richard, and this was unusual, because my father hated everyone.

"Richard!" Caroline 1 would scream from the kitchen.

But there was an earlier time, a time that I recall, when I suppose it might have seemed possible and desirable to help me. In this time, when I was ten years old, Caroline 2 chatted amiably. Caroline 1 and Richard offered me a gift of a ribbon-festooned sweatshirt printed with the image of an enlarged playing card, the queen of hearts. I could be encouraged, even if the sick winter between my parents was difficult to be around.

Later, all things changed. No one paid any attention to my parents and the sickness was with me.

While I was still on my campaign to get information out of Barbara, I mentioned them, the Lerners. I wanted to hear what she might say.

Barbara said, "The daughter is damaged."

"*The*," she'd said. I asked Barbara what she meant.

"I've seen her and I can tell. She is damaged. Damaged goods."

Barbara's manner did not invite further inquiry.

Of course, I had my ideas: from television and movies and literature. When a child is said to be "damaged" it is because someone (usually in her family) has hurt her.

But here something else is coming back. I'm remembering that at our lunch, our summit, Barbara told me about herself. She wouldn't speak to me about her children, not Elliott nor Mags, nor what has befallen them; however, she would discuss herself. At the end of our conversation, I must have said something about my mother, about how I did not understand why she did not leave my father. I must have seemed annoyed and dismissive. Maybe I was.

Barbara was at pains to let me know that I did not understand the situation. And the "situation," as far as Barbara was concerned, was that of women, the situation *for* women, which was historical.

Barbara said, "Did you know I was raped two times?"

It had happened, she told me, once in Paris and once in a basement in Manhattan. Each time the man was someone she had met on several occasions before. In Paris, he returned to the apartment he was renting her because, of course, he had the key. In New York, it was after a rehearsal, when the others had left.

"You don't understand," Barbara told me. She meant that my mother's choice to remain with my father was not all that unreasonable. "You have to forgive her."

But even in my rage I was unsure what for.

About that other family: I believe they were people we met one day when I was about ten. There was a daughter who was my age. I played with her. Also, there was an older son. The father was divorced from his first wife and had begun dating a woman who was an artist. The artist was an artist without a major career and so she was a good parent to his children. Let us say their last name was Hell, the German word for "bright," "light," or "pale." There was Abbey Hell and Josh Hell and their father, Mark Hell. And there was the artist, whose name was Laynie. (Laynie, by the way, came up very briefly earlier. It was her ass that Barbara saw my father grabbing, during that summer of the house rental and Barbara and Palmer's penury.)

Mark Hell was lanky. He was largely bald, with a few vain wisps. I recall him often in shorts, New Balances. He was a math addict, someone known to cheat at tennis. Boundaries were fungible. He worked for a powerful NGO.

My parents mocked Mark Hell, PhD. They made fun of his predictable nine a.m. phone calls, his answering-machine messages including his full name. At the same time, they went wherever he told them to go. Mark Hell extolled my mother's beauty. It was strange to see. My father was a handsome man from working-class origins whose looks and photographic memory had taken him places in the early 1960s. Now he seemed to prefer, whenever possible, not to use language at all. Mark Hell, on the other hand, spoke constantly. He filled rooms and slayed hours with his perfectly waxed sentences on the impossibility of fossil fuel regulation, the boon of developing economies, the state of certain currencies he and his colleagues hoped to stabilize through austerity. He was always going to Brussels to give another talk. He commanded the dinner party to stare at my mother. He told me that I should really consider marrying Josh, who obviously preferred men and would remain closeted well into his thirties. "Grab him!" exclaimed Mark Hell, clutching, as usual, at social straws. Mark Hell did not care that he did not understand his offspring. This wasn't important to him. Nor was it important that they would run away from him to other continents as soon as legally and financially feasible. Mark Hell pleaded with Laynie to live with him. He pleaded with Laynie to marry him. He cheated on her religiously.

He was a narcissist with an ambiguous interest in humiliation.

So I never liked Mark Hell. Given his behavior, this is probably not surprising, but all the same, there were plenty of people I knew and loved who did awful stuff, and I wonder, to this day, even, why I found him so uniquely worthy of censure. Dr. Hell was tall and thin and ugly, it was true. I was, by the standards of the end of the previous century, overweight, but I, like everyone else I have named, including Laynie, was pretty cute. Mark Hell controlled all of us, in part because he was an outsider to an in-group we didn't even know we had. We didn't realize that Mark Hell was busy collecting us. He had, after all, collected his own children, which is an odd thing to do. He took us on outings and displayed his collection to the world. My mother, he said, was beautiful. Probably he sometimes slept with her. Dr. Hell was an expert, above all, in revenge. He was an economist.

One time something strange happened. I must have been about twelve years old. We were on Long Island, walking on a beach near the cottage where Laynie had lived, largely alone, until she met

Dr. Hell. It was a cool late spring, fog hanging over the sand. We walked slowly in our collected group.

We needed something to do. It was a turbulent day, variously located; the water too cold, even for feet.

I was carrying with me a small, beaded coin purse, something I had found the previous summer in a secondhand store and purchased using my allowance. I recall it as mostly white, with pink and red and green and yellow, a shimmering flower pattern. I don't remember what I had inside. Maybe there was a folded dollar bill in there and a pebble. I must have been shifting the purse from pocket to pocket in my jeans, which were also secondhand and too tight for me, as was all of my clothing at this time. I moved it around as a way of seeking comfort. I do remember this. And I scanned the ground. Although I could not have told you this at the time, there was something that I was attempting to avoid the feeling of.

Somewhere I dropped the purse. Or perhaps the tightness of my pants forced it out, I don't know.

What I can recall is that I could not be consoled. Not for the rest of that day, nor for the next. I could not tear my mind away from the notion that this object was irrevocably gone. We spent an hour searching for the purse on the beach, retracing our steps, until my mother started screaming that she had wasted enough time already and that if I had wanted to keep something I should have held on to it.

I remember Dr. Hell as the most meticulous searcher. His voice was strangely calm, his logistical interrogations keen. He seemed to like the thought of walking backward. To him, a loss was something to be savored.

ANALYSIS II

*For the following questions, select the best answer.
You may not select more than one answer. Responses
including more than one answer will be marked as
incorrect. Incorrect or unanswered questions receive,
as before and for all foreseeable time to come, a score
of minus one.*

The narrator summarizes the myth of Cronos, aka
Saturn, on pages 115–16. This citation most likely
conveys which of the following meanings:

   a. Male aggression and violence are mostly condoned
      within modern societies.

   b. Women often behave in such a way as to enable
      male aggression and violence.

   c. We should reconsider the historical significance
      of the name of the day of the week, Saturday.

   d. Some things cannot be discussed.

   e. A and b.

   f. B and d.

The two families, the Lerners and the Hells, have
what in common?

   a. In both families, a father has a dominant role.

   b. In both families, a daughter becomes a close
      confidant of the narrator.

   c. The narrator is very interested in the actions
      of the fathers in both families. Specifically, she is
      interested in whether the fathers are faithful to
      their wives.

   d. These two families have nothing in common.

   e. None of the above.

We can assume that:

a. The narrator is telling us everything she knows.
b. The narrator is telling us everything that she thinks she knows.
c. What the narrator tells us is an approximation of reality designed to shield the narrator from overwhelming sensations, i.e., the Truth.
d. Because all of the answers listed so far amount to the same thing, all of the above.
e. Each of these answers is distinct and unique. So, not d, even if d is extremely tempting.
f. Experience has a fundamental reality, separate from descriptions of it. This reality can really be touched upon in language, no matter what the philosophers say.
g. There is no answer.

We can assume that:

a. The narrator is a version of the author who has traveled into the future.
b. The author is a time traveler.
c. Both a and b.
d. What should have been, is.

Ten: Glass

We might be tempted to think that it is those whom we know best, those with whom we live, those whom we love and who love us, in return, who have no secrets from us. We are not to be blamed for this belief, but in fact it is only those to whom we are closest in whom we can truly realize the fact of ultimate unknowability, as far as other human beings are concerned. You could think about it like a net or veil: harder to perceive this mediating item but easier to see *through* it, the closer it gets to your eyes.

I consider my coworkers at Paulette: I know the adulterers, the pathological liars, the fantasists, the addicts, the neurotics; those who have suffered miscarriages and those who have aborted. I know the chronic masturbator, the kleptomaniac, the bipolar guy who checks Twitter all day and is considered the most perceptive among us, the woman whose personality disorder has brought her social success; I know the sadists, the saints, the hoarders.

The funny thing about Cody was, when I met him he wasn't anybody. He didn't seem like anyone I knew. I couldn't type him. He was somehow blank and immediately beloved by me. It wasn't that he was flawless. It was just: his flaws didn't amount to much, as far as I was concerned. He at first slowly, and then very rapidly, came to resemble a person so familiar, and so uncanny in his familiarity, that I could only have met him in my dreams.

Cody was a shape-shifter, and thus, it's strange I found out anything at all. Which is to say, about him, his history. I have the sense that most people don't. By this I mean, I could have kept on living with Cody and it would have been a normal life. It would have been a marriage like a lot of others, civilized and rotten to the core.

That I found out. *This* is the thing. Not what. Never what. The content does not matter. That the lie became clear is a formal feat and also bizarre. It's a pleat in reality, an unasked-for singularity.

Because anyone is living at least a double life.

The only person who ever tried to tell me this was Jamie Cullinan, the boy who could see the ghost of his dead mother when he got undressed and who, in the end, decided that he did not love me. He was the only person who said anything about it, who really seemed to know.

It feels like this to me, and I'm not sure where I first read it, this story, but the story is famous so maybe that doesn't matter. The story is the story of a mountain made entirely of glass. It is a perfect idea. It is in part a perfect idea because it is so hard to say what it means. I imagine one might attempt to scale the glass mountain but then slip off. In the sun it is burning hot. At night it is silky and cold.

The glass mountain is translucent, of course, and therefore one can see an image of the world through it. But the world is distorted by the thickness of the mountain's glass. It is said, too, that some people like to claim that the mountain is not there. They refuse to acknowledge its towering influence, particularly, it's also said, because they live nearby.

In the story of the glass mountain—a made-up story, and the only place where the glass mountain exists—there is a good young person who is given a task by an evil older person. One component of the task is to climb the glass mountain and retrieve a magical item from its upper reaches. I don't remember who the good person is, or the evil person, or what the item in question is. I don't remember how this person makes it up the unscalable side of the glass mountain. I don't really remember anything about the story at all.

In real life, not so very long ago, but also long, long ago, I knew and loved a young man, Jamie. In truth, I don't know whether he was bad or good. He was young and so was I. I was living my life and would, as we know, go on to love others.

Once Jamie told me that there was a movie I should see, it reminded him of me. The movie was *The Double Life of Veronique*, by Krzysztof Kieślowski. I watched the movie because I wanted to know how Jamie saw me.

I know, by the way, that photography distorts the world. Things are expanded and compressed. Still, I tried to look at myself through this film. In it, there are two young women with the same name who are born at the same time in different countries. They are in many ways identical. Both of the young women are singers. One follows her talent to a starring choral role and, in the midst of her triumphant performance of extremely high notes, suffers heart failure. The other young woman, Veronique, or, the other Veronique, gives up singing, sensing a death in her life. She continues modestly on as a teacher of small children.

At the end of the story, Veronique, our survivor, becomes the lover of a man who somehow knows what she is. The man builds puppets and is developing a novel and related puppet dramatization. This sounds ridiculous but is in fact disconcerting. His puppet story is about a doubled woman. When he tells Veronique what he is working on, she weeps. I believe that Veronique's father also realizes that Veronique has been two people. In the last shots Veronique is touching a tree.

When I think about this movie now, it annoys me. It's the Icarus myth, of course, but here Icarus/Veronique escapes her wax wings by giving her tale over to a responsible teller, who happens to be male. Kieślowski seems to suggest that you have two options, if you are this type of woman: (1) make immortal art and die; (2) give up art, mourn, get a creative boyfriend, touch trees, have a largely menial job in which you care for other people's kids. He saves one Veronique for us. He's merciful, modern. He doesn't throw her under the bus—or, *train*, as with Vicky of *The Red Shoes*, whose already frail body is further mortified by Michael Powell and Emeric Pressburger's histrionic conclusion. Here is the message: You will be punished, you will destroy yourself, your heart will give out. The art cannot possibly be good for you. "I let," Kieślowski seems to be saying, "one of them live so that everyone can learn from her. I created two Veronicas so that one of them might serve as an example."

There's no glass mountain in this story, at least, not explicitly. But I happen to believe in its influence.

Try to scale it, and you will slip down the side. Touch it, and your hand may burn or freeze. You might walk right into it or trip over its edge. I'm familiar, of course, with the metaphor of the glass ceiling. What I'm talking about here is more infernal, since uncreated and inherited. I'm talking about the way we can't help imitating narratives. We have to repeat our ancestors' errors and withstand the awful gift of their secrets, because we have so little else to go on. So having two Veronicas is handy. Kill one of them off and you still have a protagonist. Too bad there was only one Vicky. Although one may well imagine that Vicky was pregnant with a daughter when she died.

I'm sorry, by the way, to get so dark or, I mean, sinister, here. Q.: Angry and sad? A.: Mostly sad. I am alive today and therefore am my own double. I have apparently chosen life over the realization of some self, if Jamie Cullinam knew what he was talking about, which, who really knows.

By the same token, it's hard to say. I've lived as my own other, too.

I used to have this habit, slightly ongoing, of buying used clothing in a certain way. My purchases were less about what looked good on me than locating discarded designer items that I could afford. The thing about this sort of practice is that it inevitably brings you into contact with imprudent purchases of the rich, silly clothes, stuff someone bought to satisfy a humiliating impulse. I found these platform Chloe heels and carried them off for five dollars. They were white-and-brown ice cream, a twist. They had a whiff of slut, and I wore them to two weddings.

Now, my having vaguely inappropriate clothing was nothing new. But there was something about these dessert sandals. I put them on and felt pleasing. Don't get confused—I didn't feel good about myself, exactly. I used to wear them around the house, when I was alone. This was during the very last moments when Cody and I were together.

These final moments, these months, were in the summer. There was a day I remember, when I did not know where Cody was. It was a Saturday, a morning then the middle of the day. I got to feeling strange. I wandered the house. I guess I was trying to feel like Cody, to be with him in some way.

I was in a trance, and I took off all my clothing.

It was like the feeling of the air on my skin would tell me his location, telephonically, somehow.

I put on a swimsuit. I lay on my stomach on the bed in the Chloe heels and a swimsuit, rocking from side to side.

I was there, like that, wanting something so badly, for a long time.

When at last Cody came home to this mystifying scene, I pulled aside the crotch of the swimsuit. I had no idea that Cody had spent the morning and most of the middle of the day first at the beach with, then back at her empty apartment fucking, Sophie.

But I did know that I had chosen an incredibly vile and violent person with whom to throw in my lot, oh my little lot.

And oh how it was, a month later, when I found those images on his phone.

Sophie looked a lot like me, if purer. She was a pure European version of me, thin and decorative. She had no ambitions or scruples and was up for pretty much whatever Cody requested, including housewife role-play and impaling herself with cooking implements.

Cody, I saw, had finally found his heart's desire.

Yet, this was, revoltingly, not the end of us. It took another month. I am "proud," if I can deploy that adjective with serious reservations, of my escape. Yet, it did not come without damage.

I had sex with him once, after I knew. Just that one time. This incident is now the only thing I remember about our years of coitus. I don't know how to describe this without embarrassing myself. I feel such shame: it is quite possibly the lowest moment of my life.

Cody mounts me from behind. He is a foot and I am a shoe. It is as if he hopes to knock whitish paint off the whitish walls of the hotel room we are using for this rendezvous. If, as this was happening, you were to ask me, "Is all of the paint falling off the walls around you?" I might have said yes. But I was also just a mote in the maelstrom, as Cody tried to teach me, through his actions. I remember him saying, after he was done, "*There*. That is how I like to have sex." As if I knew nothing about him. As if we had never met.

One could imagine a voice that says, "Thank you so much for showing me how."

I don't imagine I tried to speak. Vicky was inside her plume of steam. There was at this point just one Veronica.

What I remember is my brain moving inside my head, seeming to touch my skull. Someone was thrusting inside my body and so my body moved. It was harsh. I don't think I got a concussion; it wasn't quite so literal or even so real. Because what was occurring took place on another channel, in spite of its physicality. This felt like an action by means of which Cody separated me from myself. It was not painful, because I could not feel it, except formally. It was painful, if only because what Cody did was cruel. I understood, somehow, that this was the figure of history, as it existed in and around my body.

The thing was, the history was exhausted. It didn't want to keep performing itself, any more than I wanted to keep living in its sway. It had come to me in the guise of this mediocre, protean man, and now it was having its last spin with my corpse, getting its licks in.

My brain hopped against the interior of my skull, and I was not present, except that I was present and everywhere in the room. *This occurs to me. This happens,* I thought, floating near the ceiling. I fell apart again and traveled to the carpet as dust. I became the electric light that was gathering in one corner. I had no idea, then, how young I still was. I was merely an object a man I believed cherished me above all things used to strike himself.

These events continued forever. The narrow hotel room framed us, and the events were framed and reframed: Either I had lived the past eleven years in ignorance, or I had not. Either I had lived in a world with this person, my beloved, or I didn't. Or, I lived in a world but it was not the world in which the beloved existed.

I wrote it all down, was the thing. I'm so sorry. I could not help myself. Here, the infinitely small cars that are words creaked into a line. This, it, is.

So there is the story as it is told: In which a young woman fails. She fails to maintain her marriage. She fails to have children. She fails.

It's funny, I wonder if you even heard this story. Nevertheless, it's mostly true.

I was born without the right to anticipate the future. It dawned on me slowly. The human right to anticipate, to plan and know, was like a skin being lifted, drawn away from the grid of the world during the period of my young adulthood. I felt it lifting, tugged gently off, with the swarming of new technologies, their automation of language and choice. "Oh," I sighed. There was nothing before me, yet I continued to live. I was crazy, staring at this, but I was alive.

Perhaps it was around this time—even before I got my job—that the tests began. They must have started mostly in my mind. It was a way to establish a link between the story and actual events.

Q: So, how have you felt today?
A: I am trying to keep it together. But maybe it's bad to try to keep it together.

Q: What could you do instead?
A: Tell someone how I feel.

Q: Is that what you're doing now?
A: Yes and no. It gets dark very quickly.

Q: You've never stopped being angry. But about *what*?
A: It isn't what I want.

Q: What isn't what you want?
A: I don't know! This life!

Q: Which life do you want?
A: I want to be alone. I want to be with that feeling.

Q: I don't understand you, what is "that feeling"?

It's difficult to say how these questions should be scored, besides, they are so old. I wonder here, in the present, what my ideal test would be. Would it be a test that asked about the nature of events and how we should assess them? Would I offer myself, the test taker, possible interpretations, in order that I might produce a thread that could function, successfully, as a story?

Thus I write: *Once upon a time.* Once upon a time, there lived a mother. The mother was not particularly young, but she wasn't old, either. The mother had a child who was female and this concerned her. The reason she was concerned was that young girls and young women were not, as the mother thought to herself, able to tell the difference between an egg and an egg yolk.

Now, this might seem like a strange concern, but for the mother this made perfect sense. An egg is a thing, the mother thought. Meanwhile, the yolk is just a part of it. It was important to score the egg and the yolk appropriately. Because the egg is whole, it should receive three points. A yolk, being merely a part, could receive only a single point. One should hold these values in one's heart. A yolk exists, but it does not really matter. What matters is the whole.

The mother knew that her daughter was not growing in such a way so as to be able to perceive the all-important difference between an egg and an egg yolk. Her daughter probably thought that an egg and an egg yolk were the same sort of thing, if not identical.

The mother was a good mother and because of this she planned to correct her child. "Child," said the mother, "there is something I would like you to do."

"What is that?" asked the little girl.

"I would like you to leave this house and stay here, both at the same time."

The little girl thought for a moment. "But if I leave this house, how can I also stay in it?"

"I didn't say being human was going to be easy," the mother told her, opening a cabinet. "Would you like a snack?"

"No, thank you," said the little girl. "It can be hard for me to think and digest simultaneously."

The mother closed the cabinet. "That's very prudent of you. I can tell you are not going to let me down."

The little girl smiled at her mother and went quietly away. She knew from experience that it was essential to behave as if everything her mother said was intelligible and corresponded to the innate format of the phenomenal world, as well as to what famous people said. The little girl went into her room and closed the door.

The girl thought. One solution, of course, was to kill herself. It was quite possible that her mother was a dualist and that therefore the little girl's physical death and spiritual liberation might satisfy the demand. However, as a result of killing herself the little girl would be dead, and the little girl felt that she probably did not want to die, at least, not just yet. The little girl needed to find another solution.

And so she thought. And she thought and thought some more.

Finally, in the early hours of the morning, the little girl arrived at a plan. It is difficult to explain, by the way, how the little girl knew what she knew. It had to do with having a mirror—for the little girl had a mirror in her room. In the mirror, the little girl had seen something. She had seen her reflection and also she had seen something else. The little girl spoke to her reflection. She liked that after she was done speaking she could observe as an attentive look came over her face. In these moments, she could change her mind.

The little girl turned away. Her room was full of scraps and objects her mother considered refuse. The little girl gathered these scraps and objects and sat in a chair and tinkered through the night.

In the morning, the little girl was finished. She climbed out the window.

In the little girl's bed, there was a new little girl. This new little girl was identical to the old little girl in every way, except that she was not human. The new little girl was composed of refuse and she was a doll, but no one would be able to tell the difference between her and the old little girl.

The old little girl—who was, in truth, the little girl—went far away, and the doll stayed to live with her mother.

Life for the little girl far away was not easy, but she did not die. The little girl grew and became strong, and now she was a girl, and after some years she returned to her home, where her mother lived with the doll.

The girl crouched at the kitchen window and looked in.

The doll, which had also grown, was seated at the kitchen table with its back to the window. The girl's mother was at the sink and she was cracking eggs.

"What's the difference between an egg and an egg yolk?" the mother asked the doll. The mother did not seem very happy. The mother was impeccably dressed, but there was a grayish cast to her face, a sheen of sweat. A twinkling hair had escaped from her chignon.

The mother sniffed the air and the girl at the window ducked down.

The girl could hear a soft creaking sound as the doll shook its head. There came a chopping, as the mother cut up one of the doll's hands.

"Oh no," said the mother to the doll, "you don't look very well!"

The girl went away and came back the next day.

The girl was hoping to catch the doll alone so that she could speak to it and apologize to it for bringing it into this difficult world. The girl was thinking that perhaps she would also explain to the doll, once and for all, the difference between an egg and an egg yolk.

However, when the girl arrived at the kitchen window, her mother was there again. Something extreme seemed to have happened during the night. The mother was busy, very absorbed gluing the doll back together.

The girl began to leave and as she left, in her thoughts, she criticized her mother. "She takes so much trouble," the girl thought, "and for no reason at all. If she wants that stupid doll to know the difference between an egg and an egg yolk, why doesn't she just tell it?"

As the girl made her way quietly down the street, she paused to gaze at her reflection in the window of a parked car. "I've somehow always known," she thought, "that there is a difference."

This is, anyway, everything you need to know about my life in order to understand me. Each day I do my job and live alone. I have lived in the city and outside the city. It doesn't really matter.

The other day it occurred to me that no one loves me and I love nobody. Certainly, I have close friends and even a lover, whom I refer to as "my boyfriend." We speak by phone almost every day and once a week go enthusiastically to bed. I also enjoy texting sessions, lunch, dinner, drinks with various darlings, my similars, my confidants, my friends.

But what I'm saying is, it's not love in the old way, not like it used to be, not like you could die from.

D.

conEdison

BENJAMIN

Your account number: ___-___-___-___

Service delivered to: 60-19 Gates Ave.

Your electric rate: EL 1 Residential or Religious

Next meter reading date: Tuesday, Dec 13, 2014
Avoid estimated bills – please give us access to read your meter.

Your billing summary as of Nov 4, 2014

Your previous charges and payments

Total charges from your last bill	$43.07
Payments through Nov 1, thank you	–$00.00

Remaining balance $812.22

Your new charges – *details start on page 2*
Billing period: Oct 2, 2014 to Nov 1 2014

Electricity charges – for 30 days	$28.64
Adjustments	$8.12

Total new charges $36.76

Total amount due $848.98

Payment is due upon receipt of this bill. To avoid a late payment charge of 1.0%, please pay the total amount due by **Dec 1, 2014.**

Message Center

📌 Have you overlooked your previous bill? Unless you have paid it recently, will you please pay this bill promptly and help us avoid asking for a deposit equal to two months' average billing. Thank you.

¿Olvidó usted pagar su cuenta anterior? A no ser que la haya pagado recientemente, por favor, pague esta cuenta prontamente y ayúdenos a evitar que tengamos que pedirle un depósito igual al costo promedio de dos meses de servicio. Gracias.

📌 The "Adjustments" amount includes a Late Payment Charge of $8.12 calculated on the portion of your balance which is overdue.

La cantidad indicada como "Adjustments" (Ajustes) incluye un cargo por Pago Atrasado de $8.12 calculado sobre la base de la porción de su saldo que está atrasada y no pagada.

Contact us 24 hours a day, 7 days a week

Payment slip

conEdison

Please make checks payable to
Consolidated Edison Company of N.Y. Inc.

Total amount due   **$848.98**

Amount enclosed:

BENJAMIN
60-19 GATES AVE.

JAF STATION
P.O. Box 1702
NEW YORK, NY 10116-1702

E.

gives on to the notion of an "individual owing obedience." In English, as we know, *subject* operates first, foremost, and primarily as a synonym for theme, subject matter, topic, issue, query, question, concern, point, argument, statement, thrust, view, or line of reasoning; for branches of understanding, a discipline or field, or as a technical discursive mode indicating a state of being under the condition of being "subject to," in the sense of "being disposed or prone to, likely to be influenced or affected by, under the power of." However, even in English, and in American English, at that, this allegedly unmarked "being subject to" brings into play the conditions *of condition* as such; of subordination, subjugation, stipulation, attenuation, jurisdiction, deference, obligation, and attributed power, all of which implicitly carry with them a silent trace of the sovereign will. The unacknowledged sovereign inheres as a silent co-presence and collaborator with the subject of subordination, aka, reading. In considering the sub-ordinant, the subject of subordination, that which is read, the sub-*ject*, we inevitably consider how the time of subjects coincides with that of their subordination (again, reading), dialectically providing us with an impetus, therefore, for a de-absolutized vocabulary of subordination that may give rise to a new literary subject, that of "non-reading," which is to say, of refusing the knowledge of what is to be (otherwise) read, of de-subordinating literature by liberating the subject through our ignorance of it.

3
Lives

What kind of person goes home?

—Bhanu Kapil

When one is feeling very bad, it is sometimes no consequence for more bad to be added. Bad can be freely piled on. We can bear it. We stagger. We stagger gamely. What would have crushed us at another time is now merely recognizable. We nod. We say we saw it coming. We don't cry—at least, not much, not more than we have cried already. This door has been intended only for you. And now I am going to close it.

It was approximately nine p.m., according to a clock above the circulation desk.

Erin swiped her university ID. A metal arm withdrew serenely into a silver pylon.

Behind Erin, the arm slid back, locking with a dry click.

The library she entered was a gift to the university from a man whose estate had been sued, after his death, by his granddaughter, who maintained that he had sexually abused her for decades, from the age of four on. The dead man, a renowned philanthropist who had come up through the pharmaceutical industry, was also sued by his great-granddaughter, niece of the first plaintiff, for the same reason. Where Erin presently stood, at the base of the library given to the university by this individual, was a ten-thousand-square-foot chasm. This quantity of air, enclosed by the front and back and floor and ceiling of the library, was, presumably, also a bequest. It was nothing but vastness and, also, nothing. It stretched over Erin's head, concluding with a dimly illuminated glass ceiling apparently intended to counterfeit a skylight and, Erin supposed, therefore the sky.

The philanthropist, a self-made man and alleged abuser, had engaged a famous architect to design the structure. The architect had, at first, in the mid-1960s, invited librarians from around the country to inspect his plans. The librarians were not delighted by what he had in mind, which is to say the enormous hollow atrium, necessitating U-shaped floors that would severely limit the interior space that could be employed for storage of books or human-scale activity (walking, sitting, reading, writing). One consultant said that the envisioned building was a throwback to the nineteenth century, not merely inconvenient but obscene.

The architect was long since a celebrity and carried on.

After his death, the architect was remembered not just for his glass buildings and love of the aesthetic crimes of modernism but also for his sympathies with the Third Reich. The architect told his biographer that he had gotten too caught up with style, with all the young men in their uniform black leather, supple and polished; their trim pale hair and strict formations. He said that his worst mistake had been going to Germany and liking Herr Hitler a little too much. The architect claimed that, in architecture, "Danger is one of the greatest things to use." Danger was, to him, a natural building material and decoration. It was a brilliant boot around which one wrapped one's lips.

The library, completed in the early 1970s, possessed the void the architect had originally desired and placed at its center as a symbol of the progress of the late twentieth century. It was not as if the architect had not done this sort of thing before! His signature voids, the architect liked to say, were what allowed people to look at and recognize one another.

The library's nine upper stories, rising above Erin, had walkways with delicate metal railings. The railings sparkled. Below her shoes was a marble floor with elaborate stereogram-patterned tiling, alternating gray, black, and white Vs. The architect believed that the illusory effect of depth produced when these tiles are seen from above mimics, as in M. C. Escher's drawings, three-dimensional forms. He believed that the tiling resembled a series of spikes pointing up at the viewer. He apparently trusted that this trompe l'oeil, a phantasm of a pit of pointed spears where there was only flatness, would discourage anyone from jumping. The image of the pit of spears built into a library to be used by students would, in the architect's opinion, be sufficient to deter self-destruction. In this, the architect, celebrated, in truth, mainly for his use of glass, was wrong.

Two years before the architect's own demise in the early '00s, two undergraduates at the university fell to their deaths from the library's upper stories. Their deaths were ruled suicides. In this sense, it is better to say they jumped—into the void the architect had created, which was also an image, as he himself maintained. Subsequently, Plexiglas barriers were added to the delicate metal railings. Six years later, in 2009, another undergraduate, a junior, successfully climbed over the top of the Plexi wall to fatally launch himself into the void from the tenth floor. A bystander, Erin had read, had said that there was no blood. The body just lay there, unmoving, plain. The bystander, Erin recalled, had been studying in one of the library's subterranean levels and had emerged to behold a prone form. This bystander did not want to give his name.

The philanthropist, after whom the library was named, had taught himself pharmacology as a young man. He had not been born to money and never obtained a college degree. He was eventually a close friend of Richard Nixon, with whom he sometimes vacationed in New Jersey, bringing along his two granddaughters, one of whom was later to sue him. The philanthropist became a White House adviser on health issues during his friend's presidency and was instrumental in the conversion, in the early 1970s, of the US Army's former biological warfare facilities at Fort Detrick, Maryland, into the home of the National Cancer Institute. From 1943 to '69, weaponized botulism, among other agents and chemicals, was manipulated here; in 2009, the year of the third university library suicide, the fort was declared a superfund site. Today, the surrounding area is known for unusually high rates of cancer.

After the death of the philanthropist's first wife in the mid-1950s, the philanthropist married a younger woman, a social scientist and diplomat. He famously gave his new wife many jewels, including a diamond and platinum tiara formerly the property of Queen Geraldine of Albania. After the philanthropist's death in the late 1970s, his second wife caused the philanthropist's records and personal effects to be securely entombed in the library. As far as Erin knew, this woman was still living.

Given the modernity of the architect's design and the pursuant presence of the void and, thus, the inevitability of deaths, a series of aluminum panels were installed in 2009 above the delicate but insufficient metal railings on all the floors of the library. Those who had conceived of the installation let it be known that the panels, perforated in a pattern of alternating rectangles, were not only a posthumous rendition of a design by the celebrated (if personally flawed) architect but also symbolized the movement of data as zeros and ones. Data, they said, cascaded metaphorically down, from the top to the bottom of the library, reflecting at once the materiality and immateriality of contemporary knowledge. No one said anything about the pit of pointed spears where, presumably, this knowledge at last accrued.

The philanthropist, who was additionally a vociferous anti-Semite, once wrote in a letter to his good friend Dick, "Jews have troubled the world from the very beginning. If this beloved country of ours ever falls apart, the blame rightly should be attributed to the malicious action of Jews in complete control of our communications." The library, built on the strength of the philanthropist's bequest, now with its cascading zeros and ones, a fence designed to prevent self-slaughter, housed more than three million books. It provided access to thousands of electronic resources via licensed databases, e-journals, and other formats. It contained twenty thousand journals and three and a half million microforms. It cast a sizable shadow over the neighboring public park, blotting out the sun. Underneath this park lay some twenty thousand bodies, anonymous persons whom the city had buried on the cheap, beginning at some point in the late eighteenth century. The shadow raked over them, too.

Sometimes student groups organized, Erin knew, to demand that the university rename the library, given the philanthropist's disagreeable affinities and affiliations, but it seemed that the critics always graduated before anything was done, the administration having a seemingly inexhaustible ability to wait things out (or, perhaps, just an awareness of the cycles of outrage and disengagement common to quickly shifting populations). For her part, Erin found the library unpleasant. It wasn't just the waste-choked bathrooms, the grimy tabletops and seedy floors, the cracked windows festooned with bits of discolored tape and stickers from fruit. It was the obscurity of the library, which was stuffed full with the feeling of that enormous, central void by means of which at least three people had ended their lives. The void hung around in the air and not just where it actually was. It expanded and bled and traveled. It stuck to the spines and pages of books and to the keyboards of public computers. The scanners were full of the void and always out of order. The lighting buzzed and flickered; it seemed to have been done as inexpensively as possible. Cockroaches swam through the void to avail themselves of food scraps clinging to takeout containers. Students slept in the void or watched television on the internet. If you ran your finger along a shelf, you could nearly see the void's particles sitting there, on the surface of your skin. It was a film and a vapor and a veil. The void hid things, even as it invited you to see right through it. It was microscopic and yet enormous, but what the void really meant, what it *conveyed*, was that you couldn't see—and shouldn't.

Erin tried not to care that the library was unpleasant. There wasn't much she could do about the void, given its ancientness and scale. Of course, she would have preferred to do her reading and writing in a place that was not haunted in permanence by the world-historical fantasies of at least two extraordinarily mentally ill men, but the fact was she had grown accustomed to the badness of the university in general, along with the specific badness of the department that would someday, she fervently hoped, confer on her a degree. The related badness of the library was somehow a lesser of these evils, even given the obviousness of its horror. The library was, at some level, merely an object. Its horror was the horror of a thing, not the horror of a person and not quite the horror of an event. It was tempting to think of it as history made manifest, but Erin was not willing to go that far, if only because she had to sit in it. The library's horror was the horror of a clever pattern of interlocking inlaid marble Vs, upon which Erin now trod. Down here, at least, one was unaware of the spears.

Erin could not have said, at this time, how much energy she had expended attempting to ignore the void. It was entirely possible that she had expended quite a lot but was, in spite of these efforts, still suffused with it, long since infected. The void sometimes seemed to have an animal smell. The void was rich, even as it was empty. Erin was thoroughly marinated.

She tried to steel herself.

What Erin knew of her existence was as follows: She had lost the person she had for so long loved most and was currently locked out of her home without many resources or friends. Also, she had recently, as of this morning, as the contents of her bag reminded her, received an email of rejection from a literary agent. She needed to remember this, to attempt to think it through, now that she was here in the place where she did all her thinking and work. The email, received at 10:07 and opened at 10:09, read:

Dear Erin,

Thank you so much for sending me revisions of your novella and novel, and for waiting so patiently while I took some time with them. You've obviously done a lot of hard work on the manuscripts since I last saw them, and I enjoyed reading these revisions so much.

Unfortunately, as impressed as I was with the changes you've made, there are some considerable things holding me back from completely falling in love with these books. It's still not entirely clear to me what the heart of either of them is going to be, whether it's Amethyst's struggles to understand the dynamics of her family in MAISON CLOSE or the narrator's intellectual musings in HYPERGRAPHIA. As observant and unique and refreshingly strange as these narratives are, they are still difficult for the reader to connect to on an emotional level, in part because the protagonists' troubling lack of agency is never fully explained. In the end I found myself wanting more resolution, and, frankly, needing to understand the logic—what's ultimately at stake here—just a little bit better.

I'm sorry that I don't feel these current drafts are manuscripts I'm in a position to take on at this time, but I'm certainly willing to read more of your writing, or another version of this novella and novel in the future. I think you're a very talented writer, and there's a lot of smart material here. It just hasn't quite coalesced in my opinion. Of course, fiction is extremely subjective, and you may find another agent who feels differently. Whatever happens, I was so glad to be introduced to your writing, and I wish you all the best in your publishing endeavors.

Sincerely,

Erin understood that if you wanted to "sell" a book you needed someone to sell it for you; you could not sell it yourself. And so she was going to "get" an agent even if she did not understand agents. A few years earlier, she had begun gathering what she thought into prose because she saw that narrative sentences were what publishers acquired. Erin recognized that she was not supposed to think about the abstract parts of literature, if she wanted an agent. Agents, Erin could see, were put off by abstraction. They liked grammar when it was invisible, books when they made sense and also when they made the reader cry. They did not like "refreshingly strange" books. They did not like *Ulysses* or anything at all by William Gaddis. Gertrude Stein and Virginia Woolf were OK, because you could slap a flowerpot or a photograph of Nicole Kidman wearing a prosthetic nose on the cover of one of their books and it would sell a little. People wanted to own them, but usually you had to leave out the parts about them being queer. Proust, meanwhile, was long-winded, but people wanted to own Proust, too. People did not want to own Jane Bowles. They did not want to own Djuna Barnes or Nella Larsen. They did not want childlessness and death; they wanted childlessness and longing. They wanted views out of beautiful windows. They definitely did not want to hear about the void, which, Erin reflected, was indubitably within her now. Erin did all her writing within this library. The void, which seemed to make the people she described disjointed, unreal, and without stakes, was the lens through which she saw the world.

After receiving the agent's email, Erin had printed out both of her rejected manuscripts, securing them with binder clips. She'd had a definite feeling of needing to make them into concrete things, so that she could arrive at a strategy.

Seven months earlier, in a different world, when she was still, or so she had felt, securely married, Erin had gone to see the agent. The agent had an office at the top of a small and stylish prewar office building that got good light from all directions. A friend of Erin's had provided the introduction, and Erin had been invited by the agent's assistant to convey her writing electronically to the office. The writing was read. Erin was, in turn, invited to appear.

Erin had gone to a chain store that sold work outfits to upwardly mobile professionals who did not want to reveal too much of their personal taste to their employers. She used a credit card to buy a stiff, spotted dress with long sleeves and a short skirt that she wore to the encounter with the agent. The agent (Erin was offered a cup of water and an apple which she duly consumed before being ushered in) was no more than five years older than Erin. Erin marveled at the decor in the agent's office, which the agent had evidently selected and purchased using money that was earned through the activities of the agency, i.e., selling manuscripts. There was a white shag rug and a desk with legs of violet glass. Books were everywhere in vibrant stacks. The agent was a slender approximation of the nerd/sympathetic friend as imagined by Hollywood for a late-1990s suburban rom-com. Erin, for her part, was sweating and proved able to summon up very few correct answers to the agent's queries, she could tell.

After determining to her satisfaction that Erin was by no means charismatic, the agent began proposing ways in which Erin might conceivably improve her writing. The suggestions were mostly about something the agent called "arc." The agent seemed to want the people Erin described in her writing to realize things. She wanted them to figure out that bad things were happening to them and then to figure out how to make the bad things stop. Once the people had recognized that the bad things that were happening to them were what they were (i.e., bad things), then the people should use the rule of identity (bad things are *bad*) to reorient their personal systems of ethics and aesthetics. They should not experience the things that were bad! They should change their behavior! After this occurred— the great behavioral reorientation—then new events in the narrative should show how different results were obtained for the characters' lives. Subsequently, the book should end in glory.

Erin was not really in a position to respond to these pronouncements during the course of the meeting itself, given the desk's crystal legs and the many published books testifying to success, but that did not mean that Erin did not attempt to come up with many witty retorts afterward. She walked stiffly home over the Williamsburg Bridge, replaying in her mind what had transpired. She knew that the agent would never in a million years agree to represent her writing, but that did not mean that the agent was altogether wrong. For the fact was, what the agent said made sense. Why, after all, did Erin's characters persist in wallowing in dreck? The agent said that if Erin could make her characters see their confused attachment to the bad and throw that attachment in the trash, then, and only then, the agent might look at them again. And so Erin had attempted, but clearly failed, to revise.

Thus, having read the agent's confirmation of what both she and Erin had already known, perhaps even before they met, Erin had printed out her forlorn, arc-less stories with their illogical characters who would never stop accepting rotten things, even if they vaguely realized these things were rotten, and she put the manuscripts into her bag. She also put her copy of Roger Herbsweet's first book in there. It sat between the manuscripts, along with Faith Ewer's lost page and a frightening bill.

Erin had checked Roger Herbsweet's book out of the library earlier in the term, but it had taken the emergence of the human-desk scandal to make her finally decide to read it. Back when she had still thought of attempting to ingratiate herself with old Herby—because she had no dissertation adviser and was therefore in danger, then, as she still was, of being asked to leave the program—it had seemed like a good idea to have read his one critical tome. But, then, Erin had kept his monograph at home on her bookshelf and had not read it. She had not emailed him. She knew when Herbsweet's office hours were and made a point of writing them on her calendar each week in pen, but felt a kind of repulsive bounce in relation to that possible action.

The unnamed student had attended Herbsweet's office hours. Look what had happened to the unnamed student. Of course, also look what had happened to the honorable Herby.

Erin assumed, without quite knowing why, that Herbsweet had at one time been different. There was how he was now, and there was how he had once been. How he was now—which is to say, how he had lately been, given that he seemed to have been banned from campus—was: small, vaguely evil, entertaining, crude, resourceful, morose, dreamy, mercurial, loud, stubborn, ostentatious, occasionally brilliant, and directionless and insecure. Herbsweet sat at the head of the seminar table and was at once a clod and a magician. He was not very nice unless you said or did something useful to him, in which case he was briefly very, very nice, twinkling like a cone of sugar with a maraschino cherry on it. Otherwise Herbsweet was harried and bitter, forever gnashing his petite flat teeth and flaunting his whitish mustache, which he allowed to grow longer than was, strictly speaking, OK. One of his favorite games was to begin discussing some tangential historical event that might or might not have bearing on the week's assigned reading. In this game, the students' task was to guess what the relationship between the historical event described and the book they were studying might be. The only difficulty was that Herbsweet was ever at the ready to remind his students that literature had nothing to do with history and any implication of direct causation would be met with a drawn-out "Nooooooo!" This monosyllable was occasionally enhanced with pointing, with Herbsweet standing up from his chair to point, with Herbsweet throwing a book or balled-up printout in the direction of the student speaking, with Herbsweet clapping quietly once the student had finished their comment, with Herbsweet giggling into his neck.

The stupidity of the majority of his students was well understood by Herbsweet. He was experienced and saw it coming. You could not get anywhere near him with your stupidity! If you were to bring it into his presence he was going to sniff it out, and everyone was always bringing stupidity into his presence. Therefore, Herbsweet was permanently sniffing. He smelled your rank idiocy, along with the additional debility that had led you to believe that you could bring your moronic ideas near him in the first place.

Herbsweet was not credulous. You were not going to catch Herbsweet off guard. You were not ever going to put one over on him! Never! Herbsweet remained pure in his knowledge and distance, even as he appeared to have a morbid fear of showers, soap, combs, razors, and toothpaste, among other appurtenances associated with contemporary hygiene. Herbsweet attended to his facial hair with safety scissors. Herbsweet carried a stained satchel of books and papers. He rustled and jerked and shuffled as he went around in an oily ankle-length overcoat that he completed with a tall fedora fashioned from moss-green felt. But just because Herbsweet proceeded with apparent impatience and buried his body in lichenous fabrics and texts did not mean that he was incapable of sensuous, even vulpine motion. To see him traveling along the sidewalk was to believe that he might be capable of scaling walls. It was clear that Herbsweet maintained his human form only at great personal effort.

Yet Erin believed that Herbsweet had not always been so. And his having been young meant that he had at one time not been in possession of the overweening sense of superiority and related need for increasingly dicey tests of said greatness that were, today, slowly but surely converting him into a demon. While Erin had originally planned to woo Herbsweet as an adviser, the longer she was in his class, the more she saw and heard, the more confused and fascinated she became. Hers was a morbid fascination with Herbsweet's cursedness. Erin watched. She saw the prodigious struggle Herbsweet underwent to remain out of reach of his own baleful longings, his thirst for hazard. Herbsweet held himself triumphantly in check, and it was true he worked hard, if in a state of frantic disarray. But what Herbsweet had forgotten, and what he seemed unlikely to remember, was that not everyone wakes up in the morning having dreamed of apocalyptic bonfires and the crunching sounds of warm bones being ground to dirt.

Erin had begun to create her own image of the young Herbsweet. She carried this image with her to the weekly meetings of his course. She plastered this image over her eyes and said nothing all class long, and this was how she got through it. She had originally planned to render this image all the more detailed and lifelike through the reading of Herbsweet's early book, but then she had realized that the image worked better if it wasn't based on anything that might be actual.

In Erin's image, Herbsweet was idealistic. His face was hairless and smooth. He thought that European poetry could save the world. He wore sweaters with collared shirts and smoked a lot, sunk in easygoing studies in an era when to be male and white and in possession of a PhD meant decent work for life. This Herbsweet liked to make spaghetti sauce and roasts. His hobbies included research into medieval tapestries and the unclaimed shipwrecks of the Renaissance. He hitchhiked frequently in Europe.

When Real Herbsweet started on one of his episodes, she silently enumerated to herself all the things that, in her fantasy, the young, ersatz Herbsweet (her beloved invention) held dear, the poems of Ronsard and groves of olive trees, the dainty decayed faces of wooden altar statuary and the erudition of the Frankfurt School, sex alfresco with a Tuscan hippie. She strove to convince herself that she and Herbsweet were not so very different, that they both treasured cultural treasures, along with complex cultural complexity.

Even so, when the news had come, trickling in via carefully worded emails and significantly less euphemistic whispers among the graduate students in their narrow shared office (formerly a closet), Erin was surprised. It was not, of course, that she did not believe that Herbsweet was capable of, well, *anything*, but that she had begun to believe in his success—in other words, that he had successfully staved off chaotic metamorphosis to remain civilized.

That he had not staved it off and gone instead full beast was what made her blink. It gave her pause. She had begun reading *The Golden Fleece: Démocrite Charlus LeGouffre and the Search for* Reconnaissance. She wanted to know him better. In fact, she had finished the book this morning on the train. It had been good to have another thing to think about. And that was true even now, in this portion of the longest day that Erin was aware of herself as ever having lived. The book was dotty with self-indulgence. It was distended and bizarre. It was a soggy prop in a longer and as yet unconcluded personal drama. It was a relief, for the moment, simply not to be its author.

Erin went upstairs.

She took the library stairs sometimes, rather than making use of an elevator, in order to continue to be able to speak on her phone. Often, the person she was speaking to would notice Erin huffing and puffing as she took the stairs, two at a time, as was Erin's custom. Erin hoped, in so doing, to make up for her reluctance to visit the gym. The void, into which Erin climbed, seemed to resist her progress. It disliked being penetrated by human bodies, even as it could not survive without their presence, feeding, as it did, upon human thoughts, luxuriantly carving them out and roosting within them. The void brushed curiously against interior parts of Erin. Erin, meanwhile, was able to end quite a number of trivial conversations simply by making the sounds she made while climbing these stairs. Not that, in truth, Erin had so many conversations or conversation partners that, in the end, any of them could be considered trivial.

Erin had some friends. Or, Erin had had some friends. Something had begun to happen during her time as a professional student and married woman that had caused her to have fewer. People became topics in Erin's mind. Meeting them in person was disturbing. They were always doing new things, becoming difficult and unreliable and exceeding their statuses as topics, as such. Everyone had to get money. Erin did not like to think about it. Erin herself needed to get money, too, because her stipend was about to run out, which would mean no income and therefore no money and meanwhile being unemployed while ineligible for unemployment benefits, while working full-time on a dissertation, which would not be the only reason she would be unemployable. Erin, a habituée and devotee of the void, had long since ceased to have practical skills.

Erin was grunting lightly, attempting to recall what if any monetizable talents she might possess (highly literate, runs to paranoid; sees through faces, walls, marketing; skilled at typing; adores irony, sarcasm; well-developed and simultaneously fragile idealism, useful if you desire underlings capable of pedantic critique; has in earlier times been accustomed to extravagant praise from teachers . . .).

Here Erin struck something.

The something included a human skull but was also soft, as humans were, leading Erin to believe the something was human. Erin touched her own forehead, which hurt, because it had contacted the other with a certain force. "Ow," Erin said.

"I didn't see you," replied a doctoral student named Alana Harris, frowning. They were standing on the eighth floor at the top of the eastern flight of stairs. Alana Harris might have wanted to flee but was evidently coldly resisting this impulse. "Please look where you're going," Alana Harris instructed Erin.

Erin did not much care for Alana Harris. Alana somehow managed to appear undercooked. She was fetal, pale, with visible down on her cheeks, which she inadvertently accentuated through generous application of pinkish foundation and a layer of powder. She dressed like a Cold War housewife, probably also unconsciously, binding herself into sweater sets and skirts, a floral scarf at her neck. She wore berets and broaches. Was it a very specific mixture of vanity, reactionary politics, and resistance to contemporary standards of beauty that caused Alana to default to Talbots mannequin? Did someone love this mixture? Was that person Roger Herbsweet?

For everyone knew that Alana Harris was the plaintiff, the so-called unnamed student.

Erin quietly contemplated asking Alana Harris a few questions about her "boyfriend." Alana, while not exactly sensitive, had always manifested herself extremely proud and very brittle. She was always announcing something or other that she had organized or begun to participate in, a conference or roundtable, and invariably these posed nonquestions and had the ambition to do little more than add a line to the participants' CVs: the figure of the clerk in whatever, the circulation of whatever ephemera in whatever context of political persecution no one participating seemed to have the slightest genuine regard for, the long nineteenth century, our Enlightenment inheritance. Alana Harris sought volunteers. She sought others with meaningless interests who would, like Alana Harris, be satisfied by the invisible, ultra-low-worth tokens they would accumulate through this activity.

And so it wasn't, at least not precisely, that Erin Adamo was jealous of Alana Harris. Erin did not want to be Alana Harris—and she certainly did not want to be *like* her. And yet, at the same time, Erin did very much want to be Alana Harris. She wanted to possess a potent delusion that she could make use of in order to get herself to act.

But here was the thing about the void: It had already begun acting on Erin. Even as it was making it more and more challenging for Erin to do anything at all, it was freeing Erin of her delusions. It was dissolving whatever fantasies Erin might once have had of recognition or success. It was letting Erin know that if Erin wanted to accomplish anything she was going to have to do it in a world in which she, Erin, was nearly insane with doubt and meanwhile entirely mistrustful of everyone she knew. In addition to this, Erin would have to bear being considered, on account of these somehow impossible-to-dissimulate feelings, a dull liability by those who controlled her ongoing education. If they could drop Erin, they would.

Faith Ewer did not even have to bother to pick Erin up to drop her. Erin approached Professor Ewer and a few seconds later found herself on her ass. It was like running up a ramp that ended in midair. But there had, in all fairness, been a possibility with Isobel Childe. Erin had flubbed that one, too, in her ineluctable perversity, in her inability not to do things that stymied her, that caught at her and held her even as she struggled.

Erin wished for a well-oiled exercise wheel to run on and she wished for a committed academic adviser, which might not be a dissimilar device. The void, however, was having none of this. The void was obviously planning to keep Erin for itself. Erin had become addicted to the library, to the void, to its fragrant broth. She sometimes walked around with tote bags stuffed to bursting with library books, just to feel the weight of them, just to make her back and shoulders ache as she stood in a crowded, swaying train. And even then, she could not bear to read at home. She would reverse the process, returning with her brick-like books to be in the void. It was no wonder Ben had left her, given her habits.

Well, except that it was—which was to say, a wonder. But someone who stood on the outside looking in could have predicted it. Yes, Erin thought, someone like Alana Harris! And Erin laughed.

Alana Harris, for whom hardly any time at all had passed since her earlier recommendation that Erin deploy her spatial sense to avoid unnecessary collisions, did not laugh. "It's not funny."

"Hi," Erin said. Then, ludicrously, "It's good to see you."

Alana Harris, brittle and wan and proud, was momentarily appeased. Few people ever found it "good" to see her. "Yes," she confirmed. She lingered.

Erin, who was out of breath, experienced a petty joy. She became magnanimous. "How are you doing?" she asked Alana Harris.

"Well," Alana Harris told her.

"Great," said Erin.

"What are you doing here, Erin?"

"Homework."

"Are you taking a *language class*, Erin?" Harris made reference to the practice among some graduate students of enrolling in free undergraduate language classes to enhance their research portfolios.

"No," said Erin.

"I see," said Alana Harris.

"I was in the seminar today," Erin told her.

It was, in a way, a polished thing to say, because it contained acknowledgment of the scandal without naming it. This was, additionally, an offer. Erin might be willing to apprise Alana Harris of some of what was currently going down, if Alana Harris would, in return, suggest some outlines regarding her own participation. Erin could not believe her own aplomb. It was so unlike her. She watched as Alana Harris's wheels turned.

Alana Harris sparkled pastily. Little threads of electricity swam around in her colorless eyes. She said, "I'm not really able to attend coursework in person for the moment. My lawyer was not sure it's appropriate."

"That makes sense," said Erin.

Alana Harris's face quivered. "People will be reading a lot into my actions. Going forward."

"It's true."

"I'm not sure if you realize that my career is probably over. You always seem like you have something else you're counting on. It used to bother me, you know."

"Sorry to hear that," said Erin.

Alana Harris seemed to be measuring Erin's face. She took a step back. Alana Harris said, "Before this happened, I used to be afraid of you. I didn't understand why a person like you is doing this."

"Like me?"

"Someone who could do other things! I didn't understand why you were here."

Erin was simultaneously flattered and alarmed. It was as in one of her recurring dreams in which her clothing dissolved to enormous public interest.

"I'm not sure," Erin paused, "I could."

"Well, you definitely don't need to do this."

"'Need' is funny," Erin said. She was beginning to feel exhausted by Alana Harris along with Alana Harris's fears. Erin took a step to the side to indicate that their conversation had attained its meager potential and could now be abandoned.

Alana Harris, who missed nothing, failed, too, to miss this.

Alana Harris said, "My legs hurt. Do your legs hurt? Let's perch." She indicated a leather-covered toadstool.

Erin allowed herself to be directed.

"As I was saying," Alana Harris said, joining Erin on the toadstool, "my lawyer's very optimistic."

"Yes," said Erin.

Erin's lack of enthusiasm was having a strange effect on Alana Harris. Alana Harris seemed unable to stop speaking.

"He really is," said Alana Harris. "I really mean it."

Here Alana Harris began telling Erin Adamo the story of her life.

Alana Patricia Harris was born in 1982 in the United Arab Emirates to American parents who returned to the Midwest and became divorced before her second birthday. Alana's father, who ran a manufacturing business, started two additional families before Alana graduated from high school. Alana's mother, who had received a multiple sclerosis diagnosis when Alana was ten, did not have additional children or remarry. Alana lived with her, first in Lansing, Michigan, and later Oakland, California. Her mother was a professor of microbiology who specialized in intestinal microflora, with respect to which she had an additional specialization [which Alana explained but Erin did not understand]. Alana idolized her mother, who had instilled in Alana her precision and perhaps some of her fashion sense. Alana attended UC Berkeley as an undergrad, where she double-majored in French and Middle Eastern studies. She later worked for a French publisher based in Lyon and then returned to the United States where she began her PhD. Her mother had a live-in caregiver and continued to reside on the West Coast—a source of grief to Alana. Alana meanwhile maintained a formal correspondence with her father, who occasionally passed through New York, at which time he would invite her out to dinner. He had long since moved on from the relationship with Alana's mother, as well as from several subsequent relationships, and Alana remarked that it was easy enough to avoid the topic, given the complexity of his present life, which involved seven other offspring, two of whom Alana had never met.

Alana's mother encouraged Alana to go above and beyond. While she did not entirely agree with her daughter's choice to study literature, she was intrigued that Alana believed that there was a role for quantification in the humanist space.

Alana was starting to understand her position. She perceived that Roger Herbsweet could be a powerful advocate, and she had approached him. Her mother would want her to, after all. Alana knew of his reputation. She was informed that he was tough, crass, something of a drinker, but generally a reasonably good soul. Alana Harris had, unfortunately, made her queries among male colleagues, and so the portrait of Herbsweet that she obtained was, she later found, selective at best. Not that Roger Herbsweet was a bad man. He was difficult, complicated yet oddly attractive, and he was not without a sense of humor.

Alana Harris went to see Roger Herbsweet and Alana Harris's life began to change. Strange men, Alana said, began asking her for her phone number in coffee shops and in the street, and Alana meanwhile felt a new facility in all she did. She bought herself several new scarves and made some small investments in the stock market using a smartphone app. She pored over esoteric catalogues and handbooks, hoping to discover evidence of material culture of the long nineteenth century that might intrigue Roger Herbsweet. She went online to aggregators of used and out-of-print books and began to develop a library of all of Herbsweet's own offerings, his poetry translations, etc., which she arranged on a single shelf supported by cinder blocks in the leafy two-bedroom she shared with a hard-partying flight attendant who was seldom home. Alana had some idea that Herbsweet needed a gift. He must return to the implications of his early monograph! She spent a lot of time pondering this. Alana Harris began to think she knew what Roger Herbsweet needed.

Alana paused. She was breathing audibly and looking out into the library's atrium, as well as at the metal scrim that stood between her and Erin and the void.

"Have you read his first book?" she asked.

"No," Erin lied.

Erin was trying not to listen very closely. She wondered what her parents were doing at this moment. Probably, her mother had finished loading the dishwasher and was solemnly annotating a mail order catalogue with Post-it notes. Her father would be insensible in a chair. This made Erin think about Ben. Thinking about Ben, it felt like: There was a faded devil that pranced around. The faded devil was possessed but could not speak its pain. The devil would use its cell phone to get in touch with someone with whom it could go drinking or share sex. Then, satiated, the devil would dive into a bright, bottomless sleep . . .

"Hello?"

"Hi," said Erin, automatically.

"Where did you go?"

"Sorry," Erin said.

The thing about that devil, Erin was reflecting, was that it was capable of quite a lot—of thoughts and actions that even the Ben she had lived with had not permitted himself. It was a projection produced by a state of skinlessness. Ben was no longer covered, held and hosted by Erin, a woman, and he had, presumably, not yet lighted on a new vessel. Perhaps he had tried to retain Erin for a period to stave off this painful transitional state. He existed now as a partially created thing. One must be on guard wherever creation is incomplete.

"You went somewhere, Erin," Alana Harris said, her eyes tightening to a squint. "Let's be real. We both know you aren't here for 'homework.'"

"I'm pretty tired, actually."

"I'm so sorry to hear that. If you had been listening, Erin, you would know that I had a very interesting time at our meeting."

"Whose meeting?"

"Yes," said Alana Harris. "That's why it's good to listen, Erin! I gave Roger so many fresh ideas just that first time I stopped in with him he said he felt like he was renewed. A new man, he said. Roger really didn't want me to leave."

"He said that?"

"Why, yes! As we know, at base, he has disdain for most people. Obviously, I was different."

"He definitely seemed unhappy," said Erin.

"I, by the way, who was trying to help him, mind you, Erin, had to act like I hadn't known all along that things were going to go this way, that we were going to become this close. I had to be very careful about that, to have it seem like we had discovered this mutual interest and attraction on accident. I didn't want it to seem like it had been my idea."

"That's—" Erin did not know how to finish her sentence.

"Why else would I have ended up studying with him, if it wasn't all meant to be? I mean, he was always going to be there, be the person who taught me these things, who made me see myself—"

"In what way?" Erin asked.

"I don't know how to describe it. It was like I wasn't living before. Things weren't connected."

"Becoming involved with him changed that?"

"I felt—" Alana Harris's soft body seemed to thicken. "I had always felt that I was going to do something important. I needed someone to see that."

Alana Harris kept visiting Roger Herbsweet's office. She went several times a week. She looked at the books on his shelves and told him which ones she, too, possessed. He, for his part, said odd things to her like that he had gotten his own collection too cheaply. One day he gave her a mediocre gift, an issue of *Practical Textuality*, an academic journal with a name confusingly similar to a more prestigious publication. The issue turned out to be dedicated to him. When she thanked Herbsweet, Alana's voice seemed to echo, as if emanating from some source behind her. She had the impression that she was levitating. It felt shockingly good, kind of like sex.

Alana told Erin, "There was a weird afternoon where we were throwing around citations, and Roger was all, well, we don't want to make it too obvious. And I was not sure what was he talking about, although I was oddly embarrassed, or pretended to be embarrassed, and I turned my head to find myself staring at a woman's face on the cover of a novel sitting on the shelf right behind me."

"What was the novel?"

"I can't remember all of it," Alana Harris said. "It was like a seventies cover, an old paperback. There was something with a flowering tree and a skirt."

Herbsweet had a topic in mind for Alana. When she was ready to write, he said. He'd give her little practice questions and she'd run off with them, spend the weekend hunched over trying to reach him in her sentences.

Herbsweet groomed her.

Eventually, Herbsweet began dropping references to someone named Jennifer. Jennifer had been a student, although it was not clear whether Herbsweet had in fact been Jennifer's adviser. Jennifer had completed her dissertation and done well. She was now a Canadian associate professor. Or, rather, she taught in Canada.

Alana hated Jennifer.

Alana had entered terms related to Jennifer into a search engine three weeks ago and the first result was a link to a newly published article behind a database paywall. The subject of the article was Démocrite Charlus LeGouffre.

Alana had made her hands into two tight fists. She had pressed these fists against her forehead like a pair of horns and she had sat there for several minutes, as the realization that she had arrived during this play's final act dawned unpleasantly upon her.

Alana printed out the article. There was but a single citation of Herbsweet's book.

Perhaps Herbsweet had only guessed, by smell and hypothesis, that the scholarship would be so devastating. The article had appeared in the international academic ether, and his occult canine sense—for they say, no matter how unlikely this appears, that dogs are more intelligent than cats, it has been empirically proven—had drawn him to Alana and Alana to him, as a means of support. She was his little tool. In spite of his addiction to email and unfortunate online hat-shopping habit, he was incapable of setting an alert for his own name.

Alana had not read the article—it was too distressing—but she had located and highlighted that one destructive, revelatory sentence. Her job now was to break the news to Herbsweet. Alana delayed and delayed. Of course, Herbsweet could tell she was withholding. It made him more familiar with her, jovial and rash. The more Herbsweet groped carelessly and enthusiastically in Alana Harris's mind and, who was anyone kidding, her very *soul*, the more what he took to be a lucky image appeared to him. He was transfixed by this image and in turn transfixed her, memorizing the abstract movement of her thoughts, priming the supple bulb of her brain. A song came out of him, and Alana followed it, taking careful, mincing steps.

"Have you ever played hearts?" Alana Harris wanted to know.

"I'm not sure," said Erin, still remarking to herself on Alana Harris's near-pathological cowardice in being unable to read the article.

"The card game."

"No."

"Do you play any card games?"

"Uno?"

"Oh my *goodness*," said Alana Harris piously. "This is with a real deck. Do you know what a hand is?"

Erin held up her hand.

"In hearts," said Alana Harris, ignoring Erin, "they're called 'tricks,' and the idea is not to win them, because if you win you have to take the cards, and the hearts, among other cards, are worth points. You really need three people to play. But so, there is a technique in hearts, in which you win by not getting any points. Or you win by getting all the points, and then you give many, many points to your foolish opponents."

"So points are," Erin paused, "*bad*?"

"As long as you don't have all of them, yes, I would say they are. I used to play with my mom and we'd have a third hand we called 'the House' that both of us played for. The House's cards were face up."

"So you didn't look at each other's cards but you looked at the house?"

"The House, yes, we did. Anyway, sometimes the House would shoot the moon."

"I don't understand why or how it would do that."

"I guess it was interesting to watch ourselves lose."

Erin did not say anything.

Alana Harris giggled. Her life might be fucked up, Erin reflected, but that did not mean that she had lost her enthusiasm for paltry forms of control. "It's the name of what you do in play. You accumulate all the points, the bad cards, and when you win, well, you win bigger."

"Because you make other people have points?"

"Exactly. And they get a lot of them. Like, really a lot. Like, you've destroyed the only natural satellite of Earth and everyone but you lives on Earth. It's a thing where, on the receiving end, you're preeeeetty unlikely to dig yourself out."

"Sounds risky."

"Counterintuitive for sure," said Alana Harris.

Alana Harris had never, in her short and arid life, had to think about the difference between going down with a fight and going down without one. The reason she had never had to think about this was that her life had been, up until this point, so virtuous that it did not excite the tendencies that can land a person in aporia (which is to say, "an irresolvable internal contradiction or logical disjunction," via late Latin from the Greek *aporos*: "impassable" = *a-*, "without," + *poros*, "passage"). It was only through her attainment of *marvelous*, as she had for a period of time perceived them to be, heights of virtue that she had invited the attention of so adept and corrupt a figure as Herbsweet, a man who could drag her into the sulfurous mud. Alana Harris had not seen it coming, but, then again, most people never do. Which is the reason for the existence of stories.

Alana knew that any day now Herbsweet would be widely considered a laughingstock. Maybe it would even take another month or two to seep into all the cracks and crannies of the most poorly renovated sections of the ivory tower, this news item of Jennifer's. In any case, it wasn't long and there were two big problems facing Alana: (1) She was quickly becoming Roger's pet and no one else in the department would touch her after this. (2) A letter of recommendation from Roger was going to be worth only slightly more than the paper it might be printed on, which, at the going rate at the university library, came to approximately two cents.

Alana Harris did not discuss her situation with anyone. This bizarre self-sufficiency tending toward abnegation and/or strangulation of self, which was simultaneously what had made Alana Harris successful as a college student and caused her to be attracted to repellent clothing and dangerous people, what made her good at jobs and bad at friendship, was, Alana Harris realized, a quality that had allowed her to blithely enter into Herbsweet's orbit and that would now make it supremely difficult for her to exit again. It was as if she had sleepwalked into this position and now, very much awake, had nowhere to go.

It was impossible, Alana Harris felt, to simply cut things off with Herbsweet. If anything, their relationship was deepening. He had begun taking her out for drinks, calling it "your little reward," and rummaged around in her crotch with his slim, dry fingers. He knew all the restaurants in the vicinity of the university with full bars and generous tablecloths. He had smiled at her under his mustache and his pickled eyes danced darkly around the room as he repeated the same platitudes he had undoubtedly doled out countless times before to countless previous advisees, misty with delusion and ambition, over whose crotches he had lingered in a similar fashion. One night, there had been a hotel.

No, it was not enough just to stop it. For Herbsweet was a violation. He was an unmoored signifier, certainly American, definitely magic. He was pulling out all his tricks. What had ever been his job, even, other than to keep frilling the air with words? He could transform himself into breath, could journey five days or three months into the future and then leap back again; he was not subject to the laws of gravity and was barely human at all, except when he was lecherous and therefore a tremendously human, sweltering mess. Maybe Alana Harris did not care about the article with its awful sentence or, for that matter, her own future. Maybe she actually loved Herbsweet, a walking, to her mind, contradiction. Maybe she wanted him all to herself.

How much did Alana Harris think before she acted? Did she really plan or did she merely fall? She had gone to the department on a Saturday, making use of an administrative key card she had found in a drawer in a shared desk a year earlier and then kept in case it might someday be of use. And she had gone to Herbsweet's office, the door of which had been left ajar, and she had taken his key from off the top of the high bookshelf, removed the skirt she was wearing, locked it into Herbsweet's drawer, and replaced the key.

After this she had assumed the position. Her movements were

but a feather with which she brushed his cheek. She wasn't just ruining *his* life. She was telling somebody, oh somebody, how she really felt, how they had made her feel. Such actions, as we know, bring fleeting but intense relief.

Erin did not know what to say. There was a lot one could accuse Alana Harris of, not least of which was bad taste.

But accusing Alana Harris of tackiness did not seem like a good use of anyone's time. Erin knew about delusion (the true identity of tackiness), too. People didn't deal with it in a matter of minutes or even months.

Fumbling, Erin said, "That's intense."

"I know."

"I mean," Erin said, "did you ever try to talk to him?"

"But, Erin, you know very well what happened next! I had my own personal escort! They bore me away! You should try it. I'm not kidding! You find out all kinds of things. Like, I didn't even realize I already had *an adviser*! Isobel Childe showed up! There she was, because she read my master's paper. It was amazing. She was so high."

"She read your paper, too?" Erin struggled to keep envy out of her voice.

"And my paper was very good. I was surprised that Isobel didn't say more about it at the time."

"I almost worked with her, too," said Erin. "Except I said something stupid."

"I'm sure it wasn't that bad."

"No," said Erin, suddenly opting for candor. "It was very bad. I told her that I didn't want to be like her. No, wait. That wasn't it. What I said was, I *can't* be like you. I can't just write about Balzac."

"That seems like a normal thing to say if one says it tactfully?"

"It was not normal. I was not tactful. I followed it up by saying, *I am Balzac*. Like, I literally said this to her! 'I can't write about him, Isobel, because I am him.'"

"Hmm, yeah, well, I guess she inspires that sort of thing. I just started apologizing and sort of begging her to communicate with Roger on my behalf. Like, little did I know!"

"What do you mean?"

"I mean," said Alana Harris, "how extremely successful I had been. Florian stopped by."

"Oh," said Erin. Erin was afraid of Florian Cádiz, and she recognized that his appearance confirmed that Alana had become a person of great importance, at least where the department was concerned.

"He came twice."

"I see," said Erin, who felt uncomfortable.

Alana Harris was standing up. "And now, you're going to come see something! Really something."

Erin remained seated. "I can't," she said.

"Are you kidding me?"

"It's late." Erin already knew more about Alana Harris's grotesque doings than she had ever had any ambition to learn.

"Wait, do you still have the key card? I was thinking that might come in handy."

"The one you were using? Why would I have that?"

"Oh," said Alana Harris, smiling and shaking her head. "I just remembered. You left our coat at your parents' place. And then you were too scared to go back! Forget it. We don't really need it where we're going. You're not going to believe your eyes. I didn't either, not at first. But there are more things in this world, that's what I think."

Erin frowned. She put her hands on her knees and pressed herself upright. She gathered her bag.

"That's more like it," said Alana Harris.

They left the balcony and shuffled up a flight of stairs, then over soiled vinyl into a windowless shelving area where an organizational project involving ancient folios was underway. There was something mealy underfoot, as if decaying liquid cheese and muesli had been spread around with a trowel during a very sick person's very sick lunch break.

"Voila!" said Alana Harris. She was tapping on the glass pane set in the door of a study carrel, an otherwise windowless cell one could reserve online. The glass had crisscrossing wires embedded in it, presumably to reinforce it in the event of catastrophe tending to total societal meltdown. These rooms, grimy and effective, were a format. Joy, daylight: these were not ingredients in the recipe for success.

Meanwhile, there came a panting from inside the carrel. There was also a clicking, as of hopping, on clawed feet, upon vinyl, and a yipping. Hardware jangled. A blurry beige form appeared and disappeared repeatedly at the base of the glass rectangle.

"Is that your dog?" Erin wanted to know.

Alana Harris was opening the door. Alana Harris got down on Alana Harris's undersized hands and knees. "There's my good boy!" exclaimed Alana, as a cairn terrier, smiling and trailing its tongue, threw itself at her. "Yes, yes, yes!" said Alana Harris, clasping the busy little earthdog.

"He's cute," Erin observed. Presumably, Alana had smuggled the dog in in a bag, like someone on the train, feigning as if everyone who happened to see it had to be charmed by its crushed face.

Alana Harris looked up. "Oh my goodness, don't you recognize him?"

"He's nice," Erin repeated.

Alana Harris was shaking her head. "No, he's a very bad boy. Isn't that right, Roger? You are very, very, very bad?"

Erin blinked. "Why is that his name?"

The dog, who was mostly brownish with a black chin and a pronounced and rather unattractive mustache, seemed to take note of Erin for the first time. It studied her and emitted a sharp bark.

"He doesn't suffer fools," Alana Harris said.

The dog bowed, stretching its small limbs, and gazed rapturously at its benefactor.

Erin considered offering the dog her hand to smell but thought better of it. "Was he always named Roger?"

"Isn't that a silly question!" Alana Harris was not addressing Erin, at least not primarily. Her voice had devolved into a drippy, creamed iteration of its former self. It was to be used for lathering things. Alana Harris scrubbed away at the dog's head as it blinked at her, its eyes wet and dark and terrifyingly intelligent. "Yes, Roger is a good, bad, funny tiny boy," she repeated, to Roger.

Erin was ready now to depart. "That's cute you have a dog," she was muttering.

"Wait!"

"I'm sorry?" Erin was adjusting the strap of her bag.

"Don't you want my study room? Don't you maybe need it?"

"Oh," said Erin, who had not considered this.

"We're going to have a whiz. Isn't that right, Rog'? Then we have to go back to Florian's."

"Florian has a dog?" Erin was trying to remember the last time the department had been over at his place *en groupe*, the plastic trays of sliced genetically altered strawberries and cubes of speckled cheese. She could not place Roger the terrier, who would presumably have trotted, begging and shivering, among the guests.

"I'm helping Florian look after him. We decided that I could." Alana Harris paused. "Florian is on my side, by the way."

"That's nice he's lending you his dog!"

"He's not his dog."

"I see!" said Erin. She was maneuvering around Alana Harris and Alana Harris's familiar, who was now making low growling sounds in Erin's general direction.

"Come on, Roger. Let's make a tinkle." There was a jingling of the dog's tags and presumably Alana Harris was scooping it up. Erin could hear it panting with pleasure. "See you around!" Alana Harris trilled.

Erin did not reply. She went into the study carrel, which: Alana Harris was right, she did need. She shut the metal door with its peekaboo glass strip behind her and was greeted by a wave, not of doggy dankness, but of male human body odor, that spicy, thick, resentful smell like locker rooms and prehistoric gardens. Erin let the scent wash over her. Maybe she banged her head against the surface of the institutional desk. Maybe she cried.

Erin rubbed her eyes. She stood.

She used the chair in the study carrel to prop the door open. These doors had a tendency to end up locked if left unattended. Erin did not know if this was coincidence, the result of malevolent pranks, or if they locked automatically at certain times of the day. Never underestimate the institution, she reminded herself.

She went downstairs, taking her bag.

At one of the public computers, she called up a popular database and initiated a cursory search. It was not hard to find. Certainly, more students in what was formerly Herbsweet's course had either already come upon the article or soon would, depending on the topics of their final papers.

Erin commanded a PDF to be printed and went to one of the printing stations, where she used the remainder of her "printing budget" to cause pages of ten-point font to appear, lofted upward by the laboring device.

They were warm and she stacked them, cutting herself between her right thumb and forefinger, a yoke already marked from previous incidents.

She seized a golf pencil from an unstaffed reference desk and retraced her steps.

Thankfully, the door was still ajar.

She ensconced herself, let the door screech to. That odor was now, mercifully, less pronounced.

The article was by one "J. Stasulis."

Erin read:

Revelations of a Sculptural Unconscious:
Between Dimensions with D. C. LeGouffre

"Gender is the extent we go to in order to be loved."

"None of us has time to live the true dramas of
life that we are destined for."

"Life is elsewhere."[1]

They say that those were the days when images flew across the land under multiple identities. That there was nothing worse for them than to remain still, self-same, locked into a single painting, photograph, print. Nothing—no one medium, no unique language or grammar—could hold them. Marble itself was not adamant enough, nor bronze. From the very moment they came into being, they were promiscuous, never static. They were ever available to new techniques of transposition, new contexts and markets. They could, it seems, always escape under the guise of another novelty. They were eager, unashamed, and barely accountable to the dictates of taste.

I am writing here about images of the nineteenth century. This was a century of a wild proliferation of popular images, in many ways analogous to the kaleidoscope of today's virtual sphere. It was a time of

---

1. These quotations are offered for atmospheric reasons. The first two come from Robert Glück's novel *Margery Kempe* and Walter Benjamin's essay "The Image of Proust," respectively. I have used the most recent editions. The third is a translation of a phrase often erroneously attributed to Arthur Rimbaud, "La vie est ailleurs." This phrase does not in fact appear anywhere in Rimbaud's published writings.

painted oilcloth panoramas hung in photography studios, photographs derived from history paintings, and portraits derived from photographs; a time of collage, photomontage, scratched and inked negatives, painted-over prints; an era of a bizarre array of transposed images, developed, for example, on eggshells and chemically treated silk.[2] Impure, profane, unoriginal images. Keepsakes and souvenirs. Each more patently derivative than the last, each a way station for the ever-accelerating transformation of fact into fads, scandals, miracles, news.

The decades following the invention of photography saw an *image frenzy*. Images circulated from camera to easel to three dimensions and back again. A variety of technicians, amateurs, illusionists, and artists of all stripes took part. Even neoclassical sculpture with its apparent ambition to remind the viewer of the empires of ancient Greece and Rome was caught in the maelstrom. Whether through their reproduction as plaster casts or as *cartes de visite*, even figurative works in marble were hard to keep still after 1850.

But perhaps I am too quick to focus on photography. Let me put things another way: neoclassical sculpture of the mid-nineteenth century had a privileged relationship to narrative, when it came to the visual realm. Sculptors were often obliged to leave out aspects of a given scene (other persons, architecture, landscape), usually on account of limitations with respect to materials and space. Hagar, as depicted by the American artist Edmonia Lewis, for example, is identified by means of her accompanying overturned water vessel. An odalisque, produced by Jean-Jacques Pradier, a Frenchman, turns her head as if to respond to an approaching visi-

---

2. See, for example, Michel Foucault's essay on "photogenic painting."

tor. Excised from the very contexts that afford them mythical, religious, moral, and/or cultural significance, these figures demand an intervention on the part of the viewer, who must at once recognize the narrative context(s) from which they are drawn and return them to this context, reflecting, along the way, on the sculptor's use of art to make possible this double gesture of recognition and reassimilation.

Bearing this convention for viewing nineteenth-century sculpture in mind, along with the burgeoning saturation of the public sphere by photographic and other images, it is interesting to consider what takes place in a certain novella, or *conte*, apparently published without much notice in January of 1857 in a small Parisian review. In this fiction, a marble statue of the Greco-Roman goddess Diana is severely damaged when a pirate attempts to move it at sea. All that remains after this accident is the statue's right hand. Yet, this hand is so expressive that it becomes an object of obsession for multiple characters, enduring migrations and ecological as well as political stresses, before it is again recontextualized and multiplied. At the end of the story, the statue's hand is once more a statue's hand—or so we are led to believe. No longer an alien object of desire, it has become part of a series of civic markers—even as it seems to retain its status as the traumatic monument of an obliterated event. Something lingers in the air. Something resists assimilation.

Who lends a signature to this odd tale? The author's name is of no small interest: *Démocrite Charlus LeGouffre*. The archaic Charlus (meaning "free man") is preceded by an astonishing given name: Démocrite. Political suggestions aside, this moniker may cite an ancient philosopher famed for his theory of vision. Democritus, according to Theophrastus, started from a simple observation: the appearance, in the pupil of the eye of a man or animal, of a small inverted picture of the world. In answer to the question of how this picture comes about, Democritus suggested that air, the finest of all media, receives an imprint of objects, which it then confers to the eye. To quickly shift this discussion back to the nineteenth century and its images, a Democritean theory of vision was famously adopted by Honoré de Balzac in his novel *The Cousin Pons*. Balzac suggested that physical objects project themselves onto the atmosphere, producing spectral visions, which photographs capture. All bodies are, in this account, made entirely of innumerable layers of ghostlike images. Each time some thing or person is photographed, a spectral layer is peeled away and transferred to the photograph, which, in turn, becomes a sort of infinitely shallow, if information-rich, grave.

Last but not least, there is the surname, strangest of all: LeGouffre. Derived from the Greek *kolpos*, meaning "entrails," the noun *gouffre* denotes a profound and abrupt cavity, perhaps the result of subterranean erosion, an abyss. In figurative contexts it is the depths of misery and, when personified, indicates a person who spends enormous amounts of money or overeats. In one reading of the full name, we might find, by translation: *Photographer Freeman Abyss*. But of course the names of actual persons should not be subject to literary interpretation.

Erin paused. She looked up at the wall in front of her. It was bluish and festooned with dried boogers. Someone had written: *When I sit in here, I touch myself and think of you* ☺ Another individual had drawn an arrow pointing to this inscription and replied, *NO THANKS!* A third party, who had evidently arrived a little later, wrote, *i don't understand why this is life where im forced to read things like this when i just wanna a problem set!!!* Finally, someone else had circled the phrase "wanna a problem set," commenting, *If you pay attention to what you write and don't do drugs, your life will be better.*

Here ended the forum.

Erin's ass was numb and she needed to urinate. She got up. It was a little before eleven p.m.

While peeing, Erin felt relief. This was normal, but it was also, she reflected, extraordinary. She urinated, and meanwhile she thought nothing. She did not particularly think of Ben. She still knew that Ben existed, somewhere, and she believed in his existence, independent of her thoughts. What had changed, she noted, was that the thought of him did not, for the moment, inspire terror or shame. It inspired, instead, a kind of miraculous neutrality.

Erin's bladder was now empty. She did various things, exited the foul enclosure, washed her hands. She looked at herself in the mirror provided by the institution. Her image, although green under the fluorescence, seemed a reasonable distance from Erin's body. She felt capable of pertaining to it, as well as examining its mass and contours. Something like a tension had left her. She smiled.

On her way back to the study carrel she stopped at a computer and searched the catalogue for a copy of *Passe-partout* in French, then walked down to the eighth floor, obtained the book, climbed back. It was a slender, mildewy volume, with yellowing pages and a protective chalk-blue cover over the original binding. It was a post-1927 edition, rendered all the more slender by omission of the introduction by Éluard, which some editors seemed to discredit.

Erin sniffed the book. She did not know why she always felt compelled to sniff books.

She thought about a severed marble hand floating around an antebellum landscape populated by fast-moving images. She put the hand into the sky, but it did not look very good there. She put it into the ocean, briny and odiferous and free of plastics. Here it merely sank, trailing bubbles.

Erin had read Herbsweet's book and she had read a small portion of the article by "J. Stasulis," but she had not read LeGouffre. It felt strange to think now of the simple reality of the sentences themselves, written by the author, by means of the author's hand. Erin had not read the book, but the closer she came to the moment at which she, indubitably, *would have read* it, the more she felt that this compact and all but weightless slip of a book was somehow intended for her, composed for her and only her, shaped for her exclusive reading. The moments she experienced, here and now, had somehow been foreseen by the author, whose mind, in writing the story, had inclined toward Erin's, even as Erin herself had been far from existing during the middle of the nineteenth century, even as Erin's ancestors had been mostly concerned with attempting to thrive as peasants in Eastern Europe and the Middle East and were, particularly if female, illiterate.

Erin was aware of the boundless jealously that literature inspires. It was an old jealousy. There was the jealousy of writing itself, of course, the jealousy felt by writers who cannot stand one another's products, but there was also the jealousy of reading, and this jealousy was less talked about, perhaps because it was more common, even, than authorial envy. The jealousy of the reader went like this: The writer is speaking to me (and only me).

The Germans, who had a word for everything in modernity, had named the pull books exert. *Lesesucht*, they called it: the desire to read. Related is *Lesewut*, or reading mania, a term associated with the publication of Johann Wolfgang von Goethe's *The Sorrows of Young Werther*, in 1774. That short novel was passionately consumed by a public who, in addition to their mania for literature, also experienced a mania for seeing young love and obsession end in suicide, so perhaps theirs was a more general lust for scandal and personal tragedy than, strictly speaking, a passion for a book.

For Erin, who now took the stairs between the eighth and ninth floors of the library at a methodical pace, sensing the void at the center of the building continually brush, insubstantially, against her left arm, there was a stirring of desire and also a strange conviction: *Passe-partout* had been destined for Erin, but *she* was also destined for *it*. They were, in an appalling pun that nonetheless appealed to Erin, *bound* for each other. It was not that no one else could or should read this book, but that such readers were tangential. Their reading was of lesser consequence than Erin's, not because they were less intelligent than she, but because LeGouffre had had a very specific brain in mind when he'd composed his story, and this brain happened to exist within Erin's skull.

Erin's intuition did tend to raise questions about whether she really wanted to read the book of her life now. If she were to read it now, she would then have read the book, possibly the only book, written for her and only her, and then there would be no more books of this sort to read. But, on the other hand, if she did not read the book, then she would be spending each subsequent moment of whatever life remained to her delaying her arrival at the book of her life (written only for her!), which would be ridiculous.

Erin wanted to read. She did. But it was also true that Erin wasn't sure if doing something she urgently wanted to do was a good idea. Things—important things that Erin had chosen of her independent American will—had not, to engage in understatement, gone well.

When she was back in the study carrel, the inside of which had developed the fusty scent of a wet sweater, Erin determined that she would delay her reading of LeGouffre's book just a bit longer by diligently returning to the academic article. She placed *Passe-partout* on the right outer edge of the desk in the study carrel and stared down at the printout.

Erin skimmed the opening.

An image frenzy.

Part of the problem was conceiving of moments in the past, moments to which Erin had attributed a particular nature—which she now saw was not, in fact, the nature of those moments. She had lived with Ben and he had gone to work each day. More or less, in the evening he returned home. What Erin had believed, during this time, was that Ben went to work. At work, he did his job, which included the writing of emails and interaction with databases. He ate his lunch, at a desk, in a park, in a diner, at a counter. He exchanged text messages with Erin and with his friends. That such activities were possible in their simplicity, their meagerness; that life could be composed of such neutral, apparently inconsequential actions as these: this was now a possibility all but entirely lost to Erin. At moments she would forget. In the mornings, she would wake up, and for a moment she would have forgotten: that every day at lunch for many years, Ben had fucked his coworker.

This was what one's enemy did. These were not the actions of the love of one's life.

Ben drank out of anger and he lied. He said that Erin made him angry. She had made him angry for many years. Erin did not take Ben into consideration, Ben said. Erin was distracted. Erin went to the library.

Erin thought about what her mother would say. Erin's mother would want to know what Erin had done to bring these catastrophes on herself. Erin's mother would say that she did not know what Erin was doing with her life!

But Erin knew. She knew that she knew that she knew that she knew: she had written her manuscript, "Hypergraphia," long before anything had happened. It was like there were two of her, one to live and one to write. She had composed events in advance, had recorded what were in fact scenarios of the future, what she might someday live. And she had gone back in time and written the story of somebody's mother and father and called that story "Maison Close." Some shadow hand compelled these compositions. Erin both was and was not their author.

Somewhere in the heap was a book Erin had not yet read.

Erin recalled her homework: the title, she needed to translate the title.

But her mind swung back: she had not known, and yet she had. Thus, there were at least two Erins. The capacity for description had been active in her, unharmed. She had deployed this capacity in the direction of multiple wax worlds, places similar but not identical to her own future and past. If someone had asked her what she was doing during this time, the time of Ben's cheating and of her writing, she would have said that she was not doing anything.

She did not tell Ben that she wrote. Privately, she fantasized about receiving a large cash advance for her fictions. Having received this advance, she would quit her graduate program and quit the relationship with Ben. She had not, however, been able to explain to herself that if she were having such a fantasy (as she definitely was), then this meant that there was something wrong with her relationship, not to mention her professional life.

But Erin had preferred not to explain things. She had believed in the reality of her love for Ben. He went to work and at work accomplished unremarkable accomplishments. She believed they lived in New York City and would someday do better for themselves and stop spending so much of what they earned on rent. Things were going to turn out fine; one just had to wait and see. They were always going to be together.

Erin liked, anyway, to believe that her shadow hand was dormant. She was not compelled by forces beyond her rational control, forces such as the unstable, irrational meanings of literature. This was a major upside to her relationship with Ben and even why she loved him. Ben was not words; Ben was Ben.

"Trust me," Ben said constantly, while they were together.

But Erin's shadow self, along with its hand, had been as strong as ever, in spite of Erin's hopes to the contrary. The part of life that would not make itself directly known was there, running, multiplying, as it were, in the background. Life exceeded Erin's capacity to know it. Erin saw that she had lived—where and as she least expected herself to.

Erin sometimes wondered about the history of trances. Was there such a history—of human trances, where they came from, what people believed about them—and how could it be told? She wondered, too, whether, in addition to the history of human trances, it might not be possible to write, in a rhyme, a companion volume: a history of human glances.

Erin could not take more of the article. It was too . . . what was the word? It was too *dense.*

Anyway, it had not been supposed to be this complex. It had not been supposed to turn out like this, like actually *living in hell*, with Erin looking toward those who were supposed to support her, her husband, her parents, and her teachers, with these allegedly well-meaning and supportive people screaming at Erin, "You are the absolute worst!" These people were not supposed to throw stinking psychic trash in Erin's general direction, nor were they supposed, when the psychic trash had fallen, steaming and pungent, on the ground and on the furniture, getting all over everything including the walls and the ceiling, to continue screaming about how Erin was ruining everything and yell at Erin that she had better pick up all of that psychic trash pronto if she knew what was good for her, because that psychic trash had definitely not come from any of them, no way; it was all hers.

Her parents lived in a building where a child had murdered his mother, and they even seemed to like it. They could not stop talking about it. This hideous event enlivened them. It was real, yet it presented itself to them as an intriguing fantasy. Still, Erin kept thinking that there had to be a way, that it had to be possible to regain their love as she seemed to remember it, the old love that had almost certainly been available when she was young. Erin knew that she could—not just that she could get it back, this love, but that she could remember it. She could remember the old love, even though, when she flipped through moments from her childhood, she wasn't sure she saw it there. Erin squinted and she saw herself being good, striving for goodness in an image. When young Erin was good, for a moment the stricture loosened, austerity was lifted, and for an hour or so she was at peace. But being good wasn't easy. It wasn't just Erin's grades or her behavior. Erin's body had to be good, and Erin's friends had to be good, and Erin had to be a sex symbol obsessed over by boys and men, who won all of her volleyball games and did not feel sadness. She had to not feel sadness and she had to fuck. Being and/or having and/or doing few of these had-to-be/have/do things, Erin often felt the stricture, the proverbial corset. It was hard to be any good. Because Erin kept trying, she believed that she remained weakly available to love, even if it was unlikely that it would come to her, and she never questioned her parents' actions. If Erin rebelled, she did so largely in the style of harmless televised plots regarding white suburbia.

But when Erin met Ben, the story changed. Erin had to keep on striving to be good; however, now Ben loved her, he said he did, and it was a miracle. Therefore, because a miracle had been visited upon Erin, in spite of her not having really deserved it (not being truly good), she must continue to cherish Ben all her life. Because she had not deserved Ben's love, Erin must dust and coddle it, she must preserve it from the psychic trash wind that was forever blowing at full throttle.

Ben's drinking was part of this weather. His loud accusations and tendency to (expressively) break household objects were aspects of it. The weather was unpredictable.

Erin wanted to be good so badly. Given the quantity of psychic trash, it was often hard to maintain the goodness of either Erin's home or Erin's person. Erin's spiritual janitorial skills, somehow essentially sufficient when Erin was young and living with her parents, were no longer up to snuff. Ben, no dummy, could tell. Erin tried to be a better janitor.

There were many heaps of trash.

There was much for her to do! Quantities of work! Yet it remained hard to be good, to do good things, because it would never be good enough, even if Erin cleaned up all the universe's psychic trash, even if she sat there, quietly anticipating each new trash output in order to discreetly bear it away or even eat it, if there was no other opportunity for its disposal. It was not enough to wait in perpetuity with the ends of disappearing psychic trash, because, if Erin's education had taught her anything, this behavior was predictable, and anyone female who engaged in it was not good because she was allowing herself to be oppressed. If Erin *truly* wanted to be good, then Erin needed to be more productive and better, even than this. Erin needed to be the kind of good person around whom no psychic trash accumulated, ever, and also she needed to be a big success. When she was at school, in her program, each step she took and each word she uttered should be free of the rubbish tips of ill forms of subjectivity. Alas, and predictably, Erin's steps and words never were free of the encumbrances of doubt. Erin did not represent freedom from the past. She did not project girl power. Psychic trash clung to her. Erin was not good. Erin was often afraid.

Then something strange began to happen. The strangeness seemed aligned with Erin's determination to write. It was this: Erin began toying with the notion of accepting that she was not good. Erin considered the possibility. I'm not good, she thought. I'm not free of my flawed ancestors. I'm fallen. I'm complicit. My mind is pitted with shallow graves.

It felt like a style of freedom, a loosening.

Even my writing, Erin thought, is no good.

This did not, of course, mean that Erin's writing was bad. It was merely irrelevant. Although she continued to bear in mind the possibility that someone might buy her prose, yet she could not bring herself to strategize after any determined fashion. She did not try to write a work that would have commercial viability. She cultivated—to the extent that she tried at all—a bagginess she associated not with novels but with the poetry written in long, meter-less lines in New York City after the wars. She was not exactly chatty, but she did not by any means stick to a point. She trusted in some notion of force and mass: the narrative would find its own ballast. It would circle back, swing round once more. Everything that happened was repetition. But it was repetition with a difference. So she dragged along in a spiral, trusting to this form.

Erin had had her result. And she had written merely what she could. She had no agent and no publisher and no book, but she had this strange, familiar writing, a trace of what was to come, an altered recollection of what had come before. And here she was, somehow living in it, in this spiral. Things were nominally survivable.

I have, Erin thought, gone back and recoded my childhood, and I have gone ahead and seen what is to be. Anyone can do this, Erin thought. Anyone can look forward and look back. Anyone can break apart, can travel to the future. But she wondered what help it was. It was perhaps better *to* have written such things, as opposed to not to have, in order to have something to stand on. The alternative was, of course, the void. It was a very bad idea, Erin knew, to try to stand on that.

The edition of *Passe-partout* was stiff and made a cracking noise as Erin opened it. She tried to use Herbsweet's book to keep it flat, but the French book was recalcitrant and flung Herbsweet's monograph to the floor, where Erin left it.

She took her first manuscript, the text of "Maison Close," and placed it on the surface of the study carrel desk, print down. She pushed the printout of the academic article out of the way and readied her golf pencil.

It was late and Erin was exhausted, but Erin was also in no way exhausted, because the present teemed with space, granting Erin an alertness that seemed entirely new. She was trying to pay attention to this novelty.

Erin opened *Passe-partout* once more, shifting it so that she could use her left hand to turn the pages. She understood that no one was urgently requesting a translation of LeGouffre's esoteric fable by

Erin Adamo; it was hardly necessary from any perspective. Yet, it was a book, perhaps *the* book, that had been written only for her. And now she was going to translate it.

Over the course of the next four hours, without lifting the golf pencil more than an inch from the pages in question, Erin wrote the following rendition of *Passe-partout*, a single pause-less jag:

Once upon a time, in ancient marmoreal Rome, there lived an excessively innocent young man. He had studied for many years, apprenticing himself to the greatest among those who practiced the noble art of chiseling, from the unyielding earth, the human form. Educated and sure, he was now ready to set forth on his own path. He was a sculptor, in short. Overendowed neither with years nor with riches, yet he was gifted. He could counterfeit the knee dimples of amphibious nymphs; coax a pliant drape from marble, granite, or obsidian; depict with uncanny artistry the sweaty agonies of those consumed against their wills by sea serpents, whales, crocodiles. In some ways, this sculptor was extremely fortunate. Alas, his good fortune and gifts meant little to him, for the woman he loved, whom he had married in spite of her family's poverty and foreign origins, had taken ill with an incurable ailment. She had no hope save to make her peace with worldly affairs and prepare for eternity.

One may imagine the gloomy, Vesuvian days the artist spent, laboring to produce sublime effects in stone, even as he comprehended that his source of transcending joy was soon to depart for all time. Because fate is strange, it was also during this period that the sculptor began to see his first success. He received commissions from all parts and was sought after by the renowned architects and decorators of his day. Foremost amongst the requests that he received—which, one must be frank, meant little to him during the season of his despair—was a request from the Princess H＿＿＿＿ of the kingdom of Norway, who wished to have a likeness of the huntress Diana, sister to the moon and guardian of all that stirs in the forest, disguised as a young man in a summer habit of slashed leather and chatoyant silk, engaged in mending a broken arrow. So urgent was the princess's desire, that the price she proposed went far beyond tripling the largest sum the sculptor had ever received, and thus, as the commissioner had no doubt surmised would be the case, since the fee was paid in advance, he was able to turn from every other effort in order to concentrate, with exclusive earnestness, upon the princess's project.

Those acquainted with the winged creature grief will hardly think it strange if, into the mind of the bereaved sculptor, a plan began to steal. It occurred at first almost without his consciousness of it. As he devised a plot to execute the Princess H＿＿＿＿＿'s request, he could not but turn his attention all the more irresistibly toward his fatal beloved, who, in her suffering, resembled ever more an emissary of the divine.

She said: "You study me."

"Yes, my light," replied the sculptor.

"You are needed in the studio to complete the great design that lies ahead of you. You must leave me to my bed."

Though the young woman turned her face to the wall, the sculptor could not bring himself to leave. He called a neighborhood boy who served as an assistant and asked that drawing implements be brought, so that he might begin.

The sculptor's wife understood at last what her husband had in mind. She neither chided him nor expressed gladness. She seemed to realize that the Diana that would soon appear would be as a figure for her tomb, yet she bore this with the same strange silence that had first made her so lovable in the eyes of he who now strove to represent her.

The chromophobia of our own time was present also for theirs, and the sculptor prepared a form of pigment-less white marble. His Diana was a lean, shrewd-eyed youth, who stood on her left leg in a pair of intricately laced sandals, the ribbons of which were delineated with all the sculptor's skill. The right leg was nimbly raised such that a portion of thigh could serve as work surface for a pair of dexterous hands with narrow, tapered fingers. These were engaged in knotting a length of wire, fusing together two halves of the huntress's signature missile. The left held the object, while the right hovered in the air, about to redescend to its task. There were some who whispered that the fingers of this right hand were arranged in an obscene gesture particular to the language of the sculptor's wife's people, but it hardly seems likely that this was the case. The figure's fine head, meanwhile, was lowered, the chin tucked in deference to work, yet the goddess's aspect was clear, particularly if the statue was displayed upon a plinth, as the sculptor intended. In this way, the viewer might stand beneath the beautiful sportswoman and gaze up into her magic face, even as she seemed careless of being observed. Such was Diana's liberty: she pertained to a celebrated family but was frequently away from the Olympian palace. For all her enthusiasm for the hunt, she took more delight in precision than in slaughter.

The sculptor's cherished wife died not long after the completion of this masterpiece. It was therefore with a regret infinitely doubled and redoubled by loss that the sculptor bid farewell to his Artemis, in the folds of whose doublet, it is said, he inscribed a dedication to the deceased, perhaps in one last vain attempt to draw near to the retreating being whom he cherished. Inevitably, however, the statue was placed in the hold of a large vessel bound northward, and the desolate artist retired to his studio to confront his many new commissions.

Our story might end here, with the ship's successful voyage, its cargo hoisted free before the eyes of an appreciative royal. We might be content to bid farewell to the artwork, along with its author, and return to our own lives with the certainty that art has a mysterious power to assuage our woes, even as it contains our hopes and reminds us of that which is greater than ourselves. However, if we turn away now, we will fail to learn the true story of what followed, along with the vicious verity that what in fact comes to pass in life is often far, far stranger than what we anticipate and imagine—stranger even than those eventualities from which we shrink in fear.

The boat we track, destined for the coast of the nation pertaining to the Princess H_____, was, as it so happened, set upon by marauders. They were professionals and wasted no time in overpowering the sailors, who were mostly convinced to sit down in a circle on the stern, rather than be run through with pikes. Save for the impressive Dion, there was little of interest or worth in the ship's hold. It is possible that the pirates would have contented themselves with one or two rapes or a handful of captives and departed to allow the crew to continue on their way, had it not been for the unfortunate coincidence that the leader or "king" of the desperadoes had lately been to Paris, during the time of the Salon des _____, which did take place, even in those days. Here, in spite of his naturally gruff and venal nature, he had been moved by the sublimity of a certain collapsing Andromeda. He had come, reluctantly, to realize that he was not insensible to art. Although no member of the honorable crew was so disloyal to their mistress as to lead him to the sculpture, the pirate lord was drawn to it, as he would later maintain, and, although, as he also remarked, the girl was rather thin and anemic for his tastes, yet she had an irresistible pull, once the protective wrappings had been sabered off and she was revealed to him in the dark hull by the light of two dozen or so candles placed before a large mirror.

The artwork was, we must believe, brought up on deck. Here sunlight fell upon it, rendering it lactic, tender—even in the punishing, salty heat. The pirate was now seized by an obsession. He no longer took any interest in the ship itself or the men aboard it: all his concern was for Diana, whom he was determined to possess. He seemed to believe that he had at last come upon the treasure to end all treasure, and could even retire to the New World, which it had, for many years, been his ambition to do.

The pirate instructed his minions to secure the statue with rope and convey it, by means of a hurriedly devised system of pulleys, across the deck of the besieged ship onto his own. Knowing the nature of their commander, the underpirates made haste to copy his instructions exactly. Unfortunately, given that the pirate was more skilled at violence than at engineering, his method made use of a weak mast that snapped under the weight of the stone, causing the statue to plummet back down to the decks of the two ships, which had been lashed together for the purpose of the breaching. Here it struck a cannon and shattered.

An inhuman cry rose from the mouth of the pirate, unlike anything his crew had heard before. He executed several bystanders on the spot, not differentiating between his own staff and the captives. Weeping and tearing at his mustaches, he rummaged in the rubble that had once been the snowy, gleaming form, as if he might, through some miracle, be able to reconstitute the goddess, much as she had cleverly reconstituted the shaft of her arrow. This was not to be the case, of course, but amid the limbs, awkwardly severed, the bashed-in face, the pulverized garments, the pirate discovered a fragment that had, owing to some unknowable whim of fortune, maintained an integrity of a kind. This was the right hand of the deity, the hand that tensed in anticipation, gathering its forces to pluck at a wire.

The pirate seized this remnant. What happened next is uncertain, but it seems that in a single brilliant motion, a symptom of the genius for movement that had made him a success where criminal arts at sea were concerned, the pirate leapt from the deck of the captured ship onto his own, slicing the ropes that bound the two together. Then, with the skeleton crew that had remained aboard his own craft, he made rapidly and all but instantly for the Port of New York.

The fate of those who remained aboard the Princess H_____'s ship is known: they continued their voyage to the originally foreseen nation, where they were pardoned and even celebrated by the enlightened powers there. However, this bland if encouraging turn of events for the virtuous sailors and morally uncertain servants of the pirate alike cannot be of great interest to readers of novels, and we will not linger on it. Instead, we will turn to the fate of the pirate himself. His destiny is largely unknowable; nevertheless, we will enlarge on its probable form.

The pirate, a vigorous man in middle age not insensible to the charms of the fairer sex, had for some years maintained a liaison, if one may delicately term it that, with a certain representative of the half-world of the isle of Manhattan. Given that we speak of America and one of its churning cities, crowded with all the people of the world, it may be difficult to view one world as "half" of another. Let us be more precise: the pirate nurtured an affection for a practitioner of the most ancient profession. Even in that cauldron that was the gate to the massive democratic enterprise, the land of experiment and opportunity as well as swindle, bondage, and calumny, the meaning of the pirate's beloved's work was understood by all, from the lowliest stoker or stevedore to the exalted president. But the pirate was a pirate and thus felt himself well suited to his beloved.

It may astonish the reader that, in an additional twist to this incredible plot, the pirate's feelings were not returned. No matter how often he presented himself below the window of the house on Pest Street, in the herring-infused and rat-infested quarter where the lady dwelled, in order to recite one of the few poems known to him or to sing, in a surprisingly thin and too-bright voice, one of the more polite sea chanteys he had learned in the course of his trade, the pirate was always rebuffed, sometimes with the contents of a chamber pot emptied casually above him.

Given the pirate's difficulties, the significance of the uncanny statue discovered in the hull of a ship he hoped to plunder becomes clearer. Any lover believes that he understands the object of his affection better than all others who have lived. The beloved is a book only the lover can read. She is piece of music only he can hear, a phantasm that appears before him, sap green in the mist. The beloved haunts only the lover, or so the lover believes. Thus, coming upon the huntress, the pirate saw an offering worthy of the woman with whose life his own, again, according to his own estimation, was irrevocably linked. He believed that in presenting his good madam with the monument, he would succeed, by means of an aesthetic gesture, where previously his terrifying presence and passionate avowals had failed. Neither had the pirate meditated about the means he would use to convey the statue through the streets of Manhattan nor had he reflected on what sort of accommodation the demimondaine would be able to provide it, given its costliness and weight, but in the moment of his first catching sight of that delicate figure in that lightless hull, these considerations had been mere trifles and perhaps had not even existed.

Now, after many long weeks at sea, the pirate once again stalked the cobbled streets where the empress of his heart made her home. He carried with him, wrapped in a quantity of black silk, a precious lump. The voyage had not served to alleviate the pirate's suffering. Rather, it had taken his obsession, along with the keen disappointment he felt in relation to the statue's sudden destruction, and melded these two unstable sentiments together, into what was at first a noxious ore, and then, when it cooled and hardened, a small, irregularly formed dish. Into this dish the pirate released his tears, among other discharges, which he privately drank, late into the night, muttering imprecations and further solidifying his determination to be accepted by a woman who had no intention of ever responding to his pleas.

But who was this desirable creature? She was an American. Her name was Liz. Perhaps at one point she had been an Elizabeth. Liz was a creation of the port. Her father had been a sailor. Some joked that her mother had been a dray horse, given Liz's barrel chest, her legs fine as needles. The strange truth was that Liz's mother was the daughter of a banker, who, when young, had gone astray in spectacular fashion. Liz thus possessed a claim to tragedy that rivaled that of anyone Liz had ever met. The debt that was owed to Liz by Fortuna, goddess of wheels and crossroads, was staggering, and when one made Liz's acquaintance, one met this injustice first. Over her career, this quality, displeasing though it might seem, had served Liz well. Even if she was not a wealthy woman, she was comfortable by the standards of her environs and had reserves set aside, besides. In spite of her pedigree, she did not cater to the rich. Rather, she cultivated a steady list of mediocre captains, workaday accountants, and butchers, favoring quantity as well as predictability, and thereby assuring herself of an eventual retirement to that rambling territory known as New Jersey, where she intended to acquire land and possibly a younger husband to maintain it as well as her person, as she began to tend toward senescence.

The pirate, with his midnight caterwauls, did not figure in this plan. In truth, if Liz had troubled herself to expend a thought or two on his behavior, she might have said that his pretension to pain insulted her. What, after all, could a man know of longing? What did he comprehend of frustrated desire or the need for recognition? If the pirate suffered, let him do so on his own time. It was not even she who dumped excrement on his head! It was her neighbors, whom he kept awake with his rustily crooned chanteys about missing ships and creatures composed of women's torsos and squids' tentacles whose knifelike teeth devoured the briny flesh of castaways.

Liz was not, however, prepared to experience the pirate as a late-morning caller at her establishment. He appeared with mustaches shorn, in a stiff gray suit, bearing under his arm a bundle. Liz, whatever her opinions regarding justice, her own personal history, and the ongoing war of the sexes, was not one to refuse a gift, particularly one that might be convertible to lucre, and she therefore had her cook and maid usher the pirate into her salon, where he entered, only to be rendered speechless by proximity to the object of all his fantasies and hopes.

"Hello, sir." Liz was polishing a watch lately neglected in a bedside drawer by one of her admirers. She designed to have it appraised that very afternoon.

When there was no reply from the penitent, who, admittedly, was limited where English was concerned, Liz, as was frequently her lot in life to do, took the lead.

"I see you come bearing a gift," she informed the love-struck lawbreaker. "As you know, my professional life gives me little opportunity for personal amusements, and you have always known that, in any case, your request to divert yourself with me has always been denied. This state of affairs will never change during the course of either of our lifetimes, and I beg you to accept this as fact. You are without hope. If you love me as you say you do, believe me. However," Liz continued, "I am not so cruel that I will not accept what you have come to offer. Place it on the floor at my feet. Then, say nothing and do nothing but take your leave, and after this you must never return. You may depart with the knowledge that I have received you, seen your face, and understood your wishes. This is more than you deserve, and it is the utmost that I will grant willingly. Anything more you ask, you will ask against my wishes. Again, if you love me as you profess to, you will not desire to perform an act that directly countermands my inclination. Do as I decree. Leave what you have brought, know that I take it into my possession, then never let me see or hear of you again."

So saying, Liz seated herself in a sagging chair upholstered in the remnants of a flag.

The pirate, stunned, obeyed. Thus concluded this brief and unusual affair.

After the door had shut once more and Liz was left to her own devices, and after she had called for a fresh cup of coffee and gazed on her own countenance in the glass that hung above her mantel, sighing, Liz addressed her attention to the mysterious package that lay upon her carpet. How strange it was to find oneself in such a position! Even if she had

dispatched the pirate with admirable deftness, it was difficult not to feel that one's life was rather destabilized by an
addition such as this. Was it prudent to unwrap the object?
What if it turned out to be the mummified corpse of an infant
narwhal? Yet, what if here lay a chalice of gold or a ruby-
studded cuff? There was only one way to learn what sort of
fealty she had inspired in her suitor. Therefore Liz sank to
her knees . . .

Her sentiments, upon comprehending what she held in her
lap, once the contents of the cloth had been revealed, were
of a mixed nature. On the one side, she was relieved that her
admirer had not proven himself brutal and insane by offering
her a bloody remnant. On the opposing side, Liz regretted
that the token she had received was probably worth very little
on the open market. Somewhere in between these two poles
lay another feeling far odder and certainly more unexpected
than either of the other two. This was a feeling that the pirate had somehow succeeded in offering her an item that was
not only something she would never have sought out or even
known how to identify, but with which she felt an instant
kinship—an affection that was even tinged with exasperat-
ing longing. Looking at the graceful hand that lay among her
skirts, its rounded fingertips captured just as they touched
one another above the exquisite pad of a delicate thumb, Liz
was, in spite of herself, moved. She sat, for nearly an hour,
staring at this wonder as her coffee grew cold. Then, through
an act of extraordinary will, a movement of spirit characteristic of the animal nature that had permitted her to survive and
very nearly flourish in the hell of privation and social stigma
into which she had been born, Liz took the marble hand in
her own and walked upstairs to the second floor of her home.
Nothing was as it had been but a mere ninety minutes earlier.
All had changed, and this change was a metamorphosis not
of material but of understanding.

The hand, Liz noted, as she bore it to the small room where she kept her accounts, was larger than a normal human hand. It was not so large as to be ridiculous, and yet it had about it the aura of a protector. It seemed, Liz felt, to pull into it, to welcome, Liz's own feeling. It welcomed Liz's life. It was a dumb object, faceless and senseless, yet Liz believed that the hand accepted her, that it not only recognized but liked and wished to teach her however it was in its power to teach a mortal creature. Liz unlocked her study and walked to her small desk. She placed the hand on its "back," on the gilt-stamped leather blotter she had long ago purchased as an extravagant sign to herself that she was a true businesswoman. The hand rocked slightly in this position, and then stilled.

After this, Liz was compelled by other business to shut the door to her small counting room and to return to the parlor floor and, eventually, to exit her dwelling in order to attend to a number of errands. The watch was worthless, but her solicitor had pleasant news, having received word of several parcels of real estate that might be worth her attention. Liz passed by the butcher's and ordered some steaks to be delivered. She planned to spend a cozy evening at home, celebrating her evasion of the passions of the pirate with a rich dinner and a quantity of sleep, giving it to the cook to communicate to her regular customer that she was indisposed.

Upon entering her home, Liz felt a shiver of excitement. Although it was the same narrow town house she had left but a few hours earlier, now it seemed infused with novelty and possibility. She very nearly hugged herself as she walked the stairs to the second floor, where she was, and to her study in particular, drawn as steel shavings are to the surface of a magnet. Unlocking the door to this private room, Liz was at first alarmed, and then astonished, to discover that the marble hand was not in the location in which she had, earlier that day, so gingerly placed it, its fingers hanging in midair like so many strange, small legs. But the hand was not gone. It had only relocated to the windowsill. Liz flew to it, caressing it and muttering nonsensical words into the soft yet hard creases of its palm, which now she alternately kissed and gently licked, alternately dampened with her tears.

When Liz had satisfied these bizarre desires, she stood, placing the hand on the seat of her chair where she had been sitting just a moment before. She went downstairs to berate the cook for giving her such a fright, although she would willingly admit that her alarm at the possible loss of the hand was by no means reasonable. However, when remonstrations and questions were put to this loyal retainer regarding the fragment, a token from the faded pirate, the cook refused to admit any guilt. She maintained inflexibly that she had never been above stairs all day. Furthermore, even if she had, the lady knew well that she did not possess a key to the lady's small room and that, being in deficit of this key, she could have had nothing to do with the lock on its door. Having asserted this much, the cook returned to the task of salting the lately arrived steaks.

Liz had no choice but to return to the hand. Although it had no mouth, perhaps it was capable of communicating to her in some way what agency had moved it from the desk blotter to the windowsill. Opening the door to her study again, Liz perceived that a new miracle had transpired during her brief absence: the hand now sat alongside some of her books on a low shelf. Liz stood for some time staring. She felt a certain trepidation, but even in her fear there was a camaraderie with this object, which was obviously of a deeply foreign nature, since it was incapable of comprehending the rules to which all objects, or so the laws of Liz's sphere ordained, were subject. The hand was not permitted *to move*. It was the plastic image of a hand! Independent movement was strictly forbidden it. And perhaps the hand even suspected as much, and this was the reason that it moved only surreptitiously, in order not to overtly disobey the regulations of the land in which it found itself. Surely the pirate had discovered the hand on one of his voyages in some faraway nation where such magic was permitted. Perhaps the hand had even enchanted him. Although Liz was a woman of nearly infinite rational reflection, the events of this day had catapulted her into new channels of logic, upon the swells of which she began to imagine possibilities that had never before come to her mind.

Liz began to wonder if all of the pirate's imprecations might not have been inspired by the fantastic agency of the hand, which required, like the seed unconsciously transported by a sparrow or the burr that catches in the flank of a scavenging fox, to be transported across vast distances to reach her, in order that it might dwell by her side. If this was indeed the case, it would suggest that the professions of love uttered so peculiarly and unwantedly by the pirate had a foot in truth, that it was not out of the question that the words spoken by the pirate were the words the hand wished that it itself could speak, had it either lips or tongue to do so.

Again, Liz took the marble hand in her own. She stared at it, and she felt it staring back at her, returning her gaze as if it were a deity that had come to her as a lover in a dream. Liz, blushing, suspected that she was in the presence of the partner of her soul, that that fateful half of being from which long ago each of us was severed in that wise myth was now returned to her. In proximity to this fragment, Liz, in short, felt herself whole, believing that she herself provided the same function for the marble hand.

Let us not forget that these developments, which are of so extraordinary a nature as to seem improbable if not impossible to us, seemed, by Liz's lights, less outlandish than the appearance of the pirate, which was, to her, inexplicable and unpleasant in the extreme. By this example, we see how unreal events can lead us into even more unreal genres of speculation, by means of which we attempt, nonsensically, to resolve what is strange by the addition of that which cannot possibly be the case. Here is the origin of much foolishness, but also, if the reader will permit, much newness and even joy in human life. Here, perhaps, is life itself.

Liz, as the evening of this eventful day drew on, and as the time for her much anticipated dinner came and went, attempted to do a service for the hand. Softly, she promised it that she would not abandon it, even if it were to disobey the sacred laws that bound objects to absolute motionlessness and silence. She whispered to it the story of her life, the manner in which her mother had sinned against family and caste, the terrifying childhood of lack to which she, Liz, had therefore been subject, forced to live an existence beyond the legitimate world, in order to be able to have some comfort and security, a comfort and security that came only through the having of money, a substance that was, as she had already intimated through the enumeration of many ironies, obtainable via that allegedly most execrable and cruel of trades, to which Liz had inured herself with a haste and ease that astonished even her, she who thought herself incapable of surprise. But the hand must already know all this, Liz murmured. The hand must know how Liz had suffered more than any human can bear and then some, such that the life Liz led was always a mere fraction of the life she could have led, full of feeling, if her mother had chosen differently and if her mother's family had been less cruel. Liz saw the hand and was its eternal servant. She begged it to reveal itself to her. Liz said, "I wish I knew what you were called."

At this moment, there was a soft banging noise, disheveled air. A book fell from Liz's shelves. Liz trembled and nearly screamed, but she succeeded in gathering herself and stood to examine the book, which had opened to a page. It was a cheap novel Liz had come into possession of by way of a once-persistent peddler who seemed, fortunately, to have perished in the intervening years. It was nothing but loves, lovers, beloveds, persecuted ladies fainting in gazebos, messengers dying at great convenience to plot, hounds and horses slaughtered, crepuscular forests, troubled hearts, embraces, sermons, pinching, bellows, imprecations, tears, and gnashing of tiny, pearl-like teeth. The peddler maintained that it was the latest thing in France and would soon be in all the kitchens of the New World, but Liz herself, thrifty though she was and inimical to waste, had not read it. Now the uncut pages fell eerily open, and Liz saw that on the page, a recto, which sat exposed, someone had underlined a pair of words:

PASSE-PARTOUT

Liz nodded, gathering the fallen book into her hands and returning it to its shelf. Here was the name of her only love: Passe-partout.

Now, Liz had also come to learn, through this experience, that her new companion was capable of granting wishes. Liz had read fairy tales enough to comprehend that a speaking object betokened not just enchantment but an imprisoned spirit, one that was often willing to trade favors for intimacy until such a time as it should be transformed back into its original form. It was a style of exchange Liz understood all too well and she always took an opportunity when it presented itself. Sometimes, as they lay in bed together, Liz would whisper to the object, "I wish that you *will* love me forever, for you must!" On these occasions, there might be an extra sparkle in the haze around the moon, the shadows might be a slightly more piquant blue or violet, a bat might fly in at the window, uttering little cries. Liz made a spiritual request of this sort not merely to ensure the love of her object, however. She made the request in order to inform the object that she, Liz, would abide by its rules. Passe-partout and Passe-partout alone, Liz swore, governed all her hours. Liz had encountered Shahrazad's legends long ago. She was informed as to how narratives of this sort had a tendency to unfold.

Having accomplished this much, the canny professional lover undertook to change her material circumstances. She made a wish to Passe-partout that her bank account should be dramatically increased, that she should be monetarily provided for for life, even beyond her own wildest imaginings. Having uttered these words, Liz heard the cook admit a visitor downstairs who subsequently announced the death of Liz's estranged grandfather, the Hon. T_____ Esq., who, in order to assuage his own guilt over his daughter's early violent death, his own visits to his daughter's household performed only under cover of night, his granddaughter's terrible toils, had left a will in which the granddaughter stood to come by a fortune, effective immediately. Thus were Liz's means and surroundings transformed, thus did she liberate her cook, granting the woman a modest yearly allowance, and thus did she transfer her dwelling to the countryside, where she became the mistress of a small agricultural enterprise and where she hoped to live out her years.

But here we must reveal another secret: The love Liz bore Passe-partout was a love that had in fact been present in her heart since the hour of her birth. It was a love, as is ever the case for human beings, that was so similar to an unmending wound as to be indistinguishable from injury. We persist in believing this hurt-love or pang-passion is the medium by which we are most able to share our deepest selves with others. Liz had learned from the example of her mother, and so, even as she was in some ways an extremely disadvantaged person, she was also very fortunate, in that she did not, under any circumstances, wish to share her secret shattered heart, the love of her life's great laceration, with another human. Upon making the acquaintance of this living object, a traveler from afar, a sort of saint or muse, Liz became convinced that not only was she *able* to share her heart's furtive ardor-cut with Passe-partout—nay, she must. The sense of requirement brought Liz some relief, for it was a relief not to be free, not to be able, after a fashion, to err and refuse, to wonder and wander. Passe-partout and Liz lived happily together for some years.

Can a human being love a thing? To see Liz in those days was to believe that it was possible. Liz kept Passe-partout in her boudoir, in a special chest she had had constructed, sparing no expense, specifically for the object. Although Passe-partout had a tendency to remove itself of its own volition from this place, it was always to be found without great difficulty, and Liz laughed sometimes at the tricks it liked to play, retiring under a pillow, lingering gamely inside a shoe. One night, as she placed Passe-partout in its drawer, Liz muttered to it, carelessly, "I wish I knew what you are." Then she closed and locked the drawer, not even bothering to kiss Passe-partout goodnight.

The dawning of the following day brought immense sorrow, for, as the clever reader will have surmised, Passe-partout was not to be found in the place where previously it had been, nor was it in any of its other preferred hiding places. Liz's unfortunate wish was cruelly granted! Pointless to detail her searches, the resources she expended: it was all to no avail. We may imagine the future that lay before Liz.

In one scenario, she becomes a madwoman, convinced of her fault in the loss of the one valid object of her love. In this scenario, Liz never ceases in her search, upending her house and tunneling through the very soil. But we may also imagine that Liz, not entirely without her wits, which, we recall, are formidable, remembers that she herself demanded to know, the night before she lost Passe-partout, "what you are." A wise woman might well decode what came to pass.

But we will never learn which path Liz took, for our story no longer concerns her. In fact, in the story with which we are concerned, Passe-partout does not disappear by means of magic, whether its own magic or that of a god. Instead, an enterprising young man watched Liz through Liz's window one evening and determined that he was in need of this hand to make his own way in the world.

This young man was also an American. However, he was of rural origins rather than urban ones. His name is unimportant, and we will not tarry with him long, save to say that he fancied himself a poet and had the vain eccentricity of wearing a dirty wig like a fruit peel because, as he believed, it concealed his shortcomings. Passe-partout, whose true name he was too vulgar to learn, was to be his talisman.

The poet, although painfully ignorant and unremarkable in every way in which it is possible to be unremarkable, had heard of the ancient civilizations that surrounded the Mediterranean Sea. He saw Passe-partout as a relic of those days, believing the object, which was, in his mind, a "she," to have washed up on the shores of the United States as a sign of the nation's fated continuance of that variously imperial glory, even as he was to become the greatest bard of the nation. Thus did he prepare a plan to obtain Passe-partout by trickery, and thus did he avail himself of this plan, by chance—indeed, it was nothing more than chance—on the

very evening when Liz had wished to know what Passe-
partout was.

The poet, being impractical, vain, and unlucky, set a course
into the wilderness. His instincts and self-serving nature more
than compensated for what he lacked in brains, and he was
able to skillfully evade the mercenary searchers Liz had sent
out into the world. The poet traveled, deeper and deeper into
the continent. Panthers crossed his path by night and owls
rolled their iridescent eyes at him, and he was often beyond
the reach of Europeans. He began to wend his way south
without knowing it, all the while composing meaningless
sonnets and the like to his muse, which he carried in a sack
of blond hide.

Meanwhile, the Americans began a war with one another.
Who knows why they slaughtered their brothers and neighbors? Certainly it was not over lack of land. Perhaps it was
because a great many of them did not know why they were
there in that land in the first place, with nothing to do but
claim and have and build and beget more bewildered, violent
offspring. There was one war and then another. The poet had
eluded the draft through his itinerancy, but he could not avoid
the ubiquitous battles, one of which he wandered into even
as he was composing a verse in which Passe-partout was affixed to the wrist of an angel and caressed the poet's face. At
once incongruously and appropriately, immediately the poet
died, filled with buckshot and later bayoneted and beheaded.
His pathetic body was left to rot, his louse-ridden clothing
and oily appurtenances untouched, even by waves of retreating troops. Decades passed. Peace came. The arts flourished.
Women walked freely on the paved streets, arms linked at
the elbow.

A little girl, not so unlike Liz, although she must remain
nameless, happened one day to pass through the field on

which many years earlier, before her birth, a deadly battle had taken place. Animal scavengers had long since dragged away or picked clean the fallen. This killing field was now a site beloved to the young girl for the lushness of its grass, the pristine quality of the light that fell, that seemed as if washed clean by human tears. On one of her habitual rambles across this field the little girl espied something gleaming among the dandelions. Irresistibly, she was drawn to it. She ran and discovered what she described in her mind as a fairy: a large, pallid human hand, rising from the turf. The little girl gasped with glee and seized the object, which came away with little resistance, almost as if it longed to be taken up and held.

The little girl scampered off, taking with her the hand, a surprisingly easy burden. She clutched it to her chest. She took the hand to a little bower not far from the hovel where her parents, itinerant farming people and collectors of discarded objects, resided, and she set the hand on a sort of altar she had devised and commenced worshipping it.

Passe-partout heard the child's prayers. The indignities it had suffered over the years, first in the clutches of the talentless poet who despoiled it, truth be told, with more than his ill-made verses, and, then, by the side of this lunatic's moldering corpse and severed head, whose very scalp was torn to pieces by desperate beasts crazed by a sudden overwhelming availability of lifeless human flesh. It is possible that Passe-partout, surrounded by all this doom, could not help but be touched by death. Yes, this was almost certainly the case. But the beauty of the graceful fingers inspired in the little girl a series of sweet, gaunt smiles and delicate songs. Passe-partout's agony at its knowledge of the cruelty of time was in some ways assuaged. Yes, Passe-partout had become cursed, but now the curse was lifted.

Passe-partout basked. It became wise. In its wordless language it began to instruct the little girl. Go, it said. Leave this place. Go into the world and look like what they call you but be something else and never return.

Who knows if the little girl understood these commands; all we know is she was never seen in this locality again.

Thus was it that Passe-partout, who might have been transported wherever she/it wished by the little girl, instead passed many more years at its altar, infinitely alone, a silent piece of stone, no longer an object of worship but now a worshipper and penitent: of the sun, moon, and stars above, of the branches of the trees and spiraling dry leaves, of the glassy eyes of animals that came to sniff and gaze at it, but that always departed with a shrug of disgust. For a very long time, Passe-partout was abandoned.

In this time, it is possible that Passe-partout relinquished all of its/her magic. It became an object once again.

And then one day, there came an architect. The architect had been engaged to imagine in this expanse of countryside, a legendarily haunted locale, a model town to be inhabited by local workers. These were to be indentured to the owner of the land in exchange for his provision of roads and housing and to offer up their labor until this debt should be repaid. A number of squatters of various stripes had had to be removed by force before the architect's arrival, some of whom claimed ancient rights to the place, and the architect was not without concern that these stragglers were not beyond charming the place before they left or returning to commit evil acts of revenge.

Lighting upon the startling marble form of Passe-partout, the architect at first believed he saw a demonic apparition. He shrunk from what remained of the altar, but then, gathering courage and wits, approached it warily. Although a man of science, he could not believe his own eyes. The perfection of the object spoke to him of the Renaissance in Italy, the rarest species of stone, and for a moment the architect wondered if he had not stumbled upon evidence, protruding from the ground, of a mighty rational civilization that had once stretched across the continent of North America, but that was until now lost to memory, a terrestrial Atlantis. In a flash, he saw himself excavating a great temple complex adjoining the grounds of a formerly bustling marketplace, the history of the world turned upside down, his writings and pronouncements read and lauded the world over.

Sadly for this man's antique ambitions (and the fortune he rapidly expended digging holes), this was not to be. Yet, as it had done before for other seekers, Passe-partout came away from the heap of sod and glistening beetles and worms where it lay and up into the hands of the architect, who spent long minutes studying it, gently cleaning its surface with the hem of his waistcoat. Whatever the hand betokened, this was indeed a striking example of the skill of some sculptor, formed with so much grace and intelligence that the stone seemed to speak, although the architect lacked the sensitivity to comprehend what the fragment was saying. Its worth, the architect conjectured, must be enormous!

The architect bore the hand away to his camp, and, after he had finished his survey of this setting, sampled the attractions of the female members of the much-reduced local population, as well as their dishes and dances, made sure that no piece of earth had been left unturned in case of the presence of ancient ruins, and finally succeeded in establishing the grim phalanx of row houses he had promised his employer, he returned to the city in which he generally liked to make his home, that fair center of the arts, Philadelphia. Here he married without much delay and worked steadily and obtained success.

As time went on, the architect ceased to accept commissions to construct the model towns now common in the nation, and instead began to be associated with the design and erection of public buildings, many of which were graced by allegorical female figures representing the better tendencies of human striving: Peace, Knowledge, Nation, Soft Fecundity, Enduring Powerlessness, etcetera. Whenever the architect was involved in such a commission, he made it his practice to share with the sculptor the mysterious remnant he had so long ago discovered in the wilderness, far from any obvious source of art or learning. The architect then prevailed upon that sculptor to fashion the right hand of the thematic figure in question in the exact likeness of Passe-partout. The architect took these steps all but unconsciously, and it is possible that even those craftsmen who formed so many likenesses of Passe-partout did not remember even a week later whence they drew their inspiration for those surpassingly lovely five digits, gesturing with enigmatic meaning, which again and again they caused to multiply.

And so it was, not so many years later, that the Roman sculptor, the once-widower and now celebrated master, who was by this juncture an extraordinarily old man, insect-like and nearly always silent, traveled to Philadelphia at the request of one of the most honored members of the academy of the arts there in order to view the efforts of the young nation in plastic modeling. In making his tour of the city, the Roman sculptor was struck by the number of public statues, as well as their simultaneous diversity and likeness to one another. The Roman sculptor also felt, as he was driven around in a fiacre leased on his behalf, an unwonted desire to reach out and touch the public sculpture, although he found himself only drawn to the sculptures' hands, and not, for example, their nubile breasts, resplendent thighs, soft pubises, pert mouths.

Long ago, the Roman sculptor had learned of the loss of the commissioned sculpture of Diana mending her arrow and he had long since ceased to mourn this mishap, much as he had ceased to mourn his first wife. He had remarried and was accompanied on his current journey by the youngest of his numerous sons, who was himself nearing old age and whom the sculptor now asked to communicate with their driver in English, that impossibly irregular tongue.

The coach came to a standstill beside a marble maiden whose short stone plinth placed her at almost the same height as the occupants of the vehicle. They were at a cross-roads, and the naked woman wore a sash and crown of stars. Beneath her foot she crushed a broken iron chain, the symbol of some history or future the Roman sculptor could not quite convince his now-frail mind to parse. Closing his eyes, the sculptor reached out a trembling hand. He felt the cool, stern fingers, lifeless to the touch and yet pulsing with strange meaning. Where was he now, he asked himself, in what century and what city? Who was it who seemed to sigh so tenderly, echoing like waves, compounded of all the groans of all the martyrs of human history, releasing the total of heaven's grief in one moment before the universe grew still and solid once more? Whom or what had he forgotten, somewhere in his long existence? The voice was so familiar, yet it remained buried—as flesh encased in the green bark of a tree or water sealed in stone.

There came a yelp from the driver's bench, and the vehicle rolled on.

Erin set down the golf pencil. It was impossible to write with it anymore, its graphite rubbed down to a slope that was increasingly interrupted by the presence of the surrounding wood. Her translation was done. Erin felt as if she might be asleep, although she was almost certainly awake. She left the study carrel to go gaze out into the void, came back.

This was an odd hour in the library, the one time of day when a feeling of tranquility came over the building. No one spoke and nothing moved. The circulation desk was vacant. Outside, the sky was an erratic color. Dawn was still not quite possible, but it flickered somewhere, ready to expand.

Erin put the translation into her bag. She turned back to the academic article, wanting to know, now, what J. Stasulis had meant regarding the interrelationship of statues and photographs.

Erin hunted, found her place:

> . . . we might find, by translation: *Photographer Freeman Abyss*. But of course the names of actual persons should not be subject to literary interpretation.
>
> Here I must unexpectedly interject a story. Astonishingly, it moves us forward quite a span, to the next century. In the spring of 1925, a French woman named Laël Edelbrot was recently separated from a husband, one Jean Autriche, patriotic bureaucrat, who later died in a Silesian *Stammlager* after the Battle of France. The marriage was brokered by the two sets of parents but quickly abandoned by both parties. Edelbrot returned to Paris where she began a course in the history of art in preparation for a role in a cousin's antiquarian business. She was an example of the "New Woman" who had come into being after the 1918 armistice. Rendered financially independent by a small inheritance at a time when money was particularly tight in the City of Light (for an American perspective, see Langston Hughes's remarks to Countee Cullen in a 1924 letter: "The French are the most franc-loving, sou-clutching, hard-faced, hard-worked, cold and half-starved set of people I've

ever seen in life. . . . You even pay for a smile here."[3]), Edelbrot also benefited from the relatively permissive culture of the interwar period.

Edelbrot was twenty-three when she began a diary. In its first entry, dated March 1, 1925, she writes,

> It was on my walk that I began to think I
> should keep a journal and write it in this book.
> I do not know what else to do about the fact
> that I still have youth and yet do little with it.
> Not that I must be a tool. I want to say it is an
> idea of ambition. An ameliorative force? More
> simply, I must not go on approaching death
> without having made some further attempt.
> It should really be more complicated.[4]

These remarks suggest that this was a time of transformation for Edelbrot, who was the product of a liberal mixed-faith Parisian family and who now seemed ready to place her own intellectual development at the center of her life. The diary does not specify when Edelbrot first met a certain Czech expatriate, but in late March we read that at a surrealist-organized salon Edelbrot was cornered by one Matthias Dinz, a minor Alsatian poet who "displays unmerited optimism and talks of parties he went to with socially skilled people."

---

3. Langston Hughes to Countee Cullen, March 11, 1924, Countee Cullen Papers, Amistad Research Center, Tulane University.

4. In response to my advertisement in the *New York Times* requesting information regarding the life of Edelbrot (later, Edelbrot-Mélaton), a friend alerted her grandnephew, Lucien Chodkieweitz, who generously contacted me and, after learning of the nature of my project, entrusted me with Edelbrot's diary of the mid-1920s. All quotations are supplied with his permission. Translations mine throughout. The reasons for my initial request will be clear to the reader of note 11 in this article.

Attempting to escape this bard, she ends up at a café where

> we play at puns in a banquette for a couple of
> hours. Toyen and I try to play continuously,
> rally. She is wearing high-waisted pants. She
> will not take off the short red jacket she has
> on. Later we throw pages soaked in champagne
> into a potted display of pussy willows.

Here is the first mention of Toyen's name. Again, it is unclear if Edelbrot and Toyen were already acquainted before this evening. What began against the backdrop of a male-dominated scene is to blossom into what Edelbrot would call "the foundational relationship of my life."[5]

But who was Toyen? Born in 1902 in Prague to working-class parents in the Smíchov district, Marie Čermínová was subsequently to take the one-word, gender-neutral name Toyen as a mark of their[6] independence. When speaking Czech, Toyen used male pronouns and inflection, famously telling their (male) companions one evening, "Farewell! I am a sad [male] painter." (*Já jsem malíř smutnej.*)[7] Toyen's performance of gender was sometimes caricatured by the men

---

5. Phone conversation with Chodkieweitz, who was close with his grandaunt in the years approaching her 1977 death, when he was a teenager.

6. I have chosen to use the *they* pronoun series when referring to Toyen in English as a way of reconciling their use of male pronouns in Czech and what seem to have been feminine pronouns in French, according to Edelbrot's diary as well as Toyen's friend, the author Annie Le Brun. Although Toyen themself never explained the origin of their name, it is widely thought to be a shortening of the French noun *citoyen*.

7. Karla Tonine Huebner, PhD dissertation, University of Pittsburgh, 2008.

around them, who insisted that they wore "coarse cotton pants, a guy's corduroy smock, and on her head a turned-down hat, such as ditchdiggers wear," while working by day at a soap factory, only to appear in the evening in elegant, traditionally female clothes, including "silk openwork stockings." Such accounts may, however, point more to the obsessions of Toyen's milieu than their own preferences.[8] A drawing of Toyen that graced the 1930 cover of *Rozpravy Aventina* (*Aventine Debates*) portrays them in pants, while they cast a shadow as a heteroclite figure draped in a gown with a bird for a head, a pair of fish at their chest, and arms made of a drafting triangle and a picture frame.

These sometimes-sensationalized aspects of Toyen's self-presentation should not be allowed to overshadow their prolific artistic production. An accom-

---

8. We might see in the Devĕtsil group's anxieties a reference to James Allen, a celebrity of the nineteenth century who was of interest to surrealists. Allen, a British man, came to public attention after he died in a work-related accident in 1829 at the age of forty-two. An article described how Allen was found to be "in fact" biologically female and gave an account of his life from the age of eighteen, when he married his wife, Abigail. Allen was known as his employer's "smart groom," and he and Abigail opened a public house. After a theft of their savings left them impoverished, they were forced to sell this property. Allen began laboring at the docks in London. He was valued for his work ethic and sobriety and became notably physically strong. The linen bandage he used to bind his breasts was later revealed at the hospital. "As a striking contrast to the general beauty of the person, was remarked, the colour of the face and roughness of the hands, occasioned by the deceased's anti-feminine habits."

Abigail Allen, meanwhile, "never doubted that [James] was of any other than the male sex." They were together for more than two decades, until James's death occasioned many accusations against Abigail, on account of her participation in what was considered a fraudulent marriage.

plished painter first in a cubist vein and later a surrealist, Toyen is perhaps best known for their precise
illustrations, many of which are erotic in nature.

As sketchbooks from their more than four years
in Paris suggest, this erotic work was associated with
an exploratory lifestyle. In fall of 1925, Toyen apparently traveled from Prague accompanied by Jindřich
Štyrský, their artistic collaborator. The encounter with
Edelbrot may have had something to do with the decision to make a more permanent move, although it was
common for Czech artists to come to Paris during this
period for its exhibitions, café society, and unparalleled
nightlife, with such indelible clubs as Bricktop's, Chez
Florence, the Moulin Rouge, and Le Rat Mort. Toyen's
drawings reveal the artist delving into a range of explicit material, including women having sex with one
another, sailors ejaculating onto naked women and
other men masturbating in front of women, as well as
acts of bestiality. While it is impossible to know the
exact nature of Toyen's tastes and experiences, from
Edelbrot's accounts we glean that cocaine was readily
available and cocktails regularly spiked with hash pel-
lets. Nudity at parties was not unheard of and there are
indications that Edelbrot and Toyen ventured down to
the banks of the Seine in the early hours of the morning. Here hastily constructed dirt-floor lean-tos were
the sites of shabby clubs where sailors, college students, artists, and society women mingled and engaged in group sex. Lines from Edelbrot's diary, such
as "Endless day I wake into in confusion," suggest that
the lifestyle could be all-consuming.

Yet Edelbrot was not a public figure, as her friend
Toyen was. Her intellectual aspirations and desire to
"do something" seem to have been more about a private
form of identity-related work. In an explicit and wide-
ranging entry from early January of 1926 she writes:

Had decided yesterday that the dream of the vampire was an encounter with myself. As intense as sex with oneself would be. Then: this interpretation is stupid. Pursuant to this, I imagine myself as a man with an erection. Try to imagine holding this erection in my hand. In order to do this, I must think of the feeling of the lips of my vulva. Should I imagine that I have a monstrous clitoris? I envision myself as a man who is "kindly" to women. I get one alone and smack her ass. I would take her from behind to get the benefit of the nice smooth round ass.

Everything male is about connoisseurship.

But, then, if you don't have a very nice penis, masturbation is an unpleasant task. Very little difference between pubic hair and hair on the legs. The game of the hunt. One's weapon. Sock with cum rolled into it. Standing around with idiots watching idiot women standing around with idiots.

I should like to write an account of a person who is continually transformed, who is a woman and becomes a man, who becomes a dog, a cat, a flower, a pencil, a mote, an old woman, a girl, a boy, an infant. I would return to childhood as a disembodied voice and provide constructive advice. Do not think so much about the following: eating, proving your worth through sex (the possibility of engaging in sex to prove that one exists), (the hope) that others will show greater empathy or intelligence, do not pray for this.

It is impossible to know if Edelbrot shared these reflections with Toyen. The two appear to have been fast friends, meeting on a daily basis throughout late

1925 and 1926. They discussed art and literature, and Edelbrot occasionally joined Toyen and Štyrský for meals and excursions, at which time she was sometimes treated as Toyen's "little sister, the sensible one, who follows convention."[9]

Toyen, meanwhile, was making a splash among the Parisian surrealists who, like the members of the Devětsil group of their native Prague, considered them irresistible, perhaps in no small part due to their lack of interest in male suitors. Crucially for our purposes, Toyen came to the attention of the poet Paul Éluard, who had for several years been engaged in a ménage à trois with his soon-to-be-former wife, Gala (later, Gala Dalí), and the artist Max Ernst. Éluard was experiencing a period of hyperactive despair. His marriage was unlikely to survive its inclusion of Ernst, and Éluard was flailing. Infatuated with Toyen after an encounter at a café, Éluard wrote them a letter in his own semen. This document was objectionable to Toyen for a number of reasons, not least of all its odor. Toyen shared these developments with Edelbrot, and the two hatched a plan to obtain, as Edelbrot writes in a long entry detailing the above events, "some small recompense."

Here our narrative begins to align with the image(s) of the nineteenth century introduced at the outset of this article. Much as Max Ernst would later appropriate engravings of heavily draped Victorian domestic

---

9. These encounters seem to have sometimes been strained or ambivalent, perhaps due to the preexisting bond between Toyen and Štyrský, even as Toyen always claimed that this relationship was platonic. Edelbrot writes, "We spoil ourselves with Pernod, and I cannot tell if we are friends. I tell them how delicious the drinks were and walk away defeated. The twins respond to my vow to see them soon with gentle avoidance, although I cannot quite again tell if it is not some sexual matter."

scenes to construct his famous collage novella *Une se-maine de bonté* (*A Week of Kindness*, 1934),[10] and much as the practice of collaborative writing known as the *cadavre exquis* (exquisite corpse) had come into vogue in surrealist circles at some point in the late 1910s or early 1920s, so Edelbrot and Toyen availed themselves of a principle of artificial synthesis by means of which they would generate literature.

The *petit conte triste* (sad little tale) as they at first termed it was mailed back and forth between their respective addresses over a period of approximately four months in 1926, with each writer contributing several paragraphs at a time. The document grew and grew. Some might attribute to chance its elegance and strangeness, particularly as neither Edelbrot nor Toyen

---

10. A note here regarding the surrealist response to nineteenth-century mores: it is worth recalling 1933's *affaire Nozières*, when a number of male surrealist writers and artists, including Ernst, along with Éluard, André Breton, René Char, Salvador Dalí, Yves Tanguy, René Magritte, Hans Arp, and Alberto Giacometti, among others, came to the defense of a young woman condemned to death by the French justice system. Juliette Nozières was arrested on August 28, 1933, on the charge of poisoning both her parents with sleeping tablets and successfully murdering her father. Eighteen years old at the time and under interrogation, Nozières accused her father of having habitually assaulted her since she was twelve. The case became a scandal and a cause in France. The surrealists founded a publishing house, Nicolas Flamel, in Brussels and published a collection of poetry and artworks demanding justice for Nozières and crying out against the supposedly sacred closed unit of the family, the bourgeoisie, the hypocrisy of defenders of the established order, and society itself. Nozières eventually served twelve years of what had been a life sentence. Briefly an ambiguous symbol of changing times, she died aged fifty-one.

was known as a literary writer, but in truth the talent on display is undeniable.

Edelbrot saw the work as a *roman poétique*, writing,

> Lying in bed this morning, having slept for
> eight hours for the first time in as many days,
> I thought that our "poetry in prose" bears the
> marks of its "time." Its "newness" grants our
> "poetic novel" a kind of storage function even
> as it pretends to be the outmoded work of an
> obscure melancholic émigré.

This entry demonstrates that the backstory of the purported author of the *conte* was either already significantly developed or complete at this time (the last days of 1926). We read little of the project in Edelbrot's entries until February of 1927, when she records, tersely: "Well, it is done. Have conveyed the 'rarity' to P. E. Unable to contain himself, he babbles taking his leave. What a boon!"

This, then, is the factual narrative of the genesis not only of *Passe-partout* but of LeGouffre himself, who was no more and no less than a being of paper, a fantasy propped up by Edelbrot's access to the means of forgery—given, lest we forget, her cousin's trade in antique printing apparatuses. As Éluard's excitement grew at what he believed was a discovery of momentous proportions and as he hatched his plan to bring forth the 1927 *livre d'artiste* version of the novella, including the celebrated illustrations by Joan Miró, Edelbrot fed Éluard a steady diet of background information. She created the correspondence with Éduard Manet, even going so far as to publish an article on the painter, which she also shared with Éluard. And she must also have laid the groundwork for Éluard's contentions regarding LeGouffre's performance of gender, although the exact way in which Éluard came to his own conclusions is somewhat uncertain and remains one of the greatest mysteries associated with this magnificent literary hoax.

What we do know without doubt is that, before her death in late 1977, Edelbrot became acquainted with an American scholar who had traveled to Paris on a fellowship seeking material related to Éluard's early career. It was this meeting, in the days before search engines, that gave rise to the first and only major study of LeGouffre's work in English, a dense monograph titled—with a terrible irony the author himself seems, in a moment of heartbreaking eagerness, to have missed—*The Golden Fleece*.[11]

As I learned, Edelbrot, who had by the 1970s married and divorced a second time, becoming Edelbrot-Mélaton in the process, was never concerned that her deceptions—or, depending on one's point of view, creations—should be recognized as such during her lifetime. Rather, she made her diary available to a trusted relative, apparently confident that her and Toyen's ruse would be revealed to the right audience in due time. Toyen, for their part, passed away three years later, in 1980, after having moved to Paris on a permanent basis in 1947 with a new and younger male partner. Nothing further is known of their involvement in the LeGouffre affair. Indeed, Edelbrot's diary con-

---

11. Roger Herbsweet, in his *The Golden Fleece: Démocrite Charlus LeGouffre and the Search for* Reconnaissance, appears to chalk Éluard's assertions regarding LeGouffre's sex and gender up to a fascination with cross-dressing carried over from the nineteenth to the early twentieth century. Éluard, meanwhile, did not do his readers any favors. Having become ensnared in reactionary politics near the end of his life, Éluard and his archive were for a time neglected, such that it was not possible to obtain definitive proof of the source of his contentions later on.

cludes with the publication of *Passe-partout* in 1927, at a celebratory soiree at which, tellingly perhaps, Toyen is not present.

To return to my suppositions about images in the nineteenth century broached at the beginning of this text, it seems only too obvious that *Passe-partout*, the story of the journey of a fragment of sculpture, a sculptural *part*, a "part out," to read the second word of the novella's title in English, stands as an allegory of the process by means of which sculpture was seen and appreciated during the period, as well as the civilizing process itself—with, of course, a difference: This story and this work of short fiction turns the normally public experience of viewing large-scale marble sculpture into a private one and points to the aesthetic and spiritual loss endemic to the assimilating forces of the West. And it transforms a style of spectatorship generally concerned with sentimentality, as well as moral lessons, into an experience of communion with anomalous sepulchral yearnings. In this sense, this history of an art object is a very strange history indeed.

The term *passe-partout*, or *passé-partout*, as it is sometimes spelled, has a number of meanings. It may refer, metaphorically, to anything that passes everywhere or provides a universal means of passage. More specifically, it is another name for a master or skeleton key. Yet, with the advent of portrait photography, it was widely used to refer to means by which a given image might be secured or displayed. The term indicated at once an ornamental mat for a picture, a method of framing usually employing glass, and paper prepared for a passe-partout framing process. As a helpful home-decor adviser wrote in the late 1890s in *The Perry Magazine*, "A *passe-partout* mount is easily made by placing the card under glass. Fold four little gummed papers over edges to hold glass in place. Then bind together with black binder's linen or *passe-partout* paper, allowing three-sixteenths of an inch to show." Thus, while pastel and other drawings often required a passe-partout mat to prevent their being smudged by glass, photographs and in particular daguerreotypes, less in danger of being smudged than scratched, became so ubiquitous as to change the framing method to which the very term *passe-partout* referred.

If the courtesan Liz lights on the name Passe-partout for her beloved curio, she is naming it after a commercial framing method common to photography, not, as readers in the twenty-first century might believe, after a convention for referring to a mysterious (possibly magic) object that grants universal passage. Liz has, quite literally, named her sculpture fragment "Framing Device," a very modern, even metafictional name.

Matters of media and genre are inevitably interlinked. It is useful to recall that without chemical stability, the term *photograph* could apply to the most fragile and fugitive sorts of images, such as naturally occurring frost shadows of buildings on a lawn on a sunny winter morning. We also recall that it was stability, and perhaps stability alone, that delayed the invention of the photographic image until the nineteenth century. Previous to photography, it was the mold or cast that held the greatest documentary power. One has only to think of the death mask: a practice that could not, apparently, be undertaken until after death, since it required absolute stillness. Photography was an extension and improvement of this logic.

The fictional object devised by Edelbrot and Toyen under the name of a fictional author, Passe-partout is at once imperishable and fugitive. Passe-partout is as adamantine as any whole sculpture, but at the same time fragmentary, flexible, and even porous, cavernous, like LeGouffre's strange surname, seeming to take on any meaning that its temporary owner might ascribe to it. It is powerful, able to fulfill wishes and apparently move of its own volition, even as it submits to kidnapping, servitude, and neglect. It is inconsistent, nonsensical, fascinating, impossible to interpret, vengeful, and even giving—that is, until it becomes a part of a series of civic monuments, multiplied and reobjectified, stripped of its (pun very much intended) legerdemain.

The elderly sculptor visiting from Rome first looks at then touches the three-dimensional image he had himself created many years earlier in a state of grief and shock. His experience, in so doing, is not precisely one of recognition. Rather, he seems compelled to attend to a series of negative affects and muffled wordless expressions. After showing us the sculptor's vicarious reunion with Passe-partout, whom the sculptor does not acknowledge as the likeness of the hand of his first wife, the story ends with another abstract sound, a wordless cry used by the taxi driver to spur on the horses, indicating man's continued dominion.

These events suggest a skepticism on the part of the author(s), particularly as to the meaningfulness of political monuments. Yet, the role that Passe-partout plays in what I will term, by way of shorthand, romantic love, is far less clear. Where Passe-partout enters into relation with individuals, a dynamic is established by means of which Passe-partout is at once fixed in its identity and also a source of phantasmagorical projection. It is, therefore, a form of allegorical media. Its identity is photographic in nature if not also cinematic, giving rise to illusions of depth and presence.

As I have pointed out in the opening lines of this article, contemporary conventions for viewing sculpture necessitated a certain amount of projection on the part

of the viewer. The viewer had to resituate a given figure within a larger, mostly invisible scene and also to
employ inference to understand the particular moral
message communicated. Passe-partout, however, operates in a liminal space between sculpture and some
other representational format associated with repressed memory. But if Passe-partout is indeed or also
a *literary* figure, we must say that it is avowedly antiromantic, since the story explicitly critiques the hope
for personal redemption associated with romantic
love. I would argue, given the central narrative silence
of this novella along with its repetitious form, that it
contains a missing figure. In my reading, this figure
is neither the deceased wife nor an image of Diana,
goddess of the hunt, nor even its two hidden authors,
but rather photography itself, that technology for the
creation of fixed images endowed with the appearance
of three dimensions and, therefore, modern, administratively managed identity, the purview of institutions. *Passe-partout* represents an image of LeGouffre's
world that, for some unknown reason, still lacks the
affordance of photography but that is yet capable of
photographic forms of desire. That such a desire, a specifically *photographic desire* for identification, a desire
unimaginable without the existence of photography, is
summoned—anachronistically—by means of a sculptural fragment, at once foretells LeGouffre's fictional
future as a photographer and suggests an inherent dissatisfaction with the illusory fullness and completeness, relayed by the photographic format. This ambiguity stands as a quiet but powerful critique of the norms
of the time in which LeGouffre "lived" as well as those
of Edelbrot and Toyen's era. Rather than stumble,
myself, into the impasse/*gouffre* associated with Passe-
partout, one of excessive identification with a thing-

like image or image-like thing, I will join the fragment
in its profound silence and eventual multiplication.

Here the article ended.

Well, Erin thought, that might be one way. Concluding incon-
clusively—and Erin was very sleepy.

The life of the person known as LeGouffre: born in Paris and
then the teenage break. In New York and then Mexico City, with a
pause in New Orleans, perhaps until the flood. A being who operates like a footnote, hovering within events and lives of alleged central importance. Who is unaccountably present for scenes of great
literary-historical significance, but always slightly hidden, mostly
impossible to make out. The scholar grasps after that life—but it
was not real. Or was it? Which, among the various sorts of lives
intelligible to the scholar, has the now deceased, and therefore unavailable, historical person chosen? How shall we reach them?

There can be no originality in scholarship without the abandon-
ment of the principle of similarity. And yet, nearly all scholarship
is based on simple comparative gestures that derive most if not all
of their power from more or less clearly acknowledged moments of
repetition. Herbsweet's writing on LeGouffre was mediocre, celebratory. Omissions, biases, coincidences, and lacks allowed Herbsweet
to find room for his middling ruminations. Herbsweet left things
out, then substituted himself. He got in there, crammed into that
space in time past, and vibrated, sending out currents that altered an
existing landscape. It was a fabric, a technology, this thinking. But,
as they always did, new scholars came, and they set about altering
the text. They cordoned off an entity like Herbsweet. His intimations and suggestions, wily and arcane, no longer went anywhere.
He was blocked. Herbsweet sat in his little plot and did not flow. He
was no longer convincing, even to himself.

Ineffectual Herbsweet sought out new conquests. He ignored
literature and advanced in the real world instead, touching crotches,

seeing how far he could get. Yes, that was what he did, Erin knew. Literature and history became props to his wandering hands. They were screens, translating devices. He played an abstract game with social norms and youthful bodies, using the university as a sourcing mechanism. New supplicants were furnished yearly into his seminar and office hours. And he was not even unusual in this. This was true for all of Herbsweet's colleagues, as well. Each had their own metaphor for it, their own tokens and accounts, their own purposes and ends.

Erin went into the stacks. She felt dizzy, some major part of her entering a dream, but she wanted the internet. She had little energy left, and because of this a certain peace had crept in. Soon she would put her head down, but for the moment she savored having come to a point of no longer being able to fight. She was just a thing that could undertake basic movement. She was incapable of self-recrimination.

At a terminal, Erin googled "botox wikipedia" and, having satisfied herself as to the substance's makeup (interesting that it was organic), tabbed over to the university catalogue and did a search for "botulinum." This resulted in a list of items such as "Manual of botulinum toxin therapy," "Botlinum toxin in facial rejuvenation," "Botulinum toxin in urology," "Botulinum Toxins, Fillers, and Related Substances," "Botulinum neurotoxin for head and neck disorders," "Botulinum Toxin Treatment What Everyone Should Know," and "The Current Status of the Botulinum Pathogen Problem in the Canning Industry," *Biomedical Aspects of Botulism*, US Army Medical Research Institute of Infectious Diseases, International Conference on the Biomedical Aspects of Botulism (1981: Fort Detrick, Frederick, MD). There were some 411 electronic resources available, as well as several hundred books. Erin selected all of these. Next she went to a menu and clicked on an option to "Email my results." A dialogue box came up with a field for an email address. Erin entered Faith Ewer's coordinates from memory. Next, she altered the dummy subject line so that instead of "Item(s) from _____Cat," it read: "Your Impressive Work." Erin commanded the massive bibliography to be dispatched via the catalogue's daemon. Erin sighed, momentarily lighter within her exhaustion. It was hard to keep her eyes open. Although her earlier use of her ID meant that she could be placed in the library at this moment, Erin was not signed in at the computer and doubted that a prank of this sort would be grounds for combing through electronic records, which was, however, an interesting possibility, in itself. At any rate, the message raised the question, "Which *work*?"

Erin imagined, briefly, its recipient forwarding the missive to a dean, perhaps with a lengthy preamble, puffy with outrage.

Or perhaps she would forward it to Florian Cádiz. And Florian Cádiz would privately lol into his sleeve, before composing a dour message about how he could *not* for the life of him understand that cryptic subject line and the undergraduates were really getting out of hand!

And Florian Cádiz would chuckle some more and archive the thread and reach down to stroke the tawny fur of his new, small, imaginary dog, which rested its clammy face against Florian's slipper. And Florian would return to his current research project, which everyone knew was human-to-animal transformation narratives and the representation of said narratives in visual art, particularly sculpture. Florian would nod, confident that he, a new Circe, was on his way to mastering this topic.

Erin reentered the study carrel.

She pressed her phone on, checked her email.

Erin was alarmed to discover one new message, *Your Impressive Work*. Her heart tightened and throbbed, but then she realized that she must, in her fatigue, have typed her own email address into the prompt. It was not the first time she had done this. For months now, Erin had accidentally been sending messages she believed she was writing to others to herself. It happened every few weeks. Erin would pause in her inbox, marveling at the letter that had arrived to her from the very recent past, encountering herself as if she were a stranger. From Erin to Erin. Special delivery. Hermetic seal.

Oh well, Erin thought. *My* impressive work. Ha. Faith would never know how Erin felt. And that was fine; that was probably for the best. Faith did not care about Erin, and Faith did not even really care about Faith, truth be told, not if she was constantly putting poison into her face. Yet, it was a relief, unexpectedly, not to have shared that bleak emotion, not to have risked Erin's own meager privacy. Let Faith eat her own sins.

Here a pair of texts dropped down into the open email application. The first read, *sorry just seeing this.* The second, *talk soon?*

Erin powered down the device.

She seemed cushioned in something decent, although she was still surrounded by the rancid air of the study closet. She gathered up her things.

Her brain felt full of soft ropes and Erin left the cell. She was faint as she walked down the stairs, hearing voices. She paused to listen to a muted figure, what seemed to be a delicate dog-size man in a suit of gray fur. The figure had large, clear eyes.

"Life is everywhere," the figure told her.

Hmm, Erin thought, hallucinating.

The slight, humanesque figure was saying something.

Erin squinted, which seemed to help.

Tendrils swirled.

Erin crossed the lobby, exited the library. Outside it was nearly day.

Erin tried to listen. She tried to remember. She recalled lying once on the earth, on a lawn, in Melbourne, in Australia, where she had felt the presence of the surface of the planet, as well as the form of progress to which she had been raised, the worldless future.

For there was no Alana Harris. There never had been. That was the name of the daughter of one of her mother's friends. There was only Erin, surrounded by her numerous losses, humiliations, and trespasses, who had broken apart irrevocably before the closed door of the institution, who had become more than one—and so weird.

Erin was in the park now. She stretched out in the wet grass.

A translation. This was what she sought. A passage and a way. What, having nothing, Erin possessed. The mere present.

Life Is Everywhere, she thought. Not a bad title.

Now Erin is asleep. We cannot reach her. So let her rest, for soon there will be much for her to do.

But someone is still speaking.

Who is writing this book?

A funny question yet not entirely unwarranted. Some words have gathered in this narrow space, common and humane. A magic circle forms around an anomalous day that occurred years ago and really did occur.

Note (Afterlife)

As novels often do, this novel emerged in the place of a novel I could not write. A little over ten years ago, I began thinking about an imaginary French novelist born in the early part of the nineteenth century. I don't really know why I began to think about him. In my imagination, this novelist traveled to North America and suffered many failures. He wandered and never went home.

The research and acts of description necessary for a novel of this sort—which I envisioned as a doorstop to end all doorstops—were challenges, it's true. But I'm not sure that technical limitations or my multiple full-time jobs were the true death knells of this ambitious picaresque. Instead, what hindered me was that I could not stop wondering who or what this fictional novelist was, why I had become concerned with him in the first place, to the exclusion of other artificial individuals. Part of me disliked the feeling of focusing on a single figure, at all. I was always getting distracted by "unimportant" details: garments of the day, popular poetry, the history of cooking, handicrafts (the period's interest in jewelry made of human hair is still a source of fascination).

The early 2010s were a different time and it's easier for me to see now that I was having trouble with something bigger and broader in relation to literature. I couldn't keep the relationship between figure and ground in my speculative depictions stable. I couldn't keep it straight. Decorative items, parts of the landscape, background stories kept coming to the fore, kept messing with my admittedly half-hearted attempts to delineate a hero. My somewhat weird, or increasingly weird, book collapsed on itself, and in its place this novel began. Here, I allowed myself to give up on historical supermen who could be easily separated from the "noise" of their environments or even from the apparatus of the book itself. Not so much a "meta" comment on the form of the novel—or, *if* a comment on the form of the novel—this fiction attempts to think through what a world might feel like if cause and effect sometimes traded places, if figure and ground were indeed interchangeable, if story was a sort of network of users coming on- and offline, if mediating entities sometimes got very much in the way of narrative, as such.

In the spirit, if not the letter, of Ursula K. Le Guin's essay on "The Carrier-Bag Theory of Fiction," there is a bag within this book. (I'm sure Le Guin did not mean for fiction writers to make actual bags of/ in their books, but it amused me to be so literal.) There is also plenty of vulnerability here, a rehearsal of genre as carefully strategized collapse, what might even be called literary weakness—in that this book is only weakly a novel, much as it is weakly tragic, vaguely comic, barely true, only ever so slightly false. It is always beginning to be something other than its "proper" self: a confession, a dream, an email, an unpublished manuscript, an academic study, a series of historical footnotes, a literary hoax, a utility bill. Of course, such disobedience is par for the course where novels are concerned, given their track record of flexibility and tendency to compost if not digest novel (= new) forms, technologies, social spheres, and so on.

"Resilience is a wager with time," Wai Chee Dimock writes in the introduction to her study *Weak Planet: Literature and Assisted Survival*. This scholarly consideration of (mostly) American litera-ture was published in 2020, after I had completed the manuscript of *Life Is Everywhere*, but the novel could easily have been inspired by many of Dimock's observations. In particular, I am struck by her ideas regarding a literature of multifarious, informal, "weak" ties. I wrote this novel with many, many other books, articles, magazines, PDFs, and browser tabs open, sometimes imitating their language, sometimes seeing through this language, sometimes talking back. (Far from being anxious about influence, I rejoice in it; I'm quite promiscuous when it comes to that thing some writers call voice. *Please*, I think, *take me over*.) Scientific histories, histories of popu-lar photography, of sex work, of gambling in the nineteenth cen-tury, of artistic movements, of apparently atypical cognition, reviews, essays, and other fictions: I sometimes wrote around and between their letters. I drew faces in the margins. I underlined and crossed things out. I made stuff up; my own book is rather impure.

Here, in lieu of a formal bibliography, I would like to include the names of some of the writers, scholars, poets, artists, strangers, and fellow investigators this novel follows, echoes, argues with, and gazes at with love, being a minor afterlife of their writings. They are also the voices and images to which my own hands moved: bound, liberated. Through and thanks to them, I evaded paralysis:

Michael Adler, Sara Ahmed, Peggy Ahwesh, Jane Austen, James Baldwin, Charles Baudelaire, Walter Benjamin, Mirella Bentivoglio, Verena Berger, Lauren Berlant, Susan Buck-Morss, Sophie Calle, Leonora Carrington, J. Alastair Carruthers, Jean D. A. Carruthers, Alain Ceysnes, Matt Cole, Arda Collins, Consolidated Edison, Sébastien de Courtois, Douglas Crimp, Catherine Crowe, Countee Cullen, Hanne Darboven, Adeline Daumard, Moyra Davey, Zygmunt F. Dembek, Caroline Derry, Pieter P. Devriese, M. Parent Duchatelet, Andrew Durbin, John Elderfield, George Eliot, Buck Ellison, Frank J. Erbguth, Eric Finzi, Alice Weaver Flaherty, Gustav Flaubert, Jack M. Fletcher, L. Carvalhão Gil, Cora Gilroy-Ware, Madeline Gins, Renee Gladman, Robert Glück, Lisa Hager, Diana Hamilton, Elizabeth Hardwick, Jean-Louis Harouel, Rachel Harrison, Jill Harsin, Saidiya Hartman, Nathaniel Hawthorne, Georg Wilhelm Friedrich Hegel, Andreas Hennenlotter, Katie Hickman, Tony Howard, Julia Ward Howe, Susan Howe, Karla Huebner, Langston Hughes, Edmond Jabès, Fleur Jaeggy, Henry James, Jules Janin, J. Jeannel, Lee B. Jennings, Rohini Kapil, Thomas M. Kavanagh, John Keene, Justinus Kerner, Wayne Koestenbaum, Taeko Kono, Shiv Kotecha, Yutaka Kudo, Annie Le Brun, Frank J. Lebeda, Pamela Lee, Wendy Anne Lee, George E. Lewis Jr., Tan Lin, Jen Manion, J. Gama Marques, Herman Melville, Yoko Mitani, Lara Mimosa Montes, Etsuro Mori, Germaine A. Nelson, Alexander

Nemerov, Arturo Aguilar Ochoa, Oluremi Onabanjo, Meret Oppenheim, Cora Pearl, Adam Pendleton, Georges Perec, Adrian Piper, Edgar Allan Poe, A. Ponte, Norman E. Rosenthal, Virginia Rounding, Raymond Roussel, Donatien-Alphonse-François de Sade, George Sand, Francesca Canadé Sautman, T. Denean Sharpley-Whiting, Ada Smailbegovic, Himali Singh Soin, Susan Stewart, Masayasu Tabuchi, Lynne Tillman, Maria Torok, James K. Torrens, Jalal Toufic, Toyen, Edward P. Vining, Aby Warburg, Thomas Jefferson Whitman, Walt Whitman, Stanley Wolukau-Wanambwa, Virginia Woolf, Atsushi Yamadori, Frances Yates, Alejandro Zambra, Patricia Massé Zendejas

This list is incomplete
8/20/2021
11:14 am

Brief, Important, Few Last Acknowledgments

Yuka Igarashi's brilliance and care sustain me as a writer: I am so lucky to benefit from her unerring editorial eye and gracious, lively interest in the absurd in all its manifestations. Fiona McCrae generously offered balance and insight, as well.

Thank you to Ethan Nosowsky, Katie Dublinski, Marisa Atkinson, Kapo Ng, Yana Makuwa, and everyone at Graywolf who has supported this novel, wrangled its various paginations, described its bagginess to someone who might enjoy a baggy narrative, delineated a crescent moon, or otherwise shared in the kind, exacting, and thorough way of working that the press is justly known for.

Chris Clemans has sometimes said that there is no need to thank him, but I disagree.

Lucy Ives is the author of two novels: *Impossible Views of the World*, published by Penguin Press and selected as a *New York Times Book Review* Editors' Choice, and *Loudermilk: Or, The Real Poet; Or, The Origin of the World*, published by Soft Skull Press and also a *New York Times Book Review* Editors' Choice. Her short fiction is collected in *Cosmogony* (Soft Skull Press, 2021). In spring 2020, Siglio Press published *The Saddest Thing Is That I Have Had to Use Words: A Madeline Gins Reader*, the first definitive anthology of poet-architect Gins's poetry and prose, edited and with an introduction by Ives. Ives's writing has appeared in *Aperture*, *Art in America*, *Artforum*, the *Believer*, *frieze*, *Granta*, *Lapham's Quarterly*, *n+1*, and *Vogue*, among other publications. She teaches in New York University's XE: Experimental Humanities & Social Engagement master's program and was a recipient of a 2018 Andy Warhol Foundation Arts Writers Grant.

The text of *Life Is Everywhere* is set in Adobe Caslon Pro, Chaparral Pro, EB Garamond, Helvetica Neue, PT Serif, Times New Roman, and Wingdings. Book design and composition by Bookmobile Design & Digital Publisher Services, Minneapolis, Minnesota. Manufactured by Versa Press on acid-free, 30 percent postconsumer wastepaper.